ALEXANDRA BRACKEN

Quercus

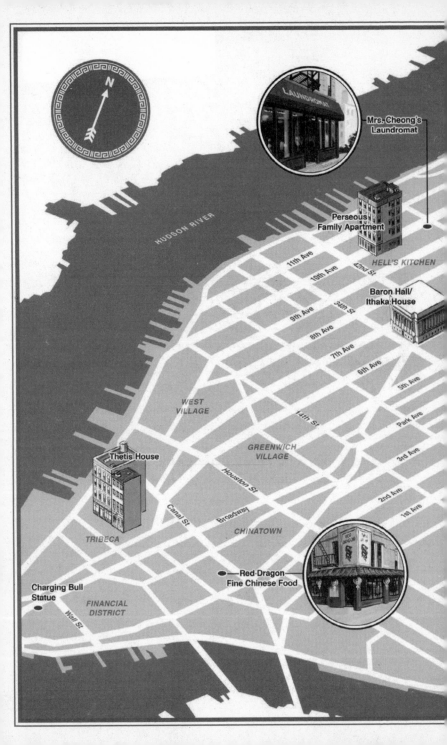

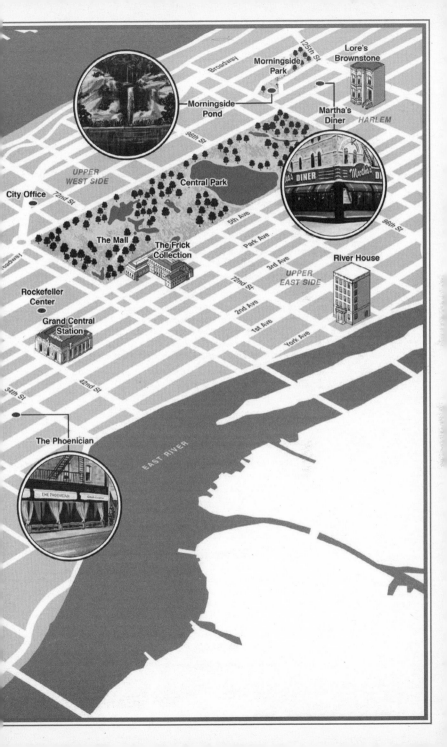

QUERCUS CHILDREN'S BOOKS

First published in Great Britain in 2021 by Hodder & Stoughton
First published in the US in 2021 by Hyperion, an imprint of Buena Vista Books, Inc.

11

A CIP catalogue record for this book is available from the British Library.

ISBN: 978 1 786 54152 9

Typeset in Minion Pro

Printed and bound by Clays Ltd, Elcograf S.p.A.

The paper and board used in this book
are made from wood from responsible sources.

Quercus Children's Books
An imprint of Hachette Children's Group
Part of Hodder & Stoughton
Carmelite House
50 Victoria Embankment
London EC4Y 0DZ

An Hachette UK Company
www.hachette.co.uk

www.hachettechildrens.co.uk

For my Greek family. Σας αγαπώ όλους.

LIVING LINES

THE HOUSE OF KADMOS — The Kadmides
Bearers of the mark of the serpent
Exalted by Wrath, Ares reborn

THE HOUSE OF ODYSSEUS — The Odysseides
Bearers of the mark of the Trojan horse
Exalted by Heartkeeper, Aphrodite reborn

THE HOUSE OF THESEUS — The Theseides
Bearers of the mark of the Minotaur

THE HOUSE OF ACHILLES — The Achillides
Bearers of the mark of the warrior

THE HOUSE OF PERSEUS — The Perseides
Bearers of the mark of the Gorgon
Exalted by Tidebringer, Poseidon reborn

DEAD LINES

THE HOUSE OF MELEAGER — The Meleagrides
Bearers of the mark of the Calydonian boar

THE HOUSE OF BELLEROPHON — The Bellerophonides
Bearers of the mark of Pegasus

THE HOUSE OF JASON — The Jasonides
Bearers of the mark of the ram

THE HOUSE OF HERAKLES — The Heraklides
Bearers of the mark of the Nemean lion
Exalted by the Reveler, Dionysus reborn

The lord of sky stood bright against the fall
of twilight and spoke: Hear me, blooded heirs
of those proud men who ventured into the
darkness to slay those monsters and kings past.
I call you to a final agon to
win your own lasting glory. Nine gods have
betrayed me and now demand cruel revenge.
For seven days at the turn of seven
years will they walk as mortal so you men,
and all your heirs henceforth, may break your own
fated path and turn your thread of life to
immortal gold. Reveal your strength and skills and
I will reward you with the mantle
and the deathless power of the god whose blood
stains your bold blade. For this chance I ask much.
Gather at the navel of the known world
and begin your hunt when the day is born.
So it shall be until that final day
when one remains who is remade whole.

Zeus at Olympia,
translated by Kreon of the Odysseides

He woke to the feeling of rough ground beneath him and the stench of mortal blood.

His body was slower to recover than his mind. Unwelcome sensations burned through him as his skin tightened like newly fired clay.

The dew of the grass seeped into the back of his thin blue robe, and he felt the dirt splattered on his bare legs and feet. A humiliating shiver passed through him, sweeping from scalp to heel. For the first time in seven years, he caught a chill.

The mortal blood that flowed through him was like sludge compared to the liquid sunlight of the ichor that had burned away all traces of his mortality and released him back into the world. For seven years, he had swept through lands near and far, stoked the vicious hearts of killers, nurtured the embers of conflicts into flames. He had been rage itself.

To feel the boundaries of a body again . . . to be poured back into this weak vessel . . . it was torment enough to make him pity the old gods. They had lived this atrocity two hundred and twelve times over.

He would not. This would be his final taste of mortality.

His senses were dulled, but he recognized the city and its grand park. The smell of mowed grass mingling with faint sewage. The sound of traffic in the near distance. The electric, restless feel of its veins deep beneath the street.

The corners of his mouth stretched up awkwardly, forced to remember how to smile. It had been his city once, in his mortal life; the streets had offered him riches, and the greedy had sold him pieces of power. Manhattan had once knelt before him, and would again.

He rolled, shifting into a crouch. When he was certain of his limbs, he rose slowly to his full height.

Dark blood flowed in rivers around him. A young girl, her mask ripped from her face, stared at him with unseeing eyes from the edge of the crater. A knife was still buried in her throat. A man's head, severed from his body, bore the mask of a horse. A dagger was balanced in a limp hand that was missing fingers.

There was a faint shuffle of footsteps to his right. He reached for a sword that was no longer at his side. Three figures stepped out from beneath the shadow of the nearby trees. They crossed the paved trail between them, their faces hidden by bronze masks that each bore the visage of a serpent.

His mortal bloodline. The House of Kadmos. They had come to collect him, their new god.

He stretched his neck until it cracked, watching their approach. The hunters were awed, and it pleased him. His predecessor, the last new Ares, had been unworthy to hold the mantle of the god of war. It had been an unspeakable pleasure to kill him and claim his birthright seven years ago.

The tallest of the three hunters stepped forward. Belen. The new god watched, amused, as the young man plucked the arrows from the bodies in a ruthless harvest.

A shame that his only surviving offspring had been born a bastard. He could not be the heir of Aristos Kadmou, the mortal the new god had once been. Still, his lips curved, and he welcomed the glow of pride at the sight of the young man.

4

Belen lifted his mask and lowered his gaze respectfully. The god reached up, feeling along the lines of his face. The boy's was so much like his own now. The scarred husk of decades had been peeled away from the god when he had ascended, leaving him young again. In his prime, forever.

"Most honored of us all," Belen said, kneeling. He offered the new god a rolled bundle from the bag at his hip—a crimson silk tunic to replace the hideous sky-blue one he wore now. "We welcome you and offer the blood of your enemies in tribute to your name, as a sign of our undying loyalty. We are here to protect you with our lives until the time comes for you to be reborn again in power."

The words were gravel in the new god's throat. "Beyond that."

"Yes, my lord," Belen said.

More hunters approached from behind Belen, all cloaked in a hunter's black. They dragged a figure also wearing a tunic of sky blue.

"Bring him to me," he told Belen.

Two black SUVs, their lights off, approached from the nearby street and drove over the grass to reach them. The Kadmides then began their work. They unrolled tarps on Central Park's grass and rolled the dead hunters onto them. They overturned the soil. Replaced the bloodied grass. Loaded the brutalized carcasses into the trunk of yet another SUV pulling up behind them.

This same ritual, he knew, was being performed by the other bloodlines across the park.

The captive lashed out again as he was drawn forward, battering the nearest hunters with his skull like a rabid animal. They had cut the tendons of his ankles to prevent him from using his heightened speed to escape. Good.

The hunters forced him to his knees. The new god reached down to rip the hood off his head.

5

Gold eyes burned as they glared up at him, the sparks of power there swirling with fury. Blood poured from a wound at his forehead, staining his once-luminous skin and tunic.

"Your last useful power has been taken from you," the new god said. He clutched a fistful of the old god's curling brown hair and wrenched his head back, forcing his gaze up.

"I know what you desire, Godkiller," the old god said in the ancient tongue. "And you will never find it."

He'd only needed to know that it hadn't been destroyed. The new god's rage was its own kind of euphoria. He brought the razor-sharp edge of his blade to the old god's soft mortal flesh.

The new god smiled.

"Trickster. Messenger. Traveler. Thief," the new god said. Then he slammed the blade through the ridged bones of the prisoner's spine. "Nothing."

Blood burst from the wound. The new god drank deep the sight of the old god's fear—that pain, that disbelief—as his power faded. A shame the new god could not add it to his own.

"It's the way of things, is it not?" the new god said. He leaned down, watching as the last flare of life left the old god's eyes. "The way of your father, and his father before him. The old gods must die to allow the new to rise."

The park was silent around them, save for the wet sounds of the new god's sawing blade, and the invigorating crack as he finally separated the head from its body. The new god thrust the head of Hermes high enough for his followers to see.

The hunters hissed in pleasure, banging their fists against their chests. The new god took one final look at it before tossing the head onto the nearest tarp with the other remains. Come morning, there would

6

be no sign of the eight gods who had appeared like lightning within the boundaries of Central Park, or those hunters who had fallen in their attempts to kill them.

The city thrummed around him, aching with barely constrained chaos. It sang to him a song of coming terror. He understood that longing—to be unleashed.

"I am Wrath." The new god knelt, dipping his fingers into the bloody mud. "I am your master." He dragged them down over his cheeks. "I am your glory."

The hunters around him lifted their masks to do the same, smearing the damp earth across their eager faces.

A new age was in reach, waiting to be seized by one strong enough to dare.

"Now," the new god said, "we begin."

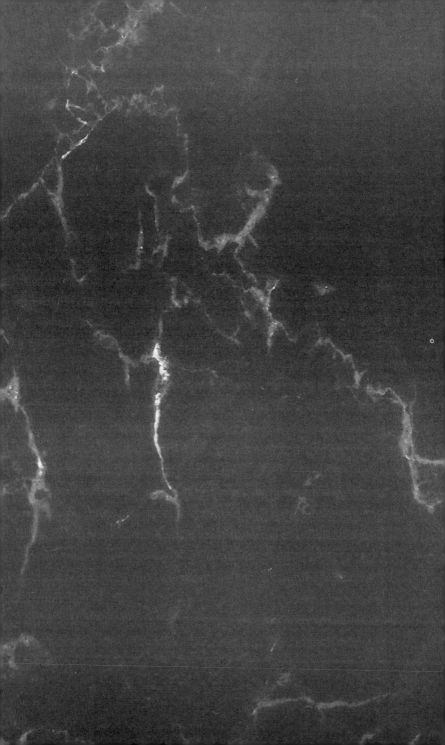

PART ONE

—

CITY OF GODS

ONE

HER MOTHER HAD ONCE TOLD HER THAT THE ONLY WAY TO TRULY know someone was to fight them. In Lore's experience, the only thing fighting actually revealed was the spot on their body someone least wanted to be punched.

For her opponent, that spot was clearly the new tattoo on his left breast, the one still covered with a bandage.

Lore brought up her fourteen-ounce gloves and let them absorb another sloppy hit. Her sneakers squeaked over the cheap blue mats as she bounced back a step. The lines of silver duct tape holding the makeshift ring together were, after five fights that night, beginning to peel from the moisture and heat. She grunted as she stamped the nearest one flat with her heel.

Sweat poured down her face until all she could taste was the salt of it. Lore refused to wipe it away, even as it stung her eyes. The pain was good. It kept her focused.

This—the fighting—was nothing more than a recent bad habit, one that had brought her a desperately needed release after Gil's death six months ago. But her original promise of *just this one match* had vanished as she'd felt that familiar surge of adrenaline.

One fight had been enough to break the deadening grief, to get her out of her head and back into her body. Two fights had disconnected

11

the deep ache in her heart. Three had brought in a surprising amount of cash.

And now, weeks later, fight fifteen was giving her exactly what she was desperate for that night: a distraction.

Lore told herself she could stop at any time. She could stop when it no longer felt good. She could stop when it dredged up too much of what she'd buried.

But Lore wasn't there. Not just yet.

The cramped basement of Red Dragon Fine Chinese Food was sweltering. The hot press of too many bodies surrounded the mats. The crowd shifted as the fighters did, forming the unofficial boundary of the ring as they clutched their Solo cups and tried to keep from spilling their top-shelf liquor. Bills and bets flowed around her, hand to hand, until they reached Frankie, the ring organizer. Lore glanced to him as he adjusted the order and bets of the next two fights, forever less interested in the winner than the winnings.

Steam rolled down the stairs from the kitchen above them, giving the air a satin quality. The smell of kung pao chicken was a delicious alternative to the reek of old vomit and beer that haunted the boarded-up nightclubs the ring usually rotated through.

The crowd didn't seem to mind; whatever it took to give them some illusion of edge. Frankie's exclusive list seemed a lot less exclusive these days: models, art-scene types, and business guys passing around their small sachets of white powder were now frequently joined by private-school kids testing the limits of their parents' apathy.

Her opponent was a boy about her age—all soft, unmarked skin and unearned confidence. He'd laughed, crooking a finger at her as he'd chosen her out of all of Frankie's available fighters. Lore had decided to destroy him and lay waste to whatever tattered bit of his pride remained well before he ever called her *baby girl* and blew her a drunken kiss.

"Let me guess," she said around her mouth guard. Lore nodded toward the bandage on the teen boy's chest, covering his new body art. "*Live, Laugh, Love*? *Rosé All Day*?"

His brows lowered as the crowd laughed. The boy swung a glove at her head, grunting with the effort. The movement, combined with his flagging strength, left his chest wide open. Lore had a clear target when she slammed her glove into his tender inked skin.

The boy's eyes bulged, his breath wheezing out of him. His knees hit the mat.

"Get up," Lore said. "You're embarrassing your friends."

"You—you stupid bi—" The boy choked a little on his mouth guard. Lore had wondered how long it would take before he melted down, and now she had her answer: five minutes.

"I'm *sure* you're not going to call me that," she said, circling him, "when you're the one on all fours."

He struggled to his feet, fuming. She rolled her eyes.

Not so funny anymore, is it? Lore thought.

Gil would have told her to walk away from the stupid kid—he had always been quick to remind Lore in that nonjudgmental, grandfatherly way of his that she didn't have to jump into every fight that presented itself. The truth was, the man would have hated this, and Lore suffered the guilt of that, too. Of disappointing him.

But Lore had tried other ways. None of them helped her move through the crushing tide of loss like a good fight did. And now it wasn't just Gil's death she needed to escape; there was a new dread clawing beneath her skin.

It was August, and the hunt had come back to her city.

Despite her best efforts to move on, to forget the shadowed life she'd left behind and step into the sunlight of a new, better one, some part of her mind was still attuned to the slow countdown of days. Her body had grown tighter, her instincts sharper, as if bracing for what was coming.

She'd started seeing familiar faces around the city two weeks before, making their final preparations for tonight. The shock had come like a knife to the lungs; each sighting was proof that all her hope, all her silent begging, had come to nothing. *Please,* she'd thought again and again over the last few months, *let it be London this cycle. Let it be Tokyo.*

Let it be anywhere else but New York City.

Lore knew she shouldn't have ventured out tonight, not while the killing would be at its most fevered. If a single hunter recognized her, the bloodlines wouldn't just be hunting gods. They'd be out to skin her, too.

From the corner of her eye Lore saw Frankie check his ridiculous pocket watch and give the *wrap-it-up* signal. Places to go, money to rub all over his face, she supposed.

"Done yet?" Lore asked.

Apparently, the alcohol had decided to hit the boy all at once. He chased Lore around the mats with his clumsy, swinging fists, growing angrier as the laughter of the crowd boomed.

As she turned to avoid a blow, her necklace swung out from where she had tucked it beneath her shirt. The charm on it, a gold feather, caught the dim light and flashed. Her opponent's glove struck it. Somehow he must have hooked on to its thin chain, because as Lore shifted again, the clasp snapped and, suddenly, the charm was on the ground at her feet.

Lore used her teeth to undo her glove's Velcro strap and slid her hand free. She ducked as her opponent swung again, quickly scooping the necklace up and tucking it into the back pocket of her jeans for safekeeping. As she pulled her glove back on, her body heated with a fresh wave of resentment.

Gil had given it to her.

Lore turned back toward the boy, reminding herself that she couldn't kill him. She could, however, break his pretty little nose.

Which, to the cheers of the crowd, she did.

Blood burst from his face as he swore.

"I think it's past your bedtime, *baby boy*," she said, glancing back at Frankie to see if he'd call the match. "In fact—"

She saw the fist coming out at the edge of her vision, and turned just in time to take the hit to the side of her head, not her eye. The world flashed black, then burst bright with color again, but she managed to stay on her feet.

The boy crowed in victory, thrusting his arms into the air, nose still bleeding. He lurched toward her, and the moment she realized what was happening was the only moment she had.

Lore instinctively brought up her gloves to protect her chest, but that wasn't what he was after. The boy locked an arm around her neck and crushed his lips to hers.

The panic was blinding, exploding out over Lore's skin like ice; it locked her out of her own mind. He pressed his body tighter to hers, his tongue clumsily licking at her as the crowd howled around them.

Something split open inside her, and the pressure that had been building in her chest for weeks released with a roar of fury. She drove her knee up hard between his legs. He dropped like she'd cut his throat, squealing the whole way down. Then she lunged.

15

The next thing Lore was aware of was being pulled up off the ground still kicking and snarling. Her gloves were splattered with blood, and what was left of his face was unrecognizable.

"Stop!" Big George, one of Frankie's security guards, gave her a small shake. "Honey, he ain't worth it!"

Lore's heart slammed against her ribs, beating too fast for her to catch her breath. Her body trembled as Big George set her feet back on the ground, holding her until she gave him a nod that she was all right. For his part, Big George stalked over to the boy moaning on the mat and nudged him with his foot.

As the pounding in Lore's ears receded, she realized the room had fallen completely silent, save for the banging and clattering in the kitchen just upstairs.

A slow horror slithered through her, knotting around her heart. Inside her gloves, her fingers curled to the point of pain. She hadn't just lost control. She'd slipped back into a part of herself she thought she'd killed years ago.

This isn't me, she thought, wiping the sweat from her upper lip. *Not anymore.*

There was more to life than this.

Desperate to salvage her night's pay, Lore ignored the bile, and the singular, sharp hatred she had for the whimpering piece of filth on the ground, and put a sheepish smile on her face. She held up her hands and shrugged.

The spectators rewarded her with cheers, thrusting their cups up in the air.

"You didn't win—you cheated," the boy was saying. "It wasn't fair—you *cheated*!"

This was the thing with boys like him. What he was feeling just

16

then, that *rage*, wasn't the world falling in on him. It was an illusion shattering, the one that told him he deserved everything, and that it was owed to him simply because he existed.

Lore tugged her gloves off and leaned over the boy. The crowd hushed, their faces as eager as hungry crows.

"Maybe your next one should be *Can't Win for Losing*?" she said sweetly as she pressed hard against his bandage, this time with her bare hand. The bell rang over the sound of his outraged cry, ending the match. Big George dragged him back toward his huddle of friends.

Lore started back toward Frankie. It had been a mistake to come here tonight. Even now, she couldn't tell if her body wanted her to break into a run, or scream.

She'd made it to the edge of the ring when he called out, "Next match: Golden versus challenger Gemini."

Lore gave him an annoyed look, which he returned with his usual unbothered smile. He flashed her five fingers. She shook her head, and he added three more. Crumpled bills waved in the air around her, fluttering by as the crowd rushed to place their bets.

She needed to go home. She knew that, but . . .

Lore held up all ten fingers. Frankie scowled but waved her back toward the ring. She pulled her gloves back on and turned. If it was one of the boy's friends, at least she might be able to amuse herself.

It wasn't.

Lore reeled back. Her opponent stood just outside the light cast by the fixture overhead, clearly welcoming the darkness. The young man stepped forward, enough for the dim glow to catch the bronze mask that obscured his face.

Her breath turned heavy in her lungs.

Hunter.

17

TWO

A SINGLE WORD BLAZED THROUGH HER MIND. *RUN.*

But her instincts demanded something else, and her body listened. She slid into a defensive stance, tasting blood as she bit the inside of her mouth. Every part of her seemed to vibrate, electrified by fear and fervor.

You are an idiot, Lore told herself. She would have to kill him in front of all these people, or find a way to take the fight outside and do it there. Those were the only options she allowed herself to consider. Lore was not about to die on booze-soaked mats in the basement of a Chinese restaurant that didn't even serve mapo tofu.

Her opponent towered over Lore in a way she tried to pretend she didn't find alarming. He had at least a six-inch advantage despite her own tall frame. His simple gray shirt and sweatpants were too small, stretching over his athletic form. Every muscle of his body was as perfectly defined as those men she'd seen on her father's ancient vases. The mask he wore was one of a man's raging expression as he released a war cry.

The House of Achilles.

Well, Lore thought faintly. *Shit.*

"I don't fight cowards who won't show their faces," she said coldly.

The answer was warm, rumbling with suppressed laughter. "I figured as much."

He lifted the mask and dropped it at the edge of the ring. The rest of the world burned away.

You're dead.

The words caught in her throat, choking her. The crowd jostled Lore forward on the mats, even as she fell back a step, even as she fought for air that wouldn't seem to come to her. The faces around her blurred to darkness at the edge of her vision.

You're supposed to be dead, Lore thought. *You died.*

"Surprised?" There was a hopeful note in his voice, but his eyes were searching. Anxious.

Castor.

All the promise in his features had sharpened and set as the fullness of youth left his face. It was startling how much his voice had deepened.

For one horrible moment, Lore was convinced that she was in a lucid dream. That this would only end the way it always did when she dreamed her parents and sisters were still alive. She wasn't sure if she would be sick or start sobbing. The pressure built in her skull, immobilizing her, suffocating whatever joy might have bled through her shock.

But Castor Achilleos didn't vanish. The aches from Lore's earlier fights were still there, throbbing. The smell of booze and fried food was everywhere. She felt every drop of sweat clinging to her skin, racing down her face and back. This was real.

But Lore still couldn't move. Couldn't look away from his face.

He's real.

He's alive.

When a feeling finally broke through the numbness, it wasn't what she expected. It was anger. Not wild and consuming, but as sharp and ruthless as their practice blades had once been.

Castor was alive, and he'd let her grieve him for seven years.

Lore swiped a glove across her face, trying to refocus herself, even as her body felt like it might dissolve. This was a fight. He'd already landed the first blow, but this was the person who had once been her best friend, and she knew the best way to hit him back.

"Why would I be surprised?" Lore managed to get out. "I have no idea who you are."

A flicker of uncertainty passed over Castor's face, but it vanished as he raised an eyebrow and gave her a small, knowing smile. Beside her, several men and women in the audience trilled and began to whisper.

There was no way to send him out without making a scene, and there was no way she was letting him out of this basement completely unscathed after everything that had happened. Lore turned to give the signal to Frankie, hoping that no one could see her heart trying to pound its way out of her chest.

The bell rang. The crowd cheered. She lowered into a fighting stance.

Go away, she thought, staring at Castor over the tops of her gloves. *Leave me alone.*

He hadn't cared enough to try to find her in the last seven years, so what was the point of this? To mock her? To try to force her to come back?

Like hell he would.

"Please be gentle." Castor raised his hands, glancing down at a split in one of his borrowed gloves. "I haven't sparred in a while."

Not only was he alive, he'd finished his training as a healer instead of a fighter, as planned. His life had played out exactly as it was meant to, without her there to interrupt it.

And he had never come to find her. Not even when she'd needed him most.

Lore stayed light on her feet, circling around him. Seven years stretched between them like the wine-dark sea.

"Don't worry," she said coldly. "It'll be over quick."

"Not too quick, I hope," he said, another grin tugging at his lips.

His dark eyes caught the light of the bulbs swinging overhead, and the irises seemed to throw sparks. He had a long, straight nose despite the number of times he'd broken it sparring, a jaw cut at perfect angles, and cheekbones like blades.

Lore threw the first punch. He leaned to the side to avoid it. He was faster than she remembered, but his movements lurched. As strong as his body appeared, Castor *was* out of practice. It made her think of a rusted machine struggling to find its usual flow. As if to confirm Lore's suspicions, he leaned a little too far and had to check his balance to keep himself from stumbling.

"Are you here to fight or not?" she growled. "I get paid by the match, so stop wasting my time."

"I wouldn't dream of it," Castor said. "By the way, you're still dropping your right shoulder."

Lore scowled, resisting the urge to correct her stance. They were already losing their audience. The basement floor shuddered as the crowd stomped their feet into a driving beat, trying to force a change in the tempo of the fight.

Castor seemed to read the room correctly, or he'd gotten splattered by enough drinks, because his face set with a newfound focus. The lightbulbs kept swinging on their chains, throwing shadows. He wove in and out of them, as if he knew the secret to becoming darkness itself.

21

He feinted right and launched a halfhearted punch at her shoulder.

Fury painted Lore's world a scalding white. That was how little he respected her now. He didn't see her as a worthy opponent. He saw her as a joke.

Lore slammed a fist into his kidney, and as his body curled, her left hand clubbed his ear. He staggered, eventually dropping to a knee when he couldn't regain his footing.

She threw another punch, this one directly at his face, but he had enough sense left to block it. The impact reverberated up her arm.

"Keep toying with me," she warned him. "See how that ends for you."

Castor stared at her through the dark, unruly hair that had fallen into his eyes, his ivory skin flushed. She stared back. Sweat dripped off Lore's chin, and her body was still pulsating with the force of the storm inside her. The swinging lights danced in his dark irises again, almost hypnotically. The last traces of humor left his face as if she'd clawed them off herself.

He shot forward, locking an arm behind her knees and pulling them out from under her. One moment, Lore was standing; the next, she was flat on her back, gasping for air. The audience cheered.

She raised her leg to knock him back away from her, only to hear Frankie's pleasant voice call out, "No kicking!"

Right.

Lore rolled hard to her left, coming to the edge of the mat and onto her feet again. This time, when she launched a volley at Castor, he was ready, meeting her blow for blow. She ducked and bobbed, sinking into the current of the fight. Her lips curled into an involuntary smile.

There was movement at the top of the basement stairs as someone came down. That one look cost Lore—Castor reeled his arm back and launched a powerful blow into her gut.

She wheezed, trying to resist folding at the waist. Castor's eyes widened, almost in fear.

"Are you o—?" he began.

Lore lowered her head and drove it straight into his chest. It was like ramming into a cement wall. Every joint in her body suffered, and her vision was dotted with black, but he went down, and she went down with him.

Castor rolled them so he was on top, careful not to crush her with his weight as he pinned her to the mat. Lore was gratified to hear him breathing as hard as she was.

"You died," she managed to choke out as she struggled against the hold.

"I don't have much time," he said. Then he switched into the ancient tongue. "I need your help."

Her blood cooled at his words, spoken in the language she'd tried to force herself to forget.

"Something is happening," he said. The fight had warmed his body until it was almost burning to the touch. "I don't know who I can trust."

Lore turned her face away. "And that's my problem how? I'm *out*."

"I know, but I also need to warn you— Damn," Castor breathed, then swore again in the ancient tongue for good measure. He shifted their positions so that Lore rolled on top of him. She was distantly aware of the audience chanting the mandatory eight count. Too late, she realized he was letting her win.

"You jackass," she began.

His gaze was fixed on the staircase, on the figure she'd glimpsed before. Evander—Castor's relative, and occasional playmate to them both when they were kids.

Van wore a simple black hunter's robe, with a glint of something gold pinned just above his heart. His dark skin gleamed with the steam rolling down behind him from the kitchen, the undertone as cool as a pearl. He'd cropped his hair close, which only better served to highlight how devastatingly handsome he was. His eyes were sharp as he signaled something to Castor.

"Time's up," Castor said. Lore wasn't certain if he was talking about the match or something else.

"Wait," Lore began, though she didn't know why. But Castor had already lifted her off him. His hands lingered at her waist a second longer than either of them seemed to realize.

"He's looking for something, and I don't know if it's you," Castor told her.

Lore's head went light as his words sank in. There was only one *he* that would matter. She fought for her next breath. She fought against the static growing in her ears.

"You may be done with the Agon, but I don't think it's done with you. Be careful." His gaze became intent as he ducked low and whispered in her ear. "You still fight like a Fury."

Castor pulled back, taking his bow, accepting boos from the crowd and a red Solo cup that was offered to him. He pushed through the audience, heading straight for the stairs. As Castor reached him, Evander gripped his arm, and, together, they disappeared into the sweltering kitchen.

Someone grabbed Lore's wrist, trying to tug her arm up into the air, but Lore was already moving, shouldering her way through the crowd.

What are you even doing? her mind screamed at her. *Let them go!*

She collided with someone near the stairs, hard enough that he

24

was sent stumbling back against the nearby wall. Lore whirled around, half an apology already escaping her lips, when she saw who it was.

Shit.

His skin was white as bone, his dark eyes almost comically wide as they met hers. Edgy, vaguely hipster buzz cut. Skinny frame and skinnier jeans. Necklace made of braided horse hair.

Miles.

Unbelievable, she thought. How the hell had this night managed to get worse?

"Wait here!" she ordered.

At his stunned nod, Lore ran up into the kitchen, weaving through the irritated cooks and the veil of steam until she found the disabled emergency door and burst onto the dark street.

The air glowed red from the taillights of the SUV speeding away. A single red Solo cup rolled toward her feet, something dark smeared across the side of it.

Ink.

She turned it toward the dim security light above the door, trying to parse the uneven strokes of each letter. Her pulse beat wildly at her temples.

Apodidraskinda.

A child's game. Hide-and-seek.

A challenge. *Come find me.*

Lore dropped the cup into a nearby trash can and walked away.

THREE

THE HEAT IN HER BODY HAD SUBSIDED BY THE TIME LORE MADE HER way back down into the basement. She didn't see Miles as she cut through the crowd and went to retrieve her backpack and night's pay from Frankie. She only half listened to his instructions on where the next week's matches would be held, counted her bills to make sure he wasn't stiffing her, and tried to ignore the thrumming in her veins.

He's looking for something, and I don't know if it's you.

A shudder passed through her. She shook her head, clearing Castor's voice and face from her mind to prepare herself for what was coming.

Miles was waiting for her outside. In the few minutes it had taken Lore to return to the street, he'd managed to make himself breathless— whether from pacing, rehearsing whatever speech he was about to give her, or a combination of both. He stilled as she came through the door, pretending he'd been checking his phone the whole time.

Whatever she'd expected him to say, it wasn't "Want to get a bite to eat at Martha's?"

Lore hesitated. What she wanted was to go home, shower, and sleep for the next six days, until this disgusting hunt reached another end and the next seven-year cycle began. But Miles had a steadying effect on her.

"Sure," she said with forced nonchalance. It still felt like there was lightning beneath her skin. "Sounds good to me."

He raised an eyebrow. "You're definitely paying this time."

"Am I?" she said, letting herself drift back into their comfortable rhythm. "Or am I going to flutter these lashes and get our meal on the house?"

"When, in your entire life," Miles began, genuinely curious, "has that *ever* worked for you?"

"Excuse you," Lore said. "I am adorably persuasive."

She fluttered them now, but her face ached from the hits she had taken, and the swelling likely didn't help much, either.

Miles opened his mouth to say something else, but changed his mind.

"What?" she asked.

"Nothing," he said, glancing up at the cloudy sky. "Should we go before we get the shower that only one of us needs?"

The air dripped with humidity and was scented with the bagged garbage piled up for collection the next morning. A taxi blazed by, kicking up a wave of gutter water. It had been raining on and off for days, and Lore knew there was more to come.

"I'm wearing a perfume of the finest lo mein and BO," Lore said. "There's no accounting for taste with you."

That, of course, wasn't true at all. Miles treated his body like a piece of art, letting it speak for him—his moods, his interests, and the people he carried in his heart. His skin was colored by an array of tattoos, from gorgeous florals and vines that wrapped around his torso, to modern art faces he'd designed himself, to mountains, eyes, and bands of shapes only he knew the meaning of. Lore had always loved the simple hangul tattoos on his neck best because of the story

27

behind them. The phrase was something his grandmother used to say to him when he called her and his parents at home in Florida on Sundays: *I love you more with every sunrise.* When he'd shown them to her, she'd chided him for yet another tattoo, licking her finger and pretending to try to wipe them away with her finger, but she'd glowed with pride the rest of the night.

They walked to the Canal Street subway station to take the A train up to 125th Street. Lore was halfway down the stairs when she heard the approaching train and felt the telltale gust of air whip through the station. She ran, sliding her MetroCard out of her back pocket and through the reader. Miles, never ready, let out a strangled sound and fumbled with his wallet.

"Wait, no—ack—" Miles swiped his card again, getting an error message.

It was half past three o'clock in the morning, but subway service slowed in the off-hours, leaving the car full. She caught the closing door with her forearm just as Miles all but dove through.

He smacked her shoulder as the train lurched forward.

"Martha's," she said. "Hungry."

"Taxi," he said. "Easy."

"Money," she said. "Wasteful."

The car emptied at Columbus Circle, freeing the seats in front of them. Miles sat down and immediately pulled out his phone. Lore took a deep breath, rubbing a hand against her forehead. With her body still, there was only the chaos of her thoughts.

He's looking for something, and I don't know if it's you.

Lore had been unsettled by seeing the hunters in the city. She'd known to be afraid of Aristos Kadmou—or whoever he was as a god— finding her. She would be even more careful now and leave the city later that day, steering clear of the fighting and of him. Of all of them.

But the overriding feeling in her wasn't terror. Lore knew she could hide because she had successfully done it these last three years. Instead, there was a restlessness in her body she couldn't purge, an unwelcome tightness in her chest every time her mind conjured Castor's face.

Alive, she thought, still feeling strangely dazed at the thought.

Miles made a noise of dismay beside her. Lore glanced over just as he closed one of his dating apps.

"What happened to the guy you went out with on Friday?" Lore asked, welcoming the distraction. "I thought he had potential. Nick?"

"Noah," Miles said, closing his eyes and taking a deep breath, as if for strength. "I went back to his apartment and met all four of his hamsters."

Lore turned to him. "No."

"He named them after his favorite First Ladies," Miles continued, sounding pained. "Jackie had a pillbox hat made out of felt and nail polish. He made me feed them. With tiny strips of lettuce. *Lettuce,* Lore. Lettuce."

"Please stop saying lettuce," Lore said. "You could take a break from dating, you know."

"You could *try,*" he pointed out. He shifted a little in his seat. "I've never asked you this before, because I didn't want to pry."

"*But . . . ?*" she filled in.

"But," he began. "It's just that one guy, and the way you reacted to him . . ."

Her hand tightened around her backpack strap.

"How was I supposed to act when he came at me like that?" Lore asked. "He deserved to have his face rearranged. Maybe he'll think twice about doing that to girls."

"Oh, no, *he* definitely deserved it," Miles said quickly. "He probably deserved at least another solid thirty seconds of it. I was actually talking about the other one."

"The other one," she repeated. Her heart gave a hard kick.

"The guy who looked like he'd been molded out of every single one of my boyhood fantasies," Miles clarified helpfully.

Castor's voice was warm in her mind. *You still fight like a Fury.*

"What about him?" Lore asked.

"You seemed to know him," Miles said.

"I don't," she said sharply. *Not anymore.*

To stop any other questions, she leaned her head against Miles's shoulder, letting the rocking of the train soothe her until she was able to take her first deep breath of the night.

The train barreled on to 125th Street, falling into its usual rhythm of jerking starts and stops in each station. But she was too afraid to close her eyes on the chance Castor's face, bright and hopeful, would be there to lead her into the memories of the world she'd left behind.

It was quiet uptown when they finally emerged from the subway and turned toward Martha's Diner.

Harlem had felt like a foreign land when Lore moved into Gil's cozy brownstone on 120th Street; her family had always lived in Hell's Kitchen, and she'd never had a reason to go north of 96th. But at that point, her family had been dead for four years, and she'd spent much of that time living abroad. Coming back to the city had felt like being handed old clothes she'd given away to someone else. Nothing fit. Everything was the same, and yet somehow different.

But Lore had treasured the three years that followed, right up until that fateful moment six months ago, when Gil died—hit by a car as he crossed the street, of all things. After, her first instinct had been to pack up and go, only to find that it wasn't that simple. Gil had left her the brownstone and everything inside it.

Lore could have sold the house in a heartbeat and gone anywhere. Miles would have been fine, even if finding a new place in the city was a headache. But each time she thought seriously about it, the streets seemed to wrap around her. The familiar storefronts, the kids playing out on the stoop two doors down, Mrs. Marks hosing down the sidewalk every Monday morning at ten o'clock . . . it calmed her. It stopped the feeling that her chest might cave in on itself from the weight of the shock and grief.

So Lore had stayed. For all its exhausting complications and crowding, the city had always been her home. She understood its difficult personality and was grateful it had given her one of her own, because in the darkest moments of her life, that resilience alone had saved her.

In a way, she felt that her new neighborhood had chosen her and not the other way around, and she'd wanted to be claimed by something. And, really, that was New York for you. It always got a say, and, if you were patient enough, it led you where you needed to go.

It was four o'clock in the morning, but Lore wasn't surprised to see another person enjoying an early meal at Martha's, even in a month as quiet as August.

"Hey, Mr. Herrera," she called, wiping her feet on the old mat.

"Hey yourself, Lauren Pertho," he said, around a mouthful of his breakfast sandwich.

Lore had used that name for years, but it still had the tendency to catch her off guard. "How are you, Mel?"

"Dry, at least," Mel said from behind the diner's counter. She looked up from where she'd been counting out the register. "You both want your usuals to go?"

"Creatures of habit," Miles confirmed. "Do you have any decaf brewing?"

"I'll put a pot on for you," she said. "Whipped cream?"

Miles had the palate of a kid who ate dessert for every meal. "Chocolate sprinkles?"

"You got it, sweetheart," Mel said, ducking into the kitchen to start on their order. One Triple Lumberjack platter for Lore, and chocolate chip Mickey Mouse pancakes with extra whipped cream and maple syrup for Miles.

"What?" Miles said. "No comment? No joke about my sugar intake?"

It took a moment for Lore to realize he was talking to her. She looked up from where her gaze had fallen to the floor.

"I'm going to get a stomachache just from watching you," Lore said, leaning back against the side of one of the vinyl-covered booths. Her pulse had jumped, as if she'd been caught doing something she wasn't supposed to.

Miles stared at her for a moment, but kept his voice light. "Rich coming from someone who eats a meal meant for three people."

"Healthy appetite," Mr. Herrera said as he paid his bill, "healthy girl."

"Exactly," Lore said, fighting to focus on him. "How's my Handsome Bo doing?"

Bo the Bodega Cat had shown up two years ago, claimed Mr. Herrera's shop for its kingdom, and never left. The first time she'd seen him, Lore had mistaken him for an extremely large rat, and seriously wondered if he hadn't clawed up from the Underworld. Now, her favorite late-Sunday-morning activity was sitting on the bench outside the store and sharing the lox from her bagel with her foul-tempered buddy.

"He ate twelve chocolate bars, vomited on the produce, and destroyed a shelf of paper towels," Mr. Herrera said, heading toward the door. "And now I have to take the demon to the vet."

"Do you need me to watch the shop for you?" Lore asked. She enjoyed doing it, especially after the morning rush-hour customers came for their coffee, and she could sit and read a book until the lunchers arrived to decimate the stock of premade sandwiches and sushi.

"Not this time," Mr. Herrera said. "My nephew is here. Maybe you'd like to meet him? He's a year younger than you, smart boy—"

"Can he do laundry?" Miles asked seriously. "Or cook? She needs someone to fill the gaps in her important life skills."

Mr. Herrera laughed, waving him off as he left to open his store.

Lore wasn't sure why she had offered, knowing that she was more than likely leaving town today. Castor's presence, never mind his warning, should have sent her running immediately, with or without supplies.

She rubbed her arms at the place he had gripped them, and was surprised to find her skin was warm despite the chill passing through her. She just hadn't expected . . . *him*. The whole of him. Those familiar soft eyes. His height. The strength of his body.

The way he had smiled at her.

"Lore—*Lore*," Miles said again, this time with more force.

She looked up again. "What?"

"I said, is it about money?"

Lore stared at him, confused. "Is what about money?"

Miles gave her a look. "If it is, I can start paying you rent. But I thought Gilbert had left you money, too . . . ?"

True to his exasperatingly kind form and his love of surprises, Gil had left both of his "honorary grandchildren" a generous sum of money, but Lore still hadn't touched it, except to do maintenance on the brownstone. It didn't feel right to use it for anything else.

"It's Gil's money," Lore said.

Miles seemed to understand. "Well, you could get a part-time barista job like everyone else. It's basically a rite of passage. You could even charge for the self-defense classes."

She shook her head, trying to focus her exhausted web of feelings and thoughts onto the single thread of their conversation.

"I'm not going to charge anyone who wants to learn how to protect themselves," Lore said, keeping her voice low. The gym owner on 125th let her use some of his equipment when it was too cold to run outside in exchange for teaching the free lessons, and that was more than enough for her. "And it's not about the money."

"Are you sure? Because you've been reusing the same three gross Ziploc bags for the last year," Miles said.

She held up a finger. "They aren't gross, because I wash them out every time. What are *you* doing to save the environment?"

His eyebrows rose. He was interning that summer with the City Council and studying sustainable urban development at Columbia.

"Don't answer that," Lore said.

Miles was doing that thing she hated where he waited for her to talk while looking extremely compassionate and understanding.

"Besides," she said, "I do have a job. I'm the super, remember?"

Lore had originally come to work for Gil as a live-in caretaker, but her role had expanded after she changed out the batteries in the smoke detectors—which said everything about the threshold of tech-savviness in their building at the time.

"By the way, *Super*, can you maybe come up and fix my window before winter?"

Lore scowled, smoothing a hand back over the mass of frizz the rain had gifted to her.

"Okay, it's a little about the money," she admitted, "but it's about other things, too."

"Gil things?" Miles pressed.

She pulled the necklace out of her pocket, examining the place the gold chain had snapped. Her neck felt strange without it; Gil had given it to her three years ago, on her first birthday after returning to the city, and she had only taken it off once since then.

A feather fallen from a wing is not lost, Gil had told her, *but free.*

It had reminded her of that, of what she had gained when she'd offered to work for Gil, every day. She had been hired to help take care of him after he had a bad fall and it became clear he couldn't keep living alone, but he had done so much more for her. He had been a friend, a mentor, and a reminder that not all men were as harsh and cruel as the ones she had grown up around.

"It's been a few months now . . ." Miles began.

"It's been six," Lore said sharply.

"Six," he said, nodding. "We don't really talk about it that often—" Lore opened her mouth to dismiss that, but he held up his hand. "All I want to say is that I'm here, and I always want to talk about him."

"Well, I don't," Lore said. Gil had told her that sometimes you had to push away the bad things until they left you alone for good. One day his loss wouldn't hurt so bad.

35

"You know . . ." Miles said in a familiar tone.

"I'm not interested in school," she told him, for the hundredth time. "You don't even seem to like it."

"You don't have to like something you need," Miles pointed out.

"You don't need to do something you don't enjoy," Lore shot back.

Miles blew out a sigh through his nose. "I just think . . . whatever happened to you, you have to start thinking about your future, otherwise your past is always going to hold you back."

Lore swallowed, but couldn't clear the tightness in her throat. "How did you find out about the ring anyway? Did you follow me or something?"

"I was out with my friend from school last night and he started talking about this super-crazy, super-secret fighting ring and mentioned a girl with a scar that ran from the outer corner of her eye down to her chin, and I said, wow, that sounds like my friend Lore . . ."

Without thinking, she rubbed that side of her face against her shoulder. The scar was thin, but it hadn't faded with age.

"Your friend wasn't the guy I beat up, right?" she asked. "Just checking."

"No, but I have never been so simultaneously amazed and terrified in my whole life," Miles said.

His phone gave a shrill ring, making them both jump.

"Is that your alarm?" Lore asked, her hand still pressed to her chest. They'd lived in the same house for years and she'd never heard anything like it.

"Sort of," he said, then answered the call with "Ma, what are you doing up? It's like four o'clock in the morning— You absolutely do *not* need to print out those forms now, write yourself a note to do it at a normal hour and— No, *you* go back to bed— Well, if I wasn't up, you would have woken me up— *Ma*. Go back to bed!"

Mrs. Yoon's muffled words were filled with the kind of energy no one was supposed to have this early. Lore watched as Miles closed his eyes and breathed in for patience.

"Augh. Fine. You checked all the cords, right?" he asked. "Made sure they didn't come loose?"

Miles sent Lore an apologetic look, but she didn't mind at all. It was nice, actually. If nothing else, it gave her the opportunity to try to picture him growing up as a baby goth amidst the palm trees and bright pastels of Florida. He was an only child, and sometimes, like now, it really showed.

Miles sucked in another deep breath. "Did you actually turn the printer on? The button should be glowing."

Lore heard Mrs. Yoon's sheepish laughter in response and her loving "Thank you, Michael."

Miles pressed a hand to his face in exasperation, whether at her question or at his given name, which only his family ever used, and told her that he loved her in both Korean and English, and hung up the phone.

"She made me change the ringtone when I went home last month," Miles said. "She thought I wasn't answering because the old one was too quiet, and now I feel too guilty to ever change it."

Lore smiled, even as something twisted deep in her chest. You never missed calls like that until they stopped coming. "She just wants to hear your voice."

She wants you to remember her, Lore thought. Her mind drifted, suddenly untethered. The world around her became haloed with darkness until she only saw Castor's face, and the way the shadows had caressed it.

37

"Hey," Miles said suddenly. "You're all right, aren't you?"

"I'm fine," Lore insisted.

She would be. For him. For herself.

For Gil.

"Ready to go?" she asked as Mel returned from the kitchen with their orders.

"Promise me you'll be safe," Miles said, catching her hand before she pulled it back. "I don't care if you need to keep fighting, I just don't want to see you hurt."

Too late for that, Lore thought.

They ducked back out into the dim light of the street, clutching their breakfasts and coffees. The storm had turned into a shroud of fine mist. New York City was one of the few places in the world that looked dirtier after it rained, but Lore loved it.

As they made their way home, Lore decided that she would tell Miles she was going to spend the next few days traveling, even if that meant catching a bus and sleeping rough out in the woods where no one could find her.

Right then, though, nothing sounded better than spending the rest of her Sunday morning in bed. Lore looped her arm through Miles's as they made their way down their sleepy street, Miles humming a song she didn't recognize. She tried not to think of anything at all.

They were a block from the brownstone when Miles suddenly stopped, jerking her back a step.

"What?" she asked.

He leaned closer to the wall of Martin's Deli, the place that had banned Lore for complaining about their shamefully stale bagels, and brushed his fingers through a smear of some dark substance. Lore pulled him back in horror.

"Okay, I think you need a refresher on the rules of New York—one, do not take anything someone tries to pass to you in Times Square; two, do not touch mysterious substances on the ground and walls—"

"I think it's blood," Miles interrupted.

Lore's hand fell away from him.

He spun, searching the ground. "Holy shit. There's so much of it . . ."

There was. Lore had mistaken the splattered drops on the cement for rain, but now she could make out the dark blood washing down the gutter as the storm began in earnest.

Miles lunged forward, swinging his head around to look for the person bleeding. Lore caught him by the back of his shirt with one hand and, after passing him her food container and coffee, pulled out the pocket knife on her keychain with the other.

"Stay behind me," she ordered.

It was like tracking wounded prey. The victim seemed to have been staggering, moving from support to support—a street light, a banister, a parked car. With a growing sense of dread, Lore realized they were headed in the direction of the brownstone.

Lore's grip on her dull blade tightened as they approached it. The bloody path turned toward their door and the cheerful flowerpots Gil had placed along the front steps.

Miles gasped, and Lore followed his gaze.

A woman sat with her back against the old brownstone's stoop beside the empty trash cans. Her sky-blue robes were drenched with rain.

Lore felt the air quicken around her, like the moment before a lightning strike.

"Show me your hands," Lore choked out, raising her own pathetic blade.

The goddess's eyes were the color of sacrificial smoke, flecks of gold glowing in the irises, drifting like embers. The only hint of suppressed divine power.

They called her the gray-eyed goddess, but Lore understood now that it wasn't for their color. It was because when she stared at you, the way she stared at Lore now, her true age was revealed. Wars, civilizations, monsters, death, technology, exploration—those eyes had watched millennia pass by, and measured them the way Lore would casually note the hour of the day.

Strands of burnished-gold hair were splayed across the goddess's face like well-earned scars. Even in her current form, she was unsettlingly flawless, her features bold and perfect in their symmetry.

The goddess leaned back, pulling her palm away from where it had been pressed to her opposite hip. As it fell into her lap, the long, elegant fingers curled like claws.

The hand was empty, but stained with blood.

Lore stared, half-aware that she'd lowered her own arm.

The goddess leaned forward, causing the tear in her side to gush with hot, reeking blood. Too big and jagged for an arrow or bullet. A blade, then. That wound had to have come from a professional.

Her thoughts were all logic, but Lore felt like she was moving through a dream.

"Someone clearly had your number," Lore choked out. "Bad luck with the landing?"

"*Attend to me.*"

Lore jumped. Half-dead or not, each of the goddess's words rang out like a sword striking a shield. They vibrated along Lore's nerves until every hair on her body rose. It had been so long since she'd heard anyone speak such a pure form of the ancient tongue, it took her mind a moment to translate it.

When she did, her voice was a thin whisper. "What did you say?"

The goddess's eyes were unfocused now, quickly losing some of their steel. There was no fear in her face as she returned her hand to her side to press against the wound, only bitter disbelief. Rancor. When she spoke again, her words were labored but the command seemed to echo across Lore's soul.

"Attend . . . to me . . . mortal."

Then gray-eyed Athena slumped to the cement, and slipped out of consciousness.

FOUR

"OH MY *GOD*!"

Miles's panicked voice pulled Lore out of her own shock. When she turned to him, his face was already illuminated by the glow of his cellphone. His hands shook as he thumbed in numbers.

Lore tore the phone out of his hands, ending the call before it could connect.

"What are you doing?" he cried. "She needs help! Ma'am? Ma'am, can you hear me?"

"Stop!" Lore said sharply. "Keep your voice down!"

"Do you know her?" Miles looked like he was about to start clawing on his face. "Oh no, the blood— I just—" He gagged, coughing into his fist.

Lore spoke without thinking. "I— Yes. She's like— She's a fighter, too."

"She has to—" Miles gagged again. "Sorry—I just— Hospital. She needs the hospital. And the police."

Lore swore, her mind racing. If they brought the goddess in, the police would want to question Lore, putting her name and possibly a photo into their system. And the bloodlines always posted at least a few hunters at each hospital, in the hope a Good Samaritan might unknowingly call emergency services and deliver a god right to

42

them. But Athena had trailed her scent and blood here for any of the bloodlines' dogs to track, right to Lore's sanctuary. Putting Miles at risk, and forcing Lore to do *something* about it.

Lore kept her fingers pressed against the goddess's neck, checking for a pulse. Right now, the goddess's ichor ran as red as any human's blood, and it was pooling around Lore's knees and sneakers.

Shit, she thought, feeling helpless for the first time in years. She had to bring the goddess inside. Now.

"No police," Lore said quickly, struggling for a reasonable excuse. "No, she's— She doesn't have insurance. Can you go unlock the door and help me carry her in?"

Lore struggled to hook Athena's arm over her neck. Even in mortal form, the goddess was over six feet tall, and as Lore and Miles quickly discovered, her body was slick from both the rain and the blood.

They made it into the entry before dropping her onto the black-and-white-checked tile. Lore left Miles behind as she ran for the linen closet upstairs, pulling out extra sheets and towels and dropping them over the banister.

When she came back down, Lore closed the shutters of the bay window in the front room, sealing it off like a fortress. Miles switched on the ceiling lights.

The TV screen above the fireplace was a black mirror as Lore cleared the coffee table out of the way. Miles spread out the dark bedsheets, and Lore realized with a pang that they had been Gil's.

"What is going on?" Miles asked as they dragged Athena's prone form over. "Lore—seriously, what the hell is happening?"

The goddess moaned. Lore glanced toward the entry, the blood smeared there, and remembered that they had another very big problem.

"I need you to do something," Lore told him as she knelt down beside Athena. "I need you to go to Mr. Herrera and ask for as many containers of bleach as he has— Wait. Not the regular bleach, the oxygen bleach, unless the regular bleach is all that he has."

"Oxygen—what?" Miles asked helplessly.

"Oxygen bleach, as many as he has," Lore said. "Tell him to put it on my tab."

"Bodegas have tabs?" Miles asked.

"*Go*," Lore said, throwing her arm out toward the door. "And hurry."

Miles seemed too stunned to do anything other than what she'd asked. He jumped over the blood, gagging one last time before the door slammed shut behind him.

The house's usual smells of sandalwood and old books vanished beneath the hot stink of blood. Lore's stomach gave a violent lurch as she turned the goddess onto her back. She tore the fabric of the ruined tunic, trying to get a better look at the wound. Blood spilled over her fingers.

"Damn," she whispered.

The liver and kidney had been pierced. Lore knew this work; it was an expert cut by a léaina—one of the young women sent out by the bloodlines to hunt gods and bring back the wounded prey for their leader to kill.

She pressed a towel to it, trying to stanch the flow of blood. "Wake up. *Wake up!*"

Athena's eyes rolled beneath her closed eyelids.

Lore did the only thing she could think of. She slapped the goddess across the face.

Her gray eyes snapped open, blinking rapidly.

"I'd say sorry," Lore managed. "But you deserved it."

The air in Lore's lungs suddenly felt scalding. She was surprised at her fear in that moment, the flash of regret she'd had as she'd struck Athena. Years of conditioning to hate the old gods faded away as she saw the sparks of power burning in Athena's gaze.

You could only convince yourself something was prey until it turned around and showed you its teeth.

The goddess let out a wet cough, her head rolling against the floor. Even in a mortal body, there was something cold, almost alien, about her appearance up close. Her body was an unnatural container. One made to be killed.

Lore pressed her hands against her thighs, trying to stop the involuntary tremble in them. She wouldn't kill her. She didn't want a god's power. She didn't want any of this.

"Feels bad, doesn't it?" Lore asked, letting a wild recklessness sweep in to replace her fear. "Man, mortality. What a bummer. Dare I ask who got you?"

This moment had been over a thousand years in the making. Athena had survived two hundred and eleven cycles of the Agon only for number two-twelve to get her.

The honey tone of Athena's skin paled as death found its way in. The goddess was one of the last of the originals still in the Agon, the others being Hermes and Artemis, and, maybe, Apollo. She had been an impossible target. She was too strong, too quick, too clever.

Until now.

They studied each other. If Athena was trying to gauge Lore's worth, her strength, Lore would have been the first one to tell her not to bother.

"I'm out." There were plenty of pretty words Lore could have used to flatter the goddess. To grovel and appeal to her kind's exhausting vanity and pride. Lore didn't care to remember any of them. "And I'm not going to let you or anyone else pull me back in."

The goddess stared, the stern line of her mouth never once relaxing. Lore expected nothing else. There would be no bending; like a blade, Athena would hold, or she would break.

"I know you speak this language," Lore said, refusing to give the goddess what she clearly wanted. The ancient tongue was a mixture of many ancient dialects that had eventually become Modern Greek, but Athena's version was epic in quality.

"Whatever you came here for, there's nothing to find," Lore continued. "If this is a trick and you're here for revenge, you're too late. Everyone else who bears my name is dead. I'm the last of the Perseides. The House of Perseus is gone."

The expression on Athena's face told Lore that the goddess already knew exactly who she was.

Fear tore through her. Lore had stopped believing in Fate and the old crones tending to it years ago, but this was too much to be mere coincidence, especially after Castor's warning.

Attend to me, she'd said. *Help me.*

"You found me," Lore said, proud of how steady her voice sounded. "Tell me what you want, and make it fast. I know this is a difficult concept for you, but your time is running out and my plans for this morning don't include an awkward staring contest with a deity. Why don't you start with who tried to kill you?"

Athena met her gaze again as she said, her voice weaker now, "My sister."

A cold dread slithered through Lore's body. "As in, Artemis?"

The goddess glowered. Her other sister, Aphrodite, had been

taken out by a hunter a century ago, and a new god with her powers had been born. That new god had lasted only one cycle before another hunter killed him seven years later. It was a morbid sort of marathon relay, with immortal power as the baton being passed between bloodlines.

"I thought the two of you always worked together," Lore said. "What happened to that fun little alliance you used to terrorize everyone with?"

"Turned . . . on me," Athena said, pressing her palm to her side again. "Betrayed. The Ares imposter . . . he . . . came after me . . . at the Awakening—Artemis slowed me, escaped."

"That's cold," Lore said with mild appreciation. "Even for her."

"Alliances form from need . . . break in fear . . ." Athena struggled for the words. "Now . . . need . . . protection. Until I . . . heal. Bind your fate . . . to mine."

Bind your fate to mine. Lore shuddered.

"Why the hell would I ever do that," Lore said, "when I can sit here and watch you die instead?"

Despite temporarily losing their immortality, the gods did retain a sliver of their might to defend themselves. In their prime, their true powers had been all-encompassing; what remained must have felt like a sad pantomime, and, worse, only Apollo seemed to have been left with the ability to heal himself and others. Athena might have been physically stronger than the other eight gods in the Agon, capable of leveling whole buildings, but it wasn't going to do her any good now.

Miles's quick steps pounded up to their front door. Lore jumped to her feet, giving the goddess one last hard look. Athena visibly bristled at the impertinence of it.

"Don't say a word to him when he comes in," Lore said.

47

"Pretend you're asleep."

"Do not forsake me," Athena said weakly. "I forbid it."

"Yeah, well, I forbid you to die right now," Lore said, her pulse jumping. "I have to go clean up after you before the bloodhounds find your trail and lead the hunters here."

Athena's gaze flickered.

Shit, Lore thought miserably. The goddess could bleed, she could slip into unconsciousness, but she would never have forgotten such a crucial strategic detail if she were not in absolute dire straits.

The front door burst open. "I've got them!"

The goddess's nostrils flared, but she did as Lore asked.

"Thank you," Lore told Miles. "Now go upstairs and go to bed."

"Wait—what?" he asked, trying to follow her back outside. "What are you doing?"

"I'm going to clean up before someone sees the blood and calls the cops," Lore said. "And you're going upstairs to bed."

Miles glanced at Athena's limp form.

"Listen to me," Lore said, her voice steel. Miles flinched, but she couldn't feel sorry, not for this. He had no idea what he'd been drawn into. "Go upstairs. Don't answer the door. If you see anyone suspicious outside, call me."

She left before he could lodge another protest, or, worse, ask another question. She bounded down the front steps of the brownstone, curving around to the gate that led into the basement apartment she now used for storage. There'd be almost no time. The sun was rising behind the curtain of clouds, and so were New Yorkers.

Lore dumped two containers of the oxy bleach into a bucket and carried it back outside to mix in water from her neighbor's hose. She used a wire brush and the power of her own terror to scrub the pool

48

of blood Athena had left near the trash cans, until her head was light and her hands stung from the chemicals.

Lore started to toss the bucket's bloodied water in the gutters . . . only to stop. She watched the rain run along the sidewalk and into the storm drain.

She wouldn't be able to mask the scent of blood, or the stench of the goddess herself, and now she was covered in both. The best Lore could manage was to confuse the hunters with too many trails, and hope they ran themselves ragged before they ever found their way to the town house, and to Miles.

Lore followed the path Athena had taken, cleaning and rinsing until the rain washed the visible stains mostly clean and everything trickled down into the gutters. She traced a wide, arcing trail around the neighborhood, leaving splashes of the bloodied bleach water here and there.

When Lore was finally within sight of Central Park, she stripped off her soiled shoes and socks, her face twisting in disgust as she stepped barefoot onto the cracked sidewalk. She took off before she could let herself think too hard about what she'd be picking up, and she set on a random, weaving path through the streets, stopping only to dump the shoes and socks one at a time in scattered trash cans and dumpsters.

As she neared the brownstone again, Lore tossed her light jacket into the back of a moving garbage truck and stuffed her jeans and shirt into the undercarriages of two different delivery trucks parked near Mr. Herrera's bodega.

Instead of going through the front door, Lore entered through the basement. The smell of Gil's sandalwood cologne was everywhere, along with faint mildew and dust. Searching through the storage tubs she'd abandoned down there, Lore set aside a box containing Gil's vast collection of holiday-themed bow ties and found an old pair of pull-on shorts and a T-shirt in the container beneath it.

Lore changed into them quickly, dumping her soiled clothes into a trash bag. She took several steadying breaths until the chemical reek faded and her panic had given way to renewed anger.

Dragging herself up the inner staircase, she stepped back into the silence of the first level of the house. Some of the tension in her back and shoulders eased as she took a look around, and she almost managed a laugh. Miles had cleaned the blood from the hallway and switched off the lights in the living room, and he'd left a glass of water and bottle of aspirin beside Athena.

Helpful, Lore thought with a surge of affection for him.

She glanced to her left. Miles hadn't just locked the door; he'd also reinforced the knob with the back of a chair—like that would stop the hunters from setting enough explosives to blow off the front of the house.

Athena's head turned at the sound of Lore's approaching steps. She opened her eyes again; they glowed in the room's relative darkness. Her hand held the towel against the wound.

The air was so still around her, the silence so unnatural.

"You want me to help protect you, and, I'm guessing, to hide you from the same people that would happily kill me, too," Lore whispered. "But you already know that. That's why you came here, isn't it?"

Athena gave a slight nod.

"So exactly what's in this for me?" Lore said, taking another step closer. "I realize this is a new experience for you, but even if you heal faster than the average mortal, you're not exactly doing well. So why would I tie my life to one that might not make it a few hours, let alone a few days?"

"I heard . . . what had happened to you . . ." Athena said. "The years between . . . Searched . . . for you . . ."

The hair on Lore's body rose.

At the end of each Agon, the gods, new and old, regained their immortality, but they remained in the mortal world, unable to return to whatever home they'd once known.

The new gods, brimming with power, manifested physical forms and lived lavishly, manipulating the workings of the world to fill the vaults of their mortal bloodlines. But the old gods, with their power ever-waning, usually chose to remain incorporeal. It made them untraceable as they set about the world, trying to plan for contingencies for the next hunt or seeking retribution against those who had tried to kill them. The threat of that vengeance was the reason hunters always wore masks.

"You searched for me?" Lore said. "*Why?*"

"I believed . . . you could be . . . persuaded to aid me . . . I heard your . . . name . . . from the other bloodlines . . . Your family . . . *murdered*. Mother . . . father . . . sisters," Athena said, her breathing labored. "They called you . . . lost. Some believed . . . dead."

Lore's throat locked until she almost couldn't speak. "What do you know about that?"

Athena looked to her again, this time with the expression of someone who already knew they'd won. "I know . . . who killed them."

51

FIVE

THE MEMORY ROSE SHARP AND TRUE, CUTTING THROUGH ALL THE barriers Lore had built around it. The way the door to her family's apartment had looked as she came toward it that morning. The chilling silence inside. The smell of blood.

Lore drew in a deep breath and pressed a hand to her eyes, hard enough that light and colors danced beneath her lids. It distracted her mind from the dark trail it had started down again, but only for a moment.

She didn't know how she kept her voice so calm as she said, "I already know who killed them. Aristos Kadmou of the House of Kadmos." The new Ares, as of the last Agon.

"The false god may have . . . ordered their deaths . . . but who held the blade?" Athena pressed. "For it was not he. He was only a newborn god . . ."

Lore's body tightened to the point of pain.

"It doesn't matter. He was the one who gave the order," Lore said. "He was the head of his bloodline, and then became their god. They are all responsible, every last man, woman, and child who kneels before him, but only *he* had the power to put it all into motion."

And his bloodline had obeyed his command, murdering her parents and two little sisters so savagely that it had taken the Kadmides weeks to clean the apartment enough to hide the evidence. In the end, they'd still had to purify it with flames. According to the New York City Police Department, the family had set the fire themselves after a rent dispute and left town, never to be heard from again.

No one in the House of Kadmos had ever claimed responsibility for the murders, or ever would. The hunters had taken a blood oath centuries ago to never intentionally kill a hunter of another bloodline between the cycles of the Agon. It had been the only way to ensure peace between them.

Her family had been murdered the morning after the Agon's completion, when that oath should have protected them. The Kadmides had broken a sacred vow, but no other house was powerful enough to challenge them, and no gods had ever listened to her prayers.

"Why did you . . . not avenge them?" Athena panted. "These many years . . . you have done nothing . . . You . . . do not recognize your . . . moira . . . You never sought . . . poiné . . . only fell . . . to . . . the worst aidos . . ."

Lore sank to the floor, her legs folding beneath her. She braced her hands beside them, fighting the familiar pressure expanding in her chest. Her moira—her lot in life, her destiny.

"Those words mean nothing to me now," she said hoarsely. But hearing them felt like scars being cut open.

Poiné. Vengeance.

Aidos. Shame.

A life without the excellence of areté and the earned possessions of timé. Of never attaining kleos.

"I was just a little girl," Lore said, barely hearing her own words. "They would have killed me, too. I wasn't strong enough to fight them all. And I knew I could never get to him, not after he ascended."

53

In the years since, she'd killed to keep from being killed. She traveled by foot, by boat, by air, only to arrive back at the city that had raised her. She'd escaped the labyrinth of oaths that had been designed to trap her until the day came when the Agon called for her to sacrifice her last heartbeat.

But Lore had done *nothing* to avenge her family.

Athena's lip curled. "Excuses . . . These lies you tell yourself . . . You were never . . . a mere . . . *little girl.* I heard . . . what the others whispered about you . . . that you were the best of your generation . . . that it was a shame . . . you had been born to a different bloodline . . ."

"You're lying," Lore whispered, unable to stop the involuntary shiver that moved through her. Years ago, those words would have meant everything to her—she'd craved recognition from the very people who had refused to give it to her.

"The Spartan . . . they called you," Athena breathed. "Little Gorgon . . . I searched for you . . . chose you . . . knowing that skill . . . knowing that you are no longer one of the hunters . . . But you have . . . never been weak . . . never *powerless* . . . So I ask . . . why did you do nothing . . . to avenge your family?"

Lore drew her arms close to her chest, throwing out Gil's words like a shield. But there was no protection against the truth. "It's not— You wouldn't understand. The only real thing in this world is what you can do for others. How you can take care of them."

The goddess snorted with derision.

"All you know," Lore continued, hating the thickness in her voice, "all you have ever cared about is power. You don't know how to want anything else, and because of it, you won't believe me when I tell you that I don't want to claim his power, either. I don't want any part of this sick game."

"Then what is it . . . that you desire?" Athena asked.

The words burst from Lore, wild and pained. "To be free."

"No," Athena said, her voice labored. "That is not it. What do you . . . deny yourself?"

A vision bloomed in her mind, blazing and pure, but Lore shook her head.

"Lie to . . . yourself . . . but not to me," Athena said. "You know . . . you shall never be . . . free while the shades of your family . . . suffer and wander . . . Never at rest while he lives."

Lore pressed her fists to her eyes, trying to find the words to protest.

"You deny your heritage . . . You deny honor . . . You deny your ancestors, and your gods . . . But this, you cannot deny," Athena said. "This, you know to be true. Tell me . . . what you desire."

The truth finally escaped its cage. "I want to kill him."

Lore had denied it for years—forced the truth down deep inside her. All in the name of being good, of deserving the new life she'd been given. She wasn't ashamed of how badly she wanted it, or how often she dreamed of his death, but of how ungrateful it made her feel for the second chance working for Gil had given her.

"But I can't," Lore continued, her throat aching. "Even if I could get close enough to try, killing Aristos would mean taking his power. I don't want to be a god. I just want to live. I want to know my family is . . . at peace."

"Then I will kill him for you."

Lore looked down at the goddess in disbelief.

"I will kill the false Ares in your name," Athena said, struggling for breath. "If you swear . . . you will aid me . . . if you vow . . . to bind your fate to mine until . . . this hunt ends . . . at sunrise . . . on the eighth day."

Lore's heart began to race again, galloping in her chest.

This was *something*. It wouldn't just destroy Aristos Kadmou, either. A god could not take another god's power. Athena would be effectively removing Ares's dangerous power from the Agon—and the mortal world—entirely.

"Bind your fate to mine," the goddess said again, offering her bloodied hand. "Your heart . . . it aches for it . . ."

Gil's face, his usual toothy grin, drifted through Lore's mind.

I'm sorry, she thought, agonized.

Then she nodded.

Athena's teeth were stained with blood as she bared them. "You know what it means, do you not? What the oath entails?"

"I do."

Her own many times great-grandfather had been a cautionary tale, having foolishly bound his fate to the original Dionysus. The old god had needed protection from the descendants of Kadmos. Though he himself had been born into that bloodline through his mortal mother, Dionysus had cursed his kin—and Kadmos himself—when they refused to believe he had been fathered by Zeus.

The instant the old god died, cornered and slaughtered like a boar, Lore's ancestor's heart had stopped dead in his chest.

The strongest of his generation, gone in the time it took to blink, remembered forever by his kin as a blade traitor—and, as her own father believed, the true cause of the centuries-old animosity between the Houses of Perseus and Kadmos.

Lore would be agreeing to protect Athena with her life, to shelter her, and to bank on the hope that the goddess didn't die from this wound or any other. It was a risk she would have to take. An oath was, after all, a curse you placed on yourself—she would be damned if she failed, and damned if she succeeded. But she would never have an opportunity like this again.

Lore tried to remember the words her father and mother had always used to make their oaths, but couldn't bring herself to invoke the name of any gods.

"I will help you survive this week, and you will destroy the god once known as Aristos Kadmou, the enemy of my blood," Lore said quietly. She took the goddess's cold hand in her own. "If that's the bargain, then I swear by the powers below that I will uphold my vow or face the wrath of the heavens."

The goddess nodded. "Then I bind my mortal life to yours . . . Melora, daughter of Demos, scion of Perseus . . . Should I fall . . . you will join me. Should you die in the Agon . . . I, too, will perish. That is the vow we make to each other."

Warmth wrapped around their joined hands, chased by a chill along the ridges of Lore's spine like the tip of a knife. How perfect that Athena's power came only in the form of steel and pain.

"Is it done?" Lore asked.

Her answer was the goddess's cruel, bloody smile.

Lore pulled back, rising unsteadily to her feet. A sensation of sparks scattered across her skin like stars in the sky, sinking into the marrow of her bones.

"We need to stop the bleeding," Lore said, looking at Athena's wound. "I don't know if I have thread to stitch it."

The goddess shook her head. "Burn it shut."

Lore rose, feeling half-removed from her own body, and went to the kitchen. She held one of the carving knives over the fire on the gas stove until the metal glowed as gold as the flecks in Athena's eyes.

Miles, she thought distantly. She needed to check on Miles once this was finished.

But he had already come down to check on her.

Miles sat on the stairs, his gaze still fixed on what he could see of the living room through the old wood banister. There didn't seem to be a drop of color left in his face, and Lore knew, even before he looked at her and the knife in her hands, that he had heard everything.

"I think," he said finally, his voice hoarse, "you'd better tell me what the hell is going on."

SIX

THEY SAT IN SILENCE FOR SEVERAL MINUTES AFTER LORE HAD FINISHED giving Miles a ruthlessly pared-down explanation of the Agon, the nine gods it had been created to punish—including the one whose wound she had seared shut in their living room—and the nine blood-lines descended from ancient heroes chosen to hunt them.

She distilled over a thousand years of history into mere minutes, feeling more and more insane as his face remained carefully blank.

It wasn't like Lore could blame him; hearing herself say the words "For seven days, every seven years, the gods walk on earth as mortals. If you can kill one, you become a new god and take their power and immortality, but you'll be hunted in the next Agon as well" had left her stomach in knots, and not just because she had been taught, from the youngest age, never to reveal their world to outsiders.

To Miles, these names—Athena, Artemis, Apollo, Poseidon, Hephaestus, Aphrodite, Dionysus, Hermes, and Ares—were ancient stories, not living, breathing monsters who had refused to fade away once a more prominent god rose in their lands.

The way the hunters told it, they had attempted to force their worshippers back into submission by stoking chaos at the fall of Rome, by having Apollo create deadly plagues, including the Plague of Justinian, which alone killed tens of millions of people. All in the hope that mortals would beg them for protection and refuge.

"And, when Zeus commanded them to stop," Lore finished, "the nine, led by Athena, tried and failed to overthrow him in order to continue their work."

Gil had always made tea when they'd needed to talk about something, and Lore found herself doing the same thing now—only, as if muscle memory had taken over, she skipped the tea bags and made a very different kind of brew.

As a joke, the hunters called their tea nektar, the drink of the gods. They used thyme—the herb for courage—ginger, lemon, and honey to fortify themselves during training and the Agon.

But both mugs had gone cold, untouched where she'd set them down on the table.

The window AC unit wheezed on, flooding the kitchen with cool air. Lore had drawn the curtains on the window above the sink, and she could tell by the way the sun was still trying to intrude on them that it was already late morning.

"Say something," she whispered.

"I mean . . ." he said, smoothing a hand over his hair. His gaze was fixed on the table. "Your name isn't even Lauren."

"You get why I couldn't use my real one, don't you?" she asked. It wasn't just about lying low, though. Lauren Pertho was the alias on the papers and passport her mother's bloodline had forged to get her out of the country after her family's murder. It was the only documentation she had to use.

"I don't know what I thought," Miles said. "Let me see if I've got this straight: every seven years this . . . hunt happens. And the location changes—sort of like the Olympics, only with more murders?"

"Basically," Lore said. "The hunters figured out that they could control the location of the Agon by moving something called the omphalos—a large stone that once resided at Delphi and marked what they believed to be the navel, or center, of the world."

"The 'navel' in the poem?" he clarified.

She had recited the English translation of the account of Zeus giving the original command for the Agon. The original version, in the ancient tongue, had been lost.

"Yes. The leaders of the bloodlines gather the year before the next Agon and vote on where it'll be, which is usually where they each have the most resources and power," Lore continued. "They have to move the omphalos without the gods seeing its destination, to keep the gods from strategizing. Lately it's been here, but they also tend to focus on cities in island nations, like London and Tokyo, because it makes it harder for the gods to escape."

And rarely, in the cycles they truly wanted to torment the gods, they would bring the omphalos back to the old country, so they could be hunted among the ruins of their temples and the people who had once feared them.

"The nine families—" Miles began.

"There are only four bloodlines still participating in the Agon," Lore said. "The others have died out."

"Like yours?" Miles clarified slowly. "Because you're . . . the last of your line?"

"The last mortal," Lore said. "The new Poseidon, Tidebringer, was once part of the Perseides—the descendants of Perseus."

"What are the others?"

"The Houses of Kadmos, Theseus, Achilles, and Odysseus are the only other surviving lines," Lore said, "but there were also the Houses of Herakles, Jason . . ." Then she added, because no one ever seemed

61

to know who they were, "And Meleager, who led the Calydonian boar hunt, and Bellerophon, who slayed monsters and rode Pegasus. Those were actually the first two bloodlines to die off."

Their annihilation had come shortly after the bloodlines had decided upon unified surnames to meet the changing legal needs of the sixteenth century. Both houses had been viewed as unworthy of the hunt, even by Jason's cursed line. Meleager's because the remaining descendants originated from an illegitimate child, and Bellerophon's because their ancestor had died hated by the gods, and only Zeus himself would have seen the fallen hero redeemed.

"I thought Hercules—Herakles? I thought he rode Pegasus?" Miles said. "Are you telling me my favorite animated film of all time lied to me?"

Lore sighed.

"I'm almost afraid to ask," Miles said. "But what exactly happened to the rest of your family?"

For a moment, Lore wasn't sure where to begin.

"There's this rule—this fundamental belief—that only men, in particular the agreed-upon head of each bloodline, should be allowed to claim the power of a god," Lore explained, anger turning her posture rigid. "Only men can be heirs, both in mortal and immortal power. Having a male leader of a bloodline means succession is clearer. Should that archon fall or ascend to immortality, authority falls to his sons, or brother, or nephew. When the bloodline gathers for the next Agon, they cast votes on the next man to hold the title."

Her disgust grew until she could taste the bitterness in her mouth at the explanation. She had once believed all of that, too—*more* than believed in it. Even as a child, Lore would have gladly died on behalf of all those men to maintain the cruel order of their world.

"They really shut women out like that?" Miles asked. "Even now?"

Her nostrils flared with the force of her next breath. "It was centuries before they allowed women to hunt at all, and now only a select few are chosen to work in a sort of pack on behalf of the archon. Tidebringer, whether intentionally or by accident, claimed godhood herself fourteen cycles ago. And not from just any god, but one of the originals. Poseidon."

It was strange to feel both deeply ingrained revulsion and sympathy for the new god. Lore had been taught to hate her, to blame her for what became of the House of Perseus. Over and over, she'd been told Tidebringer was *wrong*, as if the unnatural thing wasn't that a mortal had killed a god and taken his place, but that a woman had dared to try.

"Okay, but why would the Poseidon lady mean the death of your . . . house?" Miles asked, hesitating over the word. "I thought you said that the new gods protect and serve their family?"

"That's just it," Lore said. "She was shunned by the Perseides and was forced into hiding during the next Agon and all of the ones that came after because she had no family to protect her. The bloodlines saw her as a direct threat to the order of their world. No one had even been sure a woman *could* ascend until she'd done it. The idea was too dangerous to them."

Miles sighed. "I think I know where this is going."

"To make sure it never happened again, the other families, led by the archon of Kadmos's bloodline, destroyed almost the entire House of Perseus on the last day of that Agon, when the killing of other hunters was still permitted," Lore said. "Aside from Tidebringer, the only survivor was my great-great-grandfather, who had decided to stay at university instead of participate in that cycle."

"Holy shit," Miles said mildly.

"The other bloodlines decided to keep him alive to torment him a different way—humiliation," Lore said. "They split the Perseides' stores of weapons and armor, divvied up their lucrative shipping and textile-manufacturing empires, and gave the head of the Kadmos bloodline the family's greatest inheritance."

The aegis. The shield of Zeus, carried into so many battles by his favorite daughter, Athena, bearing the head of the gorgon Medusa, and given to them by the king of gods himself to aid in their hunt. An object capable of summoning lightning and striking unnatural terror in the heart of all enemies who beheld it.

It had been the envy of all the other bloodlines, who resented the Perseides for getting what they considered to be a superior inheritance. Over the centuries, many of the other objects of power had been destroyed by rival bloodlines to keep them from being used.

But only those in that particular bloodline who bore the house's name could use their respective gifts. The Kadmides may have stolen the aegis, but none of them could wield it. And the truth of her great-great-grandfather's survival was even more sinister than she'd let on. Lore assumed he'd been spared for the same reason she had been: the aegis would disappear when the last of the Perseides died.

"Wow . . ." Miles said slowly. "But then your family—your parents?"

"And sisters."

Miles's face fell. Lore had only told him and Gil that her family had died and she'd been taken against her will to be raised by a member of her mother's family. Both of which were true, in a very vague manner of speaking.

"Their deaths were ordered by Aristos Kadmou, the grandson of the man who had led the initial execution of the Perseides," Lore said.

"Who is now the new . . . Ares?" Miles finished. "After he killed the last new Ares in the Agon seven years ago?"

"The mortal believes you lie."

Lore startled at the sound of Athena's low voice. Miles did more than that. He leaped out of his chair, knocking it to the ground, and stumbled back against the nearby counter, clutching his chest.

"Jesus!" he gasped out. "I mean—I don't—"

Miles dropped into what looked like half a curtsey and half a bow.

"Do you?" Lore asked him. "Do you believe me?"

Athena filled the doorway of the kitchen, leaning heavily against the frame with one hand pressed to the wound at her side.

"I mean, yes," Miles said. "I do believe you. It's just going to take a little while for me to get a grip on it, you know?"

The goddess took in the sight of him with derision before turning back toward Lore.

"This vessel requires sustenance."

"You want . . . breakfast?" Lore guessed.

Athena lowered herself into the free chair. Lore stared at her there for a moment—something swirling in the pit of her stomach at the sight of her in Gil's house, in Gil's chair—but in the end, she only stood up and went to the refrigerator.

Within a few minutes, Lore set down three plates of scrambled eggs and bacon and three glasses of water. She and Miles watched, both gripping their forks, as Athena pinched a piece of bacon between her fingers and brought it to her nose to sniff it.

As far as Lore was concerned, free food tasted the best, but it was clear the goddess didn't share that opinion. She took an experimental bite, and all six feet of her shuddered.

Ever loyal, even in the face of years of deception, Miles took a big bite of his own and declared, "Best bacon I've ever had."

"If you don't want it, don't eat it," Lore told Athena coldly.

The goddess sipped at her water, her lips curling into a sneer.

"It's the *sensation*," Athena said, forcing herself to swallow a small bite of egg. "To lower myself to such . . . base needs. To *need* such bland, repulsive victuals or feel hollow. Feel *pain*. It is intolerable."

"Yeah, well," Lore said, "*intolerable* pretty much sums up a lot of human existence."

Miles looked at her in surprise but, for once, kept his thoughts to himself.

"So . . ." he began, his eyes darting over to the celestial being beside him. Athena was still covered in dried blood and grime. "Where's your owl?"

The look Athena gave him would have incinerated a city block if she'd been at her full power.

Undaunted, he pressed on. "Your shield?"

A glass slipped from Lore's hand, shattering in the basin of the sink.

"Lore?" Miles rose, coming to help her, but Lore waved her hand behind her, motioning for him to sit before carefully cleaning it up.

"The *aegis*," Athena ground out, making sure to use its proper name. "I carried my father's shield. It was given to the hunters by my father centuries ago, along with many of our weapons and divine possessions. I have not seen it since, nor could I use it if I desired to. Not unless it is in my hands by the last of the seven days as I regain my immortal form."

"Not true," Lore said. "It has to be willingly given by someone in the bloodline, which is impossible. The Kadmides have had it for decades."

"And you know all this for certain, do you?" Athena said. "What is your purpose in telling the mortal all of this, Melora? What good will it possibly bring?"

"I'm tired of lying to him," Lore said, fighting to keep her temper in check. "I realize that's a foreign concept to you. Let me know if you need an updated definition of *friends*—I realize Artemis was likely the last one you had before she stabbed you."

"I can't believe I'm about to say this, but setting aside the stabbing—which, wow, first time I've ever been glad to not have a sister," Miles said, looking a bit pained. "Is Artemis the only other original god still in the Agon?"

Athena's chin lifted, as if daring Lore to answer him.

Lore ignored her. "No, there's Hermes. Apollo, too."

"There you are most certainly wrong," Athena said sharply. "Apollo perished at the end of the last Agon."

A twinge of eager curiosity passed through Lore before she could suppress it. She squeezed her hands together beneath the table until the uninvited feeling had passed.

"Apollo was supposedly killed in the last Agon, but no one witnessed it," Lore explained. "There were only rumors, which could have easily come from a bloodline that wanted to mislead the others so they alone would know to hunt him in the next cycle. If he *is* dead, whatever house has the new Apollo has kept his identity quiet. Personally, I think it's someone in the House of Theseus. That bloodline made considerable investments in solar energy last year."

Lore had already explained to Miles how a new god might benefit their family financially by meddling in world events, to further their own interests. The current new Aphrodite, for instance, had led the House of Odysseus into vastly successful Hollywood projects. A new Ares, including Aristos Kadmou, could inflame international conflicts to support their bloodline's investments in weapons manufacturing, and a new Dionysus could start a megachurch or a doomsday cult. The opportunities were vast and limited only by the new god's creativity.

"That brings us to eight," Miles pressed. "Who's the other one?"

"It was Hephaestus," Lore said. "But he's gone."

"Eradicated by a power-hungry imposter," Athena snarled.

"Maybe your father should have considered leaving better instructions instead of trusting a few men to write crappy poems about the encounter," Lore said. "It's not the hunters' fault they had to figure out the rules for themselves."

"Of course," Athena said with a derisive snort. "It was not enough for that hubristic imposter to have the power of one god, the fool had to attempt to slay another to see if he could gain Hephaestus's as well. It is only just that he could not."

"I don't disagree with you there," Lore said. "No one has made that mistake again. The hunters want to keep as many opportunities for immortality as possible. It's the reason the Agon will never end. They won't let it."

Gil's grandfather clock ticked nearby, each stroke cutting at Lore's nerves a little more.

"So what's our plan?" Miles asked.

"You're going to your internship," Lore said. "And you're going to find a friend to crash with until next Sunday."

"What?" he said. "Then what *was* the point of telling me all that?"

"The point," Lore said, "was to make you understand how dangerous this is."

"If it's that dangerous I'm not leaving this house, or you," he said.

"I'll email my boss and tell her I have strep. But I'm not going, and you can't make me."

Athena looked on with surprise and approval. Lore gritted her teeth at the sight of it.

"I prefer the company of this mortal," she informed Lore.

"That mortal doesn't even know basic knife-fighting," Lore said, rising to gather their empty plates. "So if you go down first in a fight, good luck."

Lore turned back to Miles. "I don't know how long this house will be safe. All I've done is try to confuse any of the hunting dogs that have picked up her scent. Eventually, it might not be enough."

"I will not be a prisoner in this house," Athena told her. "I will use my power to disguise my presence if necessary. I am content to remain here while this mortal shell recovers its strength. However, to complete our oath, I will have to leave these walls. And you, Melora Perseous, know less than you believe—you do not even know what the false Ares has spent these last seven years searching for."

Castor's face lit up again in her mind. *He's searching for something . . .*

"And you do?" Lore pressed.

Athena nodded. "This . . . poem you hold so dear, the one you recite as fact, it is either incomplete, or he searches for another version of it. One which tells of how the Agon ends and how its victor will claim unfathomable power."

Lore's mind shut down, leaving her body to react. She stood so quickly from her chair that it fell back and clattered against the tile. There was nowhere to go, and nothing her hands could grip except the opposite arm. "What?"

Miles looked between them, confused.

Athena swayed in her seat, clearly unsteady from blood loss and internal injury.

"My sister and I tracked him. He desires this information above all else and has set his many hunters to search for it," Athena said. "I am sure I do not need to tell you the sort of ruin he will bring to this world if he is able to find it. We must act with haste. If we locate this fragment or . . . new iteration . . . it will bring us into his path, and I will finish him."

Finding a new version of the origin poem—if it even existed—would, of course, give Athena the same information Aristos Kadmou was after. Lore didn't like the thought of any of them having it, hunter or immortal. She would have to find it first and, if possible, destroy it or . . .

Her mind finished the dark thought. *Destroy any hunter who knows what it says.*

"You're not going to be able to kill him in your current state," Lore told the goddess. "You probably need a blood transfusion and some kind of antibiotics at the very least."

"I need no such remedies," Athena said. "Do you doubt my strength, child?"

The goddess didn't seem to notice that she was blinking rapidly with the effort to keep her eyes open.

"I doubt your mortal body," Lore clarified.

"Is there anyone you trust enough to ask for help?" Miles asked.

"Yes," Lore said, but didn't add the important *maybe.*

Castor had been trained as a healer, and he would have access to his bloodline's supplies—medicine, blood, and everything else Lore would never be able to buy out on the streets. She was more than willing to swallow her pride enough to try to find him if it meant Aristos

Kadmou's death. But Lore had been angry and somewhat unreasonable when Castor had come to find her. While the friend she'd once known had never been one to hold grudges, she didn't know this new Castor at all.

Apodidraskinda.

That had been an invitation . . . hadn't it?

"I can get help and try to find out more information about the new version of the origin poem and who might have it," Lore began. "Most of the hunters are here in the city now, but it could be stored in one of the bloodlines' archives in another country."

"It is here," Athena said. "I am certain of it, and the false Ares appears to still be here as well. Whether stored in a vault or in memory, we will find it in this city."

Lore nodded. "Are we going to have to worry about your sister coming to finish the job in the meantime?"

"Artemis only wounded me so she herself could escape the hunters of Kadmos's line who fell upon us during the Awakening," Athena said. "Our alliance may be at its end, but she will have other . . . preoccupations. I will return the favor with my blade when the time comes."

"What about Hermes?" Lore asked.

"I have not seen Hermes in some time," Athena said, her face impassive. "Nor have I desired to. Once the fool shattered our pact four decades ago, we refused him all aid, and he us."

"Can't imagine why," Lore muttered. Turning back to Athena she added, "You can try to get yourself cleaned up while I'm gone."

The goddess pulled at the hair glued to her cheek with blood and nodded. She followed Lore upstairs to the hallway bathroom. Eager to ensure peace after she left them, Lore ran a bath and added salts and oils. She set out a clean roll of bandages near the sink.

"I'll find you a change of clothing," Lore told Athena as she exited the small space and the goddess entered. "I have to warn you that it won't be up to your usual standards."

Athena looked back over her shoulder, her eyes sparking. "I'm sure whatever you find will be . . . tolerable."

Lore stopped in the doorway, her fingers curled against the frame.

"I'm going to have to leave for a while," Lore said in a low voice, "to find you a healer. Miles will be safe with you, because I don't know *what* I would do to myself if something were to happen to him."

Athena's lips curled into a mockery of a smile. "Indeed. Though—"

"What?" Lore asked.

"There is one part of our story you have misunderstood," Athena said. "We were punished not for the lives lost, but for interfering in the lands of other gods, which threatened the peace of ours—the world beyond the knowing of mortals."

"That's—" Lore began. There were any number of ways she could have finished that statement. *Terrible, cruel, unbelievable.* All true.

In the end, she didn't finish her thought. Athena shut the bathroom door, leaving Lore standing alone in the hallway. She reached into her pocket again for the necklace Gil had given her. Her palm curled over the feather charm, and, for a moment, she did nothing but stand in the dim hallway, waiting for her heart to steady.

Not lost, she thought. *Free.*

Once this week was over, and Athena had held up her end of their deal, Lore would be truly free. Of the Agon. Of the gods. Of the hunters.

She wasn't surprised to find Miles already in her small room, sitting at the edge of the bed. He was the most interesting thing in the otherwise plain space.

"All right," she began, "I know you want to stay, but—"

Miles was suddenly in front of her, wrapping her in a tight hug. Lore froze, her arms limp at her side.

"Why didn't you leave?" he whispered. "You could have left last week. I would have helped you."

Lore squeezed her eyes shut and pulled back out of his embrace to move toward her dresser.

"If something happens while I'm gone, or you see anyone suspicious out on the street, I need you to leave Athena and run," Lore said.

"I'm not going to leave," he insisted.

"You can't fight hunters, Miles. They're trained to kill gods and anyone else that stands in their way. I would never even find your body."

He gave her a strange look.

"I'm not going to *fight* them," Miles said. "I'm going hide in the basement and call nine-one-one like a normal person."

Lore allowed herself a small smile as she carefully set the necklace down on the dresser and methodically pulled an oversize white shirt, black leggings, undergarments, and socks from the drawers.

"Do you want me to try to fix that for you?" he asked.

"Could you?" she asked, passing it to him. "I don't have a chain to replace it, and I don't want to risk losing it by using string."

He examined the place the thin gold chain snapped. "I can definitely try."

"Thank you," Lore said. She had so few things she cherished. Everything she'd had in her old life had been lost.

Not Castor, her mind whispered.

She drew in a deep breath, allowing the small bit of warmth to spread through her at the realization. She still had Castor. The Agon

73

had taken so much, but it had given him back.

"You know, I get why the hunters want immortality," Miles said, looking up from the necklace. "And I get what it can do for them and their bloodlines. But even that doesn't feel like enough of a reason when they know they're going to be hunted, too."

The initial panic of telling Miles everything had worn off to a kind of exhausted relief. A small part of her even felt grateful for the fact that she'd been able to choose how to tell the story.

"It all comes down to kleos," Lore said, her hand lingering on the picture frame. "That's really what they're after. That's the only thing they're allowed to want. You can gain immortality by becoming a god, but you can also gain it through glory. Kleos is the honor that comes from becoming a legend—someone others keep alive through stories and songs. Your body can die, but your name will live forever."

"That's it?" Miles said.

"It wouldn't make sense to you," Lore said. It wouldn't make sense to anyone who was raised outside their world. Sometimes it didn't even make sense to her.

The sharp wail of Miles's phone made both of them jump.

"You *have* to change that," Lore begged.

He mouthed *sorry* as he got up and headed to the door. He answered the call with a slightly pained "Hi, Ma . . . Yeah, no, I have time. What's up?"

Lore listened to his voice as he made his way down the hall to his own room.

"No, no—you're thinking of the wrong place," Miles was saying. "It's where we used to play soccer, not at the school . . ."

The bedroom door shut, making his muffled words inaudible, but his voice still hovered in her mind, ringing clear as a bell.

It's where we used to play . . .

Of course. Apodidraskinda. Hide-and-seek. The game they used to play as kids.

"Clever, Cas," she whispered. His message hadn't been a challenge at all.

It had been instructions on where, exactly, to find him.

SEVEN

Amazingly, Lore hadn't realized she'd developed a fear of heights until she found herself three stories off the ground, balanced on a narrow cement ledge of a former warehouse in Tribeca.

"Fantastic plan as always," she muttered.

Her body shook from the strain of the climb, and her fingertips were raw from clutching the brick. Lore angled her head to the right one last time, making sure she was still outside the nearby camera's frame.

While the Achillides owned other properties in the city, this building, known as Thetis House, had been the only place she and Castor had ever played apodidraskinda.

When they were kids, Castor had shown her how to approach the building from behind without being spotted by the security cameras and snipers on the roof—a feat that involved sneaking into a service elevator in the separate parking garage to the rear, crawling through a disguised hole in an electrified fence, and using a line of dumpsters as a shield.

After that, there was only the small, death-defying matter of free-climbing the corner of the building using the decorative brickwork as grips and footholds. But there was one significant difference in this climb compared to the last one she had made seven years ago.

Now Lore knew to be afraid—not just of falling, but of what she would find inside the building's walls.

She drew herself up another four bricks, passing the third-floor balconies and windows. Before she could continue to the next floor, her ears picked up something else. Airy music, accompanied by the *clink* of crystal and a low rumble of excited voices.

Lore shifted her weight, glancing up, then down, before leaning to her left to peer through the blacked-out windows of the balcony's door. Someone had left them cracked open.

You have got to be kidding me, she thought.

A party.

Inside the building was like a dream of another, ancient life. Lore caught glimpses of it as the Achillides passed by the balcony. Women glided through the space, their bright silk gowns made in the ancient style of the chiton and peplos. Their glittering jewels were complemented by crowns of laurel leaves, real and gold.

The men mingled with one another around the ample platters of food and cascading towers of champagne and wine glasses, all wearing either a chiton or more modern robes over loose silk trousers.

Parties, the kind that turned into hazy revels of wine and ritual, were common enough—what good, after all, was a glorious destiny if you were never allowed to luxuriate in it? Some involved ceremony, such as the favor-seeking sacrifices to Zeus in the days leading up to the Agon, and more rituals later, after its completion, when it was time to bury the dead.

This was neither.

You'd better be here, Cas, Lore thought, annoyed, though she was surprised to feel a jolt of eagerness, too.

Inside the brick walls were countless rooms—bedrooms, training facilities, conference spaces—and closets and cabinets to get lost in. Officially, Lore had only ever been invited to the third floor, a vast open space filled with weapons racks, and where she had trained with the Achillides young.

While both her mother and father had tried to train her to fight as a child, they had struggled to find the time between the jobs that paid their rent and kept food on the table. Lore had never thought about what it must have cost her father to approach the archon of the Achillides about her training—the true price wouldn't have been the cash exchanged or favors promised, but the loss of pride that came with needing to ask.

Lore drew in another breath as she finally reached the fourth floor. In the past—and hopefully still—the top story had been used for storage, and with hunters patrolling the roof just above it, it had never had the same level of security as the lower, more accessible levels. That included the not-quite-secret underground entrance from the building immediately to the right of Thetis House.

There was a half-inch ledge that ran from the edge of the building to the closest balcony. Lore held her breath as she shifted the very tips of her toes onto it. Her shoulders and arms screamed in protest, but it was her fingertips she worried about now, numb from the strain of clawing at the brick.

Before she could allow herself to truly think about how incredibly stupid this was, Lore quickly shuffled along the ledge over to the balcony.

The late-morning sun burned against her back. As it had climbed up from the horizon, it had brought the city's thick, damp heat to a boil, leaving her light-headed. Lore blinked away the sweat dripping into her eyes as she stretched a hand out for the stone railing of the balcony.

She was trembling by the time she hauled herself over it, dropping softly onto its narrow block of concrete. Lore drew herself close to the doors, out of the sight of anyone patrolling above, and knelt there for several moments, waiting for feeling to return to her upper body.

You don't have time for this, she thought. *Get going.*

Blackout curtains obscured whatever and whoever might be in the room. Lore pressed her ear to the door's hot glass to listen for movement, but heard only the party downstairs and her own pounding heartbeat.

The glass panels on the doors were bulletproof, but the alarm attached to them posed the bigger problem. Or would have, if an eleven-year-old Castor had been even slightly more resistant to a ten-year-old Lore's diabolical strategy of only making bets she knew she'd win.

There was a single loose brick just above the doorframe. Lore used her pocketknife to ease it out and gave silent thanks to that lovesick hunter—the one Castor had spied using this trick to meet the man he'd been forbidden to marry.

Lore pulled out the Wheelz 4 Totz magnet from the pocket of her jeans, unwinding the shoestring she'd taped to it. Carefully, she dropped the magnet down through the opening in the wall and used the string to move it back and forth until she heard the telltale *click* of the magnet kissing the alarm's sensor.

Please work, she thought. *Please let this one thing be easy.*

The alarm sensors had always been magnetic and were triggered when the magnet on the door was separated from the stationary half. It was a simple system that was usually effective, so hopefully they hadn't upgraded to new laser-based devices.

Lore reached back into her pocket for the thin piece of plastic she'd cut from an empty Pepsi bottle. It took her a moment of maneuvering to wedge it in between the doors and pop the lower, weaker lock. She had to wait for the hunter to pass by overhead again before she inserted the blank bump key she'd bought from her neighborhood hardware store into the dead bolt. Wrapping the brick with the bottom of her T-shirt, she hit the key, forcing it in enough to be able to turn it, and, mercifully unlock the door.

Lore stood off to the side, her back flat against the other door, and pushed it open into the heavy curtain behind it with a satisfied smile. "You predictable idiots."

For all the millions these families spent on security systems and weaponry, they still couldn't bring themselves to seal these doors, or brick them up the way they had the windows. It would mean cutting off their own potential escape routes if another family or god ever attacked them here.

When it was clear no silent alarm had been triggered, Lore slipped inside and quietly shut the door behind her. She welcomed the caress of the AC and the relative darkness as she drew the shoestring through the hole, removed the magnet, and replaced the brick.

As she'd expected, the room was still being used for storage. It was a maze of boxes and old trunks, all smelling damp, as if they'd barely escaped a basement flood. Lore pawed through them until she found a moldering set of black hunter's robes. She secured them around her ripped jean shorts and sweat-soaked black tank.

At the bottom of the trunk was a chipped mask. Lore stared at it, hating that she still felt sick at the thought of wearing something other than her family's own mark.

You need it, she told herself. *Take it. Just in case.*

The one thing she hadn't been able to find was some kind of blade or weapon.

"Well," she muttered, as she pulled a lone screwdriver out of an abandoned toolbox. "It's pointy."

Lore slipped it into the hidden inner pocket of the robe. She pulled the hood up, then back down as she realized how ridiculous it would look.

"Come on, Perseous," she whispered. "Let's go seek."

The layout of the hallway was exactly as she remembered it, with the exception of a few keypads that had been installed on a number of its doors. She glanced up, searching the ceiling for disguised cameras.

A voice cut through the quiet like a blade to the back of her neck.

"What are you doing up here?"

EIGHT

Lore spun around. A man she didn't recognize, wearing robes identical to her own, stood at the end of the hall, just at the top of the staircase.

"I—" she began, saying the first thing that came to mind. "I thought I heard something."

The man's gaze narrowed. Lore instinctively slid a hand inside her robe, toward the screwdriver, but forced herself to stop. She'd only look guiltier if she didn't move toward him, so she did.

"Did he sound like he was in some kind of distress?" the man asked in the ancient tongue. A note of anxiety rang through the words. "I thought he had attendants with him."

Attendants?

"It turned out to be nothing," Lore said lightly, keeping out of the faint pool of candlelight from a nearby table. She gripped the mask tighter, wishing she'd just put the stupid thing on. "The floor is secure."

Before she'd left the house, Lore had taken a sharpie and drawn the letter alpha, along with the bloodline's mark, on her left wrist. It was a design she'd seen inked onto the chests and arms of the Achillides who had trained her. She idly pushed the sleeve up, pretending to scratch at some phantom itch.

The lines of the man's face relaxed as he noticed the fake tattoo.

While there were always spies willing to do whatever was necessary to slip past another bloodline's defenses, the hunters were superstitious enough to believe that putting another house's mark on your body would anger your ancestors, causing them to abandon you.

Seeing as misfortune had been Lore's constant companion for the last seven years, she was sure her own couldn't possibly hate her more than they already did.

"Good," the hunter said. "Let's go downstairs. We should be able to get some food before they'll want us back on watch. You're one of Tassos's girls, aren't you?"

"Got it on the first try," Lore said, letting her face relax into a smile. "How's—"

A door at the other end of the hallway opened, and several small girls, no more than five years old, were ushered out of one of the rooms.

Lore's heart clenched like a fist.

All the girls wore simple white tunics detailed with gold embroidery that matched their sandals, and belts. Different styles of diadems and ribbons had been woven into their braided hair.

A woman, her own dark curls in tight ringlets, emerged behind them. The violet silk of her long, draped gown had been printed with ancient symbols and illustrations, including one of Achilles poised for battle.

The woman motioned to the girls, and all of them, every last one of the nine, fell silent and still, their small bodies rigid with what Lore knew to be fear-honed obedience.

A man emerged from the room across the hall like a clap of thunder. Lore's nostrils flared at the sight of him.

Philip Achilleos had gone silver-haired, and his permanent scowl only deepened with age. His scars seemed more pronounced than ever on his pale face, and while the old goat was still barrel-chested, the body beneath his deep sapphire robe had clearly thinned as he'd left the prime of his life.

His wife, Acantha, trailed behind him, poised and perfectly coifed. She had always been the better hunter of the two—practically legendary by the end of her first Agon cycle. But her marriage, and the temporary alliance it had brought to the Houses of Achilles and Theseus, had clipped her wings.

"Patér," the woman in violet began, bowing to Philip. "May I present—"

He circled the girls with a look of disgust. One of them risked a glance up at him. The back of his hand whipped against her temple.

Rage swelled in Lore. She took a step toward them, but stopped as the girl straightened again, her face carefully impassive as she lifted her chin.

You have to find Castor, Lore reminded herself. *Don't give yourself away so easily.*

But the girls . . . these children . . . She couldn't stand it. Being back inside Thetis House had been momentarily disarming, but now Lore remembered her hatred—for the hunters, for this life. It shot through her like a bolt of lightning.

The sight of the girl bowing before that pig with respect he didn't deserve, in the hope of nothing so much as pleasing him, made her want to scream.

Philip didn't care about these children, just as he hadn't cared about Castor. The fact that the archon had personally denied Castor's father the funds to continue the boy's medical treatment was enough for Lore to hate him in this life, and for all eternity.

"These are the best you could do?" he hissed to the woman in violet. "I told you to select beautiful girls. Where did you find these, crawling in the subway tunnels with the other rats?"

"Patér?" the woman said, her voice smaller now.

"Perhaps," Acantha said, placing a soothing hand on her husband's arm. She shared a covert glance with the woman, tilting her head until the string of diamonds dangling from her ears glowed with candlelight. "Perhaps, Patér, the sight of them would be less offensive to your gaze if she were to paint them gold?"

Philip Achilleos let out a low growl before barking out, "So be it. Remember, it is not my disappointment alone you should fear."

"Yes, Patér," the woman said, hurrying the girls to her. "Yes, of course. They will be ready in time for the ceremony."

Ceremony, Lore noted. Not just a celebration.

Philip turned, catching sight of her and the other hunter at the end of the hall. "Why are you standing there like idle fools in need of whipping?"

Neither Lore nor the other hunter needed more encouragement to flee down the stairs.

Lore let the man fill the short conversation and kept her head down, counting the stairs as they passed beneath her feet. The smell of incense and cypress oil was enough to make Lore's head feel unnaturally heavy and her body feel drunk.

The training facility, the only open floor in the building, had been converted to host the ceremony. The entrance was draped in white silk thick enough to mask the room behind it. Two hunters in full ceremonial robes, their helms and bodies brightly painted, guarded the door.

Lore let the other hunter approach first, then she reached for the extended arm of the other guard, gripping his forearm with two fingers extended, the way Castor had reluctantly taught her years ago, when she'd won yet another bet. The guard returned the gesture.

"Welcome, sister," he whispered, then stood aside.

Lore nodded, then slid the bronze mask over her face, feeling better about it once she saw some of the other hunters had done the same. She hadn't wanted to stick out as the only one wearing hers, but the greater risk was someone recognizing her.

It might have been seven years since she had last set foot in here, but her looks hadn't changed that much with age, and anyone who had known Lore's mother would see her now in Lore's face. She had the same unruly, thick hair, her warm olive complexion, and hazel eyes.

But . . . maybe not. Her mother was dead, and while grudges could feed themselves over centuries, memories faded at the pace of years. There was no one here who cared to remember Helena Perseous.

No one but her own daughter.

Lore swept the silk curtain to the side, only to be brought up short. It took her a moment to realize what she was looking at.

A temple. She was standing inside a temple.

As Lore took another step forward, the illusion became clear. Ghostly holographic images were being projected onto the seamless mirrors that covered the walls and ceiling. Columns, real and false, rose toward the digital image of a vaulted ceiling, one decorated with bold colors and seemingly gilded with gold and silver.

Even knowing it was all a lie, a thrill rose in her—one she didn't want to examine too closely.

Lore turned to find that holographic columns at the entrance looked out onto the daylight scene of a wild, rocky seascape. The room's shadows deepened the farther she moved from it. It gave the space the feeling of a dream slipping into a nightmare.

Rows of firepots led straight toward an altar of some kind; they illuminated the decorative tile that had been laid over the battered wood floor Lore and hundreds of others had bled on, scuffed, and scratched.

"What the hell?" she whispered, unable to stop herself.

A pool scattered with floating candles and flowers stretched out before the altar. Between them was an imposing chair—a throne, really, with a delicate sun carved into its back. It looked to be cast out of gold or covered in gold leaf.

Given what she'd already seen, Lore had a feeling it might be the former.

The men and women around her swayed to the gentle plucking of a lyre, others swirled around the room armed with wine and gossip in place of blades. Long tables covered with bone-white cloth covered the right side of the room. The Achillides had brought out their most cherished ceremonial bowls and wares, and all overflowed with a vivid assortment of fresh fruits. Beside it were silver platters of thin-shaved meat and fish, cheese, pastries, and heaps of stuffed olives.

With a quick look around to make sure no one was eyeing her, Lore stole a goblet of wine, downed it, and then began to assess the feast laid out in front of her. She needed to find Castor as soon as possible, but her last meal had been hours ago, and she wouldn't ignore the sharp ache in her stomach if she didn't have to.

When the woman idling nearby—the one who'd been contemplating the amygdalota in a way Lore could relate to on a soul-deep level—finally moved on to the honeyed baklava, Lore grabbed one of the almond cookies for herself. She was tempted to take one of the chocolate apples wrapped in gold foil to bring back to Athena—just to see her reaction.

Feeling steadier with some food in her, Lore turned her full attention back to the massive room and moved deeper into its shadows, making her way along the far right edge of the room. The projected images looked like nothing more than static now that she was up close.

All right, Cas, Lore thought. *Where are you?*

She moved again, this time coming to stand near the glowing pool, just outside its halo of light. Lore searched the room for him. The Achillides, like all the hunter bloodlines, had their roots in their ancient home, but every century had brought in husbands and wives from all over the world. The faces around her, with their varied skin tones and features, reflected that.

Her pulse sped even as she stood still.

Being back here, in this room, around these people . . . this was bad for her. She wanted to leave, even as she didn't. She wanted to look away, even as she couldn't.

As a little girl, she had been awed by the bloodlines' displays of wealth, so different from her family's own situation. She had devoured the inviting secrets of their hidden world's traditions and had felt as proud, as fierce as any daemon, knowing her family, among so many, had been chosen. That they were the Blooded, heirs of the greatest heroes.

This is nothing more than a costume party, Lore thought.

This world was like the static of the projections around her. Temples had once been places of sacred worship, not self-indulgent excess. The bloodlines had stripped the actual beliefs from their rituals centuries ago; their only religion was that of fevered brutality and materialism. Only Zeus himself received any sort of acknowledgment, and even then the sacrifices were shallow gestures born out of superstition, not devotion.

Several members of her old training class were here; seeing them made her temperature suddenly spike. Orestes, that epic ass, bothering a bored-looking Selene, one of the few children who'd deigned to speak to Lore in the three years she'd trained there. And Agata, dipping her hand into the pool to retrieve an emerald bracelet she'd dropped into it, and beside her, Iesos, with far more scars than Lore remembered him having—not that she liked remembering him at all. He'd been fixated on her not having a "proper" and "real" name, and had decided to call her Chloris instead, like she was supposed to be offended by it.

Where are you, Cas? she thought again, pained.

As time wore on and Lore still didn't see Castor, desperation began to dilute her small measure of hope. Maybe he was at work healing their wounded hunters, or was resting at another one of the bloodline's properties?

While his mother had died in the Agon just after Castor was born, Lore was surprised she didn't see Castor's father, Cleon. As the longtime property manager of Thetis House, he lived in the building and would have been responsible for organizing such a fete.

You've wasted way too much time already, Lore thought, shifting toward the entrance. She'd need to use the distraction of the celebration to search for him in the rooms upstairs, and, failing that, to steal whatever medical supplies she could and get back to Athena.

But Lore had no sooner taken a step than a hush fell over the House of Achilles. The hunters angled back toward the entrance, stepping away from the lighted path to the altar. The hungry looks on the faces around her, their eyes fever-bright from wine and excitement, turned her stomach.

Philip Achilleos appeared at the head of the stairs, Acantha a step behind him. They moved with the lyre's song, their eyes on the altar as they made their way toward the throne. Rather than sit on it, Philip stood to its left and Acantha to its right.

For a moment, Lore didn't understand Philip's reluctance. But like the crash of an unstoppable wave against the shore, it came to her.

The elation of those around her. The symbols of the sun, the lyre, and all the laurel in the reliefs and garlands around her.

This was meant to look like the Great Temple on the isle of Delos.

The birthplace of Artemis . . . and her twin brother, Apollo.

"Oh," Lore breathed. A jolt raced down her spine, electrifying her. *Oh.*

The new Apollo didn't reside in the House of Theseus, but the House of Achilles.

But it's not Philip? She glanced toward the old man, trying to read his guarded expression.

Interesting. An accident, maybe. Perhaps Apollo had died before the old man could finish him. It wouldn't have been the first or last time.

Children, the same girls Lore had seen upstairs, made their way down the steps, their skin painted gold. They were almost unbearable to look at, so proud as they each clutched a candle in one hand and a small silver object in the other. One held a book, another a telescope, another a lyre, another a theater mask. She saw it then. They were meant to be the Muses.

Sing to me, O Muse . . .

They, too, formed a procession to the pool. One by one, they sat along its edges and added their candles to it. The flames floated among the white flowers.

A faint hum filled the air, seeming to rise from everyone at once.

The young Black woman playing the lyre began a new song, one that seemed to spiral to the eaves on notes of air and light. She, too, shifted in her seat to get a better view of what—or rather who—was coming.

Lore knew to turn even before she heard the faint gasps. A sudden warmth passed over her skin, an incendiary power that set every nerve in her body ablaze.

He descended the stairs the way the first ray of sunlight breaks through a window at morning. His form was immaculate—tall, corded with muscles, and a face that echoed in the sweetest part of her memory.

Castor.

TEN YEARS EARLIER

ONE WINTER MORNING, BEFORE THE SUN HAD BEGUN ITS ASCENT AND her sister roused from her fading dreams, Lore woke to her destiny.

She opened her eyes to find her father's face hovering over her own.

"Chrysaphenia mou," he whispered, using his usual endearment. *My golden.* His face was soft. "Do you still want to train? I've found a place for you."

Lore looked over to Olympia, curled up beside her like a kitten on their small bed, then back to her father. She was suddenly wide-awake. Her whole body felt like it might burst. "The agogé?"

Her father nodded. "The Achillides will accept you into their training, but you'll need to start today."

Lore threw aside her bedsheets, jumping to her feet quickly enough to make her father chuckle. He bent over her, kissing her head. She kissed him back. "Thank you, thank you, thank you!"

"Shhh," he reminded her, pointing to Olympia.

Lore pretended to zip her lips, but she couldn't stop grinning. She bounced on her toes.

"It won't be like what you've read," he said, smoothing her hair down. "I don't want you to be disappointed when you arrive and see it is not Sparta."

The hunters had adapted their training programs from those of the great Sparta, but they removed the things they didn't like. Lore didn't care; the only thing that mattered was that she would be able to fight like her parents did. That she would get to see the ceremonies and the archives and all the things they didn't have in their own small family. The big mysteries she'd only ever heard stories about.

"Today?" she said, just to be sure it wasn't a dream. "Really?"

"Really," he said. "Now wash up and get dressed. I'll take you there before my shift."

Lore raced to the small dresser she shared with her sister, yanking out the top drawer. The photos there rattled, making Olympia stir and turn over. Lore glanced back at the tuft of dark hair over the bedsheet and forced herself to quietly pull out a T-shirt, her sweater, and a pair of jeans, then shut it again. She went to the bed again and pulled the covers back over Pia, making sure Bunny Bunny the doll was in reach.

Finally, she thought, excitement swelling in her until she could barely breathe. She raced out of the room, only stopping when she realized she didn't have her shoes.

Three months earlier, her parents had sat with her at their small kitchen table and explained why she might not be able to begin her training with the other hunter children her age.

There isn't the time for it, her mother had said. *I know this is upsetting, but I also know you understand that we're not the same as the other bloodlines. My— The House of Odysseus won't open its doors to us after I renounced my name, and even then their school is across the sea. Your father and I will have to continue your training. Come summer, I may be able to work fewer hours, and Mrs. Osborne will be able to see to your sisters . . .*

Lore had nodded, letting the tears and ache build inside her skull until she could escape to her room. She'd cried silently into her pillow and shoved the book of myths her father had given her far beneath her

93

bed, so she wouldn't be able to reach for it again.

She'd fallen into a deep, deep sleep and there, her fate had come to her, shimmering. Dreams were messages from Zeus. It was important she remembered everything. She saw the edge of a shield held firm in front of her, repelling the darkness. A wing made of golden light. Bright eyes reflected in the blade of a sword.

She had kept the dream to herself. Now, it seemed, the Fates were ready for her.

Her mother was already in the kitchen, preparing breakfast. Damara was nestled in a bassinet, babbling quietly to herself. She was smaller than a doll, and her skin so soft and thin that Lore was sometimes afraid touching her would leave a bruise.

She leaned over and kissed her sister softly on the head. She liked to whisper her secrets to Damara, because, unlike Pia, Damara couldn't tell her parents what Lore said.

"I'm a little nervous," she said softly, then tickled her until Damara cooed.

Lore laughed. "She sounds like a kitten."

"A kitten?" Papa reached in, stroking the curve of Damara's cheek, letting her gnaw on his thumb.

"She's a Perseous all right," he told them proudly. "The strength of this grip!"

"A Puuurrrrseous," Lore said, giggling.

"Someone is excited, I see," Mama said as she set down a bowl of oats in front of Lore. Lore breathed in the sweet smell of the cinnamon and bananas she'd mixed into it. She'd made her favorite breakfast.

"Do you want me to braid your hair?" Mama asked.

Lore nodded eagerly, letting her mother brush out her waves and carefully weave them into a plait as she quickly finished the food in

94

front of her. Papa and Mama talked quietly about the news on the radio.

"Can we go?" Lore asked. "Can we go early?"

Her father laughed. "What do you say to your mother?"

"Oh! Thank you, Mama," Lore said, standing on her chair to kiss her cheek. Her mother helped her down, following them to the door. She handed Lore's father his coat, then helped Lore into her own.

"You've nearly outgrown this one, too," she said, bemused. "You'll be tall, like my mother."

Lore could only hope. It would help her when it came to sparring and, later, hunting.

"It will feel very hard at first," her mother told her, buttoning her up. "Take heart, and don't be discouraged. Everything will come to you in time. You are a daughter of Perseus."

The words stayed in Lore's mind as she and her father made their way downtown, taking the subway farther than she'd ever gone. When they emerged from the station, the streets were as unfamiliar as they were thrilling.

Her father held her hand, resisting Lore's attempts to tug free until they finally reached a large brick building. Her father paused a moment, checking the number, then moved his hand to her shoulder to guide her to the smaller building beside it. There, the door opened before he could raise his hand to knock.

A man met them there, glowering down at where they stood on the lower steps. His black hair was slicked down against his scalp, and Lore noted immediately that he had a face like an irritated goat.

"We are honored by your graciousness." Her father bowed his head, reaching into the inner pocket of his coat to pull out a thick envelope. The man accepted it without a second glance. "May I present my daughter, Melora?"

"You understand the terms of this arrangement? The favor I ask of you in return?" the man said, his voice rumbling.

Lore looked between then, confused. *Favor?*

"I do," her father said. "I will send all the information on Tidebringer to you."

"By tonight."

"Tonight," her father agreed.

Lore's brow furrowed. Tidebringer had caused the destruction of their family, but she didn't like the idea of giving this man, a rival of her own house, anything.

It would be fine, though. Her father was never wrong.

Finally, the old goat shifted his gaze down on her. "I am Philip Achilleos, archon of the Achillides." He turned, leaving the door open. "Come, child. Your father is not permitted to enter this place."

The weight of her father's hand lifted, releasing her.

"I will return for you this evening," he promised.

But Lore didn't look back, even as the door shut and locked, sealing off the morning sunlight. The building was not so much a building as the shell of one, she realized. There were cars parked inside it.

The man led her down a staircase into a dark hallway. They were underground and heading back toward the bigger building.

"You are a guest at Thetis House," Philip Achilleos told her. "If you reveal anything you witness here, your life, as well as the lives of your family, will be forfeit. If you fall behind the others, you will be removed from the agogé to prevent you from holding our children back with your incompetence."

Lore responded yes, as if they had been questions. She would do whatever she needed to in order to stay. She would train as long and as hard as it took to achieve areté—that perfect combination of courage,

96

strength, skill, and success—and, one day, kleos. Her destiny was a gift, and now she would manifest it.

The archon brought her to the second story of the building, a bright space despite its lack of windows. The floor was covered in wood, and there were already clusters of children there, some as young as her at seven or eight. Others were older, and older still.

A heavy silence fell over them as she and Philip passed by, moving toward the far end of the room. They bowed to him, but Lore was too awed by the racks of weapons and the training groups to really hear their hissing whispers of *Perseides* and *Perseus*.

Finally, they reached the other children her age. They all wore short red chitons and clutched small wooden staffs, like spears without their deadly point. Lore searched their faces eagerly, and was surprised to see the looks of disgust and apprehension there.

They just don't know you, she thought. *You have to prove yourself, like the stories say.*

"This is Melora Perseous," Philip said. "She will be joining your agelé as a guest of our bloodline."

That was the only introduction she was to be given. With a nod to the instructor, Philip left them.

For a moment, the instructor, a pale-haired beast of a man, merely took measure of her with his eyes.

"Perseous," he said, amused. "The great House of Perseus reduced to begging and trading in pity, it seems."

The other children smirked at one another, snickering and whispering.

Lore's jaw tightened until she thought she might crush her own teeth.

"You are weeks late to be joining the others your age," he continued, circling around her. At the opposite end of the floor, the other trainees began their day's lessons, drilling with swords and staffs. Lore resisted the nagging temptation to turn and watch them, letting the clash of metal on metal, wood on wood, flesh on flesh, be enough.

You are a daughter of Perseus. She repeated the thought until it became like armor only she could see. *You are a daughter of Perseus.*

"As it happens, so is he," the instructor said, motioning to a boy at the back of the room. He stepped forward through the other children. Lore gave him a look of appraisal, uncertainty worming in.

The boy was about her height, but his limbs were like twigs. His skin was sallow, as if he hadn't seen the sunlight in months. A shadow of dark hair was growing back along his shaved scalp. Thick bandages were taped to the bruised skin of his inner arms and the back of his hands.

He's sick, she realized. Or had been, if he was here now.

She liked the laughter of the other children even less now, and liked the boy more for not reacting to it when it began again. Lore met his dark eyes, narrowing her own. The boy looked exhausted to her, but he was here, even if the others clearly thought he shouldn't be.

"Castor will be your hetaîros for the time being," the instructor said coldly. "But he is destined to apprentice with the healers and will not always be available to you. In those instances, you will observe. In the meantime, you should be . . . evenly matched."

The others laughed again. Lore wondered if they thought she was going to be hurt by it because she'd been paired with someone coming back from illness, or if Castor was because he'd been stuck with someone born into the House of Perseus.

There are always rivalries between the houses, she thought. But with her and Castor, there would be none of that. Her blood was fizzing in her veins at knowing she had a partner. Lore lifted her chin. They had no idea what she was capable of, or what her destiny would be. She wouldn't fail her bloodline, and she wouldn't fail her hetaîros.

Lore nodded to Castor. He nodded back, his gaze soft but intent. She liked him. His calm made her calm, too.

Her only warning was the feel of the air shifting at the back of her neck, and then the crack of pain there knocked her forward. The other children shoved back at her with their staffs, keeping her within their ring. The next hit came from her right, then her left, battering her back and forth as they circled her.

Castor let out a sharp gasp to her right, lifting an arm to try to block one of the boys as he spun the staff down against his shoulder blades.

Don't fall, Lore thought, trying to catch his eye. *Don't fall.*

This was all part of the training. It hurt, but it was necessary. The blows rained down on them, relentless and shattering. Lore tried to gulp in breaths, to keep the tears from pouring down her face. The hits and pain roiled around her like crushing waves. She looked to Castor again, only to find that he was already looking back.

"This is the most important teaching you will take from this hall," the instructor said. "You must learn not to fear pain, or else it will shackle you and strip your courage. Fear is the greatest enemy."

Black began to gather at the edge of her vision as the faces in front of her blurred, splitting into two and then three like the heads of Cerberus.

You are a daughter of Perseus.

Her mother's voice echoed in her skull, thundering as a staff struck Lore behind her right ear. Blood exploded in her mouth when she bit down on her cheek.

Castor was stumbling, his body shaking with the effort not to fall. He glanced at her again and forced himself straighter, as did she.

Don't fall, she thought.

99

I won't, his gaze promised.

And as long as he wouldn't, neither would Lore.

"Pain is the essence of life," the instructor said. "We are born into it and, if you are to be hunters, if you are to honor your ancestors, you will die in it."

I won't die, Lore thought, the black crowding into her vision. She looked to Castor again, holding on to the sight of him.

"Your father and mother may have delivered you into your bloodline," the instructor said. "But they are not your family. Those around you are your sisters and your brothers. Your archon is your guardian, your light, and your leader. He is your patér. Your true father. It is for him that you learn pain. It is for him that you bleed."

Lore spat out blood, nearly choking on it. Her father was *her* archon.

"You will strive for areté, but there is no greater death than that of a warrior who has attained the immortality of kleos for himself and his bloodline," the instructor said. "Honor. Glory."

The others—everyone in the training hall—repeated it with him.
"Honor."

Hit.

"Glory."

Hit.

"Honor."

Hit.

"Glory."

They don't know, Lore thought. *They don't know my destiny.*

She would have honor and glory. She would attain kleos and restore her house. There was nothing more important than that. The House of Perseus would rise again, and her name would be legend.

Castor backed into her, still shaking. She caught glimpses of him between the blows, between the looks of disdain and amusement around her. Snot and blood poured down his face, and he was blinking, trying to clear his vision. She gripped his wrist, steadying him.

They would not fall. Together, they would prove themselves. They would prove that they deserved to be there.

When the next blow came, Lore knew how to claw the amusement from their faces.

"Thank you," she said. And again, with the next crack of wood against her shoulder, her shin, her knee. "Thank you. Thank you. Thank you."

"Thank you," Castor repeated. "Thank you."

Over and over, until their voices strained and the hits slowed, and, finally, stopped. The instructor held up his fist, and the other children fell back.

Lore realized she was still holding Castor's wrist, but was too afraid to let him go.

"That's enough. Go wash yourselves and change," the instructor said somewhere nearby. "Everyone else, we will begin with the first stance."

They limped toward the doorway, Lore following Castor up one flight of stairs to the changing room. Lore and Castor found the red chiton fabric folded in neat stacks by size and each claimed their own.

Long sinks ran along the edge of the room, and there were shower stalls at the back. Lore picked up one of the nearby washcloths and, after wetting it, began to clean the blood from his face. Castor did the same for her, his touch gentle.

Their eyes met, and they grinned.

NINE

No.

The word pounded through Lore's skull. Her back found the mirrored surface of the wall just as her knees crumpled.

Cas, Lore thought as she slid into a crouch.

Even with his powerful body, his gait had none of the rigid confidence of Athena or the steady, reserved pace of Philip and Acantha. There was only that same awkwardness she had noticed during their match, as if his muscles were strung tight as a bow, as he made his way toward the altar.

Castor—*the new Apollo*—seemed to be concentrating on keeping his arms relaxed at his side and his head high, but now and then he glanced down, as if afraid he might trip. His fingers curled one at a time, only to uncurl again, over and over, with each step.

Her breath caught in her throat all the same. His bloodline had adorned him in a glimmering white chiton, its silk embroidered with golden symbols of his new divinity. One shoulder and part of his smooth, muscled chest were exposed, and his arms and legs were left bare save for the gleaming gauntlets around his wrists and the straps of his sandals.

The effect was devastating, even before she noticed the crown of gold laurel leaves nestled in the dark waves of his hair.

The new god's face was devoid of the teasing grin he'd flashed her during their fight. It was devoid of anything; if she hadn't seen the flicker of worry in his eyes, she might not have recognized him as Castor at all.

But it's not Cas, she reminded herself. Not anymore. Whoever he had been, whatever he might have become, he was something else now.

Lore didn't understand how she had missed it before—how strange it was for him to tower over her in such peak physical form when the Blooded healers and Unblooded doctors, all those years ago, had been certain death could take him at any moment. She'd even excused the sparks of power in his eyes as being nothing more than his dark irises catching the restaurant basement's lights.

She'd woven a tale she could believe. She'd seen a ghost in place of a god.

The mask caught her hot, quick breath and fanned it back across her face until she felt smothered by it. As if sensing her, the new god began to turn in her direction, but was interrupted.

"My lord," Philip called. Castor turned to where he and Acantha still held their positions on either side of the throne. "May we begin? The sun is at its highest point in the sky, burning bright for you."

"Of course," the new god said, taking his seat. Then, stronger and firmer, "My apologies."

How? Lore thought. *How is any of this possible?*

Castor had been a boy of twelve during the last Agon. He had barely been strong enough to lift his head, never mind kill one of the last old gods. This had to be a mistake—somehow, this was a mistake.

It's real, a voice whispered in her mind.

Then why had he come to find her at the fights? Why had the

Achillides let him out of their sight after they'd gotten him safely from the Awakening?

A feeling of dread began to gnaw at her as she watched Philip sweep a hand toward the waiting throne. There had been something strained in the man's tone—something . . . *something*. Lore found herself studying the archon as the new god approached him.

Castor's words came back to her as if he'd just whispered them into her ear. *Something is happening. I don't know who I can trust.*

She still hadn't seen his father—she hadn't seen Evander either, for that matter.

Her next thought arrived with a sudden, ruthless certainty. *Philip's going to kill him.*

Castor was marked now, god or not. He'd broken his oath to his archon and shed blood that was not his to shed.

Is that what this was? An illusion to draw the golden calf to the altar for sacrifice, so Philip could take the power for himself? Castor had known. He must have.

There had been a number of kin slayers throughout the centuries of the Agon, all seeking to take power from those they had once claimed to love and cherish. Most refrained, fearing that the worst sort of curse would fall on them. Kin slayers were never allowed to survive long.

But the bloodline had honored and served Philip Achilleos far longer than the new god, who had once been no more than a weak nuisance in their eyes. Lore wondered if he had any true allies here beside her.

She reached into the depths of her robe for her screwdriver as Castor moved around the pool, glancing at the small girls gathered at its edge. The throne seemed to shimmer with delight at the sight of him.

The ancients had been horrifyingly clever in their killing of rivals and enemies. When Lore looked at the chair again, all she could see were the many ways it could be made lethal to a mortal god. A poison could have been mixed into the gold, as it had once coated the tunic of Nessus given to Herakles. Or a blade could be hidden inside a panel, ready to slide into his soft flesh.

But if Philip wanted Castor's power, he'd have to strike the killing blow himself. Lore shook her head, releasing some of the tension gathered between her shoulder blades. He wouldn't do it here, in front of everybody.

The man's face was collected, but Lore felt it—the contempt in that restraint. Philip and Acantha knelt before Castor first. When Philip spoke, it was in the ancient tongue, as melodic as a river flowing into a great sea.

"We honor you, Bright One, we thank you for guiding the sun across the broad heaven. Charioteer, slayer of serpents. Far-shooting, far-working: bringer of plague, healer of man; herald of song, poetry, and hymn; voice of prophecy; averter of evil, master of fury—"

"Yes," Castor interrupted in a droll tone that was so unlike how she remembered him. "I believe that's nearly all of them."

Lore's lips parted. She would have laughed at the expression on Philip's face, except the room had gone utterly silent.

"We . . ." he began once more, glancing to Castor. The new god propped an elbow against the velvet arm of his throne, leaning his chin against his palm. He waved him on, looking bored.

If there was one thing Castor had always been, it was respectful. Not meek, exactly, but never one to challenge. If there had ever been anyone who might have had a shred of hope in not having their newfound divinity go to their head, it would have been him.

It *should* have been him.

So much for that, Lore thought, rubbing a hand against her chest. Power was the greatest drug of them all.

"We welcome you back to the mortal cradle that bore you. We honor you and ask for your continued protection of the house of mighty Achilles," Philip said. "In gratitude, my wife, Acantha, daughter of—"

"I know who your wife is," Castor said. "Thankfully, I didn't lose my mind with my mortality, though you're making me question that."

The hunters murmured, exchanging looks of discomfort and confusion.

Philip continued, his hands curled into fists against his knees, his head still bowed. "In gratitude, we will arrange a holy hecatomb around the great altar we have built for you in the lands of our ancestors."

Lore frowned. A waste of a hundred cattle, all slaughtered in ritual sacrifice. Castor appeared to agree.

"I would rather you give the meat to the hungry of this city," he said, his voice unbearably cold.

There was a sharp inhalation of breath somewhere on the other side of the room. Philip's face bloomed red with stifled anger. His jaw worked back and forth, as if struggling to bring himself to speak.

It had likely been decades since someone had spoken to him in such a tone, and Lore decided to let herself enjoy it, just for a little while longer.

"We also offer this performance, and a song composed in your honor," Acantha said smoothly.

The little Muses stood, recognizing their cue. The woman playing the lyre began again, the song serene and joyous. The girls began to sing, dancing in carefully practiced unison. As they stole glances at the new god, their movements stiffened.

Castor gave them a small smile of encouragement, one that vanished as he saw one of the girls—the Calliope—begin to cry. They were children—younger even than Lore had been the first time she came to Thetis House. The air in Lore's lungs turned to fire as she watched the girl cry harder, snot and tears dripping down her face as she struggled through her routine, no doubt realizing how badly she'd be punished for this.

When the performance came to a merciful end, Castor did not applaud with the hunters. He merely nodded, his dark gaze turning back to Philip. The older man snapped his fingers at the girls and they fell into a neat line.

"Those before you are the . . . finest of our parthénoi," Philip said, struggling with the word *finest*. "If one of them pleases you, you may have her as your oracle. Or, perhaps, a mistress once their first blood comes."

Lore wondered where one might procure a poisoned shirt in this day and age, and how well it would hold up in its gift wrapping when she mailed it directly to Philip Achilleos.

The parthénoi were those young women kept from the Agon, never to become lionesses hunting for their bloodline, but existing solely to ensure its survival through the birth of yet more children. Becoming one of them, never being allowed to participate in the Agon, had once been Lore's greatest fear, before she knew there were far worse things to be afraid of.

Prisoners, she thought, venom pumping through her veins. That's all these girls were. That was all they would ever be allowed to be.

Lore could imagine it so clearly—cutting through the hunters around them to reach the girls, carrying them away before anyone else could hurt them. But then the new god spoke.

"They are charming," Castor said, a dark expression on his face. "However, I forbid you to offer them to anyone of this bloodline—or any other—until they have reached adulthood, and may choose their partners for themselves."

The band of fury tightening around Lore's chest released all at once.

"My lord?" Philip said, his voice echoing in the stunned silence.

"It is a despicable practice to promise children in marriage while they should be focused on learning their letters and playing with their toys. We have long since stopped the grooming of young boys. All children should be protected from it," Castor said, his voice growing louder with each word. "You are archon of this line, Patér, but I am its god. If you wish to receive my blessings, this is what I ask of you."

Lore felt the first light of hope break through inside her, then fade as she gauged the reaction of the hunters around her. Upset, anger, even confusion reigned. It was one thing to be loved and feared, and another to be feared and reviled. The only thing hunters despised more than dishonor was change.

Acantha gripped her husband's arm, pulling him back. Lore suspected she did not entirely hate the way her husband was being spoken to, but the woman was too entrenched in their terrible life to ever show it.

"Radiant One," she began, "we have longed to learn how best to honor you. As you chose not to appear to us, we could not create art in your image. The estate we built for you in the mountains remained empty, your offerings untouched. If there is something you desire from us, name it."

What? Lore finally rose, trying to get a better view of Castor's face. The new gods were notorious for manifesting physical forms as soon as they possibly could to live their best immortal lives.

"Were my gifts unsatisfactory?" Castor asked.

"They were marvelous," Acantha said, patiently. "We merely wish to please you. If you grant us the knowledge of your epithet, we will be able to do great deeds in your name."

At that, Castor seemed to lose some of the sharpness of his demeanor. He leaned back against the chair, as if considering her words. Then, he shifted his gaze back to Philip.

"Come to me, archon of the House of Achilles," Castor said. "I will honor you by telling you my chosen name first."

The man seemed somewhat mollified as he approached. Castor allowed him to lean close to him before announcing, loud enough for everyone to hear, "I will be known as Castor."

Philip finally detonated.

"You must choose a name, as tradition dictates!" he said, throwing off his wife's steadying grip. "You cannot keep your mortal name!"

Castor had pushed this beyond badgering and into baiting. Even now, his smooth tone and smile only further served to raise the old man's hackles. "I wish to use it in honor of the mortal mother who named me. Is there some rule I am unaware of, or are you questioning both the quality of the name and my decision?"

Lore released a soft sigh. *Are you trying to get yourself killed?*

"Of course," Castor continued, "you may continue to refer to me as *my lord* or *Radiant One*. I will even respond to *Your Supreme Excellence* on occasion."

Appreciation and exasperation warred inside her. Lore and Castor had both hated Philip for the way he always sneered at them, even before the old man discontinued Castor's treatments. Lore supposed Castor had over a decade of pent-up anger to work through, though she questioned if belittling the archon and taking shots at his own bloodline was the most productive way to do it.

"Have we displeased you?" Philip asked the new god. "Have we not shown you the proper respect?"

"I am satisfied," the new god said.

The whole point of this is to stay alive, you idiot, Lore thought.

As if Castor had heard her, he relented, softening his tone again as he said, "With that matter settled, tell me how the House of Achilles fares, and what favor you seek, Archon."

Philip drew in an audible breath, rolling his shoulders back. "You will be pleased, my lord, to know of recent births in the seven years since your ascension . . ."

Out of the corner of her eye, Lore caught sight of a late arrival coming up the stairs—Evander. He wove through the crowd, his left hand smoothing the front of his silver silk tunic. His other, wrapped in a black glove, remained still where he held it over his stomach.

Well, Lore thought, *shit.*

Van was too smart for his own good and missed absolutely nothing. Even a hawk would defer to Van rather than trust his own eyes.

Which meant she really should have left five minutes ago.

Castor saw him as well, quickly meeting the young man's gaze before turning his attention back to Philip, who stoically continued his report on the marriages, the deaths, their various property holdings, and business ventures.

"Your medicines and vaccinations have been fast-tracked through federal approvals, and we expect the profits will begin in earnest at the start of the next quarter," Philip continued. "In fact, I believe this to only be the beginning of what we may achieve, if you, in your power, were to increase demand."

Castor leaned forward, brow creased.

"The favor I ask of you, *Radiant One*," Philip said, "is that, when you return to your full immortal form and power, you create a disease that we alone can cure."

Lore clenched her jaw until it ached to keep her mouth shut.

"We have been blessed by your ability to heal others, but we must push beyond it now and seize a new opportunity. There need not be many deaths," Philip continued, clearly feeling empowered by the excited din of voices growing around him at the mere thought. "A few thousand would suffice to ensure global demand—"

"No," Castor said acidly. "It is not in my power to bring disease or sickness, nor would I, if I could. I will do everything in my power to serve this bloodline. But I will not be a master of death, nor of terror."

Philip reeled back. "My lord—"

"I am sure," Castor began, with that same sharp tone, "I do not need to remind you why the Agon began and why Zeus would deny Apollo and his successors such power, nor do I need to remind you of the many horrific illnesses that already exist in this world. Perhaps you might even ask me what I have done to help those afflicted with the same disease I suffered in my mortal life, and how you might continue to turn the wheels I have put in place with reasonably priced medication."

Acantha bowed. "A wise course of action. I will be glad to lead such an effort for you."

The old gods had been monsters: selfish, vain, and with an unconquerable thirst for violence. Looking around the hall now, taking in the looks of disappointment and anger, Lore saw the promise of something darker.

"Evander, son of Adonis," Castor said, looking to the dark-skinned young man. "What of the Agon? Have you been able to negotiate for our dead?"

Evander stepped up to the pool, kneeling beside it. Something flickered in Castor's expression and his lips parted, but Van spoke before he could. "I have the duty to report to you the death of the god Hermes—"

The hunters around him did not let him finish. An uproar rolled through the hall, blistering in its intensity. Lore's hands fell open at her sides, her fingers numb.

Athena and Artemis were now the last of the original gods. Another, somehow worse thought occurred to her: *I have to tell her.*

Of course, that number might dwindle further to Artemis if Lore didn't leave now and find Athena some other help, but this—this was useful information.

"Who claimed the kill?" Philip demanded.

Van had a way about him, an unnerving calm, even in the face of bad news, even now as he said, "The new Ares, who has chosen the name Wrath."

The din rose again, pulsating with a new, different sort of fury.

"He killed him knowing he would not be able to claim his power?" Philip raged.

"You're sure of this?" Castor asked.

"My drones recorded the moment of death," Van said. "There's more. The Kadmides also took Tidebringer."

Another gasp rolled through the hall.

"Alive or dead?" Castor asked.

"She was alive, but just barely," Van said. "My sources are telling me Wrath wanted to get information out of her about something, but

112

she never woke again and he finished the job back at their compound."

Lore felt . . . not sadness, exactly, just a cold sort of recognition that she was now the last of the House of Perseus. Her ancestors had to be howling in the Underworld.

"What would he have needed to question her about?" Castor asked.

"I'm looking into it," Van said then added, meaningfully, "but perhaps what we discussed before?"

For a moment, Lore thought they were talking about the new version of the poem. But then she remembered Castor's quiet warning during their fight.

He's looking for something, and I don't know if it's you.

No—that couldn't be it. Tidebringer would have no idea where she was, or how he could find her.

"He is trying to intimidate the bloodlines," Philip declared to the room, reclaiming their attention with his vehemence. "We will not be cowed."

Van said nothing, but turned a meaningful gaze back toward Castor. "I think he is attempting to do more than that, and we must be on guard. The House of Theseus has formally aligned with the House of Kadmos. They are under Wrath's command."

"What?" Philip barked over the growing buzz of voices.

"As you may remember, the House of Theseus lost the majority of their parthénoi during the last Agon after Artemis located their hiding place," Van said.

Lore's stomach knotted at the memory. Dozens of little girls, all massacred by the goddess who had once been their patron and protector.

"My spies tell me that, in addition to generous financial

compensation," Van continued, "Wrath has promised them marriages and protection in exchange for their loyalty."

"Cowards!" someone near Lore shouted.

"Quiet—*quiet!*" Philip ordered. "They do not have a new god to protect them as we do."

If she hadn't been watching Castor for his reaction, Lore might have missed it—the way his face seemed to draw into itself, his eyes squeezing shut. A tremor worked through his jaw as he gripped the arms of his chair.

"My lord," Van began. "If I may—"

The images on the mirrors jumped, distorting. Lore jumped away from the wall, her heart climbing into her throat.

The hidden speakers that had carried the distant sound of waves now roared with thunderous drumming that jolted the Achillides and sent them scattering around the room.

"What is happening?" Philip called over them. "Someone turn them off!"

The mirrors flashed to black, leaving the light of the firepots to guide them toward the stairs.

As quickly as it had arrived, the drumming cut off. Castor rose then, as if he already knew what was coming.

At the center of each mirror, a spark of red color grew, splashing out across the screens until the room was bathed in it.

"*Achillides*," came a deep, rasping voice, all but slithering out of the speakers. "*Achillides, hear me.*"

TEN

THE FEAR THAT SWEPT THROUGH LORE SEEMED TO CUT HER OPEN from the inside. Sweat broke out along her skin, cold as Thanatos's fingers.

Screams split the air. A few hunters rushed for the entrance, only to collapse to the floor. The others fell like rain, their silk clothing puddling against the ground as they clawed at the columns and one another, trying to stand again. Others struggled to reach for the small blades hidden in the folds of their clothing.

Lore's own body betrayed her. Her legs felt drained of blood and strength; she hit the polished floor in a surge of renewed fear. Her limbs suddenly felt small and hollow, and she didn't have the strength to so much as lift her head.

Aristos Kadmou—*Wrath*.

This was one of his powers. Lore seized on the thought and clung to it, trying to shake the panic before it carried her off. The new Ares could induce the feeling of bloodlust in someone, but he could just as easily steal it by weakening their will and body.

Lore tried to kick her legs out to get them straight beneath her, but they wouldn't respond. She sucked in a sharp breath through her nose and twisted around, searching for Castor.

He was standing exactly where he had been all along, seemingly unaffected as he watched the rest of the room in horror. When Acantha moaned from the ground, he went to her, trying to draw her back onto her feet. His palms glowed where they held her, but the woman was a doll in his grip.

Concern and fear raged over Castor's features. Lore heard his thoughts as if he had screamed them. *What do I do? What do I do?*

Now she understood. Wrath wanted him to watch. To know what was coming.

Then, finally, he spoke.

"Greetings to you, Castor Achilleos, and to your kin," Wrath said.

"There's no need for this. We all understand your power," Castor said sharply. "Tell me what you want."

Feeling flooded her body again. Lore gasped at the sensation, hearing the hunters around her shouting and struggling upright as his influence lifted.

"I offer you kleos," Wrath said. *"Bend your knee to me, young god. Use your power at my command, and the House of Achilles will not be destroyed. Refuse, and all will die beneath my blade, beginning with you."*

"Idle threats," Philip hissed, staggering to his feet. "We will match you blow for blow."

"Will you let the mortal speak for you, young god?" Wrath demanded. *"I offer all those willing a place in the world that will come, the one we will create together—a place of power and wealth beyond imagining. The Agon will end, but all those who serve me will be rewarded."*

Lore struggled up from the ground, supporting herself with one of the overturned tables.

Castor gripped the back of the golden throne, his eyes shut again. He forced them open. "The Achillides serve no one."

"Is that your answer?" Wrath said. *"So be it."*

116

"Shut them off!" Philip shouted. He picked up one of the firepots and threw it at the nearest mirror, smashing it. "Cut the power!"

"Your new god resents you," Wrath continued, speaking to the hunters now. *"He is weak, the weakest of the gods. Unable to manifest a physical form. Unable to tap the depths of his power. I will care for you, and serve you as you serve me. I will revel in your honor, I will share my power and strength. Only I can protect you. Only I can set you free."*

"The House of Achilles will not yield," Philip said. "You are nothing more than a coward, hiding behind screens. You'll protect them? You won't even show the courtesy of returning our dead."

The hunters stomped their feet in agreement, letting out a ferocious roar of approval.

The screens flickered again, the pulsating crimson replaced with something more horrifying.

A line of severed heads had been left in a trash-strewn gutter, their eyes plucked out and replaced with silver coins. Their jaws had been unhinged, their mouths gaping open in a mockery of the Achillides' masks.

Philip and several others smashed the remaining mirrors, but it was already too late.

"Come and claim them," Wrath said, his voice breaking up as the connection was severed. *"You will join them soon enough."*

ELEVEN

LORE TOOK ADVANTAGE OF THE CHAOS IN THE AFTERMATH OF WRATH'S declaration of war to make her quick escape.

She wove through clusters of Achillides, heading straight for the stairs. She would only have a narrow window of time to slip out before their emergency security measures made that impossible. She had to get back to Athena. She had to find her some other help, from some other place, and tell her what happened.

But Castor . . .

Lore cast a fleeting glance back at the new god, unsurprised to find him surrounded by armed hunters. He looked bone-white as one of them issued low orders and gestured toward the other side of the room.

He could heal her, Lore thought. The conversation earlier had confirmed that he'd inherited that power from Apollo. It would be an easy solution to her most pressing problem.

No. She couldn't take him with her. Lore knew that, but it didn't ease the regret that gripped her. Athena would never allow her brother's killer to live, and there'd be no way to smuggle the new god out of Thetis House without the Achillides coming after them and potentially tracking them back to her home. She couldn't put any of them—Miles, Castor, or Athena—in more danger than they already were.

Castor would be safer here, with his bloodline. Even with Philip, and even after Wrath's declaration of war. While Wrath's message had been dangerous because of the way it portrayed Castor as weak to the Achillides, it had, in a way, also saved the new Apollo. The hunters could always be counted on for their monstrous pride, and none more so than the Achillides. They would never willingly give up their new god, and they would die before subjecting themselves to an outsider's rule.

Lore stole one last look around, her mind racing.

Don't let me down, assholes, she thought. *Don't let him die.*

Van broke away from where he'd been speaking to Acantha and made for Castor, crossing the room in a few long strides. He passed within inches of Lore, close enough for her to smell the orange and sandalwood of his cologne, and she barely resisted grabbing him.

It had been such a long time since she'd last seen him. They'd been children then, running wild through the city. Where Castor had always been an open book, happy to be read and understood, Van was the journal that remained locked and tucked beneath the mattress, except for the moments he blamed Lore for getting Castor into trouble or leading him into doing something Van deemed dangerous—which, to Van, had been almost everything fun.

And the truth was, Lore's trust was a rare volume—rarely lent, and never freely. Van's loyalty to his bloodline would always surpass that of a sort-of-friendship, and Lore would have to find a way out of Thetis House herself, the way she always did.

So up she went, retracing the same path she'd taken down, feeling more unsettled with each passing moment. An unbearable heaviness anchored in the pit of her stomach. Lore fought her way up the last steps, gasping for breath as the bleak panic circled back to her.

Wrath.

His voice—it had echoed in the jagged parts of her, stirring up

119

images of her parents and sisters she had fought for years to suppress.

If the House of Theseus had allied with him, it would add hundreds of bodies between him and Athena; the old god would never get close enough to uphold her end of their oath. The thought scalded her.

It's actually worse than that, she realized.

If Wrath was working his way through the other gods, old and new, his hunters would come after Athena relentlessly. Aristos Kadmou had never been one for small purposes or quiet aims. He was clearing his enemies from the game board, and whatever he was planning wouldn't end there.

And Cas . . .

Lore had so few ties to her past life that the thought of finding another one had been a powerful drug, whether she wanted to admit it or not. She had stopped believing in the Fates years ago, but she could see it so clearly in her mind then, the gleam of their blades as they gleefully cut away everyone and everything until she had nothing, and no one.

"Get a grip, you blubbering wine sack," Lore muttered. She had a good and decent life here in the city, a real home. And she had Miles, who was still waiting for her back at the house with a god who would gladly wear his blood.

But she wanted the one person who had always been able to settle her, whether it was her temper or fear. She wanted the one person she had always been able to look to, knowing she'd find him there.

She wanted Castor.

Lore bit her lip, struggling to swallow the thickness in her throat. She found the door she'd entered through, gripping the handle. It rattled, but didn't budge.

"Oh, *perfect*," she groused. Lore tried the door again, this time with more force. "I don't have time for this."

She pushed aside her borrowed robe, feeling around the back pocket of her shorts for the piece of plastic to jimmy the lock. There was nothing in it but lint.

Shit.

She must have dropped it as she'd come through the French doors, or set it down while she was changing.

The candles in the hallway were burning low, flickering out. The smell of smoke and hot wax was everywhere, mingling with the incense still rising from below. Lore licked her dry lips, trying to assess her options through her exhaustion and nerves. She moved on to test the next door in the hallway. Then the next. And the next.

"Of course I understand," someone said, their voice drifting up the stairs. Heavy, quick footsteps followed. "The security breach—I worry—"

A curse blazed through Lore's mind as she hurried to the next door, already drumming up a thousand possible excuses for what she was doing. *Walking rounds, investigating a noise, retrieving my purse, wanted to be alone . . .*

None were necessary. The last door on the hallway, one with a security keypad, was ajar. She slid inside, shutting it firmly behind her, breathing hard beneath the mask.

The room was dark, but there was just enough sun coming through the tinted skylight to fully illuminate it. A large, impressive bed canopied with white silk sat at the center, right between two bricked-over windows. A wardrobe that looked to have been passed down through centuries was up against one wall, painted with a fading pastoral scene of cattle and farmers. Plush cushions were arranged like a flower's petals on the floor, and everywhere, scattered around the room, were elaborate candelabras waiting to be lit.

The smell of fresh paint still clung to the air, and the carpets looked too pristine to be anything other than brand-new. This had to be Philip and Acantha's room, newly restored for their residence during the Agon.

A movement on the bed drew her eye. At the foot of it slept an enormous shaggy dog. White had gathered on the muzzle of its bearlike face and the tips of his long ears. His black coat was dusted with it, as if he'd only just come in from running through a snowy Central Park with Lore and Castor.

A thin line of drool stretched from his mouth to the silk duvet. His big eyes slid open. He raised his head as if in recognition.

"Chiron?" Lore whispered.

She lifted the mask to get a better look at him, a small burst of happiness lighting through her. He was still alive—he had to be, what, fourteen now? She approached the Greek shepherd slowly, holding out her hand.

The dog had been Castor's constant companion, practically from the time the boy had been small enough to ride on Chiron's back. He'd faithfully trotted after her and Castor like a beleaguered nanny on their many adventures through the city.

His tail swished against the silk duvet, and Lore was strangely relieved when he licked her fingers in greeting.

"I missed you, too, you big dope," she said, stroking his ears. "I don't suppose you've learned how to speak human and could tell me how to get out of here?"

The dog lowered his head and promptly returned to his nap.

"Yeah," Lore muttered. "That's what I thought."

The thick rug absorbed her steps as she circled the room. No balcony—no windows, except for the skylight. The same was true of

122

the surprisingly luxurious bathroom attached to it. Lore kept catching glimpses of her irritated expression in its black marble.

She cast another look at the skylight, considering. If she could get up there, she might be able to pry it open enough to slide through, but there would still be the hunters on the roof to deal with—hunters in prime fighting condition. Lore was currently white-knuckling the last remaining shreds of her pride, but even she could acknowledge that there was no comparison between fighting hunters and beating up spoiled rich kids.

The dog opened one eye.

"Don't look at me like that," she told him. "I'm actively planning my escape."

Chiron's head swung toward the door. A moment later, Lore heard them, too.

"Be assured that we will . . ." a muffled voice said, growing louder as it approached.

Lore put her mask back on and dove under the bed, only to roll back out when she realized she could still be seen from the door. She started for the wardrobe, but Philip or Acantha would need to change at some point, and while Lore could explain away a lot of things, she wasn't sure she could pull off a decent explanation as to why she was crammed inside their armoire. Which left the worst option.

She tucked herself behind the—hopefully—decorative wood changing screen in the back corner of the bedroom as the door was unlocked and opened. There was a gap between two of its panels, just wide enough for her to watch as three men entered.

In an instant, Lore realized her mistake.

This wasn't Philip and Acantha's room.

TWELVE

CHIRON STOOD UP ON ALL FOURS AND GROWLED. LORE JUMPED AT THE sound. She had never heard him bark the way he did then, deep and rumbling.

"Easy, beast," Philip said, holding out a calming hand to him. *"Down."*

Chiron's posture was rigid, his head lowered and tail tucked . . . but he wasn't staring at Philip. He was eyeing Castor.

What little color was left in the new god's face faded. He watched the dog, his body rigid, until Van stepped between them.

"I'll remove him," Philip said. "He does not . . . seem to remember you."

"It's fine," Castor said sharply. "What I want to know is how in the hell Wrath accessed your feed."

"The technicians are being questioned," Van said. "I'll take my own crack at them and the system. Chances are, they just hacked in without any help within Thetis House. I'm more troubled by the fact that Wrath is capable of using his power this way."

"My immediate priority is the protection of our bloodline's god. It's only a matter of time before they attempt a more direct strike," Philip said. "The guards will come for you, my lord, when it is time to move to a more secure location outside the city."

"Do you think that's really necessary?" Van asked. "If they do in fact have a spy in our bloodline, they'll always know our moves before we make them. It is a huge risk."

"You are not archon of this bloodline, *Messenger*," Philip said. "This is my decision."

Messenger—of course. That was the pin Van wore, a gold wing to indicate his status as the bloodline's emissary. The role meant little more than spying now, but the Messengers were protected from the killing under an oath between the houses. That way, they could carry messages without fear of death and handle the exchanges of bodies collected by other bloodlines.

"Are you sure this isn't your rivalry with Aristos Kadmou speaking in place of your reason?" Van didn't have to raise his voice to give his words an edge.

Lore was shocked that they couldn't hear her ragged breathing.

"Evander, son of Adonis," Philip hissed. "Speak to me in such a way again and I won't merely strip that pin from you, I'll take your other hand."

Other hand? Lore leaned forward.

She could see it now—the way the fingers on his right hand were slightly longer and stiffer than the left. He had movement in them and could cup the hand, but any shift was slower and the range more limited. He, like many of the hunters, had lost a part of his body and had replaced it with an advanced prosthetic.

Damn, Lore thought.

It had to have been some kind of sparring accident. Van's right hand had been his dominant hand, at least as far as she could remember from the few training sessions he'd attended while his parents were conducting business in the city.

While some hunters fought to reenter training to learn new styles

125

of fighting better suited to their changed bodies, and thereby stay in the hunt, most were pushed into a kind of early retirement in a non-combat role, like archivist or healer, by their archon.

Lore had always found that practice infuriating; if someone wanted to fight, if they wanted to strive for kleos, they should be allowed to, no matter the circumstances.

"If we could have a prophecy, my lord," Philip began again, turning to Castor, "we might be able to anticipate the Kadmides'—"

"How many times do I have to tell you that there won't be any prophecies?" Castor said. "It is not one of my powers. I feel like I must yet again remind you that while I have some of Apollo's power, *I am not him.*"

Lore held her breath as the new god took a few steps in her direction, removing his gold gauntlets and placing them on the small table beside the screen.

Philip steeled himself, but nodded. "Yes, my lord. Of course, we all remain eager to hear the tale of how an innocent boy of twelve bested one of the strongest of the original gods and ascended. Perhaps you might speak to one of the historians of our bloodline—"

"Enough," Castor said, the word strained. He was now so close that Lore could smell the incense smoke clinging to his skin. For a moment she was sure the new god's eyes had flicked up to meet hers, but he moved toward the bed. "I would like to rest before we travel."

"Cas— My lord," Van began. "Perhaps we might discuss—"

"I said *enough*," Castor said, gripping one of the bedposts so hard it cracked. "Summon me when the time comes to leave."

Philip gripped Van's shoulder and drew him toward the door. "There are hunters posted outside. Is there anything else I can provide you, my lord?"

"Just your absence," Castor said, still not turning around.

126

"Lock the door behind us," Van reminded him.

Castor nodded, but made no move to do so until they had both left the room and several long moments had passed. He turned, knocking his knee into the trunk at the foot of the bed, and he swore. Lore would have laughed at the sight of a powerful god hopping and grimacing, except that his motions seemed even stiffer than they had before.

He tried to stretch his arms across his broad chest, to roll out his neck. He turned the door's three dead bolts and pressed a nearby button on the wall. Lore jumped as a metal door slid down to cover it. Locking himself in.

Trapping her in with him.

Chiron growled as Castor tried to approach him, offering his hand the same way Lore had. The dog's lips pulled back, his snout wrinkling viciously. Castor didn't pull his fist back until Chiron lunged, snapping at his knuckles.

"You know me," he whispered. "You do."

Lore pressed her hand to her mouth again to keep from making a sound. Of course Chiron didn't remember him. This wasn't the boy he'd loved so fiercely and protected. This was . . . something *else*.

There was nothing to be afraid of; he had come to *her* for help—he had no reason to kill her, even for trespassing in this house. But, still, Lore couldn't bring herself to move. She felt like one of the statues of old, forever trapped in one pose, eyes eternally open.

The dog's mouth relaxed and he quieted enough for Castor to try approaching again. As his hand came to hover over the dog's back, Chiron stood and moved. He curled up on the mountain of pillows, giving the new god a look of deep suspicion.

Castor stared back at him, no traces of warmth or hope left in his expression. Something dark seemed to pass deep within him as

127

he circled the room, his breathing deepening, becoming labored. He stopped now and then, running a hand along the raised damask of the wallpaper, the silk of the sheets and curtains, the curved edges of the flowers carved into the back of a chair.

It was like a silent ritual of some kind, each stroke of his fingers reverent. Lore could just make out his profile and the endless storm of emotions that crossed his face. He muttered something to himself she couldn't hear.

Finally, he stopped at the center of the room, shuddering. Reaching up, the new god slid the crown from his dark hair and held it between his fingers. There was a quiet *snap* as he broke it in two and let the pieces fall to the floor.

But there was no sound at all as a hidden panel in the wall behind him swung open and a hunter wearing the mask of the Minotaur stepped silently into the room.

Castor straightened, rising slowly to his full height, and looked back just as the hunter pulled a small gun from inside his robes. For a moment, he did nothing but stare at the hunter. He didn't move. He didn't seem to even breathe.

Shit, she thought. *Shit, shit—move!*

He didn't. The hunter fired.

Lore shoved the screen down, reaching for her screwdriver. It was no knife, but it did spiral through the air the way she'd hoped. It glanced off the attacker's mask, knocking him to the ground.

She launched forward as the hunter scrabbled back toward the secret door, too furious in her fear to let him escape.

The hunter slid a long dagger out from the hilt at his side. Chiron leaped to his feet on the bed, barking wildly—it was enough of a distraction for Lore to seize the small marble bust on the dresser and smash it against the hunter's head. Once. Twice.

The assassin slumped to the ground, unmoving. Blood trickled out from beneath the dark hood. Lore shoved it back and ripped the mask away, revealing Philip Achilleos's slack face.

"Bastard," she seethed. And a traitor, too, hiding behind another line's mask. It wouldn't have protected him from the kin killer's curse, just as it hadn't protected him from her.

Chiron whined, snapping Lore out of the fight's daze. He was near where Castor had fallen to the floor, sniffing his hand. Lore retrieved her screwdriver and scrambled over to the new god, searching him for any signs of a bullet or wound. There was only a small feathered dart near his heart—a tranquilizer.

She added *coward* to the archon's tally. He hadn't wanted any resistance from the new god as he drove a blade into Castor's heart and ascended.

"Oh, damn you!" She gripped the front of Castor's robes, shaking him. "You could have avoided that easily—snap out of it!"

His head lolled back. She pressed an ear against his chest, but couldn't hear anything over her own heartbeat.

"Castor?" she said, shaking him. *"Cas!"*

He didn't respond. Lore pressed the heel of her hand against his chest, driving it down and down and down. Castor surged up, gasping. He twisted onto his side, disoriented, his legs and arms sliding against the carpet.

"Cas . . ." Lore began, reaching for him.

The new god dragged himself farther away, throwing out a hand toward her.

Her sharp gasp was the only sound Lore managed before the air turned to fire in her lungs, and a writhing mass of heat and light blasted out from his fingertips.

THIRTEEN

Lore had been raised with a blade in her hand.

She'd drilled for endless hours and days with practice staffs, blades, spears, and shields, repeating those deadly movements until she no longer had the strength to hold up her weapons. The hilts had left dark grooves of memory in her palms, like the rivers in the Underworld. She'd nurtured those calluses, thickening her skin so it no longer shredded.

Lore had wanted her body to remember it all: the weight of the weapons, the angle of the strike, the exact power she needed to coax from her muscles. Some part of her had always understood that there would come a time when her mind emptied with exhaustion or pain, and all she'd be left with was that work, that practice. A moment when ingrained skill finally blurred into reflex.

Like now.

The armoire behind her exploded into thousands of splinters, catching in her hair and skin. She didn't feel any of it. Didn't waste a breath. She dove away, gasping.

Mask, she thought, trying to flip it off her face. Its laces had become tangled in her hair, and she couldn't pull it away, no matter how hard she clawed at it.

The wind was knocked out of her as she slammed into the wall behind her. Castor's arm banded over her chest like a steel bar.

He shifted his arm, bringing it up against her throat. Black gathered at the edge of her vision as her air supply was cut off. There was no emotion in Castor's face; it was as if he, too, was acting on pure instinct now, his body striving to survive.

She kicked viciously, trying to hit his kneecaps. Somewhere in the background, she was aware of barking, of the dark blur behind her opponent snapping and lunging.

Lore bashed her forehead against Castor's, letting the bronze mask do its work. He groaned, blood bursting from a cut across his forehead. Castor staggered back and she tackled him, all broken nails and raw, desperate strength. His weight was impossible—suffocating as it settled over her—but he was still flesh and blood.

She wrapped her legs around his torso and flipped him over so that she was on top. Lore brought the screwdriver to his throat, but Castor gripped the metal and pushed the tip back toward her face. His blood sizzled on the steel as it heated in his hand, turning molten gold. The scalding intensity of it was so near to her eye that it finally broke Lore out of her frenzied haze.

Chiron was all but howling, gripping the new god's other arm in his mouth. He didn't seem to feel the fangs or the brute force of the massive dog. Castor's pupils were dilated, ringed by the gold embers of his power. He was looking at her, but not seeing her, even as he tore her mask off.

"It's me!" Lore choked out, trying to twist away from the burning blade. "It's me—it's Lore!"

The transformation that stole over the new god's face was like the slow unfurling of a wing. Fury spread to shock, then horror.

He released his hold on her, and Lore scrambled off him, dropping to her knees, panting. The screwdriver fell to the carpet. The smell of singed wool quickly filled the room. Lore had enough sense to kick it toward the tile in the bathroom.

The silence that followed was almost as painful as the heat had been. For a long time, Castor did nothing but stare at her as she leaned forward over her knees, trying to gulp more air into her lungs. Her blood was still drumming in her veins.

Chiron trotted over to her on stiff limbs, and for a moment she did nothing but press her face into the fur of his neck. The weaker part of her wanted to disappear into it.

Finally, Lore forced herself to turn around.

"Surprise?" she said, because Lore had never met a situation she couldn't make even more painfully awkward.

"I could have . . . I could have killed you," Castor said hoarsely. "I thought . . . I was confused, and the assassin—"

No. He *would* have killed her. Her arms were throbbing with the effort it had taken to hold the screwdriver back.

"I seem to remember being the one on top, big guy," she said.

He closed his eyes, releasing a long breath. Castor rubbed at his forehead, which reminded Lore of how much her own hurt.

"Should have known it was you from that first hit," he said. "Only you would immediately go for the head. Do I want to know where you got that mask?"

Chiron licked Lore's chin, comforting her.

"Yeah, yeah," Castor said, shooting the dog a dark look. "Give the dagger a little twist, why don't you?"

Lore stroked the dog's head in silent thanks, then pointed back to the bed. He lumbered off, giving Castor a wide berth.

"Not that I didn't enjoy almost being impaled by a screwdriver,"

132

Castor said. "After your reaction at the fight, I didn't think I'd ever see you again . . . but you came."

"Actually, I was escaping before you rudely interrupted me," Lore said. "And, for the record, I had no idea this was your room."

The dog probably should have been a strong hint, but never mind that.

"If you didn't come to help me," Castor said slowly, "then what are you doing here?"

"I think I *did* just help you. Should we move on to the fact you just stood there while your would-be assassin fired at you?" Lore jerked a thumb back toward Philip. "I hope I don't need to tell you who it is."

He sucked in a sharp breath between his teeth, eyeing the man's crumpled form. "I didn't . . ."

"You didn't what?" Lore prompted, feeling the first licks of anger on her heart. "Stand there and let him try to kill you?"

Castor looked away. "You wouldn't understand."

"Well, I definitely won't if you don't explain it," Lore said. When he still didn't look at her, she added, "What's going on? Don't tell me you just wanted to see if he would actually go through with it. We both know the kind of person he is, and you weren't exactly building bridges with that act you put on downstairs."

"How much did you see?"

"I saw enough," Lore said, crawling toward him. "Even when you were . . . Even when you were at your sickest you kept fighting."

That hadn't been the real Castor downstairs, with all his bravado. *This* was Castor.

"Did . . ." she began. "Did you want him to do it?"

His hesitance was answer enough.

"No," he insisted. "It was just a mistake—I wasn't being careful."

133

Lore shook her head. "You're always careful."

He rubbed at the knee he'd hit earlier. "Not lately. It feels like . . ."

She waited for him to finish.

"Like I'm in a body that doesn't belong to me," he said, finally. "I haven't had to move . . . or feel . . . or . . ." Castor drew in another breath. "I just wasn't sure what to do, or how to avoid killing him."

"Would that really have been so bad?" Lore asked.

"During this week, when the Achillides need leadership?" he pushed back. "Without any proof of him attacking me first? There are no cameras in here. I already checked."

"Aren't *you* their leader?" Lore asked, plainly. "Don't they serve you, even over the archon?"

"They never wanted me," he said. "Not as a child, and certainly not now. Maybe I did think, just for a minute, they would be better off if Philip were to ascend. That he would—"

Lore flinched at the rawness of Castor's words, but he didn't finish his thought.

"That he would what? Become even more insufferable? Abuse even more power?" Lore pressed.

"He'd at least be able to control it," Castor said. "He wouldn't . . . They would believe in him."

"In no world is it better for you to die and for Philip Achilleos to become a god. Tell me you understand that. That you believe you deserve to live."

It didn't make sense to her—why would Castor have killed Apollo, if not for his power?

The thought came to her suddenly. *To heal himself. To be born again in a new, healthy body.*

He'd fought an aggressive form of leukemia from the time he

was four years old, pushing through chemotherapy, radiation, and stem-cell transplants throughout the years. It had returned with a vengeance just before the start of the last Agon, and everyone, including Castor himself, had believed he'd die from it.

Everyone but Lore.

"Please stop looking at me like that."

"Like what?"

"Like you're afraid."

"I'm not afraid," she said. "I'm worried. I'm trying to understand what's happening and how this"—she gestured to him, all of him—"happened."

Until now, Lore had never thought about how overwhelming it might be to suddenly bear the brunt of your bloodline's needs, or to lose the person you'd once been. Maybe that explained the heaviness she saw in him now, and the reluctance to accept what he was. But there was something else, too—something she couldn't put a finger on.

"What a coincidence. I'm *also* confused," Castor said, dodging the opening she'd given him to explain. "How did you get in the building to begin with? They locked it down and posted men everywhere. I checked. Don't tell me you turned yourself into a spider."

She made a face. "I got into the building the way I always used to."

"No, you didn't," he said, staring at her under his fringe of dark hair. "There were hunters all along the fire escape. You couldn't have used it."

"Good thing I didn't use the fire escape, then," Lore said.

"You didn't . . ." He sat up straighter. "You told me you used to come up the fire escape!"

Oh, Lore thought. *Right.*

She *had* told him that—just like she'd told him that the Furies preferred the taste of tender boy flesh and that hunter initiation involved drinking satyr piss and running naked beneath the moon.

Not for the first time, Lore realized she'd been kind of an asshole as a child. This, however, had been the one possible exception.

"I didn't want you to worry," she said gruffly.

Castor had worried over everything—the trees in the park, stray dogs, if she'd be punished for sneaking out to see him, if the cancer would kill him, and if his father would be all right without him. This had been the one worry she could relieve him of. "It was the only way inside when you were . . . when they stopped letting me come to see you."

The medicine had compromised his immune system, but Lore couldn't stand the thought of him being alone, day after day. She had always been so careful not to touch him, knowing the kind of city grime she brought in with her. Most days, she had just sat by his bed as he slept and kept watch over him with Chiron.

He shook his head in disbelief and no small amount of horror. "That's a four-story fall. You wouldn't have walked away from that!"

Lore waved her hand, turning back toward where Philip was still flat on his back, his breathing shallow.

"You said you didn't know who you could trust," Lore said. "Is this what you meant?"

"Yes." He drew in a deep breath. "But I also just . . . wanted to see you, and warn you about Aristos—about Wrath. Van brought me to you instead of coming straight here from the Awakening in Central Park."

"Why?" Lore hated the ragged edge that crept into the words. "You had seven years to come find me before then. Did mortality make you feel particularly nostalgic, or were you just in the mood to ruin my night?"

"I tried," he said. "I tried to find you for years, but it was like you vanished. There was no trace of you left."

"Yeah, that was kind of by design," Lore said, her heart giving a hard kick at the memory.

"I thought you might be dead, but Van managed to track you down yesterday," Castor said. "He was worried about Philip, and he thought—*I* thought—you might be willing to help hide me, or get me out of the city."

Was she wearing some kind of sign on her back that offered shelter to all immortals in peril?

"But you're right," he said. "You're right. It wasn't fair to put that on you. I suppose I just thought—"

"What? That we're still friends?" she finished, before she could stop herself.

He flinched and tried to hide it by rising to his feet. Lore stood, too, not liking the feeling of being caught in his shadow.

"Then why *did* you come here?" he asked quietly. "You told me in no uncertain terms you had no desire to help me, so why risk it?"

The question hung like a sword above her neck. Lore turned her back to him, struggling to answer that herself.

Because you're the only one in the world I thought I could trust.

"Desperation," she heard herself say, cutting the truth down to its core. Her eyes caught the glimmer of gold on the ground and, ignoring the pain in her body, she bent to pick up one of the fragments of his crown. The lie came easier than she'd expected it to. "To see if you know anything else about what Wrath's been searching for."

Lore held the piece of the crown out to him, keeping her eyes on

137

the intricately shaped laurel leaves and not his face.

"I see," the new god said softly. "I caught some of his movements in the years between, but I could never pinpoint what he was looking for, and neither could Van. I wish I had more of an answer for you, Golden."

"Don't—" Lore forced her voice to steady. "Don't call me that."

It had been stupid of her to choose it for Frankie's ring, but it was the first thing that had sprung to mind, and Frankie had liked it too much to let her change it the next week. It was a play on the endearment her parents had used, *my golden*, which itself had been an ode to honey. Lore had been named for both of her grandmothers, Melitta, meaning bee, and Lora.

"I think I know what it is," she told him. "What he's looking for."

Castor's hand hovered alongside hers. A hint of warmth brushed her bruised knuckles a heartbeat before he did. The touch was soft, hesitant, gone almost as soon as she'd felt it.

"What?" His eyes were on her. She couldn't say what it was that kept her there, waiting, her hands still outstretched. But then the touch came again, the very tips of his fingers drawing down from her wrists, over the curve of her thumbs, until, finally, they hooked around the piece of the crown and Lore remembered she was supposed to let it go.

"Another version of the origin poem," she said. "One that explains how to win the Agon."

Castor's grip noticeably tightened on the thin band of gold. She couldn't bear the thought of looking up at his face for his reaction. "Why do you think that?"

A rattling dread passed through Lore as the reality of her situation sank in.

Before coming here, Lore had wanted to find the new poem for two reasons. One, because she knew Wrath was searching for it himself, and would risk venturing out of hiding for it, giving Athena the rare chance to cut him down. The second, to keep it from falling into the hands of any god, new or old, who could use it to become a true immortal with unimaginable power to crush or subjugate humanity.

Now, it seemed, she had a third: for Castor.

If the poem revealed the Agon could only end when a single victor emerged, it would have to be him.

But she had already allied with another god. One who wouldn't hesitate to kill Castor at the first opportunity.

"Lore?" Castor prompted. "Why do you think that?"

"It was another warning I got this morning," Lore said. "From someone else."

"I'll see if Van's heard anything," Castor assured her. "This will at least help focus his search."

When she risked a glance beneath her loose strands of hair, Castor was looking at her jaw. At the long scar that ran down her face.

Her lungs felt like they had been wrapped in burning steel. They spasmed painfully as she took in her next breath.

Scars, her father used to tell Lore and her sisters, *are tallies of the battles you've survived.* But Lore hadn't earned this one; she'd been branded with it.

"I don't remember that one," he said.

She ignored the question in that.

"I heard about your family," Castor began. "Your parents . . . the girls . . ."

"I don't want to talk about that," she said sharply. "Isn't one of the perks of godhood that you get to stop caring about the lives of pitiful mortals outside your bloodline?"

139

His jaw tightened. "Lore, I'm still Castor."

She shook her head with a sad laugh, even as her whole chest seemed to clench.

"I am. I *am*." The crown fragment fell to the ground again as his hands closed over her wrists, as if the touch could somehow make her understand. It seemed to spread through her blood, sparking her nerve endings, and was more than enough to prove the lie in his words.

As if just realizing what he'd done, he released his hold on her and took a step back.

This was Castor, but somehow it wasn't. She only had to look at his eyes to know that for sure. He may have retained some of Castor's genetic destiny with his looks, but he'd been . . . enhanced. The imperfections that had made him as messy a human as the rest of them had been smoothed over, and the result was devastating, in more ways than one.

Then again, she wasn't the Lore he had known, either.

"I'm sorry," Castor said, an edge of desperation in the words. "Just . . . talk to *me*. Why do you want to know what Wrath's plans are?" His eyes widened. "Tell me you aren't going after him . . ."

Silence hung between them, dividing the distance between past and present. It was the only line in her life that Lore had no idea how to cross.

He closed his eyes, his whole body strung tight. "Why did he have them killed?"

Lore wondered, then, if it was possible the Kadmides had kept what she had done a secret all this time. She supposed pride might explain that, too. Sometimes, when the memories of that night surfaced and she replayed it all in her mind to punish herself, Lore took comfort in knowing how humiliating it would be for Aristos Kadmou—to all of the Kadmides—to know he had been bested by a little girl.

"Van thought you might be with your mother's bloodline, but no one was willing to say," Castor said. "No one would risk the Kadmides punishing them for protecting you. But why would he come after your family in the first place?"

They had risked it, and she'd repaid them with blood. Interesting, too, that Van's searching hadn't turned up that gruesome story, either.

"Isn't it obvious?" Lore said. "Wrath wanted to finish what his grandfather started. He wanted the House of Perseus taken out of the hunt."

"Why wouldn't he have ordered it before?" Castor asked. "Why wait until he ascended? Why not come and do it himself as an immortal?"

"I don't want to talk about this," Lore said sharply. "I don't know why he did it, okay? Because my father rejected his offer. Because my father embarrassed him. Because he just felt like it! All I know is that the Kadmides took them from me. They took *everything*."

But that wasn't true, and she had the proof of it in front of her. They hadn't taken Castor. The Agon had.

Her throat thickened, but Lore wasn't a little girl anymore. She would control her emotions. "And I thought . . . I thought you were dead, too."

"I'm sorry. Gods, Lore," Castor said quietly. His voice slipped into a tone she'd never heard before, one of anger and self-contempt. "I couldn't help you. I couldn't help them. I couldn't do anything, for years. Even if I had found you, you never would have known."

"What do you mean?" Lore leaned toward him, staring up into the sparks of power glowing in his dark irises. Her hand opened at her side and started to rise, as if needing to smooth away the harsh lines setting into his face.

"I couldn't manifest a physical form." Castor let out a dark, humorless laugh. "It turns out that I'm just as weak and useless as a god as I was as a mortal."

Lore frowned. Acantha had said as much during the ceremony. *The estate we built for you in the mountains remained empty, your offerings untouched.*

"You are *not* useless," she told him. "And you've never been. Not ever, no matter what anyone in this horrible bloodline told you."

Castor looked as if he desperately wanted to believe her.

"I couldn't even save my father." He looked down at his hands. "He's dead now, did you know that? I saw it happen—I was there, drifting between the places I used to go and the people I wanted to see."

"I didn't know," she said softly.

"A heart attack. I watched it happen." Castor's hands curled into fists. "And the thing I can't get over, the thing I can't accept, is that I had the power to heal him. To save him. But back then . . . it was too new. At least I've learned how to invoke my power, but controlling it . . ."

Lore pressed her hand to her chest. In her mind, the final image she had of her father's body braided with the last moments she imagined for Castor's. She had to close her eyes and breathe deeply to keep from being sick.

"I came back for answers," he told her, his voice as intent as his gaze. "It's reason enough for me to stay alive. You don't have to worry about me."

Lore tried to gather her thoughts as she bent down to pick up a thick leather-bound book that had tumbled off a nearby table. She caught sight of the door out of the corner of her eye and Lore stopped.

Her grip on the book tightened.

"What's wrong?" Castor asked, coming toward her.

"The guards," she began. They should have heard her and Philip fighting. They should have heard her and Castor fighting. They should have heard *Chiron* the way he'd been carrying on. She shouldn't have been able to land one hit on him without a bullet or blade slicing through her. "Where are they?"

"There were never any guards, Melora," a ragged voice said.

Philip rose, clutching the knife in one hand and the wound on his head with the other. He advanced toward the new god.

"I've always remembered you as a stupid child," Philip continued, "but I never thought you would be foolish enough to show your face here."

"Funny," Lore said, "I've always remembered you as an asshole, and I definitely thought you'd be foolish enough to try to kill your new god."

The archon spat at her. Castor took a step forward, furious.

"Leave now," Castor told him. "No one has to know what happened, and you'll run no risk of the kin killer's curse."

"I will gladly curse myself," Philip told him. "I will welcome it, if it means that this bloodline will survive. You know it, as do I. You are too pathetic to bear the mantle of Apollo, and you will *never* have the respect of the Achillides. If I had known what would become of you, I would have spared us all and smothered you as a boy."

The words landed, a perfect echo of what Castor himself had said. The new god's hands curled into fists at his side, but he didn't deny it.

"I will try to protect them," Castor said.

"*Try?*" Philip repeated with derision. "Try! Don't think I don't know that you had planned to abandon us—to leave the city and your

143

bloodline behind. You have always been weak, but now your selfish spinelessness has shamed us all."

Castor flinched. Lore gripped his arm, hoping to steady him.

"I will offer this but once," Philip said. "I will release you from this life with a quick, clean death. You know this is the only way. *Try?* You will never be enough."

Lore gripped the book tighter, debating which soft spot on the old goat she should hit. She saw the flicker of fear in Castor's face—the worry that what Philip was saying was right, and that he wouldn't be enough—and settled on two strikes: throat, then loins.

Philip lowered into a fighting stance. "I will never know how *you*, a dying whelp of a boy, killed an old god, but I'm certain of one thing: if I allow you to live, you will fail them, and they will all die cursing you."

A thin band of sunlight slashed across the carpet near Lore's feet. She glanced down, confused, and missed the arrow as it tore through Philip's heart.

The old man stared at Castor, his eyes bulging as one hand came up to touch it. He was dead before he even hit the floor.

Castor instinctively moved to catch him, but Lore swung her gaze up, toward the open skylight. Another arrow appeared in the sliver of blue and released without so much as a whisper—ripping through the air, flying straight toward the back of Castor's neck.

FOURTEEN

Lore lunged, swinging the heavy book up into the arrow's path.

Her arms shook as they absorbed the impact of its strike. Instead of bouncing away, or catching on the leather cover, the steel head pierced through the hundreds of wafer-thin pages and tore out through the back. It hit the reinforced doorframe and finally stopped.

The book fell from her hands.

"Get back," she heard Castor say. When she didn't move, he gripped the front of her robes and spun her behind him. There was a heavy *slam* against the floor as someone jumped down from the skylight; it rattled the furniture and Lore's unsteady legs.

A voice rose like a cold night wind through trees. *"Godkiller."*

The woman—the being—looked as if she'd been carved from the darkness of a deep and ancient wild. The goddess's blond hair was matted with leaves and caught in pale, almost snow-white clouds around her dirt-streaked face. Even dulled by mortal blood, there was a pearlescent quality to her ivory skin, as if she radiated moonlight.

It was Artemis.

The goddess bared her teeth, but Lore's gaze fixed on the way her fingers were curled into claws around her compound bow. Stolen from a dead hunter, most likely.

Chiron leaped down from the bed, growling. The goddess turned as he lunged at her, her eyes flashing. The dog suddenly stilled, as if hit by a tranquilizer dart. His body relaxed as he rolled onto his side, exposing his soft belly to her.

"Lady of the Hunt," Castor said, neutrally.

Artemis gave him a baleful look as she prowled forward. Each step revealed a new, horrifying detail.

It wasn't dirt on the goddess's face, but dried blood. It had doused her front, speckling the sky-blue fabric of her robes. Lore's gaze fixed on the quiver strapped to the goddess's back—the one held in place with a strap not of worn leather, but of braided human hair. All different colors and textures, all sticky with blood and flecks of scalp.

Lore's stomach churned violently.

Artemis raised her bow. Another arrow was already notched. "You must have known that I would come for you. That I would hunt you, into the House of Hades, into the deepest depths of Tartarus, into whatever infernal darkness you hoped would hide you."

Without thinking, Lore put a warning hand on Castor's shoulder and felt the muscles there tighten in response.

"Please," he said. "You are not my enemy, and I'm not yours. I need to ask you something. If you were there that day. If you saw what happened."

Lore's gaze shot to the locked door behind them, and she knew.

No one is coming, she thought.

Lore began to search the room in earnest, her eyes landing on a floor mirror. She could knock the glass out of the frame, use the shards. All she needed was to get close enough to cut one of the tendons or arteries in the goddess's leg. That would at least buy them some time to escape.

"I've waited seven years for this moment," Artemis seethed. "My brother's death is your ruin. An evil fate is upon you now, Godkiller. When I am finished, there will not be enough left of your mortal corpse for the carrion birds."

The twins had been two halves of one soul, in a constant ebb and flow around each other, like night shifting to day, and day into night. They had jealously guarded and protected each other, rarely separating in the Agon if they could help it. Now the goddess looked as if Apollo's death had shredded the last bit of her sanity. Her eyes blazed with the embers of her power.

"Were you there?" Castor asked, a note of pleading in his voice. "Answer me."

"Leave, girl," the goddess said, addressing Lore directly. "I have no quarrel with you. Yet."

Lore felt the words like cold drips on her skin. She didn't understand why Castor hadn't attacked the goddess yet, why he kept asking her that question.

"Let me get her out," Castor said, slowly walking them backward toward the door. "Like you said, you have no quarrel with her."

It was a horrible parody of the way they used to drill, mirroring each other's steps. Castor reached for the goddess's arrow, splintering the wood of the doorframe, pulling it free. As he returned his hand to his side, he twisted his wrist so that the arrowhead pointed up at his woven gold belt—to the small knife he had tucked there, against the small of his back.

Lore drew in a deep breath, knowing exactly what he wanted. She stepped in close to him, her fingers curling around the hilt. It had absorbed the heat of his skin and now burned her fingertips.

"You'll choke on your own blood before I hear another word from you—"

147

Castor bent forward and Lore moved faster than she ever had in her life, sliding the blade free and throwing it.

Either because the knife was slightly bent, or because Lore was simply out of practice, the blade winged farther to the right than she'd meant for it to go. It spun toward the goddess's arm instead of her shoulder. Artemis jerked her bow up to block it. The knife rebounded onto the floor, spinning away.

Lore didn't hear or see the arrow until its razor tip was hissing through the air toward her, but she was already falling, only registering the force of Castor's shove the instant before she hit the hard floor.

Blood ran down into her eye from where the edge of the arrow had sliced along her temple and scalp. She swiped it away against her shoulder and stood, ignoring Castor's worried glance.

The goddess turned back toward the bed, hissing. Her eyes fell on Chiron, who'd tried his best to squeeze his massive body beneath the bed to hide.

"Don't," Castor began, "please—"

Chiron whimpered, then yelped as if she'd pierced him with a blade. The dog went rigid, his hackles rising to spikes. He bared his fangs, and his growl rolled across the room like thunder.

"Chiron, *no*," Lore said. "No!"

The dog barreled toward them with a sound unlike anything Lore had ever heard before. Strings of spit flew from his snout and foaming mouth. His eyes glowed gold with the goddess's power and there was no awareness there, no understanding—just rage.

Hunger and rage.

FIFTEEN

Lore's view of the dog disappeared as Castor stepped between her and Chiron. A blast of power exploded from his outstretched hands, bleaching the air white as it raced toward Artemis.

Lore threw an arm over her eyes, shielding them. Cement and brick splintered and the wall of the bedroom roared as it was blown out.

Somewhere nearby, Chiron whimpered. Lore felt blindly for him, clutching his fur and drawing him closer to her, behind the protection of Castor's body.

As quickly as it had come, the immense light was gone. Lore lowered her arm. The room cooled around her as the power disintegrated into hot, drifting sparks.

Castor was already at the smoldering hole in the wall, his face grave. Lore scrambled up, staggering slightly as she came to stand beside him. She leaned over the edge of the building, searching for the body.

There was a large indentation in a dumpster's lid where Artemis had struck it and rolled off. The goddess was on her feet again, melting back into the shadows of the side streets. Shouts rose from inside the house, chased by the screech of emergency sirens.

"You missed," Lore said hoarsely.

"No," he said. "I didn't."

Castor's jaw tightened again as he turned to look down at her.

"Are you all right?" he asked, running a soft touch along the outer edge of her eye. She pulled back from him.

"Why didn't you just do that before?" Lore said, feeling like she was gasping for every word.

He looked at her as if the answer was obvious. "Because Chiron was in the way."

The dog whined from beside the bedroom's door, scratching and digging at it to get out.

"Artemis will be back," Lore said. "Generally speaking, whenever carrion birds enter the conversation it usually implies a level of certainty about the slaughter."

"Don't worry about me, Lore," he said with a sad smile. "I'm not some stag she can run to ground." Castor gestured to the missing wall. "And at least I'll see her coming?"

"One, not funny." Lore dragged a hand back through the snarled mess of her hair. "Two, that's not what I meant."

The door rattled as someone pounded against it from the other side. Lore stepped in front of Castor as the locks scraped, ignoring an agonized muscle pull in her lower back, and the warning trilling in her mind.

What are you doing? she thought, furious at herself. *You can still get out if you go through the skylight.*

Athena needed her, and Lore needed Athena to stay alive. She had to find her a doctor, or some kind of off-the-books health center to treat whatever internal injuries she still had—and soon, if they wanted to catch Wrath as he emerged from hiding to strike at Castor and the other new gods.

Cas . . . Lore stole a glance. Uncertainty clawed at her. She didn't like the thought of leaving him, but what else could she do? Try to reason with Athena, to show her the logic of accepting help from a bitterly hated enemy? Lore would have a better chance of soothing Cerberus.

The room's metal blast door lifted, allowing the wooden one to open and slam against the smoldering plaster of the nearby wall. Van hovered in the doorway, his dark skin ashen and his mouth tight with worry.

"Castor?" he called into the drifting clouds of smoke between them. Chiron pushed past his legs, finally escaping the rubble of the room. "Where are you?"

"Here," the new god answered.

Van whirled toward them, dagger in hand.

Castor held out an arm in front of her. "It's all right, Van. It's just Lore."

"Lore," Van repeated, taking in a small breath.

Lore saw the growing accusation in his eyes and bristled with a familiar annoyance.

"This is *not* my fault," she insisted. Then she added silently, *For once.*

Van lowered the weapon. "How did you get in here?"

"Here's a better question," Lore shot back. "How the hell did Artemis? Why wasn't the skylight bricked over?"

"Artemis?" Van looked between them, the stray arrows, the upturned furniture, and the hole in the wall. His gaze landed on the hidden door, and Philip's body sprawled nearby. "Something tells me he didn't die valiantly defending you from her attack . . . ?"

"No, he did not," Lore said. "Did no one even think to check for hidden entrances—?"

Van held up his hand, stopping her. "While I'd love to stand around and argue, there are at least two hundred Kadmides heading this way, and half of our hunters are out searching for our dead. Castor, you need to leave. *Now.*"

Lore's pulse jumped, but her feet still wouldn't move.

Castor set his jaw. A shadow passed over his face, and Lore could only guess that Philip's words were playing through his mind again. *You will fail them, and they will all die cursing you.*

He might hate the Achillides, he might hate the Agon, but he wouldn't be Castor if he left knowing that death was coming for them and he could prevent it.

"You don't have anything to prove to them," she tried.

"I'm not going to leave," Castor said. "It doesn't matter what I think of them, or what they think of me. I *do* have a responsibility to them."

"Are you a complete idiot," Lore asked seriously, "or has the smoke gone to your head?"

"Charming as always, Melora," Van said. "Dare I ask what you're even doing here? You wouldn't help him before."

"I came for the food," Lore said. "You?"

But even then, her mind was screaming at her to go.

You need to leave before he and his serpents get here, she thought, a cold fear slipping through her. *You have to get back to Athena. You have to tell her about Hermes and Artemis and Tidebringer and Wrath . . .*

Van turned a cool, assessing look on her now. Lore fought the urge to duck away from that close scrutiny or demand to know whatever it was he was looking for. That look, and that stillness, even as a kid, had always made her feel loud, dirty, and simple.

"She came to find out if we knew anything about another version of the origin poem, one that might explain how to win the Agon," Castor told him. "Someone warned her that's what Wrath is looking for."

"Who told you that?" Van asked.

"That's my business," Lore said.

"You haven't heard anything about it?" Castor pressed him. Lore felt a strange sort of guilt that, even now, he was still trying to help her, to put her needs first, the way he always had.

Van shook his head. "No . . . if—and I mean *if*—it exists, it could be something the Odysseides know about. They have the most in-depth archives of all the families. I'll talk to my source there, but you need to go, Cas. Immediately."

Shit, Lore thought. She should have thought of the Odysseides' archive—then again, she generally made a point to avoid thinking about the House of Odysseus at all.

"I have a duty to help this bloodline," Castor insisted. "I still have some sense of honor, apparently."

"Your honor would be adorable if it weren't so stupid," Lore told him. "Is self-preservation the first thing that gets stripped from you when you lose your humanity, or is it common sense? This city hasn't changed that much since you left it. You know it better than most of the hunters out there. The safer thing is to go into hiding and wait out the next five nights, or see if you can get to one of the outer boroughs. It's not ideal, but at least you wouldn't have to constantly defend yourself on two fronts. The absolute last thing you need to do is stay here and die for people who—"

"Exactly," Van said coming to stand beside her. "Which is why you're going with Melora."

It took Lore a moment to process this. "Wait—what? *No.* He can't come with me."

"I'm not going," Castor said.

"It has to be you," Van insisted, ignoring him.

Lore was disgusted. "Still sitting out whatever fight you can, I see."

"You know that's not true," Castor told her sharply.

Lore grew heated, and forced herself to take a breath. It had always been this way—even as kids, Castor would try to pull her back from any edge, regardless of whether or not it had something to do with Van. The difference was, now she was more than capable of deciding when to jump. "If I wanted a moral compass, I would have stopped at a store on the way here."

She couldn't explain it all to them—she couldn't tell them about the deal she'd made and manage their outrage, and she sure as hell couldn't bring more trouble home.

Van raised his gloved hand and tilted his head, studying her in a way Lore hated. She had to resist squirming as he said, "The real issue here is that *you* don't believe that *you* can protect him, isn't it? I never took you for a coward, Melora."

"Oh, go to the crows, Evander," she said. "I have enough problems as it is."

Lore knew he was baiting her. Knew that her temper was quick and her regrets after the fact long, but there was something about that word, *coward*. It wasn't that he'd thrown it at her like a knife; it was already inside her like a painful infestation. At the sound of its name, it began to claw its way out.

May all cowards be devoured by their shame, her mother used to say.

"Will the two of you listen to me?" Castor said. "I can't leave. I refuse to turn the old man's words into prophecy. My bloodline has considered me a failure from the day I was born. I'm not about to prove them right."

Lore turned to him, startled by the vehemence in those words. Even Van looked slightly taken aback.

"Cas—" she began.

Brakes screeched outside, the sound followed by revving engines and shouts from the lower levels of Thetis House.

Lore's hands curled at her sides, her head warring with her gut. Castor's stubbornness was bound to get him killed if she left him here. There *had* to be a way to make Athena see reason. And if not, well, Lore had the entire way home to think of a backup plan.

"*Leave*, Cas," Van said.

Castor shook his head, pained. "I can't."

"You have to," Van said. It was the smug tone of someone who knew they'd already won the fight. "You may be willing to give up your life, but I know you're not willing to risk hers."

Van nodded toward Lore. Her lips parted in protest, but Castor drew in a sharp breath and closed his eyes.

"Van—" he started.

But the Messenger had already found the right place to slip the blade in. "She won't leave you here now, knowing they're coming to kill you. Are you going to risk them finding her?"

Lore and Van exchanged another look; she read his perfectly. *I'm entrusting him to you.*

She groaned. "If you're coming with me, we're leaving right now." Lore looped her arm through Castor's and pulled him toward the hole he'd blasted in the wall. "I don't know how the hell I'm going to get you across the city without leaving a trail—"

"Take a cab," Van said. "Pay in cash."

Lore blinked. "For the record, I would have thought of that eventually."

Van turned back to the new god. Castor had angled his body toward the door and the screech of clashing metal blades.

Footsteps pounded up the stairs.

"What about you?" Lore demanded.

"Come with us," Castor pleaded.

"Not until I learn whatever I can," Van said. "I'll ask about the poem. Where can I find you when it's over?"

Lore's jaw clenched. Castor trusted him, but that didn't mean she had to. "Martha's Diner, Harlem. Wait there."

Van nodded, slipping back out into the hallway. The locks clicked into place, one at a time. The metal blast door snapped back down, cutting them off from the rest of the house. Castor stared at it, the muscles of his shoulders bunching with his horror and frustration.

Lore was overwhelmed by the speed of the seconds slipping by. "Come on. This is a fight you're not going to win. Sometimes you have to forget about honor—"

"This is *not* about honor," he told her sharply. "It's about the people I'm leaving to die."

She released her hold on his arm, feeling as if he'd burned her with his words. Lore moved to the edge of the fractured wall again, turning her gaze down onto the dumpster.

"Shit," she swore.

The fall was no longer their biggest problem. Hunters wearing the Kadmides' serpent masks were gathering around the debris from the wall, looking and pointing up. She leaned back, avoiding an arrow fired from a metal crossbow. The beat of helicopter wings forced her attention back up to the roof. Thunder coursed through her veins at the sound of the heavy footsteps walking toward the open skylight.

Castor was suddenly beside her, holding out both arms.

It took her a moment to understand exactly what he wanted.

"You're joking," she said.

"And you're afraid," he said. "Do you think I'll drop you?"

"No, I think I'm going to have your scrape your *mortal body* off the cement," she said. "Are you *serious*? We're four stories up."

"Trust me," Castor said.

The voices were loud enough now that she could make out fragments of what they were saying.

"He's just below us . . ."

Lore scowled. "If you do drop me, I swear I will come back as one of the Keres and leave you nothing more than ash and blood."

Castor nodded, his expression grim. "I'd definitely let you try."

Lore reluctantly stepped up beside him, rising onto her toes to loop one of her arms around Castor's neck. He reached down, lifting her with irritating ease, his own strong arms wrapping around her shoulder and under her knees without the smallest quiver of effort.

Castor glanced down at her face. "Ready?"

He didn't wait for her answer as he stepped up to the edge of the wall. Ropes dropped down from either side of the wall and the last clear thing she heard was a deep, familiar voice snarling, "Take him! Don't let him get away!"

Castor freed one hand and sent a blast of power at the hunters scaling the walls from below and firing up at him from the ground.

Lore turned, pressing her face against Castor's shoulder as the stench of burnt hair and skin and metal flooded her nostrils.

"Ready?" he asked again.

She nodded. Then Castor tightened his hold on her, gripped one of the dangling ropes, and stepped into the air.

The drop robbed Lore's heart of several beats, and seemed to yank the oxygen out of her lungs. It was the only reason she didn't scream.

Castor grunted as the rope gave a sharp jerk, stopping them. Lore's eyes snapped open. They had landed in the melting, smoldering trash heap that had once been the dumpster.

"You okay?" she gasped, dragging herself out of his grip. Castor's hand was flayed open by rope burn. He grimaced as a glow emanated around his palm and the skin mended itself.

Lore took a big jump down to avoid the charred bodies that surrounded them. "Let's go—*Cas!*"

Castor looked back one last time, even as bullets and arrows rained down again from above them.

Lore grabbed Castor's wrist, dragging him away from the building, and didn't let go until he matched her pace. She led him back around the other dumpsters, through the fence, toward the parking garage— one of a thousand secrets that had knotted their lives together.

"Don't lose sight of me," Lore warned. "I'm not stopping for you."

"I'll do my best to keep up," he said, still visibly upset.

Lore accepted a boost up from him into the elevator shaft's window, then turned back, offering him a hand in return. "I'll definitely let you try."

He took it, even though she knew he didn't need to, and they set off again.

Lore's blood raced through her body as they ran, coming alive with the flush of heat through her muscles and the familiar rhythm of Castor's steps, just behind her. Their old, hidden route still waited for them, as if they had never left, and had never lost one another.

In that moment, the past became the present, and the present the past, and it was just the two of them in the shadows of their city, the way it had always been.

The way it should have been forever.

PART TWO

—

CARRYING FIRE

SIXTEEN

THE SUMMER HEAT LINGERED IN THE CITY, DRAWING OUT THE WORST smells Manhattan had to offer. As they made their way west, toward the Hudson, Lore felt like she was trapped inside a damp garbage bag.

She'd stripped off the hunter's cloak, but Castor was another story. New York was one of the few cities in which a man in full ancient costume wouldn't be even the third-strangest thing people saw while going about their day. And yet everything about him, from his height to his physique to that face, conspired to catch the eye.

Lore instructed the cabdriver to drop them off a few blocks from her town house. She still had the cash from the fight in her pocket and struggled to part with it, counting out the fare from her dwindling stack of twenties. She wasn't sure what she was more anxious about— being spotted by one of the bloodlines, or the reaction she'd get walking through the door.

Castor hadn't said a word since they left Thetis House. He didn't need to.

The pulse of the city had slowed with late afternoon. Now and then they'd pass someone on the way to the grocery store or laundromat, or kids relishing the spray of an open fire hydrant, but as she hurried them along, Lore was relieved not to see anyone she knew. The fewer lies she had to concoct, the better.

Some of the pained tension bled from Castor's face as he watched Lore stoop to pick up stray Duane Reade bags fluttering along the sidewalk like aimless ghosts.

"What?" she asked, defensive. "I don't like litter."

She would always take care of the neighborhood that had taken care of her. It was part of the contract that came with being a New Yorker.

Lore felt Castor watching her again as they rounded another corner. She spied Bo the Bodega Cat waiting on their usual bench, but hurried Castor past the storefront to avoid Mr. Herrera seeing her bloodied and covered with dust and smoke residue.

Lore hesitated as they approached Martha's.

"Come on," she told him, leading Castor around to the side door. She knocked, trying to keep one eye on the street around them.

It took a few minutes, but Mel's face appeared behind the door as it cracked open. Her eyes widened in shock at Lore's appearance.

Lore gave her a hopeful smile.

"I thought you were my fruit delivery. Are you all right? What happened?" Mel blinked as she finally caught sight of Castor. "Um, hi."

"Bike accident," Lore lied. "I ate dirt when I collided with him. Do you mind if we use the bathroom to clean up? You know Miles—he'll freak out if he sees me like this."

"Of course." Mel ushered them inside, hurrying past the kitchen, where Joe, the diner's cook, was starting preparations for the dinner crowd. "Here, use the back one. Are you sure you shouldn't go to the hospital?"

"We're both fine," Lore promised as she shut the small bathroom's door behind them. "Thanks for this."

"Yeah . . ." Mel said, her brow creased. "Call if you need anything, hear me?"

Castor waited until Lore was at the sink, splashing water on her face, to ask, "Who's Miles?"

She looked up at him from underneath the paper towel she was using to dab at the cut on her forehead. "Friend and roommate."

The new god nodded, leaning back against the door. He watched her silently, and Lore wondered if she had ever been so aware of another person outside a fight in her whole life. The size of him, his sheer immense presence, overwhelmed the small space.

She glanced up at him in the mirror, taking in his troubled expression and the tattered remains of what had once been luxurious robes.

"It's not your fault," she told him. "You had to go."

"Did I?" he asked faintly.

"You're no good to them dead," Lore reminded him.

"As it turns out," he said, "I'm apparently no good to them at all."

Lore threw her wet paper towel at his face. He startled, looking at her in shock.

"You are the best thing to come out of the House of Achilles," she told him. "Maybe the only good thing. Sometimes you just have to survive to fight another day. Even I knew those were bad odds, and you know how I feel about running from a fight."

He sighed, resting his head back against the door. "I've been weak my whole life. And when I finally did get power—when I finally became strong—"

Lore cut him off. "You are the strongest person I've ever known. Always have been."

"Now I know you're lying," he said. "I could barely keep up with you most days."

She fought to control the rising heat in her words. "You are the strongest person I've ever known, Castor Achilleos, and it wasn't because of how fast you ran or how hard you hit. It was because even when you got knocked flat on your back, you fought your way back up. You have to do it again now. Whatever you're feeling, you have to leave it on the mat and get back up."

Lore had let the Philip incident go because of the chaos that had come after, but she hadn't forgotten it.

"You have to stay alive," she told him. "If you want to help them, you have to live."

Castor's face was so beautiful, it was almost painful to look at. So she didn't.

"And what about you?" he pressed. "Is that what you're doing— getting back up and into the Agon after escaping it?"

"That's rich coming from someone who wanted to rope me back in himself," she told him.

"It was a mistake," he told her. "You were out. I should have let you stay there, but I was selfish, and I wanted to see you. I needed to know that you were alive. But if I'm the reason you got this idea about going after Wrath into your head . . ."

Lore said nothing. She couldn't, not with her jaw clenched so tight.

"Your parents wouldn't want you to avenge them, and they wouldn't want you to get trapped in the hell of being immortal. Of being hunted," Castor told her. "They'd want you to live a free, full life."

A cold tingle moved up from Lore's fingertips and spread throughout her body. Her breathing hitched as she fought for the words against the familiar, crushing tide that rose in her. "You have no idea what you're talking about. They deserve to rest. They deserve— They were— It was a mistake."

The words felt slow, almost lethargic compared to the speed of her thoughts. Castor put a hand on her shoulder. Lore tried to shrug it off,

166

to step back, but the memory of her sisters' faces rose up in her mind. The way they'd looked when she'd found them . . .

"Lore?"

"I'm— It's fine. I'm *fine*," Lore managed to get out. Her pulse beat hard and fast, until it clouded her vision with black. She tried to breathe through it, tried to remember where she was, but all she could see were Olympia and Damara, the dark holes where their eyes had been. The blood still wet on their cheeks, like tears.

Not now, she thought, the words spiraling, screaming, *not now*— she had to keep it together. The pressure was building in her again, the strain of it turning her brittle. Lore couldn't find her way out of the darkness growing around her.

"Have you ever heard the one about the turtles on Broadway?"

The words struck her mind like a torch in the dark, sudden and bright, interrupting her thoughts.

"Have I . . . what?" she asked, blinking to clear her vision.

"The turtle show on Broadway," Castor said softly.

Lore still didn't understand. "No—what are you talking about?"

"Really?" he said, his gaze still intent on her. "Because it was a shell-out."

The pressure receded, easing out of her shoulders and chest until she could take a deep enough breath to snort.

Lore looked down at her feet, at the old tile beneath them, and tried to hide her embarrassment. Gil used to tell her stories about his life as a professor, the antics of his former students, or his extensive world travels in low, soothing tones until she came back to herself. They would drink tea and talk, as much as Lore was able to.

But she didn't want to talk about it now. Castor, at least, seemed to sense that.

"It's easy to be overcome with exasperation when dealing with immortals," he said simply.

"Tell me about it," she said when she trusted her voice to be steady. "You're all more trouble than you're worth."

"Absolutely," he agreed.

"That was a terrible joke, by the way."

"Don't worry," he said. "I've got seven years' worth saved up."

"Is that a threat?" she asked.

The air warmed around her. That was the only reason her skin heated with the smile he sent her way.

There was a sharp knock on the door. "Honey? There's someone here asking after a girl that sounds a lot like you. He's tall, Black, looks like he stepped out of a cologne ad—"

Lore and Castor exchanged a surprised look. Van had moved fast.

"Can you send him back?" Lore asked. "Sorry. I promise we'll be out of your hair soon."

"You want something to eat before you go?" Mel asked. "Something to take with you?"

"Pancakes?" Castor asked, before Lore could stop him. She gave him a look, but he stared back at her, shameless.

"No problem," Mel said.

The new god took his turn at the sink, splashing water over his face and arms. Lore opened the bathroom door a crack and shut it again when she saw that it was, in fact, Van coming toward them. He was dressed in jeans and a nice linen shirt, the sleeves rolled up. For a moment, she wondered how he had made it all the way uptown without a wrinkle or sweat stain.

Van ducked inside the bathroom, relief breaking over his features.

"What happened?" Castor asked. "Are you all right?"

"I'm fine," Van told him, though he looked uneasy. "I got out. So did some of the others. I'm waiting to hear back about our hunters that went to look for the bodies." He handed Castor the plastic shopping bag he'd been clutching. "Here, for you to change."

Castor pulled out a pair of tennis shoes, basketball shorts, and an athletic shirt. "Nike? Really?"

"You're not exactly easy to shop for," Van told him, gesturing to Castor's size. "It was the only thing I knew would fit. Besides, we could use a little victory on our side."

"Were you able to get in contact with the Odysseides?" Lore asked.

Van shook his head. "Not yet."

"Pass me your old clothes when you're done with them," Lore said to Castor as she opened the bathroom door and stepped out.

"Why?" Van asked sharply. "What are you going to do with them?"

"Van," Castor said, forever the peacemaker between the two of them. "It's all right."

"I'm getting rid of them in a way that'll confuse the hunters and their tracking dogs," Lore told him. "Is that answer good enough for you?"

She didn't bother to make sure that it was. As promised, Castor passed her the old set when he had changed.

"I'll be back in a few minutes," she told them. "Don't leave."

Lore tore the warm, blood-stained fabric into smaller strips and distributed them into trash cans, sofas left out on the curb, in bus stops, and down in the subway, making as wide of a circle around her neighborhood as she dared. By the time she returned, Castor and Van were in the back hallway of the diner; the Messenger was pacing, the new god savoring each bite of pancake he put in his mouth.

"Finally!" Van said.

"Let's go," she said, then, calling to the front of the restaurant, added, "Thanks, Mel! I owe you!"

"Where are we going?" Van asked as soon as they stepped back out into the street.

Lore forced herself to stop. This wasn't a conversation for out in the open. "We're going to my house. But you're going to have to listen to me very carefully and do exactly what I say when we get there."

"Why?" Van asked. "Because if we break your rules, you'll kick us out?"

"No," Lore said evenly, "because, if you don't, the god who's already in the house is going to kill you both."

Castor choked on his food, pounding a fist to his chest.

"Surely, I just misheard you . . ." Van began. "Surely."

"Now do you see why I didn't think it was a great idea for Cas to come with me?" she asked.

"Who—" Van began. His eyes widened as he answered his own question. "No. I can't believe this. She's never sought out a mortal's help before . . ."

"She's never *needed* a mortal's help before," Castor said, tossing the rest of his meal into the dumpster. "What happened?"

"Wrath came after her and Artemis," Lore said, keeping her voice low. "And Artemis decided to slow her down the best way she knew how. Blade to the gut."

"Damn," Van said, in mild appreciation.

"I found her on my doorstep," Lore continued. "Apparently she'd kept track of me over the years and took a gamble on whether or not I'd want her dead."

Van opened his mouth to speak again. Closed it. Gave himself a moment to think.

170

"I came to find you because I thought you'd finished your healer's training," Lore told Castor. "I stopped the blood loss, but she's in bad shape."

"And why do you care?" Castor asked. "She's a snake. Let her die, if she hasn't already."

Lore glanced down. "She's still alive. I'm positive."

Van did not miss that, either.

"You didn't," he began slowly. "Tell me you weren't that stupid."

"What else was I supposed to do?" Lore demanded.

"Let her die?" Van suggested. "Smile in satisfaction at knowing a hunter wouldn't claim her power?"

"I wasn't alone when I found her," Lore said, hearing the way her voice pitched up. "And she offered me something I wanted."

A moment later, Castor had also figured it out. The color leached out of his tan skin, either from anger, or fear, or both. "You bound your fate to hers? What the hell did she promise you to get you to agree?"

She thought about lying, but it seemed pointless given the danger they were in now. "She promised to kill Wrath."

They both stared at her, silent.

"Oh," Van said. "Well, that's great. Aside from, of course, you dying if she does during a week when that's the principal goal of almost a thousand people. Otherwise a stellar plan, Melora."

"I don't need a lecture," Lore snapped. "I made a choice, and I'm living with it."

"I'll say," Castor said, the words rippling with frustration. "Show us the way to your house, then."

"You still want to come?" she asked.

The look he sent her cut Lore to the quick. "Am I supposed to just

171

let you die? You wanted me to heal her, so I'll heal her."

She turned stiffly, letting them exchange their looks behind her back. When Lore was sure they weren't being watched by any hunters on the street, she led them to the town house in silence.

"This is it," Lore said. "We'll go in through the basement. It'll get you off the street and give me time to prepare her."

There was an extra key hidden behind one of the bricks on the town house's facade. Lore retrieved it with a soft sigh. "Just stay behind me, all right?"

She ushered both of them into the crowded basement, locking the door behind them. Castor and Van looked around, taking in the stacks of boxes and plastic tubs.

"Is this stuff all yours?" Van asked.

"Are you always this nosy?" Lore groused. "No. And before you ask, I inherited the house from the man I worked as a caretaker for. Gilbert Merrit."

"You were someone's caretaker?" Van said in disbelief. *"You?"*

"Van," Castor said. "Don't."

For once, Lore kept her sharp retort to herself. She turned toward the staircase leading up into the house and called out, "It's me!"

Castor made as if to follow her. Lore held out an arm, blocking him. Van, at least, had the sense to hang back.

"You need to wait," she whispered. "Just give me a few minutes to preemptively put out the fire your presence is going to cause."

Fire was very likely an understatement, given the bloodcurdling glimpse she'd had of the old god's feelings toward her newer counterparts. She hurried up the stairs, giving Castor one last meaningful look to *stay* before she opened the door and said, loudly, "I'm coming in."

172

It happened so quickly, time split into snapshots. One, Miles and Athena standing near the fireplace of the living room, the television on behind them. Two, Athena reaching back for something leaning against the wall. Three, her face hardening with a snarl and her arm craning back. Four . . .

Something long and thin flew from her hand, whistling as it cut a bold path across the room. Lore jumped right with a startled gasp, but the weapon had never been intended for her.

Castor caught the spear just before it lodged in his heart.

SEVENTEEN

THE PIECE OF GUM MILES WAS CHEWING FELL OUT OF HIS OPEN MOUTH.

"Is . . . is that my broom?" Lore gasped. The wooden body of the spear was a distinctive green, worn in the places where it was meant to be gripped.

She glanced to Miles, both for confirmation and to ensure that he was all right. His mouth stretched into a pained rictus.

"Yes, it is," he said between his clenched teeth. "She is *very* resourceful."

Heat flared to her right. Castor's power surged along the make-shift weapon until the wood turned to ash in his hand. His fierce, unblinking gaze never broke away from Athena's.

"That was my broom," Lore said mournfully.

"Godkiller!" The room vibrated with the thunderous word. Athena reached behind her once more, feeling for another crudely formed spear.

Lore stepped back between the two gods, holding her hands out. "*Stop*—stop it!"

"You dare to bring this . . . this *abomination* here, into this sanctuary?" Athena growled.

"Well, it's my sanctuary, so yes," Lore said. "Listen—"

"This was not part of our agreement, Melora." Athena did not need to shout to drive her words home like an ax to the skull. "You swore your allegiance to *me*."

"He's here to heal you," Lore said, trying a different tactic. "He's going to help us. It's a strategy. I thought you'd like that."

"Unless you have brought him here for me to kill, I see no strategy," Athena snarled. "I heard, pretender, that even with Apollo's power you could not manifest a corporeal form. That you wasted the last pathetic years you have been granted dithering about like a lost yearling."

It was only when Miles looked back and forth between them, visibly anxious, that Lore realized they'd all been speaking in the ancient tongue.

"Well, I've never turned a skilled artisan into an arachnid, thrown an infant off a mountain, or cursed anyone into a lifetime of having their liver pecked out by an eagle," Castor said, "so I suppose I do still have a few things to learn about being a god."

Athena wasn't at her most terrifying when her skin was flushed with fury, or she was snarling deadly promises. It was in moments like this one, when her eyes cooled and her body went still with a predator's confidence that nothing would escape it. Castor's hand landed on Lore's shoulder, as if to gently move her aside.

She pushed it away, and spoke in English, enunciating each word. "*Enough.* We don't have time for this."

Lore approached Athena slowly, eyeing the spear that, it seemed, had previously enjoyed a short life as her mop. "I need to tell you what happened. We need his help."

"I do not *need* his aid," Athena groused. "The others—"

Lore pulled the one card that would matter most to the goddess, and laid it down without a single word to soften it. "Hermes is dead. Wrath killed him during the Awakening."

It was Miles who reacted, gasping a "What? Really?"

Athena merely stared at Lore, as if waiting for the lie to crumble to dust at her feet.

"Impossible," she said, finally.

"He's dead," Castor confirmed. "Tidebringer as well."

Van crowded behind them on the stairs.

"He speaks the truth, Goddess," he said, finally, mostly in acknowledgment. "We both come here not as your enemies, but as allies."

Lore felt the smallest bit of satisfaction when the goddess sized him up with the same intensity Van did others. Maybe because of it, he chose to focus on someone else.

"Who are you?" he demanded.

Miles straightened as Van's gaze fell on him, his ears rimmed with pink. "Hi—I'm Miles. I mean, I'm Lore's roommate. And friend."

"I'm Castor," the new god said. "This is Evander . . . Van."

Van's streamlined leather backpack looked like a beetle's shell. He adjusted its straps, giving Lore a sideways look. "What the hell are you thinking, bringing an Unblooded into this?"

Miles recoiled at the edge of cold disapproval in Van's words.

Lore's anger, though, was still too close to the surface. "He was with me when I found her. In case you've lost your grip on it, let me remind you—the real world doesn't work like the bloodlines. You get a choice on how to live your life when you're on the outside."

"I may be new to all of this, but I'm not useless," Miles said. "How about you get to know me for longer than ten seconds?"

"I don't need more than ten seconds," Van said.

Lore's hands curled into fists at her side. She'd already struggled with the thought of Miles being drawn into the Agon, but the

176

condescension laced through those words—as if she'd intentionally endangered him, as if Miles were *nothing*—infuriated her.

"Van," Castor said, his tone chiding.

Evander Achilleos had grown up in an elegant home in London, and had been raised by parents who spoke in cut-glass accents and ate their meals on gold-trimmed china, but you would never have known it in that moment. The handful of times his parents had brought him to New York on business trips and he'd trained at Thetis House or joined Lore and Castor in Central Park, he'd at least been polite—even as it was clear he couldn't stand Lore, for whatever reason.

He had no idea who Miles was, and he sure as hell had no idea who Lore had become.

"I enjoy this mortal," Athena said from beside Miles. "He stays."

Lore glanced to Van's prosthetic hand, his rigid posture as he kept it close to his stomach.

"What will you tell his family when you bring his body back to them?" he asked her.

"*Geez*," Miles said. "I'm standing right here."

"If you're going to insult my friend, you can leave," Lore said. Her gaze shifted to Miles, to see how he had taken Van's words. Rather than fear, she saw open defiance—the kind previously only reserved for witnessing strangers stealing cabs from other people and the price of kimchi at the bodega.

Athena's long, cold stare finally lifted from Van. "Tell me how you are certain Hermes and the imposter Poseidon are dead."

Van drew in a breath. "I captured the footage on— I saw it with my own eyes. The new Ares, Wrath, killed Hermes in the park and left his body there. Some of his hunters—the Kadmides—took Tidebringer with them when they left the park. My sources in the

177

House of Theseus confirmed she was later killed by Wrath at their current compound."

The goddess was as rigid and straight as the weapon in her hand. "And you believe these . . . *sources*?"

"Yes," Van said simply. "Because they know what I would do to them if they lied."

"Your sister is still alive," Lore added. "That, *I* witnessed firsthand. She attacked Castor in one of the Achillides' compounds."

Athena's nostrils flared. "As is her right. She will not stop until the imposter is dead."

"Fantastic," Lore said grimly.

"His presence ensures my sister will find us sooner than I foresaw," Athena said, nodding toward Castor. "Nothing is beyond her arrow's tip."

"Are you afraid of her?" Lore asked. As much as she'd wanted to bait the goddess, there was a part of her that truly wondered if a being like her was capable of fear. To be afraid was to accept you were not infallible.

"Fear is a foreign land I shall never visit and a language that will never cross my tongue," Athena said. "Where were the descendants of godlike Achilles to protect you?"

Castor's gaze narrowed. "Concerned with other matters."

"And yet you are here, alone, far from their protection," Athena said. She had the full picture in mere seconds.

Castor advanced, one fist rising, but Lore held him back again. "The compound was attacked by the Kadmides. Wrath tried to recruit the Achillides by sending Castor a warning. The descendants of Theseus have already aligned with the Kadmides and serve him."

"Then they dishonor their ancestor," Athena said, her lip curling in obvious disgust. "How many Achillides remain living and free of Wrath's control?"

Both Lore and Castor turned toward Van expectantly.

"The number is irrelevant," he said carefully, avoiding Castor's gaze.

That bad, huh? Lore thought.

"How many do we have left?" Castor's words rolled through the otherwise silent living room like a thundercloud, darkening it.

The weight of the word seemed unbearable on Van's tongue. It fell into the heavy silence like a bronze shield. "Twenty-seven."

Lore watched Castor process that number. The tendons in his neck bulged as he turned away and braced his hands on the back of one of the winged armchairs.

"How many did you begin this Agon with?" Athena pressed, not bothering to hide her pleasure.

"There are three hundred and seventy-eight hunters from the House of Achilles in the city this cycle," Van said, his voice remote. "Nearly a hundred were killed at Thetis House as the Kadmides over-ran it. The traitors join nearly five hundred Kadmides and the entire House of Theseus, which at last count was four hundred and thirty."

"I need to go heal the survivors," Castor said, his voice strained.

"No, you need to stay here," Van told him. "I brought them supplies. They have at least one healer."

"Van—" Castor started.

"I know," Van said. "I *know* you want to help, but you can't. Not right now. Wrath is out to kill all the other gods and combine the bloodlines into one force under him. He's not going to stop hunting you until he himself is killed, so that has to be our priority. If you die, the remaining Achillides are at his mercy. Tell me you understand that."

Castor's shoulders slumped. "I do."

At the mention of the defecting Achillides, derision turned Athena's perfect features monstrous. "My, how the flock flees to the shelter of a better protector."

Castor spun around, his expression wild with pain and anger. "You would know something about that, wouldn't you?"

Athena rose to her full height, meeting him eye-to-eye. Lore bit back a noise of frustration.

"You two are going to have plenty of time for blood and thunder and staring contests when you're both happily immortal again," Lore said. She turned to Athena. "Those were hunters that would have followed Castor and helped us. Now we're going to have to deal with a bigger circle of protection around Wrath and more hunters on the street searching for *you*."

"I will never cower before an imposter's blade, nor will I retreat from a binding oath. I tell you now, as I have before, the Ares pretender will die by my hand. I do not require any assistance."

"Yes, you do," Lore said. "Take it from a mortal who's had her fair share of injuries. All I did was stop the bleeding. If you agree to this alliance, he'll heal you and restore your strength. You won't need to waste days resting."

"Perhaps I shall let the false Ares do the work of eliminating my rivals for me," Athena said, "before taking his life and finishing this hunt once and for all."

Lore wasn't a fool; she knew that any partnership between the gods would only last until the end of this Agon, and that eventually Athena and Castor would stand between each other and full release from the hunt. This was just delaying the inevitable, especially if the new version of the poem existed and confirmed the victor would be the last god standing.

"You won't," Lore said to Athena meaningfully. "Because you wouldn't make it to the end of this cycle."

The others fell silent at her words. Athena lifted her chin, but her gaze was one of approval.

"I won't swear a binding oath to you," Castor said, finally. "But as your life is tied to Lore's, I cannot—and will not—allow you to die."

Athena nodded. A cold prickle crossed the back of Lore's neck as the goddess studied Castor.

"The imposter will heal me," Athena said at last, taking a seat in the middle of Gil's velvet settee. The goddess raised the hem of the shirt Lore had given her, revealing the angry wound. "And we shall begin to plan in earnest."

Castor gave a sarcastic bow. "But of course."

The others took their seats around the living room, Van in one of the chairs, and Miles and Lore on the ground beside the glass coffee table.

Castor brought a hand to the goddess's wound. Light flowed out from his fingertips; not the crackling, fiery energy of the blasts he'd thrown, but a soft, pulsating glow.

Athena hissed in a breath as the light sank deep into the red, puckered skin. She turned to meet Lore's gaze.

"Were you able to learn more of the poem the false Ares searches for?" she asked.

"Nothing particularly useful. But as Van pointed out, if anyone has a record of a different version of the poem it would be the Odysseides," Lore explained. She rolled her shoulders back to ease the tension building in them.

"I see," Athena began, hissing again as Castor shifted his hand. "I suppose the false Ares will know this as well?"

"Definitely, just like he knows they have the new Aphrodite," Lore said. "I'd bet anything they're Wrath's next target. The only question is when."

"Tonight," Van said.

"Tonight?" Lore repeated. "How can you be so sure?"

"Deductive reasoning," Van said quickly—too quickly. "The House of Kadmos won't want to risk another daylight attack that could draw unwanted media attention."

"Your reasoning is flawed. If they were willing to strike the Achillides in the waking hours, they will not hesitate to do the same to the Odysseus bloodline," Athena said. "Did any city guardians respond to the assault on your bloodline?"

"That *is* weird," Lore said, glancing at Castor. "I would have expected, at the very least, someone would have called in about hearing your blast, even if they didn't see it."

He made a soft noise of agreement, but was still focused on his task.

"It's not weird at all," Van said. "All the bloodlines pay off different members of the city and emergency services to look the other way. It's possible Wrath and the Kadmides are in deeper than the rest of us."

Miles blinked. "That's . . . horrifying, though I guess not totally unexpected."

"Then they would not fear being seen by those outside of the Agon," Athena said to Van. "Tell me, then, how you speak with such certainty that the House of Kadmos will attack this evening. Your 'sources,' I presume?"

Van's armor of self-possession and composure had always seemed unassailable to Lore. But from the moment he had walked through the door and laid eyes on the god, she'd sensed the nerves firing deep beneath his skin. Even now, as he remained silent, Lore saw him shift under the force of Athena's probing gaze.

"I detest half-truths and shadows," the goddess warned him.

Castor sat back, his work finally done. He looked to Van. "Tell them."

Van's nostrils flared as he drew in his next breath. "One source, yes. After years of trying, I managed to develop an asset in the Kadmides—an elder. When I spoke to him an hour ago, he confirmed the reports about Tidebringer's death, and that they would move against the Odysseides tonight. The final timing still hadn't been decided, but he believed it would be closer to midnight."

"An elder?" Lore said, surprised. Those men tended to be the most loyal to their bloodline, because they reaped the bulk of its many rewards. "Why would he help you?"

His smile was unfeeling. "Because I learned something about him, and he would die before revealing it to his bloodline. Because I always get what I want in the end."

"Hm." Athena did not seem impressed.

Castor stood, crossing the room to sit in the other armchair.

"You're welcome," he muttered.

The goddess ignored him, focusing on Lore again. "It seems we will have a true opportunity to kill the false Ares tonight, and perhaps even collect information on the poem ourselves."

Lore pressed her lips together at the mention of the poem, hoping her face didn't betray her thoughts. Neither Athena nor Wrath would be learning anything about the poem if she could help it.

"And even if he doesn't show up to kill the new Aphrodite himself," she said, "the Kadmides would have to bring the new god back to wherever he's hiding. We could follow them."

The settee creaked as Athena leaned back against it. "Indeed."

She felt Castor's gaze on her, but Lore refused to look—to see the concern or worry she knew she'd find there. "Sounds like a plan to me."

"Really? I didn't hear a plan in that," Castor said. "We don't know where the Odysseides are—their New York base has never been identified. And even putting that aside, we're going to have Wrath, his combined force of hunters, and the Odysseides trying to kill us." Before Lore could protest, he added, "And yes, I mean *us*, because I'm not going to be left behind."

"It is a simple matter of asking the Odysseides and their false god for a truce of a few hours," Athena said. "Surely one of you has ties to the bloodline and could approach them?"

"Don't you have a friend in the Odysseides?" Castor asked Lore. "Iro? I remember you talking about meeting her . . ."

Lore wanted to fade into the air when both Castor and Van turned to her. She might be able to get through to Iro, if they could find her . . .

No.

Their mothers had been the best of friends, training partners who had become like sisters, and it was only at Iro's mother's insistence that Lore came to live with them after her family was murdered. Came to be hidden by them, really.

In those four years she had lived with the Odysseides, Lore and Iro had gone from strangers who had met once to becoming as close as their mothers had been.

Whatever Iro felt about her now, Lore knew that Iro would feel duty-bound to kill her for what Lore had done the night she'd fled their estate.

"I think I know where the Odysseides are," Lore told them finally. "But I can't approach them. They'd kill me before I got over the threshold."

"What?" Miles said. "Why?"

She didn't regret what she'd done, but she also didn't feel like she needed to share it with an audience. "Family problems."

Athena tilted her head, deepening her resemblance to a raptor. "Would the death be justified?"

"In their eyes? Yes," Lore said. "It's not like the old way, when you could compensate them or exile yourself."

"Are you not exiled now?" Athena asked. "Is that not enough to satisfy their anger?"

The ancient law had been focused on anger—the anger of the wronged, and the need to answer to it. Anger was like a disease to the soul, and no aspect of it was more contagious than violence. If it could be avoided, it would end a vicious cycle before it began. But this was a vicious society.

"I don't know," Lore said. "I wasn't planning on ever finding out."

"So you *were* with them," Van said. By the way he was looking at her now, Lore knew that he had a good idea about what she had done, even before he said. "The new Aphrodite, Heartkeeper—"

"Heartkeeper?" Lore repeated, making a face. "Is it just me or are these names getting stupider?"

"If Lore can't approach them," Castor said, "a Messenger might be able to."

Van shook his head. "The asset in the Kadmides wants to meet again tonight. I can't be in both places at once."

"I can do it," Miles said. "The asset meet, I mean."

"Wait—no," Lore said. "I don't think that's a good idea."

185

"It's a terrible idea, actually," Van said. "It's not just a meet. I have to retrieve one of my go-bags for the cash."

"So? Tell me where it is and where to meet him," Miles said.

Van said nothing.

"What, is there some elaborate handshake I need to learn?" Miles asked. "Does he not speak English?"

Lore sighed, pressing a hand to her face. "Miles . . ."

"Let me *do* something," Miles said. "I can't fight, but I know this city and how to get around it."

"No," Van said firmly.

"You claim to be a disciple of logic," Athena said. "Surely you see that this is the best course. He is unknown to your kind and familiar with the city. The task itself does not require unique skill so much as discretion."

"Exactly!" Miles said. "I'll go straight there and come straight back."

"And what if the asset tries to kill you and take the money?" Van asked.

"You've still got the dirt on him," Miles shot back, more than willing to meet Van's cold gaze. "He's not going to do anything that risks you releasing it in retaliation."

"Miles does have a point . . ." Castor began.

"I was planning on linking up with the twenty-seven Achillides after," Van told him. "And trying to find them a place to shelter. All of our safe houses and properties are compromised, along with most of our vaults and stockpiles—"

"I know a place they can use," Miles cut in. "That is, if you can find it in yourself to accept help from a mere Unblooded."

Van said nothing, and his face betrayed little more.

"Where is it?" Castor asked.

186

"An abandoned warehouse," Miles said. "In Brooklyn. I sat in on a meeting about it at my internship. The building's been empty for over a decade because of a dispute between the city and its developers."

"That'll work," Castor said. "Thank you."

Miles smiled. "It'll at least give them a chance to regroup. What's the best way to get them the address?"

"Van?" Castor prompted.

The other young man sat stiff-backed, gaze fixed on the light seeping through the bay window's pale curtains. "I can text them the address."

Lore sighed. "Are you really up for this, Miles?"

"I am," Miles said.

"You have to promise to bail if something—anything—seems strange about it," Lore said.

"Everything is strange about your world," he reminded her. "But I'll be careful."

"Fine," Van said, rising.

"Fine," Miles said, doing the same.

"That's our plan, then," Lore told them.

"We still don't know where to find the Odysseides," Castor reminded her, bracing his hands on his knees.

"I do," Lore said. "Or I can at least make an educated guess." She glanced at the grandfather clock. "I'm going to take a shower and close my eyes for a few minutes, so I'm not completely dead on my feet. Let's aim to leave no later than five, before sunset."

"Do I have to wait that long?" Miles asked.

"Are you really in that big of a hurry to get yourself killed?" Van said. He picked up his phone. "I'm just going to tell the asset to change the meet to tomorrow—"

"*No,*" Miles said. "Discussion over. Lore is going to lead everyone to where the Odysseides are, so that you can approach them about a truce to trap Wrath and get information about the poem. Castor is going to play defense against Wrath. Athena is going to play offense. And I'm going to do this meet and get whatever information the asset has because you have no other option."

All of that depended, of course, on the occupants of Lore's house not killing one another first.

Van's lips parted and he stared at Miles, just a moment more, before he busied himself with his phone.

"When did we decide I'm defense?" Castor asked at the same time Athena said, "There shall be no *play* in my offensive—"

Lore left the others and went upstairs, shutting the door to her bedroom behind her. She set an alarm and crawled into bed.

She lay atop the covers, listening as the sound of the voices below faded to a dull murmur. After a few moments more, her heavy eyelids slid shut.

Iro's face appeared there, emerging from the darkness of her memory. That last glimpse Lore had had of her, smiling in encouragement.

Oblivious to the monster in their midst.

EIGHTEEN

LORE WOKE TO THE FRANTIC BEEP OF HER PHONE'S ALARM, LURCHING out of a heavy, dreamless black. She squinted at the time on the phone—a quarter past four o'clock in the afternoon—and immediately regretted having ever slept. Her muscles felt stiff over her bones, and no amount of stretching helped.

After changing into a clean pair of jeans and a black T-shirt, Lore stepped out into the hallway, listening for the voices of the others. But the town house was silent.

One last moment of peace, she thought, taking a steadying breath.

Even if things went right for them with Heartkeeper, nothing would ever be the same for Lore. Once the Odysseides knew she was alive, there would be no respite for her. After tonight, she might not be able to stay in the city, let alone the town house. There would be no safe place for her here.

Lore took one last look around, gripping the smooth banister. She was about to continue down the stairs when a movement in Gil's master bedroom caught her eye.

Van stood studying something on Gil's dresser—an old silver figurine of a tortoise that Gil had cherished despite its objective hideousness.

Lore didn't remember crossing the distance between them, only that she was suddenly there, pulling it from his fingers. "That's not yours."

With care, she returned it to its rightful spot beside an old wooden box and a photo of her, Gil, and Miles taken shortly after Gil had offered Miles the empty third-floor bedroom after striking up a conversation with him at a coffee shop. Gil and Miles had been cut from the same fun-loving, all-too-trusting cloth, and despite her early suspicions, their game nights and endless teasing over dinner had made the house feel warm and safe in a way Lore wasn't sure she'd ever experienced.

Lore looked around the room. Before Gil had died, she'd come in here hundreds of times, whether to harass him to take his medicine, to help him get in and out of bed on the days when age robbed his body of strength, or just to bring up tea or a board game to distract herself from the shadows of her own mind. He called her "darling," a word Lore was fairly certain no one else, not even her parents, would have used to describe her.

Though Lore had never met either of her grandfathers—they had both died years before she was born—she had loved the idea of them, the fantasy she had created using her parents' stories. But she had loved the *real* Gil, as exasperating and obstinate as he could be. She had only meant to stay with him for a few months, until his broken leg and arm had healed and she'd saved enough money to start over, but like the city itself, she couldn't bring herself to leave him. He had been gentle, brilliant, and had the unfailing ability to make her laugh. He had pierced through all her defenses.

And now, to her shame, the space felt dark and stale. His collection of canes, each with a different carved animal head, hadn't even made it into the closet with the rest of his things, and his shelves of academic books were coated in a thick layer of dust. As much as she'd tried to keep the brownstone exactly as Gil had left it, she hadn't been able to bring herself to step inside his room in months.

"This house isn't what I would have imagined for you," he said. "The style is very . . ."

"I would recommend not finishing that sentence," Lore said.

"I was going to say *grand*," he said, gesturing to the ornate dark oak furniture set around him, all inlaid with bone and finely carved flowers and vines. "How in the world did you end up working for him?"

Lore turned, her jaw set and her heart hammering. "Figure it out, if you want to know so badly."

His voice caught her in the doorway. "I was always jealous of you, you know."

Lore froze. "You were jealous of me?" she said, turning back toward Van. "Was it the poverty, the endless cycle of ostracism and humiliation, or the ongoing threat of extinction you coveted?"

Van clasped his prosthetic hand with his other, letting both rest in front of him. It would have been a relaxed posture if he hadn't been gripping it so tightly. "You always knew exactly who you were and who you were meant to be. Everything seemed to come easily to you because you wanted it so badly," he said. "I used to think that if I could find a way to want it as badly as you did, I could find something buried deep in me. Something that would make me run as fast, hit as hard. To want to pick up that sword."

"I was a stupid kid," Lore told him. "I thought I knew everything, but I knew nothing."

Van gave a faint smile. "And you know what the truly ironic thing is? Even as I ran after you, trying to catch up, you did the one thing I wanted more than I wanted my next breath. The thing I told myself was impossible. You got out."

Lore drew in a sharp breath, her stomach giving a painful clench. "I did it because I had to."

"You did it because you've never known fear," he said. "Because you wanted to live."

"I know fear," she told him. "I know it better than my own reflection."

"I don't know what happened to you," he said. "I used to wonder about it all the time, but I never doubted that you were still alive."

Van moved toward the room's attached bathroom, likely to the waiting shower. It released her from the quiet pain of the moment before it suffocated her.

"You know, some people get so used to looking out at life from the edge of their cage that they stop seeing the bars," he said. "I've never forgotten them, I've just learned how to live inside on my own terms. Don't . . . don't let your friend get trapped in here with the rest of us."

Her throat tightened at his words. She reached up, smoothing a loose piece of hair away from her face, unsure of what to say.

Van had grown up with financial comforts, but he had never completely fit in as a hunter. She felt guilty for the way she had judged him for it, both in the past and even a little in the present. His attitude toward Miles made more sense to her now, and a part of Lore wondered if what she had sensed as a kid wasn't a dislike for her, but his own frustrations—with himself, and with their world.

"It's just one job," Lore said finally. "After tonight, I'm going to figure out how to convince him to leave."

"Good," Van said.

But just before he closed the door to the bathroom, Lore heard herself say, "You can still get out. It's never too late."

"I chose to stay in," he told her. "I'm not leaving before I get the ones who caged me."

The words followed Lore back downstairs, all the more unsettling for the way they echoed her own circumstances. She thought about going back upstairs, about telling him what the last few years had taught her—that the cage was only as strong as your mind made it.

She had chosen to make the vow to Athena. She had chosen to step back inside the cage this one last time to get to the man who had taken everything from her.

Not lost, Lore told herself. *Free.*

Lore reached the bottom step and stopped.

Castor had taken the settee, stretching his long body out over it and letting his feet hang off its edge. He'd laced his fingers together and rested them on his chest. Now they rose and fell with each deep, even breath.

Athena stood over him, watching. Her hands rested open at her sides. Her face wasn't cast in its usual mask of hatred. What Lore saw there now scared her more.

Curiosity.

"What are you doing?" Lore asked sharply.

As Castor opened his eyes, Athena made her way over to the line of makeshift weapons she'd neatly arranged on the wall. He sat up, looking between them.

"Making preparations," Athena said smoothly. She held out one of them—Lore's former curtain rod, she noted with a grimace. "Have you been trained to fight with such a weapon? I won't let you dishonor it with incompetence."

Castor snorted at the question, rubbing a hand over his face. "I've never known Lore to be incompetent at anything she's tried."

"Potential incompetence aside," Lore said. "We are at least a thousand years past when it was socially acceptable to casually carry one of these around on the street."

"You will not leave this sanctuary without a weapon with which to defend yourself," Athena told her. "Not while our fates are bound. So I ask again, have you been trained to fight with this weapon?"

It wasn't a mere spear—it was a dory, the weapon carried by the ancient armies of Greece, and many of its greatest warriors. Athena had created the leaf-shaped spearhead out of some shred of metal, but she'd balanced the weight of the weapon using another metal spike as the sauroter. The construction was crude, but thoughtfully made. Lore had no doubt that the weapon would feel as solid and deadly in her hand as any that had come from a trained blacksmith.

"Yes," she said, letting her annoyance drain with the word. "I trained with one for over six years. I will take care of it."

Athena eyed her, two silver flames burning in her gaze. Whatever she saw in Lore's face convinced her. She passed the weapon to her.

Lore tested the weight and grip, hating how familiar and *good* it felt in her hand.

"It is not a gift born from the anvil of Hephaestus, he of many devices," Athena said, "but I will hold you to your word."

"How are we going to get around with these?" Castor asked, retrieving the dory Athena had given him earlier from where he'd left it near the door. "Are we supposed to tell people we're going spearfishing in the Hudson?"

That wasn't half bad, actually.

"I think I have a plan," Lore said. An extremely stupid one, maybe, but a plan nonetheless.

She took the stairs to the basement two at a time, only to reel back

194

a step when she realized she wasn't alone.

Miles was pacing down a narrow pathway between the boxes, hands on his hips. He seemed to be muttering something under his breath.

"You okay there, buddy . . . ?" she asked.

Miles spun, nearly knocking over a stack of tubs. "What? Sorry—yes, I mean—"

Lore hopped down from the last steps, giving him a sideways glance. "Are you positive you're up for doing the meet? It's not too late to back out."

"Yes!" he said, then lowered his voice. "Yes, I'm fine. And contrary to Evander's opinion, I will continue to be fine."

"Don't let Van get to you," Lore told him. "He's right about one thing, though. It's only going to get more dangerous from here. You have nothing to prove—not to him or to me."

"I know," Miles said. "I won't get in your way."

She shook her head, her throat tight. "That's not what I mean. After tonight, I need you to leave. Go visit your parents. Take a trip. Just get out of the city. Promise me."

"I'll promise you one thing," Miles said. "And that's a new broom. Okay, two things, because we need a new mop. And, actually, you're going to need a new rod in your closet."

"Anything else?" she asked, pained.

"I promise I'll check in with you," he said. "If you start sharing your location with me again."

She pulled a face. "I don't like feeling like I'm being watched."

Miles picked that old argument right back up again. "It's a safety thing—wait, what are you looking for?"

"This, actually." Lore retrieved an unused shaggy mop head and a container of feathered yellow duster sleeves. "Have you seen that old box of rags Gil refused to let me throw out?"

"Yeah, it's over here . . ."

Miles pulled Lore's phone out of her back pocket as he followed her upstairs. "Password? I'm setting up the location sharing."

She sent him an annoyed look, but told him. Upstairs, he handed it back to her and watched, alongside Castor and Athena, as Lore slid one of the dories' ends into a yellow feather duster and fixed the mop head to the other.

"Are we— What is that?" Van asked as he came down from upstairs.

Lore held up the dory, sweeping a hand down beside it. "Ingenuity. We good to go?"

Athena held one of the duster sleeves up to her nose and smelled it, then touched her tongue to it. Her face twisted in disgust. "What creature was this shorn from?"

"A Big Bird," Lore told her seriously.

"Are we . . . pretending to be a cleaning crew?" Castor guessed.

"Do you think a bucket would help sell it better?" Lore asked. She bent to tie several rags around one end of his dory.

Athena held out the other weapon to Van, but he shook his head. The goddess visibly bristled at the rejection.

"I'm off," Miles told the others. "I'll see you guys in a few hours."

Van moved to block his path to the front door.

"Don't screw this up," Van warned. "I need to keep this asset."

"Get out of my way," Miles said, shouldering past him. He looked back at Lore one last time and said, "Don't forget to text."

"I won't," Lore said. "Be careful."

"Take a cab," Van told him.

"And pay in cash," Miles finished. "Yeah, amazingly enough, I grasped the concept the first time you explained it to me."

He lifted a hand in farewell, stepping outside and shutting the door behind him.

"So where is this place?" Castor asked her.

"Broadway and Thirty-Sixth Street," Lore said. "Let's go."

But as they made their way to the street and hailed the first cab, she suddenly looked back at the town house, just in case it would be for the last time.

NINETEEN

THE ODYSSEIDES OWNED ONE PROPERTY IN MANHATTAN LARGE enough for the entire bloodline to use for meetings during the Agon. It had been a recent acquisition, purchased during the first year Lore had lived with them. The only question left was whether or not they might have sold it in the meantime.

She had her answer as soon as her and Athena's cab stopped at Thirty-Seventh Street and Sixth Avenue, and she caught a glimpse of the building a block south.

Lore and Athena carefully slid their weapons off their laps in the backseat, ignoring the way the cabdriver stared in the rearview mirror. Athena cast her gaze around, searching for threats as they walked to the neighboring building. Castor and Van's cab pulled up behind them.

The Odysseides property, Baron Hall, had another name within the family: Ithaka House. The landmark building had been created in the ancient style, both of its gray sandstone faces decorated with Corinthian columns. In its last life, it had been a bank. Now, in the years between the Agon, it was rented out as a grand event space as a cover for its true owners.

Parked beside its Sixth Avenue entrance was a large bus with blacked-out windows. A tent had been erected to connect the door of the bus to the entrance, but Lore could see the light inside shifting as people were hurried through. The bus rocked as it was loaded.

Castor came up alongside her, keeping his back to the wall.

"What are they doing?" he asked.

"They're moving something?" she guessed. "Or evacuating?"

Van approached them. "What do you know about the building?"

"There are two entrances, one on Sixth Avenue and the other on Thirty-Sixth. A few small windows on the facade," Lore said. "It's a converted bank, so it was built with security in mind—there's one large central hall and smaller lounges off that, including a vault they were planning to convert to a safe room."

"Is there a way to see inside the building without exposing ourselves?" Athena asked. "We must assess before Evander approaches the entrance."

"There's a large glass dome that looks down into the hall, but they would be stupid not to cover it," Lore said. "And I'm sure they have hunters up there to keep an eye on things."

Van slipped his sleek leather backpack off his shoulder and dug through it until he retrieved a small case. He popped the clasp on it.

Inside was a black device, shaped like a bird and no bigger than the size of Lore's fist. Leaving it in place, he retrieved his phone, entered the longest password Lore had ever seen, and pulled up an unfamiliar app. He scrolled through the images of a prosthetic hand and selected one, which changed the shape of his grip. Then he opened another. After tapping a few more buttons, the mechanical bird whirred to life and lifted out of its case.

Athena looked away in disgust. "Of course. I should have expected your . . . technology in the place of cunning and skill. This is truly the worst age of man."

"Of course, anything not gods-given is terrible," Lore said, rolling her eyes. "Well, I'm impressed."

"Thank you," Van told her as he flew the drone up toward the roof of Baron Hall. She and Castor leaned in closer as the device's camera switched on. "I designed it myself."

Heat radiated from Castor's body as he hovered near her. "I count three hunters. No masks."

A prickle of dread slid along Lore's spine.

"That seems unusual, given what I know of the cowardice of the hunters," Athena said.

"It *is* unusual," Van confirmed.

"And unhelpful," Lore said. "It may simply be that the Odysseides didn't want their masks spotted by people in the nearby buildings . . ."

"Or they might not be of the House of Odysseus," Athena finished.

Lore had been right about another thing. The Odysseides had constructed a cement cover to sit over the massive stained-glass dome. "Is that a door?"

"Looks like it," Van said, bringing the drone closer.

There was a small hatch embedded in the cement structure. There would have to be, she realized, to give access to the dome's backlights. It was secured by an electronic keypad and what was likely a blast-resistant door.

"There's no other way to see in?" Van asked her. "The infrared sensor is only going to tell us if there are people there, not who they are."

Lore shook her head. Whatever windows existed in the building would have been reinforced and fogged.

"All right, then," Castor said. He strode over to the ground-level glass doors of the neighboring building. The door handles glowed under his grip, the metal locks going soft enough for him to pull them open.

"Cas!" Lore hissed, but he had already disappeared through the entrance.

"At last," Athena murmured. There was an eager gleam in her eye as she took several long strides to the door.

The building had no security guard, let alone elevators. They took the stairs at a full run until they reached a dark room on the top floor. When they entered, Lore startled at the shadowy outlines of mannequins and dress forms. Of course—they were in the Garment District. The building wasn't made up of apartments, as she'd assumed, but fashion studios and workrooms, all seemingly empty on a Sunday evening.

Castor crouched beneath the line of windows that overlooked the roof of Baron Hall.

The two buildings were nestled together, side pressed to side. It would just be a matter of opening a window and jumping down two or three feet.

Lore ducked, moving to stand at one end of the windows, just out of sight of the hunters below. Athena took her position opposite Lore, shaking the dusters off her dory's blade with obvious petulance.

"How are we going to do this?" Lore asked, stealing a glance at the hunters as they paced from end to end.

"Just like tag in Central Park," Castor said. Lore snorted at the memory, but knew what he was talking about. They'd have to cluster the hunters together while still keeping them turned away. "If one spots us and radios it in, we're done."

"Got any new godly tricks up your sleeve on the distraction front?" Lore asked him. "A little razzle or dazzle?"

Van tapped a few buttons on the phone.

Castor and Lore turned back toward the window as the hunters, cloaked in their black robes, drifted together, drawn by the sight of the bird drone bobbing through the air in strange, irate patterns.

One of them reached to press his earpiece, making to report the strange sight. Before he could, the drone froze in the air and shot out three darts in quick succession. The hunters staggered away from one another, but then collapsed.

Athena turned toward Van as he calmly ran his finger over the surface of the phone, guiding the drone back to them. "While I do not approve of this false bird, I appreciate its lethality."

"They're not dead," Van told her. "Just knocked out for the next hour or so."

Castor broke the seal on the window frame and opened it. The bird buzzed inside, settling back into its case.

"What else do you have in there?" Lore asked him, eyeing Van's backpack.

Van raised his brows as he pulled out a small dagger.

They made the jump between buildings and kept their steps light across the roof. Lore gripped the dory hard enough for her fingers to ache. Castor and Athena went to solve the problem of the hatch while she and Van approached the unconscious hunters. He passed her several zip ties.

With a grunt, Lore flipped one of the hunters over onto his back, pushing up the loose sleeve of his robe. A tattoo of the Kadmides' mark, a serpent, coiled up his arm.

"Damn," she whispered.

Van met her gaze, holding up another hunter's arm to reveal the same.

They were already too late.

"We're in," Castor called softly.

Lore bound the hunters' hands and feet together, then rose, her heart stuttering in her chest. As she turned, a faint buzzing caught her attention—muffled voices, crackling with static. Lore pulled the earpiece from the closest hunter and, after cleaning it, put it in her own ear. Van did the same, then retrieved the third and pocketed it.

They rejoined Castor and Athena at the cover's hatch, which now looked like a half-crushed aluminum can. Lore stopped at the sight of it, almost unable to understand it. The sheer, brutal strength that would take . . .

Her eyes drifted over to Athena. The goddess stared down through the massive glass dome, her tight-lipped expression grim.

The central chamber of Baron Hall was its round lobby—an expansive, lavish space. The old teller stands had been converted into bars, including one at the very center, directly below the dome ceiling. Blue, gold, and green lights artfully lit the space, as if none of the Kadmides swarming the building had figured out how to turn on the overhead set.

It didn't matter. Lore saw everything.

The Odysseides, their hands bound and heads covered with hoods, each kneeled, waiting for their turn to be dragged to the bus outside. The Kadmides, meanwhile, were helping themselves to the other bloodline's weapons and stores of cash, food, and antiques that had been hidden elsewhere in the building.

And Wrath, standing at the center of it all, had his hand around Heartkeeper's throat.

TWENTY

WRATH LOOKED MASSIVE TO LORE, AS TALL AND SOLID AS THE STONE columns that circled the room. His sense of calm as he stood there, ready to break the neck of another god, was terrifying.

"The informant was wrong about the timing," Van whispered, stunned. "Or they changed it last minute."

Lore didn't realize she was gripping Castor's hand until he gave it a reassuring squeeze.

"Why is the false Aphrodite still alive?" Athena asked quietly. "Why hasn't he been killed?"

Heartkeeper's dark skin was slick with either sweat or blood. His face, which had always been handsome, even before immortality, was now swollen almost beyond recognition. Ivory robes twisted around his legs, both of which were bent at unnatural angles, unable to support him under the influence of Wrath's power. His mouth had been sealed shut with tape, preventing him from speaking—from using his power of persuasion on the other new god. A crown, one made of pearls and pale blue stones, lay in pieces nearby.

"This does not need to be difficult." Wrath's voice crackled through the earpieces they'd stolen from the hunters. *"Tell me how to open the vault and I will allow those men who kneel to me to live. I will allow you to serve me in the new age."*

204

Lore moved, circling around the dome to see the other side of the room. The vault's massive silver door was sealed shut. It had been designed to withstand almost anything, including bomb blasts.

"I think the poem is in the safe room," she told them.

Wrath signaled to one of the nearby Kadmides. *"Find his mortal child. Perhaps she can provide the necessary pressure."*

Heartkeeper clawed at Wrath's hands, but it was a feeble effort.

"Where is Iro, daughter of Iolas?" the hunter demanded of the Odysseides gathered under guard. *"If she is too cowardly to reveal herself, she does not deserve your protection, nor will you deserve the swift suffering it will bring."*

It was a knife designed to slip through the ribs, to lodge in the heart of their pride. Lore closed her eyes, waiting.

"I am she."

Lore's eyes snapped back open. Van shot her a surprised look, but Lore shook her head. That wasn't Iro's voice.

"I am her," came another.

"I am Iro," said a third.

Wrath turned, dropping Heartkeeper to the ground. The new god could barely lift his head, let alone crawl away. *"Kill five of them for every minute she remains hidden. Take them off the bus if you have to."*

"Where is Iro, daughter of Iolas?" the hunter called again, circling the group.

Several struggled against their restraints, but there was no hesitation as one of the prisoners said, his male voice ringing out, *"I am Iro."*

He was the first to die. His blood sprayed onto the marble floor and whipped across the resolute faces of the hunters around him.

Wrath bent over Heartkeeper, turning his head to face the killings before pinning it in place with his foot. He leaned forward, applying pressure. *"Tell me how to open the vault. The information is not worth the cost of all of these lives. Not worth them remembering you as the sniveling coward who let them die."*

Lore's mind spun, trying to catch an incomplete memory before it had a chance to slip away. There was something about the vault—something about the construction of the safe room. Lore and Iro had once broken into the archon's office to look at the documents and plans for the space.

"Please!" a hunter begged as he was dragged forward toward the line of corpses. *"Please, no!"*

The Kadmides hunters sneered with laughter. The one holding the blade drew it near to the terrified young man's throat. *"Do we have one who wishes to serve his new lord?"*

"Yes!" he cried out. The Odysseides around him snarled. *"Yes— the girl, Iro. She's in the vault."*

Castor looked to Lore. She shook her head, her panic swelling.

But there was something . . .

"Perhaps if her father will not tell us, his daughter might be inclined to," Wrath said, returning to Heartkeeper's prone form, only to glance back. *"Kill him, too."*

"My—my lord—" the Odysseides' hunter cried.

His scream blistered Lore's ear as it burst from the earpiece.

"I've never liked rats," Wrath said simply, and turned before he could see the head severed from the hunter's neck.

He made his way to the vault, raising his hand to give a mocking little knock on it. *"Child. Perhaps you would like to join us? I can't imagine you would enjoy watching me bleed the life out of your father, nor snuff out the whole of the House of Odysseus. It is a terrible thing to be the last of your bloodline."*

The memory returned to Lore in a flash. *Another entrance.*

"There's another entrance to the vault," Lore said quickly.

"You're sure?" Castor asked.

She nodded. "I saw it on the plans for the building when I lived with the Odysseides. Iro told me it would help her father escape because safe rooms usually have one entrance, and any enemies wouldn't be expecting another."

"Do you remember how to access it?" Van asked her.

Lore hesitated, but nodded. "There's a tunnel connected to a shop—I think it's on Thirty-Ninth Street."

"There may still be a way to kill Wrath and rescue the girl and what knowledge she may possess of the poem. Perhaps even the false god and other Odysseides as well," Athena said, drawing out the words slowly. "Surprise is our ally, but timing will be our master."

Lore looked down again, to where Wrath lingered near the vault door.

For four years of Lore's life, Iro had been the only person she could completely trust and confide in, and Lore had been the only true friend Iro had as her bloodline jockeyed for power and favor from Iro's newly ascended father. They'd both spoken that secret, quiet language of grief as they lost everyone close to them.

Lore had always idolized Iro—how perfect and calm she seemed in the face of uncertainty when Lore's own emotions felt too big for her body. Except for that last night, they had always protected each other, and Lore knew Iro's insistence on training with her had been the only thing standing between Lore and a life as a servant at the Odysseides' estate.

Leaving her behind had been one of the most agonizing decisions Lore had ever made. She wouldn't do it again.

Iro, she thought. *Just hold on a little longer . . .*

TWENTY ONE

VAN WENT TO GET TO THE ODYSSEIDES HUNTERS ON THE BUS. LORE didn't like it—it wasn't that Van couldn't defend himself or talk his way out of most trouble, but they had no idea how many Kadmides were on that bus, or what they were willing to do to keep their prisoners contained.

Don't die, Lore thought. *Please don't die.*

She reached up, adjusting the earpiece. Static crackled over the frequency, punctuated by a few scattered updates from the Kadmides hunters keeping watch from nearby buildings.

"All clear, no movement on the street—"

"He wants us to check the transport for the girl—"

"Shit," she mumbled, looking down at the glowing screen of her cellphone again for the hundredth time in five minutes. "Get going, Van . . ."

If ever Lore needed more evidence the Messenger always worked alone, it would have been clear from the fact that he carried an advanced drone in his backpack, but not something that would let him covertly communicate with her and Castor, who was waiting to attack from the roof if Wrath got to Iro before Lore did. In the end, Van had just given Castor a burner phone and linked into a three-way call.

208

"Are you certain this is the entrance?" Athena asked, her voice low.

Lore glanced across Thirty-Ninth Street, eyeing the shoe-repair shop again. They'd done a frantic search of the streets before Lore had spotted the vacant storefront.

Given that Manhattan commercial real estate often didn't stay empty for long, it seemed like a good bet, even before she'd noticed the small uppercase lambda beneath the historic site plaque beside the door. The Odysseides used it as a secret mark—lambda for Laertides, the patronymic epithet for Odysseus, son of Laertes.

Now, crouched behind a line of parked cars, they waited. The signal came sooner than Lore expected.

"It's a go," Van said suddenly. *"Approaching now."*

Lore drew in a sharp breath and turned to Athena. "That's our cue."

They darted across the street and took up position on either side of the empty shop. The windows and door had been papered over to obscure the inside. Lore held Athena's dory as the goddess bent to break the lock on the metal security gate.

As it rolled up with a growl, Athena pulled on the door behind it. The lock snapped with ease.

Once they were inside, the last of Lore's doubts faded. The shop was barren, save for a few packs of supplies and water, clearly meant for emergencies.

"This way," Lore said, heading into what appeared to be the back storage room. There, beneath a hatch hidden by a rubber mat, was a set of stairs.

Lore held up her cellphone to illuminate whatever was below, but it wasn't necessary. A few scattered lights flickered to life as they passed by a hidden sensor, revealing the crude tunnel hidden beneath the buildings and streets.

"Clever," Athena noted.

"We'll see," Lore whispered.

Van must have muted his cellphone before entering the bus, because it was Castor who gave them the update. *"Van's on—it looks like . . . they're off—"*

The words broke apart into static, then cut off as the call dropped.

"What is the matter?" Athena asked, her expression alert.

"No cell service down here," Lore said, sprinting forward.

The phone's light bounced around the tunnel, keeping time with her steps. There was a slight rise to the pathway now, bringing them up out of the deepest part of the tunnel. More lights flickered on, revealing a massive silver door ahead.

As soon as they were within a few feet of it, Lore's earpiece started catching fragments of the updates being shouted over it.

"What the hell is going on?"

"—headed west on Thirty-Sixth—"

"—grab the bikes—"

"Kyrios, Dorian—anyone have eyes from the roof?"

A slightly pained voice answered, *"We didn't see anything until the bus drove away. One of them must have gotten free—"*

"Can you open it?" Lore said, trying to redial Van's number. The phone still wouldn't connect her calls, even as the voices in the earpiece became indistinguishable while they shouted over one another.

"Iro?" Lore tried calling through the door. "Can you hear me? It's Lore."

Athena felt along the edges of the seamless door, then stepped back, raising a fist. Lore jumped as she slammed her hand into the dead center of it. The skin over her knuckles broke open, leaving a smear of blood across the metal. She hit it again.

"It's reinforced to withstand a bomb blast. You're not going to be able to smash your way through—" Lore protested.

But Athena didn't need to. As the center of the door bent in, it created enough room between the ground and the bottom of the door for Athena to slip her fingers beneath it. Her body shook with the strain of lifting it.

"Iro!" Lore called. "Come out!"

But there was no one inside. Iro had opened the vault door.

Adrenaline spiked in Lore's system, making a frenzy of her pulse as she ducked beneath the door, into the safe room. Just beyond it, Lore saw the grand hall.

And death.

The Kadmides were too fixated on the scene in front of them to notice Lore and Athena. They beat their fists against their chests, hissing as Wrath leaned an ear down toward a young woman in hunter's robes. He held Heartkeeper's head firm in one fist and pressed a knife to his throat with the other.

Iro looked exactly as Lore remembered her—her dark curls had been scraped back into a low bun, revealing the patchwork of bruises and fresh cuts on her face and neck. Her brown skin had gone sallow, and even as her lips moved, her face, a portrait of severe beauty, was livid with contempt.

It was the last thing Lore noticed before the world exploded.

The glass dome shattered as Castor let loose a raw blast of heat and light, sending shards of glass and metal onto the Kadmides still gathered below.

"No!" Athena growled.

Castor had waited as long as he could—Lore knew that, but a tiny part of her echoed Athena's frustration as his power raged down through the dome. His attack would help them save Iro, which Lore desperately wanted, but it would also force Wrath to retreat again to the shadows, and Athena would lose her best chance to kill him.

We can still do both, Lore thought. *We just have to act fast—*

Athena lowered her head and charged into the fray with a ferocious cry, only to be brought up short as the heat of Castor's blast threw her back.

Screams filled the air. The Kadmides fell to the ground, pierced with glass and shrapnel, and others fled, but not far—Castor's power split, crackling and writhing across the ground like lightning scoring the land. It caught them in its snare.

Lore stumbled forward, shielding her eyes as she searched for Wrath and Iro. The tile and cement caved, sending the escaping hunters down into the lower level. They disappeared into smoke and darkness.

"Where is he?" Athena thundered.

Four Kadmides rushed toward her, blades raised, but Athena was faster, slashing them across their chests with her dory. Lore struggled against the waves of heat roiling off the molten core of Castor's power blast. She caught sight of Wrath's outline through the wall of smoke.

A hunter charged toward her, and Lore ducked to avoid his sword. A sharp pain lanced through her shoulder as the blade narrowly missed her neck, and he spun away again, vanishing so completely it was as if the swirling clouds of ash had swallowed him.

But Lore forgot him as she heard Iro's desperate voice call out, "Papa!"

"Here—" Lore called to Athena. The goddess was still cutting through the remaining Kadmides, her eyes burning, the lines of her face set deep with the pleasure of her fight. "They're here!"

Lore swept her dory beneath the feet of a nearby hunter, sending him stumbling into a vein of burning power. She coughed, choking on the thick smoke as she struggled forward.

"Iro!" she called. *"Iro!"*

But it was Heartkeeper's stricken voice that reached her first. "Don't look! Iro, don't—"

Iro screamed.

By the time Lore reached her, Heartkeeper's remains were at her feet, his torso cleaved into two. The girl knelt slowly, her face rigid with shock. Her hands shook as they reached for his face.

And Wrath was nowhere.

Castor's power abated, leaving fires and a few last lashes of fury in its wake. Lore looked up, searching through the rising smoke and the dome's burnt-out frame, a fresh wave of dread rolling through her. The only reason Castor would stop attacking was if the Kadmides had reached the roof and he himself was in danger.

"Where are you, Godkiller?" Athena bellowed into the dark chaos around them. "Stand and fight, coward!"

Lore banded her arms over Iro's chest, pulling her back. "It's me— it's Lore! We have to get out of here! Iro, we have to run—"

Iro broke free of her grip, spinning around to face her. She had the dory out of Lore's hand and the tip against her throat in the span of a heartbeat.

Lore saw the exact moment her shock wore off, and the other girl recognized her.

A tremor grew in Iro's body as she held Lore's gaze. There was a bruise beneath her left eye, and her skin was streaked with sweat and grime. Her eyes were wide and bloodshot, the tendons in her neck bulging with the panic of a trapped animal. "You can't be here! You need to leave! He can't see you!"

Athena stormed toward them from behind, scattering the smoke and embers. Without a word, she lifted the shaft of her dory and knocked it into the back of Iro's head. The girl slumped forward into Lore's arms.

"The imposter has fled," Athena told her, visibly aggravated. "And now so must we. If the false Apollo could *control* his power, he may have been able to stop him. Whether intentionally or not, he has sabotaged our efforts."

"That's not true—" Lore began.

The goddess strode toward the waiting vault, stepping over the bodies and debris in her way. Lore knelt, lifting Iro over her shoulder. She bit back a cry of pain as the girl's weight settled there, but it disappeared as soon as she began to run.

They had just reached the safe room when Lore felt a pressure at the base of her neck. She turned slowly.

Wrath appeared again amidst the destruction and eddies of thick smoke. He came toward them, that slow, long stride, closer—closer—

Her hand found the door's security panel and stilled. She forgot the reason they had come. She forgot the weight of Iro, and the burning in her lungs. She didn't call out to Athena. She couldn't speak at all with terror's cold hands wrapped around her throat.

Behind him, the remaining Kadmides were regrouping, gathering like shadows.

The goddess realized Lore wasn't following and turned. Seeing Wrath, she reached for Iro's blade and threw it with all her strength. Wrath turned, letting it graze his cheek as it tore through the air beside him.

Aristos Kadmou had been the monster inside the maze of her mind for so long, she had a near-perfect memory of his scarred face and the way his coarse, dark hair had been shot through with gray. He looked younger now than Lore remembered, as if immortality had drawn him back through the decades.

But there were echoes of him lingering there—the low, thick eyebrows. The deep olive tone of his skin. A face shaped like a cut diamond.

Through the maelstrom of glass fire swirling around him, his golden eyes met hers, and he smiled.

Found you.

Lore punched her fist against the security panel and the door slammed shut.

SEVEN YEARS EARLIER

HER FATHER WOULDN'T TELL HER WHERE THEY WERE GOING.

Lore dutifully carried the small parcel her mother had handed her and trailed a step after him. Her father loved to smile, but he hadn't laughed at all that morning. He and Mama had barely spoken at all. Now his shoulder blades were bunched together like wasp wings. Judging by the expression on his face, she was afraid to ask for their destination, on the chance she might get stung by a sharp word.

She didn't like it. Not at all.

April had drawn out all of the city's secret life. Lore carefully avoided the small flowers and grass that pressed themselves up through the cracks in the sidewalk. The songbirds high up in the trees along their street greeted her as she passed. Lore smiled at them.

Though Lore was older, and taller, her view of her papa never seemed to change. He looked as big and strong as any of the midtown buildings that cut at the sky like shining glass knives.

Lore hurried to match the pace of her father's long strides. After a moment, though, he stopped to wait for her. When Lore reached him, her father cupped a hand behind her head, then wrapped an arm around her shoulder. She finally relaxed.

"Tell me," he began, keeping his tone light, "how's your Castor?"

With the sun behind him, Lore couldn't see his face.

"He is not *my* Castor," she said. "He is my hetaîros."

"Ah," her father said, innocently. "I never had a hetaîros of my own, just my father. Do hetaîros see each other outside their training, or must they meet only within the walls of Thetis House?"

Lore bit the inside of her mouth so hard she tasted coppery blood. She saw Castor outside Thetis House all the time. On the days there were no lessons for their class, or they were let out early, and neither her parents, nor her babysitter, Mrs. Osbourne, knew it.

Lore was grateful for her little sisters. They may have stolen her old blanket and Bunny Bunny, but they kept Mrs. Osbourne's gaze constantly turned away from her.

"He is training more and more with Healer Kallias now," Lore said, trying not to sound as hurt as she felt by it. One day, Castor would be the best healer the Achillides had, but until then, she didn't want to work with any of the others who had lost their partners to training for the archives and weapon-smiths. "I *guess* I wouldn't mind seeing Castor outside of training . . ."

"Outside of training—for instance, when you went to Central Park last Tuesday?"

Lore slowed, her mind whirling with panicked excuses. She could say she had to walk home a different way because of traffic, or construction—

"Ah-ah," he said. "No lie was ever righted by another lie."

She opened her mouth, then closed it again.

"Promise me that you won't go again without an adult," her father said.

Lore made a face and received a warning look that instantly erased it.

"Why?" she asked, confused.

217

"Because I said so, Melora," he said. "And because it's not safe."

Lore's jaw dropped. Not safe? Yesterday her instructor had showed her which ribs to slide her blade through to strike the heart. She had practiced the move this morning in front of the bathroom mirror. "I'm fine, Papa. I always bring my knife with me."

Her father stopped again, drawing in a sharp breath. A look passed over his face that Lore didn't understand. Not fear, exactly—more like she'd punched him in the stomach and he was fighting not to double over. He was silent for a long while.

"I'm sorry?" she whispered. That was usually the answer he was looking for.

He shook himself out of his trance, taking her hand again. "What have I told you about your knife?"

"I can only use it at Thetis House or home," she dutifully repeated. Which was stupid. All hunters needed their weapons on them at all times, even between the Agons. But the words still didn't make him happy.

He glanced around at the people walking by them, oblivious or checking their phones. Then he switched to the ancient tongue. "Because the Unblooded will not understand. They will take you away if they catch you with a weapon like that."

"I can defend myself!" The words burst out of her. "I am the best in my class. Instructor calls me the Spartan—"

"Not even the Spartans were Spartan, Melora," her father said.

Lore pulled back, out of his reach. She hugged the parcel to her. Her thoughts became a confusing tangle. "What do you mean?"

He knelt down to look her directly in the eye. "It's not always the truth that survives, but the stories we wish to believe. The legends lie. They smooth over imperfections to tell a good tale, or to instruct us

218

how we should behave, or to assign glory to victors and shame those who falter. Perhaps there were some in Sparta who embodied those myths. *Perhaps.* But how we are remembered is less important than what we do now."

Lore's heart began to beat very fast. She clutched the parcel hard enough to rumple its brown paper. "But our legends are true. Our ancestors, the gods—"

"If there were once heroes, they are all gone now," her father said, rising. "Only the monsters remain. Your courage has always been great, chrysaphenia mou. For some monsters, that will be enough to scare them off—but there will be others, bigger beasts who will delight in the chase. Do you understand?"

Lore said nothing. Her anger growled in her chest, bold and gnawing. She could take care of anyone—or anything—that tried to strike at her. Monsters had fangs, but that was why lionesses were given claws.

"Do you understand?" he repeated, sharper this time.

"Yes, Papa," she said sullenly.

"Castor's father is an acquaintance of mine," he said. "I'll speak to him about arranging times for you to see him outside your lessons and ask Philip Achilleos for permission, if I must. But you—you must promise me."

"I promise," she said, then silently added, *To be more careful than I was before.*

They started walking again, rejoining the flow of people making their way across town. Lore stayed close to her father's side, trying to avoid being jostled by roving school groups as they crossed Fifth Avenue. Lore didn't spare them another look. They weren't like her.

"Your sister will join you at Thetis House soon. Would you like that?"

Lore shrugged. She couldn't imagine Pia, with her wide eyes and her little fingers always stained with paint, taking the hits from her classmates' training staffs. The thought made Lore's chest growl again, though she wasn't sure why.

"What shall we do for her birthday?" he asked, switching back into English.

Lore shrugged again. She already knew what she would get her sister as a gift—a promise to make their bed and braid her hair every day until summer was swept away by autumn winds.

"A movie?" she ventured. Her father didn't like them much, but maybe this once . . .

"A picnic?" he suggested instead.

"A trip to Central Park Zoo?" she offered.

On and on, they traded ideas, until they ran out of things they had done and had to invent things that they couldn't ever do.

"A trip to the moon?" Lore said.

"A dance with winged horses?"

Lore shifted the parcel in her hands. It wasn't heavy, but the clinking inside made her wonder.

"A walk to wherever we're going?" she suggested innocently.

One corner of her father's mouth twitched, but evened out again as he pursed his lips.

"No, chrysaphenia mou," he said, looking ahead. "We won't take her there. It is a place of monsters."

Lore didn't recognize the restaurant. She didn't even think it was open. The shades were drawn and the door was locked. She glanced over to the name stenciled onto the larger of the two windows. The Phoenician.

She gasped.

"Say nothing," her father told her in a low voice, taking the parcel out of her hands. "Do you remember what I taught you about the way guests have to behave? The Kadmides have invited us as a gesture of goodwill and peace."

Lore recoiled. "Not them, Papa—they're the ones who killed—"

"Melora," he interrupted sharply. "Do you really think I've forgotten? We are alone in this world now, the five of us. Your mother's people will not ally with us for the next Agon, and neither will the Achillides or the Theseides. They would all gladly watch the last of Perseus's line leave the Agon. We need allies."

She drew in a long breath through her nose, holding it to keep from saying anything.

"Aristos Kadmou, archon of this bloodline, wrote to me himself and asked that I come with my eldest daughter," he said. "I could not refuse without it being perceived as an insult. They are not known for their graciousness when it comes to being slighted."

The air exploded out of her. "But, Papa—"

"We must release the past if we are to ever find a future," he told her. "Don't be afraid. I am with you, and we are strangers here. Zeus Xenios will protect us."

Like he protected the rest of our bloodline? Lore was surprised at her mean thought. Of course he would protect them. They were Zeus's chosen hunters.

Lore knew her family wasn't like the other bloodlines. But it was one thing to train with the house of mighty Achilles and another to go to the Perseides' worst enemy for weapons and armor and information. She hated that it had to be this way. Perseus was a greater hero than Kadmos ever was.

Her father raised his hand and knocked.

A voice called back through the door in the ancient tongue. "Who comes here?"

"Demos, son of Demosthenes, and his daughter, Melora, of the Perseides," he replied. "At the request of the archon of the Kadmides."

The door's lock slid open. Lore clutched the bottom of her father's old leather jacket, then forced herself to step away and straighten. She wasn't a little girl anymore. She didn't hide behind anyone.

The woman who opened the door was well into her years of white hair and worn skin. She locked it behind them.

The restaurant was dark, with only muted sunlight seeping through the screens. It was smaller than she'd expected, and, to make room, all of its tables and chairs had been pushed to the far sides and stacked. The gathered Kadmides moved, creating a narrow aisle between them. They hissed and smirked as Lore and her father passed by them.

Lore stared back defiantly. A hunter never showed another hunter their fear. Not if they wanted respect.

Familiar smells coated the air—oregano and garlic, roasted meat, oiled leather, bodies. Sitting near the back of the restaurant, elevated above the others on a small stage, was a middle-aged man, his dark hair shot through with silver.

He leaned back against his throne as they approached. An old, powerful tree had been cut down to make it; Lore's eyes fixed on the carved dragons protruding from either side of it, warning anyone who came too close.

The man looked the way Lore had always imagined Hades would as he oversaw his kingdom of the dead.

Sitting near his feet was a boy that looked about Lore's age. He wore a similar outfit to the man—a dark silk tunic, dark pants, dark boots, a dark smile. He looked down his snub nose at her like a dog he intended to kick away.

"Welcome, Demos of the Perseides," the man said. "I am glad you accepted our invitation."

Lore had heard stories about Aristos Kadmou. His dead wives. His near-kill of Artemis. His ruthless rise through the ranks of his own bloodline to become archon. His face told all of these stories, the deep lines and heavy scars making it seem as if it had been carved from the same tree as his throne.

From what Lore knew, he was only a decade older than her papa, but she supposed a black soul would rot you from the inside out faster than Khronos ever could.

"I thank you for extending it," her father said. "May I introduce my daughter Melora?"

Lore glared.

"Welcome, Melora," Aristos Kadmou said with a small smile.

"My wife has sent us with a gift," her father said, holding up the package. Aristos nodded to the boy, who rose with a look of annoyance and went to retrieve it. He was the one to open it, and the one to hold up the two jars of honey inside.

Lore balked at the sight of them. Her mother kept a hive on the roof of their building and sold the honey at one of the city's farmers markets on the weekend. It was liquid gold to them, but the boy, Belen, wrinkled his little pig nose at the sight of it.

"What do we need this for?" he sneered. "We can just buy it at the store for a few dollars."

Hot blood rushed to Lore's cheeks, and it was only her father's grip on her shoulder that kept her from clawing the boy's face.

223

"Now, Belen," Aristos said lightly, giving the boy a look that was anything but chastising. "All offerings, even the most . . . *humble*, are welcome here."

Muffled laughter followed. Lore felt her father's body go rigid beside hers. The hand he'd placed on her shoulder tightened, and though his head was still bowed, she saw him struggle to master his expression.

Aristos snapped his fingers at one of the nearby women, who bowed to him in acknowledgment and brought forth an old bottle.

"My favorite Madeira," the archon said. "Aged over two hundred years."

Her father nudged her forward to accept it. Lore stared the woman down as she slinked forward, all muscle and sinew. Her eyes were rimmed with black kohl, as were the eyes of many of the other women and girls nearer to her own age gathered around them. It made their eyes seem to glow.

They are the Kadmides' lionesses, Lore realized, taking the bottle.

"You are very generous," her father said, the words stiff. "I thank you on behalf of my family."

"But of course," Aristos said. "Think of it not as generosity, but as a sign of my good faith in the business we will conduct here."

"Business . . . ?" her father repeated.

"Of course," the other man said. "Why else would a man surrender his pride to come to the den of those who nearly extinguished his bloodline, if not for pure business?"

Lore's nostrils flared, but her father held on to his calm. "Why, indeed."

"I'd heard that you were going from bloodline to bloodline like a beggar seeking comfort and aid," Aristos said. "A pity they did not see the opportunity you offer."

"For an alliance?" her father questioned, ignoring the whispers and snide laughter around them.

"An alliance?" Aristos leaned forward on his throne, tilting his head. "No, Demos. I have an offer for you. An arrangement that will change your fortunes."

"If such a thing is within another man's power," her father said coldly.

"I asked you to bring your daughter, for I would like to bring Perseus's noble blood into our line," the man continued. "I wish to purchase her from you, for marriage."

Lore's pulse began to thunder in her head. Her temples throbbed.

Her father looked to Belen, who was smearing his snot across the front of his tunic. "Surely the children are too young for their futures to be decided—"

"Our fates are decided at birth," Aristos Kadmou said. "As you well know."

"I am less certain of such things," her father responded. "I believe we choose what we become."

"Then you stand against the Moirai?" the archon said. "Perhaps that has been your mistake these many years. I recognized my destiny as a boy. I inherited it, along with the vast timé and vaunted kleos of my sire."

"And yet you have decided young Belen's fate," her father said, "by requesting my daughter's hand on behalf of your bastard son."

There was a hiss of surprise and clattering of weapons at the slight. Belen slunk back, his face red with the anger of shame. But when the archon of the Kadmides spoke again, he silenced even Lore's father.

"I do not want her for Belen," he said. "I want her for myself."

Lore's fingers went slack, and it was only reflex that allowed her

225

to catch the bottle before it hit the floor and shattered. She twisted around to look up at her father, silently begging for them to leave now, before another vile word could pass from the man's snake lips.

"She is only ten years old," her father said. "You are her senior by half a century—and your other wives—"

A quiet murmur passed through the Kadmides. Some hissed, others thumped their chests, but it was the archon Lore watched. A thunderous expression passed over his face at the mention of his six wives, all departed to the Underworld without giving him a true heir.

"I will wait until she is twelve, as ancient custom permits, to wed her, and wait until her first blood to bed her," Aristos Kadmou said, not looking at Lore. "She will be fostered with me until then to ensure that she is brought up *correctly*."

"No!" Lore barked. Her father held her back, squeezing her shoulder again.

"Forgive her, she is very spirited," he managed to get out. "Your offer is . . . generous. However, Melora has already begun her training with the Achillides."

"Why?" Aristos asked. "Why bother, when you've known all along that there was but one future for her?"

"I don't see it that way," her father said. "She is my heir—"

"She is certainly not," Aristos said. "How many daughters do you have now, Perseous? And no sons. No one to pass on your name. She will never receive a better offer than to serve the archon of the Kadmides. You know this to be true."

Fury billowed up inside Lore.

"Be wise, Demos. You have two other whelps to unload onto other bloodlines," Aristos said. "Rid yourself of one leech and you will breathe easier. I will pay you handsomely for her."

226

It was a moment before Lore realized the faint growling sound was coming from her.

Her father, to her surprise, let out a hollow laugh.

"Do you think me such a fool," he began, "that I don't know the real reason you've offered for her?"

The room fell silent again. Aristos Kadmou leaned forward, bracing his elbows on his knees and raising a brow in challenge.

"It must haunt you, as it haunted your father and his father before him," Lore's father continued, "to have such an inheritance in your possession, and to have it be nothing more than decoration. How heavy is it in your hands? Can you lift it unassisted the way any of my *girl whelps* could?"

The other man's eyes flashed, his expression darkening.

"And how it will haunt you to know that the inheritance you lost lies beneath your feet, just one floor down," Aristos said. "Waiting. Waiting. *Waiting* for you to try to take it back."

Lore's vision flashed red as the heat inside her grew. They were talking about the aegis, the shield of Zeus carried by Athena. The inheritance Zeus had given her bloodline at the start of the Agon, the one the Kadmides had stolen from them. It was *here*.

"Does it call to you?" Aristos wondered. "Can you hear it, even now? Or do you hear the wailing of your ancestors, slaughtered like pigs?"

"I hear only the desperation in your voice," her father said evenly. "But my daughters will never give you a child who can wield it."

The archon's face passed into the shadows on the stage as he rose to his full height. "I don't need to mix your inferior blood with mine to use it."

"It will never be willingly given," her father said. "If we are to die, then it will disappear with us. How unfortunate for you that the most stubborn of the Perseides families was the one to survive."

Aristos descended from the stage slowly. His arms had been tattooed with a snakeskin pattern, and the thick veins there bulged as he crossed his arms over his chest. "Is that right? Tell me, girl, what it is you desire?"

Lore glanced up at her father and mimicked him. She stared straight ahead, refusing to look at the archon.

"I cannot imagine it is the squalor you live in now. Would you not like to live among the most powerful of the bloodlines—to have the gold and jewels and silk?" Aristos asked.

Her father had told her not to speak. She knew she shouldn't have, even now, but she couldn't help it. Pride flared in her heart.

"I will be a léaina," Lore told him. "My name will be legend."

The laughter of the Kadmides clawed at her from all sides, but Aristos Kadmou's small smirk was somehow worse. Lore felt like her whole body might burst into flame. Her father's hand stayed on her shoulder, but she no longer felt it. She no longer felt anything other than the pounding of her heart.

"You, a léaina?" Aristos said. "I have many of them, as you can see. All braver, faster, stronger than you—"

Lore released the scream that had built in her lungs, swinging the bottle against the stone pillar beside her. Wine flooded the floor like blood, turning the air sickly sweet as she lunged toward the nearest little lioness, clutching the broken neck of the bottle like a dagger. The other girl's kohl-rimmed eyes widened, but Lore was faster, she was stronger—

Her father's hand clamped down on her wrist, yanking it back before it could pierce the girl's throat. For a moment, Lore saw nothing beyond the look on his face, the horror there. Her chest heaved, and she didn't understand why it made her want to cry.

He drew her away from the lionesses, from the Kadmides who came toward her. For the first time in her life, Lore heard true fear in her father's voice.

"Please," he began, "she's just a child—she doesn't know her own temper, and there was no insult meant to you as a host. If there is to be punishment, I should face it, as I have failed to teach her better."

The Kadmides gathered closer, tightening around them like a noose. Someone gripped Lore's braid and gave it a vicious tug. She pressed her face to the small of her father's back, gripping his shirt as a blow struck her between the shoulders.

Her father pushed them away from her. A whip snapped against his arm, instantly drawing blood.

"Stop," she whispered. "Stop—"

It was another command that brought the room to silence. To stillness.

"*Leave.*"

The Kadmides obeyed the way Lore should have obeyed. They brought their leader pride as they left the restaurant, where Lore had brought her father shame. She knew about xenia, about the way a guest was meant to behave. She had violated something sacred.

When the last of the Kadmides had left, Aristos Kadmou began to circle them. His steps were slow and heavy as he clasped his hands behind his back.

"I apologize for my daughter," her father said. "I will make any reparations you see fit."

"There is but one thing I want," Aristos Kadmou said. "It's lucky that I enjoy fire in my women"—he leaned in closer—"and the

229

challenge of extinguishing it."

The archon slid an envelope into the pocket of her father's shirt. "That is my offer for the girl. Send me your answer by the end of the Agon."

Her father gave a curt nod, gripping her hand so tightly that Lore had no choice but to follow him to the door. She didn't dare look back, not even as the other man spoke one final time.

"This is her future," he said. "There is nothing more for her in our world. I will ensure that, one way or another."

A few of his serpents lingered outside. They hissed and spat at Lore and her father as they passed. The humiliation made her heart feel sick and her body small, but it was nothing compared to knowing that she had shamed her father.

I will never gain kleos, Lore thought, her throat thick and her eyes stinging. *I will never be anything at all.*

They had been walking for nearly twenty minutes when her father slowed. He said nothing as he knelt and drew her into a fierce embrace.

"I'm sorry," she whispered, pressing her face against his shoulder. "I'm sorry, Papa . . ."

He picked her up, clutching her to him the way he had when she was smaller, and carried her the rest of the way home.

TWENTY TWO

THE VAULT'S DOOR SLAMMED SHUT.

Athena rounded on Lore, incandescent with rage.

"Why?" she snarled. "When our enemy was there, within reach—"

Lore somehow managed to choke the words out around the cold hands of terror still gripping her throat. "Too much time . . . too many of them—Castor—"

The door vibrated with a deafening *bang* as something slammed into it. Athena straightened at the sound, mastering her anger enough to growl, "If we are to retreat like cowards, then we do so now."

Lore turned back, watching the door rattle. Indecision tore at her. They could take a stand. They could still kill Wrath here and end this nightmare.

Iro moaned, shifting against her.

Lore swallowed the bile in her mouth, her heart still raging in her chest. No—it was too big of a risk now. They needed to help Castor and get Iro to safety.

"Let's go," she told the goddess.

The pounding followed them down into the underground path, even after Athena bent the second door back into place behind them. Two hits, like a heartbeat. *Bang-bang.* It drowned out every thought in Lore's mind, until she was sure she heard a message in it.

Bang-bang.

Too late.

Too late.

Lore's phone vibrated as soon as they reached the empty shoe-repair shop. The message came from an unknown number, blocked by her service.

Safe.

A moment later, she realized who it was. Relief crashed through her as she texted back, **Safe. Meet at Van's place.**

"Castor is all right," Lore told Athena. The goddess had crept over to the door of the shop and had peeled back a corner of the brown paper covering it. She gazed out into the street, searching it for hunters.

"A shame," Athena groused. "For now he must answer to me for our ruined hope."

Lore adjusted Iro's weight. The girl was taller than Lore, making carrying her awkward.

"It . . ." she began. "It didn't work out this time."

Athena's gaze snapped toward her. "Why did you close the door? Does your belief in our objective falter?"

Lore shook her head. "No. He just—it left both of you too exposed. There's a difference between a long shot and a no-win, and this became the latter."

The goddess's expression didn't soften, but turned contemplative as she studied Lore. When she spoke again, the words were calm and measured. "Are you frightened of him?"

"No," Lore said. "I—"

"Your fear will feed him," Athena told her. "It will bring him pleasure. Do not grant it. He is as mortal as you these next six days. If you falter again, remember what he took from you. He may possess power, but you have righteousness. And should even that abandon you, remember that I am beside you, and I will not let you fail."

Lore tried to gather some response. Seeing Wrath coming toward her, knowing that he'd recognized her—it had sent a wave of doubt crashing through her confidence. It wasn't that she wanted his death any less. It had been the sudden, hard realization of what the Agon might ask of her to see his death through.

I can still get back out again, she told herself. *I'm not doing the killing. This is an end, not a beginning.*

"We need to meet the others," Lore said. "Is the street clear?"

"Yes," Athena said. "I will carry the girl."

Lore passed Iro over to her, and Athena stepped out into the darkness.

Lore lingered a moment, taking in the sight, and tried to remember what it felt like to be unafraid.

The address Van had given her and Castor before they'd split up turned out to be for a laundromat about twenty blocks north, in Hell's Kitchen.

They approached the waiting side door, letting the heat from the vents wash over them. The air was choked with the smell of detergent.

Lore blinked against the fluorescent lights as they stepped inside, but Athena had already pivoted toward the sound of a familiar voice.

Miles leaned against a desk in the laundromat's cramped office, his face animated as he chatted in Korean with the gray-haired woman there. But when he spotted them, his expression fell.

"What happened?" he asked. "Where are the others? Who is that? Why are you late?"

"Which question do you want answered first?" Lore asked, tired.

The older woman sighed and stood from her chair. She switched off the monitor on her ancient computer, pulled her purse out of the drawer, and said, "I'll close for the night. Tell Evander to leave payment in the safe and vary the bills this time."

She shuffled off, and within seconds, the lights across the laundromat dimmed. Only a few machines were still churning as she stepped out and locked the door behind her.

"Look at you, making friends wherever you go," Lore said as Athena lowered Iro into the room's other chair. The goddess stepped away, allowing Lore to feel for Iro's pulse and try to rouse her.

"Exactly how hard did you hit her?" Lore asked. Iro had been unconscious for almost twenty minutes.

"Who was that woman?" Athena demanded, ignoring her question.

"Mrs. Cheong," Miles said. "Really sweet lady. She told me I reminded her of her grandson, with all my tattoos." He took a breath and nodded at Iro's limp form. "Okay, tell me who this is."

"Iro of the Odysseides," Lore told him. "Daughter of Heartkeeper."

Miles gave them a pained look. "Why do I get the feeling things didn't go as planned?"

"The short version?" Lore began, leaning against the wall. Her body was quivering as it tried to regroup after the strain of carrying Iro. "Wrath is alive and Heartkeeper is dead and Iro may know the alternate poem or where to find it."

The side door creaked open again. Athena was out of the office with her dory against the newcomer's throat before Lore could even draw her next breath.

Van held up his hands. "Is everyone here?"

Athena lowered her weapon, stepping aside to allow him to pass.

"The false Apollo is yet to come."

Van looked less troubled by that fact than Lore was. He stopped in the doorway, taking in the sight of Miles. His lips compressed, but he said nothing as he studied him.

"Yup, still alive," Miles told him in an uncharacteristically sardonic way. He picked up the plain black backpack at his feet and shoved it at Van with some effort. Van's arms bowed slightly under the weight.

"Your contact was a real gent," Miles continued. "He only called me 'Unblooded trash' twice, but still said he preferred dealing with me to you."

"Possibly because you don't hold the key to his eternal shame," Van said.

"Mrs. Cheong wants her money," Miles reminded him. "And for you to vary the bills. Says you're a good business partner, whatever that means."

"It means I know how much to pay to ensure she forgets everything she sees and hears," Van said.

He unzipped the bag and dumped out its contents onto the floor of the cramped office. Lore jumped as at least three dozen stacks of hundred- and twenty-dollar bills hit the tile. He gripped the laptop at the bottom before it could slide out with them.

Lore covered one stack with her foot and attempted to slide it over to herself unnoticed.

"Nice try," Van said. "We're going to need this money to survive the week." He retrieved two stacks and turned to the safe beneath the desk, where he deposited them. "Did you run into any trouble?"

"Just a few weird looks when I insisted on that particular karaoke room and then didn't stay to sing more than one Whitney Houston song," Miles said.

There was a spark of something to his words—an exhilaration, like a kid who had just gotten away with breaking the rules for the first time. His eyes were bright, almost feverish at the memory, and his cheeks flushed the way they always did when he was excited.

Van's hands stilled over the pile of money. His tone turned accusatory. "There's almost three thousand dollars missing. Did you buy something on your joy ride?"

"Yeah, I stopped to treat myself to a nice meal," Miles sniped back. "I'm not a thief. He had another bit of information, but he wanted more for it."

"And you gave it to him?" Van snapped. "Without bothering to check in with me? He probably sold you a lie—"

"All *you* got was confirmation that the Kadmides bought a new property on Central Park South, and that they bought it using a shell corporation," Miles said. "What *I* got him to tell me was that the new Dionysus, the Reveler, was allied with Wrath and had been working with him and the Kadmides since the last Agon. But the Reveler fled at the start of this year's hunt and hasn't come back. Wrath's after him now, too."

Lore's lips parted. Even Athena looked mildly disconcerted at the thought.

"So, you tell me which information is more valuable to us now," Miles said triumphantly.

Van stood, but Miles didn't back down, not even to escape Van's glare.

"This isn't a game," Van told him. "There's nothing to win and no rules to protect you."

"I know that," Miles said. But Lore knew her friend, and she recognized the look of eagerness and accomplishment that buoyed his mood.

236

Van was right. Miles was liking this too much.

The side door opened again, this time with more force.

Castor, Lore thought, slipping past Athena.

He braced a hand against the wall and leaned forward, exhaustion crashing down over his face.

Lore went toward him, ducking down to try to meet his gaze. Aside from a cut across the sharp line of his left cheekbone, he seemed to be all right. The tension in his face eased as he saw her.

"Are you okay?" she asked. "What happened?"

Castor wiped the sweat off his face against his shoulder, but his shirt was already clinging to every line of his chest and arms. "It took me longer to lose them than I—"

He straightened suddenly, gripping her elbow. The slight movement jarred Lore's shoulder, sending a fresh wave of pain shooting through it. Warm blood trickled down her front, and she swayed, suddenly light-headed.

Castor ripped open a nearby laundry bag waiting to be delivered and dug through it until he found a towel. "How did this happen?"

"Charged when I should have ducked," Lore managed, trying to focus on his face.

"What— Oh no—" Miles began retching as he saw the blood-stained towel. "Is she—"

"Heal her, imposter," Athena ordered.

"No," Lore said, pulling back. "Iro first. Iro. She's— She needs to wake up."

"I'm not going to watch you stoically bleed to death," Castor said, exasperated.

She pressed the towel to her shoulder, stepping farther out of his reach. "Iro first."

Castor pushed past Athena and moved into the office. Lore didn't join them there until the light of Castor's power filtered out into the dark hallway. He worked quickly, nodding as Miles repeated what he had learned from the Kadmides informant.

"We need to get out of here as soon as possible," Van said. "If Wrath and the Kadmides are still tracking us, they won't be far behind."

"We can take a second to catch our breaths and figure out our next move," Lore said.

"Let's start with what would have spooked the Reveler enough to break an alliance with Wrath," Castor said. One of his hands gently cupped the back of Iro's head, but the girl showed no signs of waking up, even as he healed her.

"The death of Hermes," Van said.

Castor sighed. "That *would* do it."

"Why?" Miles asked.

"They were lovers for decades," Lore explained, leaning her good shoulder against the doorframe. "They lived it up in the years between the hunts, enjoying themselves at parties, traveling the globe, visiting old relics of the ancient world in museums. Supposedly they managed to steal a few of them back." She glanced at Athena. "You said you hadn't been able to feel Hermes's presence these last few years—do you think it's related?"

"Hermes would never agree to an alliance with the false Ares," Athena said. "I find it more probable that the false Dionysus's choice to do so created a rift between them and Hermes had to seek shelter away from his known hiding places."

"Didn't help him in the end," Lore said. "Well, regardless of what happened between the two lovebirds, if Wrath is looking for the

Reveler we need to find him first. I think we can rework our last plan and potentially get a do-over in setting a trap."

"Indeed," Athena said, having already thought of it. "The imposter Ares will not suffer him to live after his betrayal."

"That's only if he agrees to help us," Van said.

"He does not need to be a willing participant," Athena said. "He does not need to know we are there until the false Ares arrives and the trap is sprung."

"We're assuming that Wrath hasn't caught on to what we're trying to do," Castor pointed out. "And that he won't see this coming."

"No . . ." Lore said slowly. "I don't think he will. Not this. He may know we're coming for him, but he has no idea that we know about the Reveler bailing on their alliance. Even Van hadn't heard they were allied, and he apparently has sources everywhere."

The Messenger looked displeased at being reminded of that fact.

"Okay," Miles said. "But how are we supposed to find the Reveler first when Wrath most likely has hundreds of hunters out searching for him?"

Castor glanced back at Van, seeming to convey a question. Van said nothing, only shook his head in answer.

"What am I missing here?" Lore asked, looking between them. The towel was growing heavier, and so was her head. She had to lean her temple against the doorframe to stay vertical.

"Wouldn't it be faster?" Castor asked him.

"It could take forever," Van told him. "We'd be too late."

He dragged the backpack over to Castor, retrieving the laptop from it. Rather than plugging it in or booting it up, he used a small screwdriver to remove its back panel.

Both Miles and Lore leaned forward, intrigued, as he removed a small silver gadget from beneath the battery. It plugged into the base of Castor's last burner phone.

"This is a copy of the Kadmides' tracking program," Van explained, waiting for it to load. "The one they use to note sightings of the other bloodlines and the gods. I'll see if they've posted anything about the Reveler, but I can't stay logged in for too long without their Messenger or someone else noticing."

"What else do you know of the false Dionysus?" Athena asked.

"Almost nothing," Van said, "beyond what's common knowledge. He ascended a little over a hundred years ago. He was known as Iason Herakliou in his mortal life, son of the archon, Iason the Elder. He killed his entire family once he ascended and destroyed all of their records to make it harder for the rest of us to hunt him."

Miles looked genuinely shocked. "All of them? Everyone in his family?"

"All of them," Lore confirmed. "The Purge of the Heraklides remains as gnarly as ever."

"And yet totally in character for that bloodline's brutal nature," Van noted. "They celebrated all of their ancestor's worst traits. It's amazing they survived as long as they did."

"He's had a long run as a new god," Castor noted. "I suppose it helps he no longer has a bloodline to punish him for being a kin killer."

"On top of that, he's been the least enterprising new Dionysus we've seen, meaning we can't try tracing him through business affairs," Van said. "No vineyards, no new mind-altering substances, no cults, religious or otherwise . . . I can't predict how he'll react to us, but we need to be prepared for anything. Don't forget his power can induce a feeling of intoxication and frenzy. He's been known to cast illusions in hunters' minds in order to escape."

"Do you have a picture of him, Van?" Lore asked. "I've never seen one."

While the Kadmides program loaded on the burner, Van turned to his real cellphone and, after a moment, pulled up a grainy photo from an old newspaper clipping. It showed a man with one hand tucked into the vest beneath his old-fashioned suit. His round face was half-hidden beneath a magnificent mustache as he posed, stone-faced, between two bowling lanes.

"Is that a man or a mustachioed pug in a suit?" Miles asked carefully.

To Lore's surprise—and even, it appeared, Van's—Van let out a sharp bark of laughter. He recovered quickly, pressing his lips together as if to completely erase the smile.

"There have been rumors he was an architect," Van said. "I've also heard he lived here, in the city, but there's nothing left to substantiate that. As I said, we know next to nothing."

"Well, we do know one other thing," Miles said. "He's standing in the Frick."

Lore had been so focused on trying to study the man's face she'd barely paid attention to the room around him. "The what-now?"

"The Frick Collection," Miles repeated. His eyes went wide and his face lit up with delight as he took in Van's look of surprise. "You didn't know? Really?"

"Clever," Athena said. "Once again, the mortal's knowledge of this city far outstrips what the rest of you bring."

"How can you be sure?" Van asked, his tone sharp.

"The bowling alley—those arches, the distinct honeycomb ceiling," Miles said, trying not to crow. Van truly looked at a loss as he zoomed in on the ceiling. "That's the Frick. It used to be an old mansion belonging to a Mr. Frick who used his endless stacks of sweet, sweet industrialist money to buy art. They turned it into a museum after his death. The bowling alley is in the basement. I would bet money on it, and if it's true the Reveler was an architect, it wouldn't surprise me if he worked on it."

"How the hell do you know all of this?" Lore asked.

"You would know it, too, if you had come with me when I asked if you wanted to go last month," Miles said pointedly. "I get free tickets through my internship, remember? You said, and I quote, 'Real New Yorkers don't play tourist.'"

"That sounds nothing like me," Lore said indignantly.

"That sounds *exactly* like you," Castor said. "It's like your whole thing about how 'authentic' New Yorkers don't get their bagels toasted."

Lore was aghast. "Only monsters toast their bagels."

"This means nothing," Van cut in. "Just because he was photographed there over a hundred years ago does not make the information relevant to us today."

"It is all relevant," Athena said. "For it is very near to where the Awakening took place, and familiar to him."

"Which would make it feel like a safe place to hide," Lore finished. "He might not still be there, but it's worth investigating."

"Oh, I didn't even tell you the best part," Miles said, pausing for dramatic effect.

Lore gave him a look. He smiled.

"It closed two weeks ago for renovations," he finished. "The museum won't reopen until January."

"Well, damn," Lore said. "I think we should start searching there."

"Agreed," Miles said.

"I'm still going to check the Kadmides' program," Van said flatly.

242

"We can't bet on one hunch."

"Good," Castor began. "And while you do that . . ." He carefully released his hold on Iro. "She should come to in a few minutes."

He turned toward Lore, eyebrows raised. Lore pressed the towel to her wounded shoulder and, just to make Castor feel better, allowed him to help her down the hall, toward the miserable-looking employee bathroom.

"Make it fast," Van called after them. "We've got ten minutes before we need to move."

Only, Lore thought, *if Wrath doesn't find us first.*

TWENTY THREE

Lore had almost forgotten what it felt like to be looked after by another person.

She had taken care of Gil for years, and had grown used to playing that role. The strangeness of being looked after—the reluctance she felt—reminded her of something Gil had told her three years ago, on the night they'd met.

Lore had walked day and night after leaving the Odysseides' estate, trying to reach Marseille and start begging for enough money to travel back to the United States and set up a new life. Once there, her forged papers would at least give her some choices about school and starting over. Gil, then eighty-seven, had been mugged on the outskirts of the city, and she had found him beaten half to death with a broken arm and leg. He'd been hoarse from calling out for help that hadn't come.

Lore had been outraged, and despite her own fear and exhaustion, she had carried Gil on her back to the nearest hospital and felt compelled to stay there with him, not wanting the vulnerable man to be alone. She pretended to be his granddaughter to sign him in, and she listened as he told her about himself—how he was an unmarried professor from New York City, and he had known this would be his last trip abroad. By the time the doctor had stitched up Gil's wounds, and tended to the cut on her own face, the idea was fully formed in Lore's mind.

Gil wasn't from her world, and he was alone in his. What Lore proposed was purely business: she would travel back to New York City with him and work as a caretaker until he no longer needed a wheelchair. He'd mulled it over with enough obvious reluctance that Lore had steeled herself for disappointment. As they waited for him to be discharged, Lore asked him why he'd changed his mind. *Sometimes,* he'd said, *the braver thing is to accept help when you've been made to believe you shouldn't need it.*

Lore held the words in her heart, using them to ward off the last measure of her reluctance as Castor brought her into the laundromat's dingy bathroom.

He had to duck to accommodate its low ceiling. Lore's thoughts became warm and small as she watched his throat bob and his fingers become unsure of where they should rest on her hip as he supported her.

He really is beautiful, she thought. Not just for what he'd become, but in a way that was undeniably Castor.

In one swift movement, he lifted her so she was sitting on the narrow edge of the counter surrounding the sink. Like many bathrooms in the city, it verged on inhospitable, most likely to discourage people from spending too much time in it.

"Very macho, big guy," she told him.

He gave her a quelling look as he took the towel from her hands and dropped it on the floor. Carefully, without disturbing the wound, he pulled the collar of her shirt over to better see it. "Can we focus on the traumatic injury in the room?"

His attention was as earnest as it was anxious. It reminded her of when they were young, the quiet way he'd watch her after sparring as if needing to reassure himself she was fine.

"Easy, tiger. It's hardly traumatic," she informed him. "Stupid on my part, but not traumatic."

He shook his head. "I swear, you are truly the only person I know who would pick a fight at a time like this."

"That's because, unlike you, I can multitask," she said with a wink. "What's the prognosis, doc? Am I gonna live?"

All at once, she realized how that would sound to him. "Sorry— Cas, I'm sorry. Me and my big mouth."

He seemed to brush the comment aside, but she could tell that something about it had landed. "Can I rip the shirt to get it out of the way?"

She nodded, cringing as he carefully split the fabric from the collar to the edge of the sleeve. It was only then that she saw the full extent of the deep, jagged wound. Several small pieces of glass were embedded into the muscle there, and for all the many gruesome wounds Lore had witnessed in her short life, this one still turned her stomach.

Her bra strap was in the way, stuck to the crust of one of the more shallow wounds. His fingers hesitated on it, hot against her slick skin. The bleeding had slowed, but the cold she felt gathering beneath her skin was setting in deeper.

She nodded, swallowing. He snapped the strap, watching her face the whole time.

"It doesn't hurt anymore," she told him. "That has to be good, right?"

"That is the opposite of good," Castor said, his voice tight. "Who managed to get you?"

"Why? So you can avenge me?" She tried to look down at it. "Is it really that bad? It doesn't seem that bad."

"I think you're in shock," he told her. "Who was it? I lost sight of you once the dust and smoke got too thick."

"I don't know," Lore admitted.

In one quick movement, Castor had gripped the biggest of the glass shards and pulled it out. The pain was so scalding, Lore couldn't draw a breath deep enough to scream, even as he removed the remaining pieces.

But then his hand was there, pressed tight to the blood pouring from the wound. Lore felt heat, a sharp burn that faded into a numbing warmth.

"Son of a—" she managed to gasp out.

"Don't speak," Castor said. "Just try to breathe."

"Could have . . . warned me . . ." she said.

"You would have tensed the muscle, and it would have been hard to remove the glass," Castor told her. "I do remember a few things Healer Kallias taught me, it seems."

She knew he was right, but it didn't mean she wasn't going to be bitter about it for a few minutes.

"Just breathe," he told her.

So she did. And with each breath she felt his power stitch her torn flesh back together. His power had an almost drugging quality to it. It wrapped around her body and mind, lulling her with its softness.

Castor caught her hand in his. Lore shut her eyes and leaned her head against the mirror behind her. She held on to him, wanting to stay in the moment, wanting to steady herself with something real before his power turned her mind soft.

"Was it me?" he asked quietly. "Did I do this to you?"

Lore forced her eyes open. The gold in his irises swirled, bright in the dingy bathroom's darkness.

"Did I do this because I couldn't control the force of it?" he asked her again.

"No," she told him. "It was one of the Kadmides."

Castor didn't seem convinced. She squeezed his hand again, pulling on it until he looked at her.

"This power is a new skill," she said. "And just like any skill, you have to practice in order to master it, right?"

His thumb began to absently stroke along her collarbone as he healed her, leaving a warm, shimmering trail on her skin. She leaned into the touch.

"I wish it were that easy," he said, "and I could explain this better, but . . . ever since I regained physical form, it's like I can't fully catch my balance. There's a disconnect between what my mind expects and what my body actually does."

"Why didn't you just tell me that before?" Lore asked.

"You confuse me," he said plainly. "It's always been this way. I want to tell you everything, but there's a part of me that's still afraid of seeming weak."

Lore gripped his wrist. "I've never seen you that way."

"I know," he said. "But I *was* weak, for a long time, and it wasn't the fault of anything or anyone. It was just my body. Strong or weak—I hated those were the only things we were allowed to be. I wanted to be defined by the life I lived."

The life he'd lived. The one that would have been cut unmercifully short, if it hadn't been for his ascension. She could almost feel the story he was holding back. The way it rippled beneath his skin, as if desperate to be told.

"Cas," she said softly. "How did you kill Apollo?"

His Adam's apple bobbed as he swallowed hard. He seemed to be debating something, and Lore almost wished she hadn't asked. For all the things that had changed between them, she wasn't sure if she could take him lying to her for the first time.

"I don't know."

Lore's gaze shot up. "What?"

Castor glanced at the door, as if worried someone might be listening. "I don't know. I have no memory of what happened."

Her mouth opened, then shut.

"I know," he said, strained. "There were no cameras in my bedroom. Van told me that the other security cameras malfunctioned when Apollo entered Thetis House. I was alone when it happened."

"Van knows?" Lore asked. She had no reason to feel hurt by the revelation, but she was.

"Van doesn't know about the lost memory," Castor said. "I can tell he's been fishing around, trying to figure it out himself. I just . . ."

"That's why you were trying to talk to Artemis?" Lore said, finally putting it together. "You think she might know?"

He nodded. "I don't know what their connection was like, or if she saw what happened. Athena doesn't seem to know, though. Would Artemis have told her if she witnessed Apollo's death?"

"Artemis tried to stab her no more than five minutes into this Agon, so let's not bank on sisterly love for anything here," Lore said.

Castor's smile was small and fleeting. Lore took his free hand in hers again and squeezed it.

"I need to figure it out," he said. "I have to. I can't . . . This has to have happened for a reason. It has to mean *something* that I have this power."

Lore felt something in her chest crack open at the quiet desperation in his words.

"I don't believe in the Fates, but I do believe in you," Lore said. "Whatever happened must have happened because you were you.

249

We'll figure out what it was, I promise. You can hold me to it."

Castor nodded.

The heat faded from his touch as he finished healing her, but he didn't pull away, and neither did Lore. He wet a small washcloth and began to clean the blood from her new pink skin—stroke by stroke, with a tenderness that came close to breaking her heart. Lore widened her legs, letting him step closer, and closed her eyes.

"Are you all right?" he asked her. "Really?"

His long fingers grazed up along the curve of her shoulder, coming to cup her other cheek, to brush her old, long scar. The tight muscles in her neck eased as he stroked the hollow where the base of her skull met the ridge of her spine.

"I saw him," Lore murmured. "I told myself I would never come back to this world—that I would never let it force my hand or drive me to kill. I thought I could get back out clean if Athena was the one to do it, but . . . I don't know if I can do this, keeping one foot in the ring and one foot out."

"You can," Castor said. "Don't let them pull you back in. There's nothing but shadows for you here now."

Lore knew exactly how easy it was to get lost in that darkness. To *need* it.

Even now, she could imagine her hands wrapped around Wrath's throat, choking him until the sparks of power faded in his eyes—or her blade flashing as it plunged into his chest again and again and again. But Lore didn't feel sick at the thought.

She only wanted it more.

Lore leaned forward against his chest, hearing the powerful drumbeat of Castor's mortal heart.

"I used to believe in this world," Lore said. "I used to want

250

everything it promised so badly."

"I know," Castor told her. "But I never thought you would win the Agon. I thought you would destroy it."

Lore looked up at his words, her brow creased in confusion. But before she could ask, a crash tore through the silence, then a ferocious scream.

Iro was finally awake.

TWENTY FOUR

BY THE TIME LORE REACHED THE OFFICE, IRO HAD HER ARM WRAPPED around Miles's throat and the sharp tip of a letter opener pressed to his jugular.

Van had his hands out, speaking in a low, soothing tone as the girl dragged Miles toward the door. Athena watched from the corner of the office, arms crossed over her chest. She looked amused, but her dory was within reach.

"*No!*" Lore knocked the blade out of Iro's hand, giving Miles a moment to drop and crawl away. "Iro, listen to me—"

She tried to lock the girl's arms at her sides, but Iro had always been faster, and her instincts sharper. Lore didn't see any awareness register on the girl's face as she gripped one of the heavy binders off the bookshelf and launched it toward Castor.

He shifted, letting the book smash into the wall behind him. He turned his wide eyes toward Lore, uncertain of what to do.

Seeing her, Iro lunged—not to attack Lore, but to shield her from the others. "Get out of here, Melora!"

"Hey!" Miles barked. "That was Mrs. Cheong's!"

The words caught Iro off guard. She turned toward him. "I—what?"

Lore pushed through her shock at Iro's protectiveness and

252

managed to wrap her arms around the other girl before she could recover.

"Let me go! You need to get out of here!" Iro said between gritted teeth, straining and thrashing to throw Lore off her. Her faint French accent was never more pronounced than in the rare instances she raised her voice.

"*Stop*"—Lore forced them both to the ground with a hard drop— "*it!* No one is going anywhere. You're safe here—*I'm* safe here."

"Iro," Van said, crouching beside them. "This is Castor Achilleos. Like Athena, he is working with us to try to kill Wrath. He used his power to help you escape. He's not going to hurt you. None of us are."

Iro wrenched herself free from Lore, rolling up onto her feet to face her. Her black hunter's robes were askew, revealing the slim body armor she still wore beneath them. It seemed to take her a moment to understand what Van had told her. "Castor Achilleos is dead. You told me yourself—or did you lie about that, too?"

"That's what *your* people told me," Lore reminded her, shoving up from the ground. She felt like she might retch at the memory—the sheer pleasure on the face of the House of Odysseus's archon as he leaned down to tell her, *One less Achilleos for us to kill.*

"You know what happened to the Achillides," Van said. "Everyone who stands against Wrath has to stand together, otherwise he'll wipe us all out."

"That is not Castor," Iro spat. "That is *not* your friend."

"Yes, he is," Lore said, coming to stand beside him. "He's Castor the way Heartkeeper was your father."

"He—he wasn't—" Iro said, struggling for the words. "He is—he *was*—my lord. Our protector. He . . ."

"He was your father," Lore repeated.

253

He had been archon of the Odysseides for years before ascending to become the new Aphrodite in the last cycle of the Agon. Lore had come to the family after, and she had never been present when the new god manifested a physical form and appeared to them.

From the stories she'd gathered from Iro and a few other members of the family, he had been a strict but not entirely unloving parent to his sole child.

The problem had always been the bloodline's determination to uphold logic over everything else, including emotion. But Iro hadn't been like that—not always. Lore had met her just once before seeking refuge with the Odysseides, but Iro had always treated her as if they had known each other from the time they'd slept in cradles, assuming the role of big sister though she was barely a year older.

In Lore's first few weeks at the Odysseides estate, she had been so shell-shocked by her family's murders that she had only survived because Iro had gently forced her to. She had made her eat, stayed up talking to her after Lore woke screaming from nightmares, and let Lore trail after her day in and day out. It hadn't been Iro's strength and skill as a fighter that Lore had admired, though she respected it. It had been her compassion within a bloodline that strove to rid itself of that.

"She won't understand," Castor said. "She doesn't want to."

"You know nothing of my mind," Iro seethed. "Come closer and see how well I understand what you are, killer of Apollo. Tell me, did you feel clever when you set your trap for him? When you killed him from afar like a coward and stole his power from your archon?"

Everyone in the room seemed to pivot at once toward Castor, whose face shifted like the sky at sunrise. Shock became denial became desperation.

"Who told you that?" he demanded. *"Who?"*

Iro looked victorious. "It is true, then. There was no honor in your ascension."

"That's . . ." Lore's words trailed off as she looked between the two of them. Iro's outright hatred, Castor's sudden uncertainty. "That's impossible. Castor was confined to his bed at that point."

The new god blew out a harsh breath, his hands curling at the memory of it.

"You're speaking from a place of rumor," Van said. "The Odysseides always spread mischief and lies to make themselves feel better for their own failures."

"If she does not speak the truth," Athena told Castor, "then tell it yourself."

"I don't have to tell you anything," Castor said. "The Odysseides can distort the truth all they want. I've never had any honor, and I can't bring myself to care about it now."

"*You* may not," Iro said, shifting her gaze between the two gods. "But I will do what Melora failed to. I will ensure your deaths are delivered by the House of Odysseus and win back the kleos stolen from my lord in death."

Athena snorted, but Lore's lungs tightened at Iro's words.

She heard herself in them.

She heard her parents and her instructors. She heard the lines from the ancient texts she'd read over and over. Even logic wasn't going to break through seventeen years of careful psychological conditioning.

"You have the look of him about your eyes," Athena said evenly.

"Don't speak of my—of Heartkeeper," Iro warned.

"I do not speak of him," Athena said, "but of the man of many ways."

A long stretch of silence followed.

255

"We're trying to kill Wrath," Lore said finally, echoing Van's earlier words. "No one is going to hurt you. We went to Ithaka House tonight in the hope that we could call a truce with your father and the Odysseides before he came for all of you. We were too late."

The tendons in Iro's neck bulged with her panting breath.

"The Odysseides on the bus are safe," Van told her. "I got them away, something I could not do for most of my own bloodline. Our archon lies dead with no one willing to take his place. At least you are alive to serve your kin."

"I cannot be the archon," Iro said sharply.

"Why not?" Lore challenged.

"No woman will become archon of an ancient bloodline. But if the others live, then . . . I will go to them."

Iro softened her rigid stance. For the first time, Lore sensed something of an opening.

"We need to know what you told Wrath," Lore said. "Was it about the origin poem? An alternate version of it?"

Iro stood, feet rooted to the ground, hands curled into fists. Wanting to run, wanting to fight, but held in place by her mind.

"Will you talk to me alone?" Lore asked her. "Just the two of us?"

The other girl hesitated, and nothing hurt Lore more than that.

"We always used to be able to talk," Lore said softly. "Do you really hate me that much now?"

Iro went ashen. "I don't hate you."

Van's phone beeped, cutting through the tension. His dark eyes flicked over to Iro before he said, carefully, "No sightings. But there is a new category that might interest you, Lore."

He turned the phone around, holding it up for Lore to see.

"What the hell?" She took it from him in disbelief.

Melora Perseous was listed just beneath the Reveler's name, but before Castor's. When she clicked on it, the map of Manhattan lit up with glowing pins that marked supposed sightings. Some were frighteningly accurate—near the restaurant that hosted the fighting ring, outside Thetis House—but others were scattered in lower Manhattan, in places she hadn't gone.

Lore pressed her free hand against her jeans, trying to hide how slick it had become. The static was growing in her ears again. She tried to speak, but no words came.

"Only Wrath could have demanded something like this," Van added. "He must have a good number of hunters searching for you if they're turning up this many leads."

Lore forced herself to draw another breath as she returned Van's phone. "I wounded his pride by escaping his attempt to wipe out the House of Perseus. He's not going to let it go lightly."

"No," Castor said quietly, "he's not."

The worry was back, turning his gaze soft. Lore hated that for all of his power, for all of his obvious physical strength, her choices could still bring him back to the boy he'd been. He already had enough to handle this week without needing to fear for her.

"Which is why we're going to have to get him first," Lore said.

Athena nodded. "Indeed."

"If we're going to find the Reveler, we need to get going," Van said. He stood and quickly split the remainder of the money between his leather backpack, which he handed to Castor, and the other, simpler one Miles had picked up. "I'll meet you all there. I'm going to regroup with the remaining Achillides and bring them supplies."

"Are you going to take the Ody—" Miles began.

"*No,*" Van said sharply. Lore gave him a pleading look, but he refused to acknowledge it. He wasn't going to reveal the location of the Achillides to anyone, not even to offer the Odysseides aid. She didn't know why she had expected anything else this week.

Lore followed Van through the side door to make a case for sharing the location of the warehouse, only to find that Iro had followed her. Iro stepped out into the street, hugging her arms to her chest.

Lore watched Van disappear into the darkness, and was tempted to call after him. Iro, however, spoke first.

"They say his father did that to him."

"Did what?" Lore asked, turning to her.

"His hand," Iro said. "The story told to me was that his father was so ashamed of his boy's unwillingness to fight, his ineptitude for it, that he severed Evander's sword hand to give him an *honorable* excuse not to."

Lore blanched. "No. Tell me that's not true."

"I think he did it to himself," Iro said, her expression turning thoughtful. "Not out of weakness, but strength. The will to decide his own path."

The words gave Lore her first glimmer of hope that she could get through to Iro. If the girl believed an act like that could be courageous, and hadn't dismissed it as cowardice the way they'd been taught to believe, there was something for Lore to work with.

"And this hunt, these families who would have Van fight against his will—that's the world you believe in?" Lore asked her. "The one you feel such loyalty to?"

"No world is perfect. God, mortal, hunter," Iro said. "I believe in our divine purpose. I believe in honor, and in kleos, and that we will never be destroyed. I believe in it, even if you've allowed yourself to be led astray."

258

"You know why I left," Lore said. "Everyone knew what that man was, and no one said a word. Where was the honor in your bloodline elevating him to its highest position? Where was the kleos in that, Iro?"

The girl looked down. "You should have stayed. I would have protected you from them."

"It wouldn't have been enough," Lore told her.

"I don't believe that," Iro whispered.

"You don't have to for it to be true," Lore told her. "Can you honestly tell me that they wouldn't have killed me for what I did?"

"I don't know what they would have done," Iro said. "We don't speak of what happened. It is acknowledged only as a terrible accident."

Of course, Lore thought bitterly. To tell the truth would have dishonored the dead—because it meant admitting that their family's monster hadn't been confined to a labyrinth or exiled to some far-off place. He'd walked freely among them.

"I know it feels wrong to you that I'm working with gods," Lore said. "But look at Prometheus—he brought us fire, even knowing what it would cost him. There comes a point where you have to decide what's right for yourself and act, no matter the consequences."

Iro drew in an uneven breath beside her. "We were not born to carry fire."

"The rest of my family is gone," Lore said. "I don't want to lose you again. Please stay with us. *Help* us."

Iro closed her eyes and was silent for a long time. "My family is gone now, too."

"Even your mother?" Lore asked. "You're sure?"

Dorcas's presence had lingered like a ghost at the estate; she'd vanished a few days after Lore had arrived, and no one, save Iro, was ever willing to acknowledge or question it. It wasn't until months later that Iro and Lore had broken into her locked chambers to look for answers. Inside her empty jewelry box they found a slip of paper with a single word on it.

Mákhomai. I make war.

"I can't go with you to find the Reveler," Iro told her, her accent softening the words until they seemed to run together in a whisper. "I have a duty to my bloodline. But there's a debt that has to be paid, even I know this, for none of us would have survived without you."

The girl stood, her hands clenched before her. Lore waited, struggling to hide her impatience.

"The poem you asked about before," Iro began. "There is another, more complete version of what Zeus told the hunters at Olympia when he first gave the command to begin the Agon."

Lore's lips parted in surprise. "And you know it? The complete version."

Her heart fell like a stone in her chest as Iro shook her head.

"Our archivist found a letter from centuries ago, forgotten in a safe-deposit box in the Alps," Iro continued. "From one of your ancestors to one of mine."

"About its existence?" Lore pressed.

"About where to find it," Iro said. "Lore, it claims the full text is inscribed on the aegis."

Lore drew back a step, static burning in her ears as disbelief emptied her thoughts. It felt as if she had run here, to this moment. "That's impossible. That's . . . I would have known about it. My father would have known it. I would have—"

I would have seen it myself.

But—would she have? In those few precious moments she'd laid eyes on it?

260

"Does Wrath know what it says?" Lore asked. The Kadmides held the aegis in their possession for decades. They had to have studied every inch of it to discover its secrets.

"I don't think so," Iro said. "The letter describes the text as being hidden or disguised in some way. The only reason he found out about it is because some of his hunters raided the archive vault where we kept the original letter."

"Then what did he need you for?" Lore asked. "What information did you have that he didn't?"

Iro looked pale. "His hunter didn't just find the letter. There was record of the fact that we sheltered you."

"No," Lore breathed.

"He wanted to know where you were," Iro said. "I think he believes that you know how to read the inscription, and, whatever he's planning, he needs you in order to see it through."

TWENTY FIVE

THEY SPLIT UP INTO PAIRS TO MAKE THE JOURNEY UP TO THE FRICK, approaching the museum from different directions. Lore tried to keep her composure, but she was struggling to hold on to her threadbare nerves.

She passed Athena her dory as the goddess stepped out of the cab several blocks north and east of the building. The driver had eyed their staffs—the ends of both covered by pillowcases stolen from someone's laundry—with some suspicion, but not enough to jeopardize his fare.

"This way," Lore said, hurrying along the sidewalk. She turned around when she realized Athena hadn't followed.

The goddess had stopped near the steps of St. Jean Baptiste Church, her gray eyes glowing in the deep violet of late night. The church, with its classical pediment and columns, Renaissance-style bell towers and domes, and statues of Christian angels, suddenly struck Lore as an embodiment of history itself. The way it marched ever forward, each civilization devoured by the next.

"Do you feel something?" Lore asked her. "Or someone?"

The goddess shook her head.

"Okay," Lore began slowly. "Then why do you look like you want to tear the place apart with your bare hands?"

Athena leveled her with a look that came like a blade across the neck. "How shall I look upon the temple of a god whose followers destroyed the culture of the Hellenes, defiled our images, sanctuaries, and temples, and ravaged the people's faith in their gods?"

"Fair enough," Lore said.

Athena cast one last look at the church. "But this god did what we no longer could, even at the end. He made them fear him, and it took control of the hearts of our people."

"Maybe," Lore said. "But that's only one interpretation of *fear*. To some, it just means that they respect their god and stand in awe of that power."

"Do you not feel angry?" Athena asked her. "Your own way of life has been threatened."

"Good," Lore said. "Good riddance. It's a horrible way to live. It can't end soon enough."

A flicker of true surprise moved across the goddess's face. She seemed to change her mind about what she was about to say, though her voice didn't betray it.

"Do not deny your birthright," Athena said. "You are no mere mortal. I have seen you fight. You may silence her, you may suppress her glorious rage, but a warrior lives in you still."

My name will be legend.

The memory of her declaration, the confidence that had powered it, made Lore feel sick to her stomach. She hadn't thought of the dream in so long, but now it crashed through her mind. The edge of a shield. The golden wing. Eyes in the blade of a sword.

Bullshit. All of it.

"The Fates—" Athena began.

Lore shook her head. "The Fates have nothing to do with any of this. I don't accept that anything is outside of my control."

263

"You may deny the Fates, but they will not deny you," Athena said. "Fighting them will not save you from what is ahead. It will merely quicken the course of things."

"So you say," Lore said. "But that would mean you think you were always destined to fall from favor and be hunted. The Ages of Man have all come to an end in one way or another, with the exception of this one. Why can't we see the end of the Age of Gods?"

"The Age of Gods is eternal." Athena gripped her dory, and Lore wondered if she would ever become used to the goddess's eyes, the way they seemed to raze her defenses. "I may have been meant to fall, but it is so I might prove my worth to my father once more."

If you say so, Lore thought.

Athena finally followed her as Lore started down the street again, this time at a quick clip. "Take heart, Melora. If Wrath believes you hold the key to unlocking the secrets of the poem, we will survive this hunt. He cannot kill you. Your death as the last of the Perseides would remove it from this world."

"Yeah, real comforting," Lore muttered.

But still the thought sent a shiver rippling over her skin. With Tidebringer dead now, Lore truly was the last of her bloodline.

After Iro had left, leaving only a phone number she could be contacted at, Lore had told the others about the inscription on the aegis, which had, as expected, brought on more questions she didn't want to answer.

"Still, the thought of the imposter Ares possessing my father's shield . . ." Athena began, her expression darkening. "If only your family had been stronger—wiser—and had not lost it."

Anger sparked in Lore, too quick to smother. "They didn't lose it—it was stolen, along with everything else."

"It occurs to me now that this is why he did not immediately kill the false Poseidon," Athena said. "He may have believed she, as one of your line, could decipher the poem on the shield."

Lore bit the inside of her mouth hard enough to taste blood. "You're probably right."

The truth was, Iro had only seen a sliver of the greater nightmare. As much as Lore hadn't wanted to tell Athena about the poem being inscribed on the shield, she'd seen an opportunity in it. If the goddess believed Wrath already had the poem—that he already held her key to escaping the Agon—it would give her all the more reason to focus wholly on pursuing him.

Of course, the problem would be dealing with what happened once Wrath was dead, and Athena realized he didn't have the aegis after all.

But that was a problem for the future, and for the first time all day, Lore felt calmer. Secure, at least, in the knowledge that neither god would ever find the shield or the secrets it possessed.

Athena mistook her expression for worry. "Do not trouble yourself, Melora. It is to our advantage that he seeks you out. It will draw him directly into the path of my weapon."

"Great," Lore said. "Can't wait."

"What I cannot abide, however," Athena continued, the words edged like blades, "is the knowledge that your ancestors would sully the perfect form of the aegis with any inscription. Defiling my father's shield, yet still praying and offering for his blessings . . . It is little wonder he does not protect these hunters."

"We've never needed gods to protect ourselves," Lore ground out.

Athena turned her sharp gaze on her. "When true darkness is upon you, you will remember us. But if the world persists in the way it is now, who will be left to answer you?"

"Who says," Lore answered sharply, "that we'll even remember you?"

The goddess had no answer for her.

"You don't care about this city or any other," Lore continued, unable to stop herself. "All that matters to you is power."

Lore hated her temper more than she hated any other part of herself—how quick she moved from spark to flash, incinerating everyone around her.

"Listen," Lore began, slowing her steps. "I didn't mean—"

But before she could turn, something sharp pressed against her lower back, right against her kidney. She turned, looking over her shoulder.

A Minotaur mask stared back at her.

Lore gripped her dory, lifting it.

"I wouldn't do that," he warned. "I wouldn't do anything other than drop your weapon and come with me quietly."

Lore searched the street around her, but Athena was nowhere to be seen.

"Working with gods," the hunter continued, edging her forward. "I should have expected you to become a blade traitor eventually." His tone shifted as he began to speak to someone else, likely through his earpiece. "Yeah, tell him I've found her—"

Lore leaned left, letting his blade graze her, but giving herself enough room to jab her dory back. She spun it, bringing the covered tip around to bash against his mask. Its straps broke, sending the mask to the ground.

"You bitch," the hunter snarled.

She jabbed him with the dory, but he brought his blade down and cleaved the wood staff in two. Lore spun forward, avoiding his reach as he came at her with the blade again. The only thing that finally stopped him was the feel of the dory's kitchen-knife tip cutting through the pillowcase to press against his windpipe.

Breath heaved in and out of her, and her arms strained with the need to push forward just a little more and end the fight completely.

"You should have killed me when you still had the chance," Lore hissed.

"Can't," he told her, an unnerving excitement in his words.

The hunter spun left, kicking her chest with enough force to knock her to the sidewalk. The piece of the dory flew from her hands, rolling beneath a nearby parked car.

He was on her in an instant, bringing his dagger down toward her shoulder. Lore blocked it with one arm, trying to buck him off, even as she felt along the ground for the head of the dory. Her hand found something else instead.

Lore brought a broken chunk of cement against the side of the hunter's head, knocking him sideways off her. She slammed it into his face and heard the satisfying sound of gagging as blood filled his mouth. He crawled back, desperate to get away from her.

She brought the piece of cement up again, her gaze narrowed on his temple. Olympia's small, singsong voice in her mind repeating the words they'd heard a thousand times, *Kill, or be killed—Kill, or be killed—Kill, or be killed—*

Lore clambered off him. The hunter lay spread out on the ground, his face bloodied. He wheezed, his lungs wet and desperate for a breath.

I could have killed him. Icy needles pierced her skin, instantly cooling her blood. She shuddered.

After everything . . . after what Gil had helped her through . . .

Someone peeled out of the shadows beside them. Athena.

"*He,*" Athena said, "will never have her."

She was the last thing the hunter saw.

The young hunter's body jerked as the goddess slammed her spearhead through his rib cage. The wet suck of muscle as she pulled it out was even worse. His eyes widened, blood pouring from his mouth as he tried to speak.

Athena dragged the hunter and leaned him against the nearest building. She wiped the blood from his mouth with his black robe, pulling it tighter around him to disguise the wound.

"When you see him," Athena began, leaning down to bring herself eye level with the hunter, "tell Lord Hades that the rest of Theseus's line will soon join you in the world below, for today you have cursed them all."

Lore turned her gaze down, her hands clenched tight around her upper arms.

"Do not look away," Athena told her. "You are no coward."

She wasn't. In that moment, though, Lore almost envied Athena for the hollow place inside the gods where a mortal's humanity would be.

Athena handed her the hunter's dagger, then collected the pieces of Lore's dory. She kept one of the kitchen knives but threw the other one, along with the splintered wood, into a nearby gutter.

"Sorry," Lore said softly. Her life wasn't completely her own this week.

"There is no forgiveness in the Agon," Athena told her. "There is only survival and what must be done."

TWENTY SIX

THE MOMENT LORE LAID EYES ON IT, SHE REALIZED SHE HAD SEEN the Frick before—many times. She'd walked by it and hadn't bothered to stop and investigate the large, handsome building that stretched from Seventieth to Seventy-First Street. The city was a place where you only saw what you were looking for.

The lock on the construction fence was broken. Lore pushed it open to reveal the museum's nondescript entrance a few feet away, and Miles crouched on its steps. He looked up at the sound of their approach, his face wan.

"Are you okay?" Lore asked.

Miles hugged a water bottle to his chest. "I should have listened to Castor and stayed outside . . ."

Athena shifted uneasily behind her.

Lore looked through the windows of the entrance's two wooden doors, startling at the sight of two security guards sitting in high chairs, their backs to her. Castor stood between them. His grave expression turned Lore's lungs to stone.

She smelled it as soon as she pushed the door open. Stale air and decay and blood. The hair on her body rose.

"Do you want to wait for Van outside?" Lore suggested to Miles.

Miles shook his head. "He's not coming. He texted Castor to say

269

he'd meet us back at the house."

"Why don't you go meet him?" she said. "You don't have to go back inside."

"No," he said, forcing the words out. "I can handle it. I don't need to leave."

"I don't want you to have to *handle* it," she told him.

But Miles moved past her, heading inside.

Athena's breath came light and quick behind Lore as they stepped into the entry. The goddess approached the guard on the right. The young woman's hair had been braided down her back, much like Lore's own. Her head rested against the wall, as if she'd merely dozed off.

Lore saw the truth as they came to stand by Castor's side.

The woman's throat had been cut so deeply, Lore could see the white bone of her spine through the gaping flesh. It would have been a quick death, but a brutal one. She wouldn't have been able to scream.

The other guard's face had been battered, but whatever suffering he'd felt would have been over as soon as he'd been stabbed through the heart.

"A léaina?" Castor guessed. "The Kadmides might have beat us to the punch again."

"Or a desperate god," Lore said.

She wasn't sure which would be worse.

There were four more bodies. One police officer and three more uniformed security guards. The killer had brought them into the Garden Court and arranged them in a grotesque pattern around the dry fountain. Their lifeless eyes watched the heavens through the domed glass ceiling. There were no signs of blood or struggle

270

anywhere else in the museum, and the monitors in the security booth seemed to be on some sort of loop.

Which meant the likelihood of hunters being behind the deaths went up significantly.

Miles leaned against one of the nearby pillars, hugging his arms around his body.

Maybe this will be enough for him, Lore thought. Maybe Miles would see that Unblooded mortals weren't spared from killing when they stood in the path of the Agon.

"They've all been"—he seemed to be searching for a nicer word to describe the small massacre in front of them—"cut up. Do hunters not use guns?"

"Some do," Lore told him, giving his shoulder a quick, comforting touch. "Mostly on other hunters. Gods are killed with arrows or blades."

"Why?" Miles asked.

"Zeus's words at Olympia were interpreted as a command," she said. "*I will reward you with the mantle and the deathless power of the god whose blood stains your bold blade.* No one has been willing to risk losing out on a god's power by testing other methods."

She watched as Athena used one of the security guard's batons to thread through the door handles, reinforcing their busted locks.

"Based on their condition they've been dead for a few hours," Lore said. Castor nodded. Aside from the color of their blood darkening as it oxidized in the air, and the faint smell of death that clung to them, there wasn't any noticeable decay. Rigor mortis hadn't set in.

Miles gave her a look that was half-amazed and half-horrified.

"No museum staff or construction workers . . . this has to be the night shift," Lore said. "Otherwise someone would have come

271

looking for their loved ones, right?"

"Do you think the Reveler is capable of doing all of this?" Castor asked, astonished. "Alone?"

"Yes," Athena said, gripping her dory. "He has not survived this long because he possesses a gentle nature."

"Can't wait to meet him," Miles said, pained. "But we should probably get on that now, before the next security shift comes in."

Lore and the others had pulled the chairs with the security guards away from the doors, wiping their fingerprints from the seats, and Castor had melted the door's locks shut, but Miles was right. Every moment they wasted standing around was another opportunity to be caught surrounded by bodies.

If the Kadmides were responsible for these deaths, one of their crews would be by before sunrise to clean the scene—in a strange way, she hoped they would. While she and the others wouldn't have DNA or fingerprints in the system, there was every chance Miles did and could be linked to the scene.

"You will keep an eye on the entrance, imposter," Athena said. Her eyes shifted to Lore. "You and I will start searching below and work our way up."

Castor looked as if he wanted to protest, but acquiesced. "All right, but if you do find him, don't approach him yet. We need to see what kind of state he's in before making a call on how to use him as bait."

Athena gave an unfeeling smile. "Imagine lecturing one such as me on strategy."

"You're with us, Miles," Lore said. "Now—how do we get downstairs?"

The lower levels were as still and dark as the upper one had been. Lore reached out a hand, feeling along the walls. The corridor there would have been pitch-black if it wasn't for the light of an emergency exit sign.

Lore pulled the phone from her back pocket and turned its flashlight on. She led the group as they moved into the first of two galleries connected by the long hallway. Paintings and documents had been removed for the renovation, leaving empty walls and small information plaques behind.

Outside the lower galleries and the vestibule connecting them, there was no signage to help direct them, just doors leading into some kind of administrative area.

Doors that had been kicked in by force.

Athena moved one of them aside, lifting her dory like a spear. Lore motioned for Miles to stay farther behind her. Her phone's light passed over an office and a storage room. Both looked like they had been gutted, and had bled out with storage boxes and scattered papers.

They followed the trail of broken furniture through the rooms beyond it. Shipping crates had been smashed open, the paintings inside shredded, the vases and clocks smashed.

They passed the infamous bowling alley and continued their search, until, finally, Lore saw signs for what lay ahead.

The museum's storage vault.

She jumped as a booming crash split the air. It was followed by another, and another—glass shattered, and a single voice let out a ragged scream of frustration.

Lore pulled the dead hunter's dagger out from where she'd tied it to her thigh with a strip of fabric. She switched off the flashlight and passed her phone back to Miles. He nodded in understanding when she pressed a finger to her lips, but ignored her when she motioned for him to stay back as she approached the door and nudged it open.

Paintings had been stored on sliding walls of thin metal fencing, all lined up like stacks in a library. Beyond them, the dark walkway continued to the left. Lore stuck her head around the corner, only to quickly pull back at the next splintering crash.

Miles shot her a questioning look, but Athena urged her on with a nod.

Lore approached the door at the end of the hall. It had been left ajar, and if she kept close to the wall, she had a view of what was waiting for them inside.

A titan of a man careered around the storage room, moving between the shelf-lined walls, all brimming with boxes, clocks, and smaller figurines. Stone busts and bronze statues watched the man with lidless eyes from a platform at the center of the room, and narrowly survived an angry sweep of his arm.

He dragged one of the storage boxes off a nearby shelf and threw it to the ground with a grunt. It broke apart in an instant, leaving him to rummage through the padding. He kicked the remains of a broken vase aside. It skidded through the shards of glass and tufts of packing material littering the floor.

Iason Herakliou. The new god still wore his sky-blue tunic and sandals, both filthy with grass and dark grime.

The photograph had shown a middle-aged man who, while fit, was still balding and showing other signs of age. Yet this man—this new god—looked as if he had been carved from sun-warmed sandstone. His hair was nearly the same shade as Athena's dark gold, and his skin was a deep olive but was caked with dirt and dried blood.

The Reveler reached for a handle of whiskey he'd left on one of the shelves, sucking down a long draw of the burning liquid. Then he upended the bottle, pouring the rest of the contents over a massive gash in his thigh. He growled and snarled through the pain, beating a fist against the cinder-block wall until it passed.

Lore reached behind her, and, without looking, grabbed Miles by the shirt. She pushed him back, then pointed down the hall, to safety.

Which, of course, was the exact moment Miles's phone let out an earsplitting ring from inside his pocket.

"Shit—" He fumbled for it, hitting buttons as he did. His mother's voice poured through the device. *"Miles, I need your help with something—"*

Lore stared at him.

He hung the call up, breathing hard as he switched it to silent and pressed the device against his chest.

The storage vault's door slammed shut in front of them, the sound echoing through the terrifying silence that followed. Lore gripped her knife, straining her ears to try to track the new god's steps, but heard nothing.

Where is he? she thought, sweat beading her upper lip. *Where the hell did he go?*

A torrent of plaster and shards of cement exploded out of the wall to her right. Lore was thrown by the force of it, momentarily stunned by a blow to the head—only to be caught by a hand that reached through the jagged hole and locked around her throat.

TWENTY SEVEN

Lore clawed at the hand choking her, head throbbing and half-blinded by the veil of dust choking the air.

His fingers tightened, and as her vision began to go dark, Lore felt her spine compress, ready to crack. She thrust her dagger up again and again until it finally stabbed through the Reveler's forearm. He howled in pain, his grip loosening just enough for her to drop down onto her knees and roll away, coughing.

The Reveler retracted his arm through the wall. The hole it left revealed the rest of the room, the way a section of it extended to nearly the exact spot she'd chosen to stand.

Lore grimaced. *Great job as always.*

Athena glowered and moved Lore out of her way. She tore at the damaged wall with her hand and dory, widening the hole until it was large enough to step through.

"Reveler! We're not here to kill you!" Lore got out, her voice raw. A bestial snarl answered. Inside the room, shelves fell in an earsplitting cacophony.

Athena ripped one last cinder block away and ducked into the vault. Lore scrambled after her, turning to face Miles through the fractured wall. "Go get Castor!"

She didn't wait to hear if he actually listened.

"I knew you'd come for me eventually, you big, hateful bitch!" The Reveler gnashed his teeth at them. Athena had backed him into a corner, and all he had to defend himself was Lore's dagger, pulled from his arm, and a crate's lid for a shield.

Athena watched, stone-faced, as his body heaved with his hatred.

"No one is here to kill you," Lore said again, holding out her hands to show him she was unarmed, and to placate him.

"I may yet alter course," Athena said coolly.

The Reveler's face screwed up, twisting with rage and disgust. The sight of him, drunken and stripped down to the chaos of fear and self-preservation, might have stirred a trace of pity in Lore, if he hadn't just savagely murdered six innocent people upstairs.

"My name is Melora Perseous," Lore began.

The Reveler let out a dark laugh. "Of course. Gods damn it all. Don't know why I expected anyone else, given how shit this cycle has been."

She wasn't sure what to do with that, so she continued. "I appeal to you, a descendant of mighty Herakles, himself the most famous and renowned of the ancient Perseides—"

"That shit doesn't work on me, idiot child," the Reveler snapped. "I don't give a flying feck, and even if I did, Eurystheus of the Perseides attempted to destroy all the children of Herakles before the Agon was ever born."

"Okay," Lore choked out, having forgotten that dark bit of history. "Fair point. But we're just here to talk."

"Unless you would prefer to fight?" Athena said. "We will have answers from you either way."

"You think I don't know that you and the psychotic huntress aren't out to collect all the new gods' heads?" he growled. "Try it. Dare you."

277

"If that truly were the case," Lore said, "then why would she be working with the new Apollo?"

The Reveler turned the dagger toward Lore. "*Liar.*"

"She's not lying," came Castor's voice from behind them. He stepped through the opening in the wall, his gaze darting once to Lore before turning to the other new god.

"Then you're the biggest damn fool in the room," the Reveler said, staggering forward a step. "Whatever your plans are, hers are ten leagues ahead. You—you have no idea. The things he would tell me about her—"

He, Lore thought. *Hermes.*

"Be that as it may," Castor said, coming to stand beside Lore. "Wrath is the one killing new gods, not her."

The Reveler scoffed.

"Wrath didn't just kill Hermes," Castor continued. "He took out Tidebringer and Heartkeeper, and tried to come after me. We're trying to stop him—"

"*I'm* going to kill him." The Reveler growled, swiping the sweat from his paling face. "*Me.* Not anyone else. I'll kill any little shit who tries to get in my way."

"It won't happen if Wrath gets you first," Lore said.

"You think I don't know that?" he sneered. "I knew what it would cost me to escape him."

"Hermes—" Lore began.

"Do not say his name!" he snarled. "*You*—don't you dare!"

"Me?" Lore pressed. *What the hell does that mean?*

The Reveler swiped the back of his hand over his mouth and said nothing.

"You're alone," she reminded him. "You need help. If you're just going to bleed out down here, then what's the point? What's the point of any of this?"

"I have an alliance with the imposter Apollo," Athena said. "I will temporarily extend this to you, so long as you agree to serve as our means of drawing out Wrath."

"Bait? Is that what I'm reduced to?" The Reveler shook his head with a sardonic laugh, struggling to stay upright without the support of the wall behind him. Lore wasn't sure that he knew he was making such a low, mournful sound. The wound in his leg was far worse than the one she had given him. It was already turning red as infection set in.

"I'd rather you just stick a knife in my gut and kill me instead," the Reveler hissed. "End this farce of an existence. This is—all of this, this *bullshit*—it means nothing. Even the supposedly great Apollo knew. He *knew*."

"What does that mean?" Castor demanded, unable to hide his surprise and eagerness. "What do you know about Apollo's death?"

The air seemed to evaporate from the Reveler's chest. He slumped forward, sliding down the wall.

"I know nothing," the Reveler said, his turmoil and drunkenness sinking into exhaustion. "Just that the hunt is long, and there's only so much anyone can take."

Castor approached him slowly, taking the dagger from the other god's slack hand and passing it back to Lore. He looked at the Reveler with sympathy the god didn't deserve.

"Why did you come to this place?" Athena asked. Disgust settled into her countenance as she took in the destroyed art around her. "What is it that you seek so desperately?"

"Thought he left something for me. That he hid it," the Reveler said, looking between Athena and Lore.

Lore drew in an unsteady breath, her free hand curling into a fist at her side.

"Why did you decide to work with Wrath after the last Agon?" Lore pressed. "Why did you agree when Hermes didn't?"

The new god didn't respond. Lore wiped a hand against the place the shards of cement had cut the side of her head, sending an uncertain look in Castor's direction. He crouched down in front of the Reveler.

"Swear to me that you won't kill anyone in my party and that you will answer our questions," Castor told him, "and I'll heal you."

The Reveler scoffed.

Lore's temper immediately sparked, but Castor never lost his easy, reasonable tone. "You'll have a better chance of surviving if you can run from the hunters, Iason, and an even better one if you help us."

The Reveler looked up at his mortal name, his nostrils flaring. Lore was sure he would say no—that ichor, power, and unending violence had carved out every last trace of his humanity. Instead, the feral look faded from his features.

"You see the logic in a temporary partnership," Athena noted. "Perhaps there is hope for your survival yet."

The Reveler sneered at her. "Superior to the last."

"Do we have a deal or not?" Castor pressed.

The last traces of amusement faded from the Reveler. He stared at Castor, at all of them, and Lore could practically feel the strain of his mind searching for another option.

Finally, he said, "I will answer two of your questions, but I won't help you kill Wrath, and I won't be your fecking bait."

Athena rested a cold, heavy hand on Lore's shoulder. The touch stilled both her thoughts and her outrage. "Two answers will suffice."

"Working with mortals," the Reveler said, his smirk turning his perfect features hideous again. "You poor old dear. You once ruled civilizations, and now you're nothing more than a story that fades with every generation. You must long to rip out these mortals' hearts with every miserable beat."

Athena took a hard step forward, buckling the cement beneath her foot.

"Ah, *there* she is," the Reveler taunted.

"I would shut up before I let her kill you," Lore said coldly. "She's what she's always been. But for someone who used to be mortal yourself, you had no issue murdering six people upstairs who had nothing to do with the Agon."

The Reveler rose slowly, his eyebrows drawing down in confusion.

"What the hell are you on about, kid? I haven't killed anyone since the Awakening," he said. "If there are dead in this building, it wasn't my blade that did them in."

TWENTY EIGHT

CASTOR HEALED THE REVELER'S LEG WELL ENOUGH FOR HIM TO WALK out of the storage room on his own two feet. The new Dionysus had been anxious to see the bodies, but was visibly repulsed at the thought of being supported by anyone else on the journey upstairs.

Athena walked at the front of the group, searching the dark hallways and rooms. Lore brought up the rear, her eyes shifting between the dark shapes of the others as they walked a few feet ahead, one hand resting lightly against the knife she'd strapped to her thigh again.

Miles met them near the stairs, clutching at his arms.

"Okay?" Lore mouthed.

He nodded, but there was no color left in his face.

"Imposter," Athena began, keeping her voice low. "How is it possible the killers did not find you and that you know nothing of their identities?"

Lore had been wondering that herself. It had been hunters—the only question was which house they belonged to.

"I hid myself in one of the crates and stayed there until things got quiet upstairs and the security guards stopped doing rounds— *Shit!*" The Reveler stumbled as his injured leg buckled. Castor's hands flew out to catch him, but the other new god twisted away, growling.

"Let me finish healing you," Castor tried again. "I'd prefer if you didn't pass out or die before you give us the answers you oh-so-generously promised."

"Then ask your questions, you stupid ass," the Reveler said, drawing himself up to his full height again. His eyes flashed. "And let me be done with you all."

Castor gazed back at him, unimpressed. But he was silent for the same reason Lore was—neither one of them wanted to waste an answer by asking the wrong question.

Even Athena seemed to be preoccupied by whatever strategy she was inwardly developing. Her posture was so rigid that Lore was beginning to fear that one more snide word from the Reveler would be answered with a dory driven into his gut.

"Okay, well, I'll start," Miles began. Lore opened her mouth to stop him, but it was already too late. "Why did you agree to work with Wrath while Hermes didn't?"

"Because I saw potential in his vision," the Reveler spat. "Hermes neither liked nor believed him."

Lore was about to ask what, exactly, that *vision* was beyond Wrath killing his rivals and searching for the poem, but Miles spoke again.

"That must have really stung, him effectively calling you a fool and turning his back on you," he said. "But you didn't bail until the Awakening, even though you had to have known that Wrath would kill his enemies, which included Hermes—I'm assuming that means that part of your agreement was that Wrath couldn't kill him."

Even in the darkness, Lore could still see the way the Reveler's top lip curled, baring his teeth.

"And if you're so sure that Hermes hid something *here*, in a place that's meaningful to *you*," Miles continued, "it means you were in contact with Hermes before the start of the Agon and knew what he

283

was doing in the years between the Agon. Unless you're just guessing he left something for you and didn't abandon you, which is obviously also a possibility."

"He didn't *abandon* me." The Reveler lunged forward, only to be blocked by a shove of Castor's hand. Lore gripped Miles by the arm and drew him back behind her, but she suddenly understood what he was doing—getting answers by testing assumptions, not by asking questions.

Lore clucked her tongue. "So, in the end, Hermes wanted nothing to do with you. He didn't leave you anything. He probably didn't even say good-bye."

The Reveler lurched toward her. "You stupid—!"

Castor shoved him again, this time up against the wall. He pushed his forearm into the god's exposed throat. "Don't touch her."

Athena slashed the dory down between them, breaking Castor's hold. *"Enough."*

But she, too, had figured out Miles and Lore's game. A frisson of satisfaction worked its way down Lore's spine as the goddess gave her a small smile.

Hermes had disappeared, not necessarily to hide himself from Wrath, but to hide something—something that the Reveler now assumed Hermes had left for him to find. To use.

Lore was about to ask for clarification on Wrath's plans when Athena spoke first.

"What is Melora's involvement in all of this?"

"Wait—what?" Lore began.

Athena held up her hand, silencing her.

The Reveler's eyes were defiant. But when he spoke again, his tone was more measured. "All of you are fools. Wrath's plans stretch back decades. He plans to end the Agon, but he needs one last thing to put it all into play."

"The other origin poem," Lore said. "We know."

The new god hesitated, clenching his jaw.

"You are not nearly as hopeless about the hunt as you would have us believe, imposter," Athena said. "Otherwise you would end yourself or invite a mortal to do it. You want to survive. I see it in your eyes. That longing, that need to feel the ichor burning through you once more."

The Reveler glared at her, but didn't deny it.

"You have given answers you know we want, yet not the one to the question I have asked," Athena said. "What role does Melora Perseous play in all of this?"

"Don't you already know?" the Reveler asked her.

"Answer her question," Castor said.

The Reveler spat out blood at his feet. "Fine. Wrath needed me for one thing and one thing alone. And before any of you brainless gnats ask, I don't know the rest of his plans. I just want to find the deepest crevice in this fecked-up world to try to wait it all out."

"Still not an answer," Castor said, this time with a new warning in his tone.

"I made a promise, and I'm not going to break it for you assholes," the Reveler said. "I can only tell you, girl. That's what he said. Come with me if you want to know, or don't. I don't care."

The Reveler turned and limped up the steps. Lore looked back toward the others, taking in their alarm and confusion.

"We will keep our distance," Athena said. "But will not be far."

Lore trailed behind the new god. The others followed, hanging back as they reached the top of the steps.

The new god stopped once he reached the fountain in the center of the indoor courtyard, forcing Lore to close the distance between them herself. He examined the bodies, his expression odd.

Lore heard the desperation in her own voice as she asked, "What is this about?"

"My one job for Wrath was to find you," he said without preamble. "He thinks you have the aegis, and he's going to do just about anything to get it back."

The black at the edge of her sight grew, and a prickle of numbness found her fingertips. It wasn't anything she didn't already expect, but the seed of fear her conversation with Iro had planted finally bloomed.

"Why?" Lore managed to say. "The Kadmides have it—"

"There's no point in lying to me." The new god turned toward her, and she couldn't tell if it was revulsion or pity that crossed his face. "You humiliated him. His entire bloodline knows the truth, even if they won't reveal it to the others. Aristos Kadmou, bested by a young girl. But it creates a problem for you, doesn't it?"

Lore shook her head, unable to speak.

"I did find you, you know," the Reveler said. "It was a hell of a thing—a total fluke in the end because I went looking for him, and he'd found you first."

"Who are you talking about?" Lore breathed. "Who found me?"

"Hermes," the Reveler said. "You know where he was those years he *disappeared*—you know, because he was with you."

286

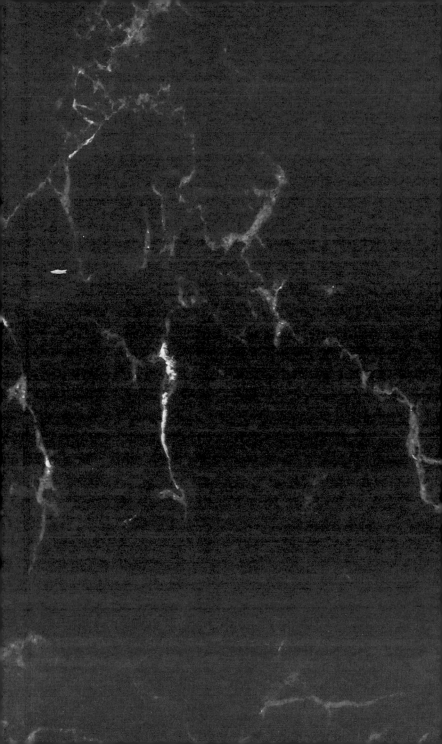

PART THREE

—

DEATHLESS

TWENTY NINE

Lore took a step back. "No. I never saw him. I didn't . . ."

"All of those years, he wasn't making plans for his own survival. He was protecting *you*," the Reveler said. "An idiotic move."

The Reveler looked at the fountain, the bloodied water.

"He picked such a pathetic form, but it worked on you, didn't it? That frail old man. Made you feel sorry for him. Made you want to help him."

"I . . ." Lore said. "No, he . . . no . . ."

"Did you really think some stranger would go to such great lengths to pay you back? Give you a fecking new home and sweet little life?" His tone turned mocking. "He protected that house, and you. No one could come inside unless they were invited. Took me days to work it out once I found that brownstone. That there was something—*someone*—there I couldn't see. He used his power to turn you invisible to all us gods. Clever Hermes. You're just a lucky little shit that no one else figured it out."

"That's impossible," Lore said, struggling to keep her voice steady. But Castor's words had already risen again in her memory. *I tried to find you for years, but it was like you vanished. There was no trace of you left.*

"Is it?" the Reveler cooed back. "Gods can fecking shroud themselves in mist and disappear from the sight of mortals and other celestials. He gave something to you, didn't he? Something you wore all the time that used his power to invoke the averting gods. 'Course, he would have enchanted it to make you feel inclined to keep it on, no matter what. He would have made your stupid little brain think it was your idea all along. That you *loved* it."

Lore's hand drifted up to her bare throat. *The feather necklace.*

Her head began to pound, hammering in time with her heartbeat.

"Its protection lasted until his death," the Reveler continued. "That's the only reason any of us, including your two godly friends, can see you now."

Lore curled her hands into fists to keep them from trembling. She shook her head, but her mind was already beginning to make the connections, to find the truth in his words. It couldn't have been a coincidence that the necklace's clasp had broken the night of Hermes's death . . .

"Even after I found the house, Hermes still wouldn't see me," the Reveler said. "Hermes wouldn't say a word to me, no matter how many times I came, no matter how hard I tried to convince him to come with me and serve Wrath. No matter how many times I swore on the River Styx I'd never betray him or his secret." He whirled on her. "And all because of you—a little piece of shit who should have been snuffed out with her family."

The Reveler drew up his hand, as if to grip her neck again, but left it hovering in the air.

With each heartbeat, the Frick began to disappear. Colors and light swirled around her, painting the image of her street, of the town house. Lore's head felt as heavy as if she'd drunk an entire bottle of wine.

"You . . ." Her lips had lost all feeling. "You're— That's not right—Gil—"

She saw Gil in the living room, switching on his creaky record player, pretending the broom was his dance partner as music filled the air. But as Lore came closer, she saw that the old man's feet were hovering over the floor.

"Gil?" The Reveler let out a wicked laugh. "Is that what he called himself?"

The image of Gil transformed before her. He grew taller, his arms and legs muscled, the skin soft with youth. A faint glow rose around him.

"I saw his disguise," the Reveler said, sounding far away. "No wonder you trusted him. It must have felt like a fecking fairy tale."

Lore felt herself start to double over as the tide of memories washed through her, all rinsed of their happy lies.

"No," she said. "You're lying—"

But . . .

What were the chances that Gil had lain in the street for hours that night and no one else had heard the attack or his cries for help? That he would have been violently mugged in a small, peaceful village? Even the doctor had been shocked that an attack had happened there.

Gil had never pressed Lore about her own injuries, then or years later. He never questioned her motives. He had welcomed her into his home. He had left her everything when he'd died . . .

When he'd died, just months before the start of the Agon.

Hermes would have known that he—that Gil—would vanish at the start of the week, brought to wherever the Agon would be held that cycle. That there was a chance he would die during the hunt, leaving Lore to wonder what happened to Gil.

Maybe the "death" of his disguise was a kindness, but it only made Lore angrier. He should have told her the truth. He should have revealed himself.

Lore thought she heard Castor call to her, but she couldn't bring herself to turn around. Her body wouldn't move.

It was a lie.

But so was this. The new Dionysus dealt in madness. In illusions.

"Stop it," Lore said, clutching her head. "I don't want to see this!"

The town house burned to black around her and the Frick returned, dull and flat compared to the vividness of the hallucination.

"Tell me," the Reveler began. "How much green velvet is in that town house? He always had the worst taste."

Lore pressed a hand to her mouth.

"All I wanted to tell him was why Wrath wanted the aegis, but he must have already known, otherwise why the hell would he bother to protect *you*?" the Reveler said. "I thought he might have brought the shield here—not for me to give to Wrath, but to destroy it. I don't understand why the idiot didn't just destroy it and be done with it and you!"

"Because I don't have it," Lore told him again. "None of this makes sense!"

"No, you little shit," he snarled quietly. "What makes *no sense* is why you've—"

A spray of blood slapped across Lore's face as the Reveler lurched forward, falling into the fountain. The stone darkened as it drank the fresh gore. Lore watched, stunned, as the arrow that had passed through the new god's throat rose to the surface of the water.

A heavy body fell over Lore's, knocking her to the ground as glass from the roof rained down over them. Castor was breathing heavily, each release of air stirring the loose strands of hair on her face. His hands felt her head, her neck, her chest for a wound.

"I'm okay—Cas, I'm—"

Another arrow ripped through the air, embedding in the tile beside her head.

Castor dragged them back through the columns surrounding the fountain, until they were out of the line of sight of whoever was firing through the domed roof. Out of the corner of her eye, she saw Miles run for the museum's entrance.

"Is it Artemis?" Lore gasped out, craning her neck up.

"Lionesses!" Athena shouted, flinging one of her knives from where she had taken shelter behind a column. The hunter shifted, avoiding the blade—but not the dory Athena threw. Her body fell into the museum, her serpent's mask cracking as she struck the marble.

Lore ignored the grip Castor had on her shoulder and leaned forward, just enough to see where one of the dome's larger panes had shattered. Two more figures in black emerged—one pointing to Athena. The other raised her bow again, this time toward Castor.

Castor threw up a blast of energy, crumbling the roof beneath the hunters' feet. The two lionesses fell, trained too well to scream, even as their bones broke over the debris.

A look of crushing guilt crossed his face, and he made as if to rush toward them. Lore pulled him back.

"I need to heal them," he said, yanking his arm free.

"They don't deserve that," Lore said, a terrible rage blooming in the words. "Let them die."

Castor stared at her, and she resented his shock. What did he expect?

"Guys," Miles shouted. "We need to *go*!"

With one last look at her, Castor extracted himself from her grip and shot across the courtyard toward the two lionesses. Lore would have gone after him if not for the low moan of agony that reached her first.

She spun around to find the Reveler's feet struggling for purchase against the slick tile as he tried in vain to pull himself out of the fountain.

They weren't trying to kill him. The thought electrified her. These were lionesses. They needed to incapacitate him, but keep him alive long enough for Wrath to finish him off.

Lore rushed toward him, calling out, "Castor!"

The new god turned at the sound of his name, releasing his hold on one of the lionesses. The glow around her faded.

"Fool!" Athena shouted to Lore. "Stop!"

"He's alive!" Lore said, gripping the Reveler by the shoulders and yanking him back onto the ground.

The Reveler's eyes were wild as his hand flopped against his blood-soaked skin, trying to press against the wound in his throat. Somehow, the arrow had missed the carotid artery. Lore covered his hand with her own, pressing harder to try to stanch the flow.

"Try to relax," Lore told him.

He shook his head, wild with pain. "It . . . must be . . . given . . . must give . . . it . . ."

"What are you trying to say?" Lore asked.

Athena pried Lore's hand away and replaced it with her own. The new god's skin had turned gray and clammy. All Lore now saw in his face was fear. Athena stared down at the Reveler, her expression remote.

"Cas!" Lore called again. The new god was within feet of them, but seemed to be moving in slow motion. She focused on the Reveler again, saying, "Hold on—just—"

A *crack* echoed through the stone columns as Athena clenched her hand and snapped his neck.

"Why did you do that?" Lore asked, choking on her shock.

The goddess rose, wiping her bloodied hand against the Reveler's sky-blue tunic. "He was beyond saving. Would you have the killer gain his power? Would you have taken it yourself?"

No, she wouldn't have.

"I could have saved him!" Castor said, furious.

"That fool was never going to help us," Athena said. "Better him dead by my merciful hand than by his enemy's."

"He didn't have to die at all!"

Footsteps pounded on the roof overhead. Lore spun, tracking them as they raced toward the corner of the building.

"There's another one?" Miles asked.

Lore's mind blazed with possibility. Maybe the lionesses hadn't been the ones to fire on the Reveler after all.

Maybe it had been Wrath himself.

Lore bolted for the entrance, ignoring Miles's startled cry as she knocked the baton out from the door handles.

She burst outside, her feet skidding against the sidewalk. A dark figure climbed down the wall from the roof. He dropped the last five feet of distance, landing hard on the patch of grass nearby.

It wasn't Wrath. The hunter turned, his serpent mask gleaming in the moonlight. He scaled the construction fence and dropped down onto Seventieth Street.

She followed.

"Lore!" Castor called. "Wait!"

She couldn't. Not anymore.

The hunter was a shadow against the darkness of early morning as he headed west, crossing Fifth Avenue and jumping the low stone fence that marked the boundary of Central Park.

Lore's hands scraped against the wall as she slid over it. The park was closed this late at night, but its streetlamps were still on. If the hunter thought he was going to lose her here, in her park of all places, he was about to be extremely disappointed.

"That's right," Lore murmured, "keep running."

She would follow him to the ends of the city, and he would take her to wherever Wrath was hiding.

Gil . . .

No, this was good. She would keep her gaze ahead now, and she wouldn't look back. If she didn't acknowledge the pain, it would leave her, just like everything else. It would. Her anger would be useful for once. It would keep her going.

Not lost, she thought. *But never free.*

It wasn't just anger that Lore felt, but humiliation—all this time, she'd believed that she existed outside the reach of the gods, that she was finally in command of her life.

None of it was real.

Not the love she'd felt from Gil, not the hope, or even the good days. Lore hadn't wanted to change a single thing about the town house or move a single object. She'd felt like she owed it to Gil to preserve his memory, but all she'd done was create another shrine for a god.

He must have laughed at her every single day.

Building a new life, a better life, Gil had told her, *will keep you looking forward, until, one day, you'll find you're no longer tempted to keep turning back toward everything you've lost.*

Hermes. *Hermes* had told her that. And for what? To see if she would eventually give him the aegis?

298

For the first time in seven years, the thought of the shield didn't send her body into lockdown the way it usually did. She could almost imagine herself holding it—how the leather strap would feel tight against her arm, the purr of its suppressed power stroking her senses . . .

She could get it. She could take back what was meant to be hers. If the Agon wouldn't let her go, she would beat them at their own game and break them before they ever broke her again.

Lore would send Wrath and all the others a message they couldn't ignore.

Where are you going, little snake? she wondered, watching him race through the trees of the empty park. *What hole are you slithering back to?*

Lore had her answer soon enough.

The hunter had stayed away from the park's established paths, preferring to keep to the grassy hills and weave through playgrounds and statues. Now he slowed as he approached the fence that edged the Mall.

The broad walkway was lined with park benches and dark elm trees. She hung back, but he had already stopped at the center of the path. Waiting for her.

The hunter lifted his mask.

"Come on, Melora," Belen Kadmou said. "Come out and play."

THIRTY

ADRENALINE, HOT AND SWEET, SURGED THROUGH HER.

Belen had all the same markers of arrogance as his father. The easy, unafraid posture. The smug smile of someone who had never been knocked off a throne. Even as a bastard, Belen had been afforded some measure of respect as Aristos Kadmou's only child.

More respect than Lore had ever been given as girl.

Belen tossed his crossbow aside, but pulled out a long knife from the sheath strapped to his inner arm. Lore gripped her own knife, taking quick stock of him. Lore was tall, but he was just that little bit taller. Fighting with small blades would give him an advantage. He would have the longer reach.

But she had more fury. Belen was a gift. There would be no better way to send Wrath a message than leaving the young man's body for him to find in the park.

Lore stepped out from the shadows. "Don't mind if I do, you over-dramatic asshole."

"Is that how you want to greet your old pal after all this time?" he crooned.

"The last time I saw you, you were sitting at your father's feet like an obedient puppy," Lore said, giving him a quick look up and down. "Seems like nothing's changed."

"You've always talked too much for a woman," he said, watching her jump down over the low fence.

"Ironic, given that this is the first time I've actually heard you speak for yourself," she said. "Did Daddy loosen the leash?"

"He is my lord and father," Belen said. "An unfamiliar concept to you, I realize, as you have neither."

Lore let the insult go as she began to circle him. "How will your *lord and father* react to knowing that you didn't manage to kill any of the three gods who were in that museum?"

"I wasn't aiming for the Reveler." His gaze bored into her. "I was there for you."

She tried not to let her shock slip into her expression. "I'm flattered."

"He wants it back, Melora," Belen said. "He won't stop until he has it again."

"I don't have whatever *it* is," Lore told him, drawing closer as she circled him again. "You're wasting your time."

"I told him as much," Belen said, holding out his knife. "That you would have used it if it were still in your possession, or given it to the gods you're hiding behind."

"And yet here we are," Lore said. "Seems he doesn't care much about what you think."

Belen's expression darkened. "You are a distraction. *It* is a distraction. All I need to do is blame it on the gray-eyed bitch. She's loyal to no one but herself. And once you're dead, it disappears forever, and he can focus on what he should be doing."

"Which is?" Lore asked.

Belen only smiled, then lunged.

Lore blocked his jab with her free arm, dropping onto a knee

301

and spinning away before he could lock her into a vulnerable, bent-forward position. She righted herself again, keeping her own weapon moving to avoid letting him get too close.

He'd have another blade slipped into the top of his black boots, and likely another strapped to his back or other hip, but both were hidden by his hunter's robe. She drew a breath, trying to settle the rapid rise of her pulse. The problem with knife fighting was that so much of it was grappling. There was no way to escape unscathed.

But Lore had never been afraid of getting cut.

"I don't know how you slipped away the first time, but it won't happen again," he said. "I heard they took the little girls' eyes first, but kept them alive long enough to hear their parents die, just so they'd know that no one would be coming to save them."

Lore surged toward him, slashing, forcing him to keep one hand high to protect his neck and chest. Her mind disconnected from her body, and all she was left with was the deep well of raw pain that had simmered inside her for years.

Artery, she thought viciously, and lunged for his leg.

It was a stupid mistake, a clumsy one. She knew it, even as her body wouldn't listen, and kept attacking. Belen caught her arm and slammed it against his thigh, sending her blade flying through the air. Lore dove for it, but Belen tackled her with a guttural cry. He dug his knees and full weight into her lower back until she thought he would break her pelvis.

Lore bucked, kicking and screaming. She stretched her arm toward the knife. It glinted like a claw, just beyond her fingertips.

Belen's weight lifted just enough for him to turn her over roughly. His chest was heaving, blood running down his arms from where she'd brutalized him. They rolled over and over, grass sticking to her face and arms as Lore grappled, struggling to pin him down. She took a chance, reaching down toward his boot to feel for a hidden knife, and found one. Gripping the hilt, she slashed it across his forehead.

He released a choked cry—it wasn't a deep cut, but it sent a curtain of blood down into his eyes. The distraction gave her enough time to grip his wrist and fingers, breaking his hold on his own knife. She jammed it into his left calf muscle. This time, Lore was satisfied to hear him scream.

With a burst of strength, she flipped their positions, trapping him beneath her. Belen tried to twist enough to throw her off, but Lore had locked her legs around him and tightened their pressure on his arms. His spit flew like a rabid dog's. Lore lifted the knife again, watching the rapid rise and fall of his chest, where his heart would be beating beneath the armor, skin, and bone.

Lore would have driven the blade in, if it hadn't been for that whisper of logic that slipped through the more animal part of her brain.

Killing him won't be enough.

It wouldn't. Wrath deserved to know the pain of losing family again, but killing Belen would do nothing but bring Belen glory. Kleos came through battle, and there was no greater kleos than for those who died bravely.

There was another message she could send his father. A better one.

"You ever heard the one about Phaethon?" she asked, leaning close to his snapping teeth. Blood covered his face like a second mask. "How he was desperate to prove his divine parentage—so desperate that he demanded to drive his father Helios's chariot across the sky?"

"Shut up, bitch," Belen growled. "*Shut up*—"

"He was warned he wouldn't be able to control the chariot's wild

303

horses, but his hubris demanded he be able to try," Lore continued. "Do you know what happened to him?"

Belen hissed, trying again to rock her off him through the brute force of his body.

"He couldn't control them. The horses climbed too high. The earth began to grow cold as the sun god's chariot grew too distant," Lore said. "Zeus had to strike him down with a lightning bolt. He paid the price for his desperation and pride with his life."

Lore released some of the pressure around his arms; she let him think she had slipped up, that he had an opportunity. Belen's hands rose with a tremendous scream from his chest, reaching for her—to shove her, to strangle her, she didn't know. Half-blinded by his own blood, he didn't see the angle of her blade until it had sliced off both of his thumbs.

Belen howled in pain and rage.

"You may live," Lore sneered. "But good luck holding a blade."

She had cut him with a knife, but her true weapon had been the Agon itself—all its cruel realities that men like him and his father relished inflicting on others. Now he would know them himself.

Belen would never gain kleos, not from this Agon, and likely not from any other. Maybe one day they could fit him with prosthetics and he would be back in the hunt, but he would always carry the scars of losing to her. He would know what it meant to be followed by whispers. *Beaten by the Perseous girl, the last of her name. Beaten by a gutter rat who should have died years ago. Beaten.*

She had written his story for him.

"Lore!"

Castor stood a short distance away, his face pale with shock.

She pushed away from Belen, rising to her feet. Her chest tightened

304

at the way Castor was looking at her. He brought the world into sharper focus: the brightening sky as the hours tilted toward morning; the blood on her hands, arms, and jeans; the breath flaring in and out her.

Lore saw herself through Castor's eyes, how she must have looked half-wild to him. As if she were a monster.

Something in her stirred, angry and frightened.

A branch snapped and she turned back toward Belen. He was crawling, struggling to his feet. He choked on every breath, hugging his arms in tight to his chest, his hands still gushing blood.

Castor started after him, but Lore stepped in front of him. He took stock of the cuts on her arms, half of which she hadn't noticed or felt, and reached out to heal her. Lore resisted, not wanting to be touched just then, or to feel anything gentle.

"Where are the others?" she asked.

"Going back to the house. Lore, what did the Reveler say to you?" Castor asked. "What could have caused . . . *this*?"

His words rankled her. "*This*? You mean actually doing something?"

"Lore," he began again, with a new intensity to his expression. "What happened? What's going on?"

Lore said nothing. He moved to get around her, only for her to block him again.

"Was that Belen Kadmou?" he asked her. "Why did you let him get away?"

Lore shifted, blocking his path for the third time.

Castor's expression turned from shock to anger then, in a way she'd never seen. "We could have interrogated him. Why did you let him go?"

"He'll make a better message than a body," Lore said.

Castor shook his head, releasing a sound of frustration. "Except you're not just risking yourself by enraging Wrath," he told her plainly. "You're risking all of us, including Miles."

The trilling was back in her mind, turning the air to static in her ears. Her pulse jumped as the edges of her vision darkened. *Miles* . . .

She hadn't even thought of Miles.

"What did the Reveler say to you?" Castor asked. "What made you so angry that you'd do this after everything you told me earlier? This isn't who you are!"

"Maybe it is," she shot back.

"No," Castor said. "You are a good person, Melora Perseous. You're not what they tried to make you, or even what you tried to be for them. Neither of us is."

"We are *exactly* what they made us," Lore said, not caring that her voice had cracked, that the words were trembling with long-held pain. "We're monsters, Cas, not saints. And, no, killing Wrath won't change what happened, but it's the only thing I know how to do. It's the only thing any of us were taught to do."

Her hands turned to claws against his chest, but his grip on her wrists remained light, as if daring her. The heat of him burned away the cool air and the smell of the grass. He blotted out the rest of the world. He created his own eclipse.

"I want Wrath to suffer," she whispered. "I want him afraid, and I want to be the one that steals the life from his body."

"We'll find other ways to deal with him," Castor said softly. "Better ways. Don't let them take that hope from you."

Castor drew closer. This time Lore did step back. That seemed to alarm him more than anything else. He pulled away, giving her distance when Lore didn't want that—when Lore wasn't sure what she wanted.

He closed his eyes. "Lore—"

The way he said her name . . .

The storm broke open inside her. Lore struck at him with her arm and he blocked, as she knew he would, leaving his center open, the way he always did.

Anger became confusion became instinct became need—she gripped his face and pulled him down to bring his lips to hers.

Castor went still as stone, his lips parting. He didn't pull away. Neither did she. Her fingers slid into his thick hair, curling. "Lore—"

She wanted him to keep saying her name that way, like it was the only word he knew.

She was clumsy and raw and wild, but so was he. His hands covered her, the same hands that had helped her up from the ground countless times. The same hands that had lifted her up to reach higher as she climbed. The same hands she'd held as he lay dying.

Lore didn't want to think. She wanted to disappear into the sensation of him. Lightning wove down her spine as he groaned.

Castor overwhelmed her until there was nothing else in the world but his lips and touch. The heat inside her rose, absorbing the feeling of his skin and turning her body soft against the hard lines of his own. His tongue stroked against hers and he drew her closer, until she felt his blatant need for her, and a heaviness settled low in her stomach in response.

In the years they'd trained together, Lore had come to know his body as well as her own. But every part of him felt like a revelation to her now, something she needed but hadn't known to want. They were back to sparring, trying to gain control, to drive the kiss.

"Lore," he murmured. "Lore—"

Castor pulled back so suddenly it left her unsteady on her feet.

Lore was still reaching for him, disoriented and desperate, when he held up a hand to stop her. There was something almost heart-breaking in the way he looked at her then.

"Do that again when you mean it, Golden," he rasped. "When it's not to distract me."

He didn't wait for her response; he set off, searching for Belen. Lore tried to catch her breath, dragging her hands back through her hair and gripping it.

"Shit—" she breathed. "*Shit.*"

She ran after him.

Belen had crossed down and out of the park and was heading into midtown. He was moving faster than she expected—then again, the body could do amazing things under the influence of adrenaline.

Lore and Castor followed the trail of Belen's blood to Fifth Avenue, eerily empty without tourists shopping and a crush of New Yorkers trying to get into office buildings.

She carefully avoided looking at Castor as they ran, too confused, too flushed with stinging embarrassment and longing at what she—they—had done. It felt like she had broken a bone and it hadn't been reset in the right way. For a moment, she was terrified that it would feel that way between them forever. That she had done something that could never be taken back.

Belen was a good four blocks ahead, but still staggering. His phone lit in his hands as he struggled to hold on to it.

Castor clenched a fist until it glowed with power. He raised it, as if to send a blast of it toward the hunter, but stopped. The crackling light faded as he eased his grip.

"What's wrong?" Lore asked, hesitating behind him.

"He's too far," Castor said. "And I—I can't be sure I wouldn't blow out the block."

He was right to worry. As they approached Rockefeller Center, several people were already heading into work, or out of it after late shifts. The massive bronze statue of Atlas, struggling with the weight of the world on his shoulders, watched them come and go.

There was a faint whirring like bees nearby. Lore turned, spotting Belen standing directly across the street.

"Hey, Melora," he called, his voice ragged. "You ever heard of the one about the Stymphalian birds?"

A drone dropped down in front of them, feathers etched into its silver wings. A small arm dropped from beneath it and released something—a device, a streak of silver—

The air around Lore roared, exploding into a wave of pressure and heat that devoured everything in its path and dissolved the ground beneath her feet.

Lore jumped in front of Castor. The blast slammed into her and she was flying, falling, down into the raging light.

THIRTY ONE

Somewhere, just beyond the high whine ringing in her ears, Lore heard a sound like the rushing of sand. With her next breath, she realized she was still alive, and that her back was burning.

Lore reared up with a gasp, her back slamming into the wall of flames hovering above her. Sparks of color and light burst in her vision.

The explosion . . .

"Lore," came the strained voice above her. "It's—all right—"

Pain flared in her, coming alive with her mind. Her palms were skinned raw, and her jeans and shirt shredded. There was a dull ache throughout her body, but it was nothing compared to her skull, which pounded like it had been cracked open.

"What . . . ?" Her mouth was coated in dust and ash. Lore coughed, struggling to remain upright, to escape the heat billowing behind her. She couldn't understand what she was seeing.

Heaps of dark asphalt, the mangled yellow remains of a taxi, and blocks of concrete had fallen in a ring of destruction around her. The chaos was just outside a circle of intense, crackling light that surrounded her like a protective barrier.

Lore craned her head back. She knew this power.

"Cas?" she choked out.

Castor stood hunched over her, his arms up, his palms outstretched. Above him, trying to drive down through the new god's barrier, was a massive slab of concrete.

It bobbed in the air, riding the blasting heat and light. It was the source of the sound she had heard before, not rushing sand. The concrete was being incinerated to a fine dust. It poured down along the edges of the barrier and piled up around it.

"Don't. Move," Castor got out between gritted teeth.

The tendons in his neck bulged with the effort of keeping his power stable. As the concrete burned away, patches of morning sky and smoke were revealed just beyond Castor's broad shoulders. His body was taut with strain, as if he truly held the whole of the heavens on his back.

Sweat dripped from his chin, and Lore realized her own body was drenched with it.

The word whispered through her. *God.*

Lore stared up at him, her thoughts in chaos. He met her gaze for a second, the embers of his power brighter than she'd ever seen them, then squeezed them shut, turning his face away.

"Stay. Close."

The burning ring of light shrank closer to her, flickering like a flame on the verge of going out.

Lore turned so she faced him and drew close enough to rest her cheek against his shoulder and wrap her arms around him.

Belen.

They shouldn't have gone after him.

"All of those people—" she began, choking on the words.

The explosion flared in her mind again, searing with terrible detail. The bystanders who slowed to stare at the drone. The ground

311

erupting like a wound. Shattering glass. The bellow of metal being tortured and bent.

Castor shook his head. "Tried—"

The light quivered around them again, sweeping in closer.

"Are you okay?" she asked. "Are you hurt?"

"Fine," he promised, turning to rest his cheek against the top of her head.

Lore forced herself to breathe in and out, hoping to steady her heart. Or was it his she felt now, beating hard and steady for the both of them?

Alive. Somehow, he'd— Lore tried to imagine it, how he'd crossed that distance and shielded her, not just from the blast, but the fall as well. She pictured it a dozen ways, but each made less sense than the one before it.

The sand kept slithering down the light barrier. A faraway siren wailed. Lore fixated on the familiar sound, using it to ground herself back in the moment. They needed to get out of there before any emergency services arrived.

That fear, at least, was a tool. Lore turned it into her ballast as the terror finally released its grip on her mind.

"Can't." Castor sounded pained. *"Please."*

The last few feet of the cement block broke in half over their heads, slamming into the debris around them. The protective barrier vanished like a breath in the air.

Castor slumped forward, his arms wrapping around her, burying his face in her hair. Lore swayed, absorbing the enormous weight of him.

"Can't," he began weakly.

"Cas?" she said, her throat aching. When he didn't respond, she gave him a hard shake. *"Cas!"*

Her knees buckled, but Lore fought it, searching for a way out of the crevasse and back up onto whatever remained of the street.

"Don't make me drag you, big guy," she said hoarsely.

Lore tried to shake him again, but he was gone. For a terrifying moment, she was worried that the power she'd been so in awe of had burned out his mortal body.

Castor's weight was impossible, but Lore didn't have a choice. She pulled him toward the left, where there was a more obvious, if unsteady, way up and out through the collapsed rubble.

Now and then, the loose cement and ash shifted, but Lore's footing was steady, and her grip on Castor didn't waver. She struggled, dragging and pushing and lifting him until her whole body shook and the edge of the crater came within reach.

Lore looked up.

Athena stood a dozen feet away. Her arms were raised above her head, bearing the weight of a massive piece of a nearby building's stone facade. It hovered over those carrying the victims and the injured away from the site of the explosion. If anyone noticed the massive display of power, they were too grateful to be alive to fixate on it.

The dead littered the street and sidewalk around them, some blown into grotesque shapes, others stretched out in pools of their own blood. It had become a battlefield. Ash and cement dust clouded the air, swirling in mourning patterns before settling over the bodies like funeral shrouds.

Athena waited until the last of the wounded was removed before she lowered her arms, releasing the smoldering debris onto the sidewalk with steadfast care.

Defender of cities. Something uncomfortable stirred in Lore at the thought, and she shoved it away before it could fully take form.

Lore braced herself for the goddess's fury, to be told how selfish it had been to risk both of their lives. Instead, as she passed through the wall of smoke to reach them, Athena looked at her with those gray, knowing eyes.

"I will carry him," Athena said. "Let us leave this place."

Behind her, a tide of uniformed officers and firefighters arrived and fought their way toward the victims and wreckage. Those who had survived fled in pure, primal panic. The dust and powdered debris had painted them pale as ghosts.

Athena lifted Castor onto her shoulder with ease, and they took off at as much of a run as Lore could manage, narrowly avoiding the barriers being set up around the building complex.

"Miles?" Lore gasped out.

"He returned to the house," Athena told her.

Lore nodded, trying to swallow the bile and ash at the back of her throat.

"Tell me what has happened," Athena said urgently. "Who was it you pursued?"

Lore relayed the story, her voice halting. She had braced herself for the goddess's disapproval and fury at the actions Castor had clearly seen as reckless. Instead, Athena gave her a nod.

"What you have done was necessary," she said. "While it will make the false Ares angry, it will also make him impulsive, and that, Melora, we can use to our advantage."

"Castor thinks all I've done is put a bigger target on everyone's backs," Lore said, glancing to him.

"Then it may be time for us to part ways with the others," Athena said. "They will not understand what must be done now. I see that you blame yourself for what has happened, but is it not the false Apollo

314

who shoulders the blame? You were not the one who wished to follow Belen Kadmou."

"It's—" Lore had to draw another breath, her chest was so tight at the thought. She could have fought harder to change Castor's mind. She *should* have.

What had happened had been the result of a cataclysmic series of choices, and she couldn't deny the role she'd played in it.

"And the false Dionysus?" Athena ventured. "What was it he could only tell you?"

All of her thoughts were too frayed, and her head was still pounding. Lore didn't trust herself not to let the truth slip. "Later. I promise."

The goddess gave her a curt nod, turning her attention back toward the street.

"I'm sorry for what I said earlier," Lore said. "About you not caring. Thank you for helping those people."

Athena might have hated the mortals who had rejected her, but she hadn't relinquished her sacred role. Pallas Athena, the dread defender of cities.

"I shall always do what must be done," Athena said. "Yet the question remains—will you?"

Don't let them pull you back in, Castor had warned her. *There's nothing but shadows for you here now.*

But he didn't understand what Lore finally did. Monsters lived in the shadows. To hunt them, you couldn't be afraid to follow. And the only way to destroy them was to have the sharper teeth and the darker heart.

THIRTY TWO

I<small>T WAS WELL PAST SUNRISE BY THE TIME THEY REACHED THE TOWN</small> house. With the crush of emergency vehicles around midtown right at the start of the morning commute, traffic became too unmanageable to try to take a taxi or call for a car.

Lore could only imagine how they looked to everyone they passed by on the street, especially with Athena carrying Castor, but she didn't care. She couldn't even think about how they might be tracked, or who might be following them.

Despite the need to get inside and out of sight again quickly, Lore's feet dragged as they turned onto her block, and all but came to a stop as her home for the last three years emerged through the morning haze.

Looking at it now, its old brownstone, the potted plants lining the steps, the lace curtains peeking through the window—all she felt was revulsion. It suddenly reminded her of the false temple at Thetis House: an illusion made up of static and lies. All the memories she had there were tainted, and for a moment, Lore couldn't handle the thought of stepping through the front door.

She didn't fight her anger this time. She let it speak to her.

Use the house. Use it the way he tried to use you.

"What is the matter?" Athena asked her.

Lore shook her head. "Nothing. Let's get inside."

Van met them at the front door, ushering them inside with a concerned look. "Is he all right?"

Lore nodded. Hoped. Then she noticed who wasn't there. "Miles?"

Van sighed. "His internship boss wanted him to go downtown to City Hall to take a shift helping out with media requests and briefings about the attack. He said he'd be back in a few hours."

The TV was on but muted, flashing with reports about the explosion at Rockefeller Center. But it was the screen of Van's laptop that caught Lore's eye from where it faced them on the coffee table. It was playing through a series of videos; every few seconds the view would jump to a different angle. Some shots were clear, others were fuzzier, but they were all tracking a single figure as he made his way across streets.

Miles.

"What the hell is that?" Lore demanded.

With obvious reluctance, Van turned toward his computer, then back to her. His shoulders slumped as he shut the laptop and picked it up. "Let's . . . let's get Cas upstairs. I'll explain."

Athena did as he asked, carefully navigating the hall without knocking Castor into the walls the way Lore knew she wanted to. She set him down on Lore's bed, leaving Lore to arrange his heavy limbs into a more comfortable position. His long legs hung off the end of her bed.

"The program is called Argos," Van said, placing the laptop on her dresser. "I've spent years coding it. It was meant to be used to search for gods and enemies through its built-in facial recognition—it can tap into any live security camera footage as long as the camera or its backup system is hooked into the internet."

Athena leaned toward the screen, watching the small image of Miles on a subway platform, and tried poking it with her finger. Van slid it back before she could accidentally crack the screen, earning a withering look from her.

"You're telling me," Lore began, trying not to lose her grip on her last thread of patience, "that we wasted all that time going in circles about where the Reveler was, and you could have just used this system to search for him? Any other secret programs you want to belatedly reveal?"

"It's not perfect," Van said. "I have to upload a photo for it to work, and the one I had of the Reveler in his mortal form wasn't clear enough—and before you ask, I've already tried searching for Wrath. If he's getting around the city, he's wearing a mask. The system can't find him."

Lore drew in a steadying breath. "What is the news saying about the attack?"

"Not much, other than that it's suspected terrorist activity," Van said. "Now would be an excellent time to tell me what *did* happen, because all the chatter among the Messengers is that the Reveler is dead and the surveillance footage near the museum, the park, and Rockefeller Center was wiped."

Of course. Lore had no doubt that the Kadmides had gotten into any footage in Central Park and deleted that as well. She tried to tell him about what had happened at the Frick, about Belen, about the explosion, but it was like her mind couldn't put the thoughts into words.

"I will tell you the tale of these last hours, Evander," Athena said.

Lore shot her a grateful look. "I'll take care of Castor."

The goddess nodded. "As well as yourself. Rest for now."

She waited until Athena's heavy steps pounded out a steady rhythm on the stairs before she ventured into the hall bathroom. Lore braced her hands against the sink, staring at the black soot and bloody scabs caked onto them. Then, when she felt brave enough, she looked at herself in the mirror.

Her hair was wild and covered in pale dust. Her skin had lost most of its color and her eyes were bloodshot and rimmed with bruises, as if she'd fought the night itself with fists and lost. She was surprised no one they'd passed had tried calling emergency services on them, because Lore had never looked more frightening in her life.

Or more like a hunter.

She quickly washed her face, dampening her brush to work through the tangle of her wavy hair before braiding it back. It took a few minutes to clean and disinfect the cuts on her arm, and to wrap the deeper ones with bandages. Knowing the towels she'd used were beyond help, she threw them away and set about wetting new ones to tend to Castor.

Her room smelled of the rancid smoke that radiated off both of them. She stood there a moment, looking down at Castor, at the way his big body overwhelmed the bedframe. Despite the bold lines of his face and his square jaw, he seemed almost boyish to her then. Vulnerable.

Lore brought one of the washcloths to his arms and legs. The cuts there were already healing thanks to his power, but he was covered in grime. She worked slowly, methodically, letting her thoughts unwind and slip away so she wouldn't have to face them. Feet. Legs. Hands. Arms.

She had done this countless times at Thetis House after sparring, when it had been nothing more than taking care of her friend and hetaîros. But as she moved to clean his neck and face, Lore felt suddenly untethered at the realization that it wasn't the same as it had been back then.

Her hand shook as she drew the cloth over and around his lips, struggling with the flush of heat that wound through her. She was angry at herself for kissing him—for crossing a line, for upsetting him, for changing everything.

"Don't hate me," she whispered. "Please don't hate me . . ."

When she'd finished, and Castor looked like himself again, Lore slumped down beside the bed, leaning back and drawing her knees to her chest. She let her head fall against the mattress and closed her eyes. Athena's voice found her there, echoing a warning.

They will not understand what must be done now.

When Lore opened her eyes again, the light in the room had changed, deepening to the violet of early evening.

She was disoriented for a moment, trying to remember how she had gotten there and why her body was so stiff. There was a warm weight resting lightly on her shoulder. Castor's hand had slipped down from the bed, as if needing reassurance, even locked in a deep sleep, that she was still there.

Lore gripped it, pressing it against her forehead as she tried to clear the lingering sleep from her mind.

Her thumb stroked along his knuckles, and she felt—she wasn't sure what she felt. Before, she'd been so convinced the feelings moving through her, an almost painful fusion of tenderness and longing and protectiveness, had been different from what had existed between them as children. But were they really? Or had absence and time simply drawn them out in a way she could finally understand?

She had had her family. Her bloodline. Her name. Lore had borne the weight of those responsibilities from the moment she first learned the word *Agon*. Castor, though—Castor had always been different. It felt as if he had been given to her by the gods, and she to him.

And now I'll lose him to the same gods, she thought, her throat tight. Whether he died or won the Agon, the outcome would be no different. He would never be with her like this again. She would never feel the pulse at his wrist, or press her ear to his heart and hear it echo her own.

Her grip on him tightened. Castor let out a soft, reassuring noise in his sleep, and she thought her heart might shatter as he turned to her, lashes dark against his cheeks. Lore forced herself to stand then, to gently drape his arm to rest against his chest, because the only other option was to give in to the need to sob like a child and beg the gods for a mercy she knew she didn't deserve.

Quietly, Lore gathered clean clothes and changed in the bathroom. There, she heard the front door open and shut and Miles's faint voice call out, "Hello?"

She started down the stairs, eager to see him, more than a little desperate to make sure he was all right, but slowed as she caught the sound of kitchen cabinets opening and shutting and the beginning of a quiet conversation.

"—into any problems?" Van asked.

"Would you care if I did?" Miles shot back. Then, a beat later, "Sorry. That was rude. Subway service was screwed up, but otherwise everything was okay. But Lore and the others—?"

"Just resting."

Lore inched down the last few steps, careful to avoid the one that squeaked. She edged into the hallway that led to the kitchen. There, she could see the two of them reflected in the kitchen window. Van at the table on his computer, Miles at the stove.

"Want anything?" Miles asked. "I'm making a cup of regular tea, but I can also attempt the weird one Lore made."

"Nektar? No thanks. I've always hated the taste of it," Van said, not looking up from his computer. Lore heard the clattering of his fingers over the keyboard. "I could use a warm glass of milk, though."

There was a long stretch of silence. The typing finally stopped.

"What?" Van asked.

"A warm glass of milk," Miles said, amused. "Okay. Coming right up, grandpa."

Van snorted, but turned back to whatever it was he was working on. Behind Lore, in the living room, the TV was on, but the volume was at a low murmur. She focused on the sound of it, on the breath that eased in and out of her chest.

After a few minutes, just as Lore was tempted to announce herself, Miles set the two mugs down on the table and opened his own laptop. Knowing him, Miles picked the seat right next to Van just to playfully annoy him, but Van couldn't resist trying to steal a look at Miles's screen.

"Can I help you?" Miles said, moving it away.

"Are you . . . are you searching *Greek mythology* on Wikipedia?" Van asked in disbelief.

"What?" Miles said defensively. "I'm a little behind the curve in this group. The last mythology unit I had was in sixth grade."

"You could just ask me whatever you want to know," Van said.

"Oh really?" Miles asked, leaning back to sip his tea. "I can ask you anything and you'll actually give me an answer?"

"I didn't mean *anything*," Van said, uncharacteristically flustered. "I meant anything related to the Agon."

"Okay, here's one," Miles said. "A good number of hunters from

322

your bloodline abandoned Castor, so why are you so loyal to him?"

Lore about fell over when Van actually told him.

"Castor is the only . . ." Van seemed to struggle for the right words. "He's the only friend I've ever had. The only one willing to be my friend, all right?"

"All right," Miles said softly.

"No—" Van said. "Don't do that. Don't feel sorry for me. It's just the way it was. Unlike everyone else, he never looked down at me for not wanting to fight, and for being relatively bad at it. He didn't—still doesn't—like fighting either."

"I was going to try to draw an analogy to me in PE, but I'm going to rescind that," Miles said. "Given that your physical education involved learning how to murder people."

That got a soft laugh out of Van. "I know you think I'm being . . . hard. But all I care about is protecting him and making sure he stays alive this week. I couldn't help him before, when he relapsed and his cancer came back. I couldn't convince him to stop going to training when we spoke on the phone, even though it was exhausting him."

"Why did he stay in training if it was that bad?"

"Because of *Lore*," Van said. "He didn't want to let her down, because she would have lost her training partner and had to leave the program. But more than that, he always wanted to see her. He always wanted to follow her, even if it was right into trouble."

"Hey now," Miles said. Lore's heart swelled at the edge of warning in his voice. "That's my friend you're talking about."

Van blew out a long breath. "I was always a little jealous of how much attention she got from Castor. It sounds stupid now that we're grown . . ."

"Oh," Miles said. "So you're in love with him."

Van choked on his milk.

Miles rested his chin on his palm and waited, eyebrows raised expectantly.

"It's not like that with Cas," Van said.

"As if you'd be the first guy with a secret, unrequited crush," Miles said. "Mine was a high school quarterback who was so painfully straight he was practically a pencil. Well, a pencil with bulging muscles and the tendency to answer anything anyone ever said to him with *dude*."

Van laughed. Miles grinned.

"I don't have those feelings for him," Van said, finally. "I never have."

Miles let out a soft, knowing hum. Van took a sip of his milk. Miles did the same with his tea.

"And anyway, why are *you* so loyal to Lore?" Van pressed. "You barely knew anything about her past, and what little you did know was a lie."

"Not all of it," Miles said. "I always knew her family had died, but none of the details about how, or what happened to her in the years after. It took a long time for her to open up to me at all. Like . . . months after Gil let me rent the spare room. I had to dig little by little, and it was worth it, because I love the soft heart I found under the somewhat surly surface. *That* part was never a lie. It's really rare to find someone who accepts you completely, and I try to give that back to her."

"So you do understand," Van said quietly.

Miles nodded. "I know you think I'm being a reckless idiot—"

"I don't think you're—"

Miles didn't let him finish. "And maybe I am. But I'm in this for her."

Lore leaned back against the wall, closing her eyes.

"That was a good speech," Van said, a smile in his voice.

"Thank you," Miles said, sipping his tea. "I thought you might like it. Everything is life and death and epic stakes with you people. I need to get on your level."

"It would be a far better world," Van said, "if we all got on yours."

The sounds from the TV changed, becoming louder and more pronounced as it trumpeted out the breaking-news-alert tone. A moment later, Miles's and Van's phones vibrated and chimed.

Lore went straight for the living room, scooping the television remote off the coffee table. There were footsteps on the stairs—Castor coming down, and Athena coming up from the basement.

The local news channel flickered on. This time, instead of being posted at the security perimeter around Rockefeller Center, a familiar-looking reporter—this one a middle-aged white man—stood in front of a gorgeous stone building. People milled around him, crying or visibly stunned. Their faces flashed red-blue-red-blue with the lights of a nearby police car. Smoke wove out through the dark air like silver snakes.

Lore leaned closer. The chyron streamed with words that stopped the blood in her veins.

The bodies of two children discovered inside vandalized Charging Bull statue . . .

Miles sank onto the couch slowly, his hand pressed against his mouth as the newscaster spoke, clearly distraught, *"Police made the gruesome discovery when witnesses called nine-one-one after noticing first smoke and then fire beneath the statue. It—it appears that the statue, which is hollow, had a panel cut out of it so that the bodies could be sealed inside. There are several unconfirmed reports by other eye-witnesses that*

325

they heard screaming once the fires began, but the NYPD has not yet determined if these children were alive or dead when they were placed in the statue."

Castor hung back, his face turned so he wouldn't have to watch. But Lore refused to look away. She already knew that, whoever the children were—Blooded or Unblooded—they were two little girls.

"Oh God," Miles said. "They're just . . . they're just kids."

Lore had known Wrath would retaliate for what she did to Belen, but she had made the mistake of assuming he would strike back at her physically. Directly. Not emotionally. Not like this.

She wouldn't make the same mistake again.

Athena moved closer to the television, studying the images flashing across the screen. The sight of her blurred in Lore's vision, and the newscaster's voice disappeared beneath the pounding in her ears. Her whole body flamed with rage.

Miles might not have recognized it, but every other living soul in that room knew that Wrath and the Kadmides had turned the famous statue near Wall Street into a brazen bull—an unspeakably evil torture device from the old country that roasted its victims alive in the belly of a bronze bull.

"Police have erected tents around the crime scene, but an eyewitness gave us this exclusive photo taken moments before they arrived," the newscaster said. *"Please be advised that this image will be upsetting, and that the NYPD has asked us to blur a message left by the perpetrator until they've gathered more information."*

The screen shifted, showing the statue surrounded by embers and smoke. There were several people rushing around with fire extinguishers, but one woman had stopped to read something written on the wall closest to the bull.

Lore turned to ask Van if he could tap into a camera, only to find him one step ahead, passing a fresh mug of warm milk to Miles with one hand, and his laptop balanced, program searching, in the other.

Miles looked up in surprise, taking the mug from him.

"It'll help," Van said. His hand touched Miles's shoulder, but he moved away quickly, before Miles seemed to notice the touch.

"I know it's not a game," Miles said. "I *know* that. But why would they do . . . *this*?"

Lore bit the inside of her mouth hard enough to taste blood.

Van's fingers trailed over the trackpad, rewinding whatever footage he'd just seen.

"What?" Lore asked. "What is it?"

Van turned the screen around and pressed Play. The night-vision footage was grainy and shot from a high angle. Its green tint gave an eerie feeling to the scene below. Six hunters stood around the bull, their serpent masks partially obscured by the hoods of their black robes. One knelt to light the fire, which caught and flared quickly. Another stood near the wall closest to the bull, using a brush and a small bucket to paint words onto the pale surface. The crimson letters dripped, as if weeping.

BRING IT BACK

A message meant for only one person. Her.

"We need to take this monster out," Lore heard herself say. "Now."

"Wait a second," Castor said. "That's exactly what he's hoping for—an emotional reaction. What does that message even mean?"

Athena looked to Lore, waiting.

Don't do it, her mind whispered. *Don't tell them . . .*

327

But what choice did she have now? She had to tell them something—if not the truth, then a version of it they could believe. One that wouldn't stoke Athena's suspicions or put Lore in the position of doing something she swore she never would.

"The Reveler . . . he told me that Wrath is searching for me because he believes I have the aegis," Lore said, her pulse thundering until her body nearly shook with the force of it. The static was growing in her ears again, but she pushed through it, trying to keep her voice as even as possible. "The Reveler's job was to try to track me—and it—down."

Van blinked. "And just to clarify—"

"I don't have it," Lore said firmly, avoiding Castor's concerned gaze as it fell on her. "No one in my family has since the Kadmides purged our bloodline. The Reveler said it went missing at the end of the last hunt. My guess is that it was an inside job."

"I see the logic in the false Ares's assumption," Athena said.

"I was ten years old during the last Agon," Lore reminded her.

"He could think one of your parents took it," Castor said, his brow creased with worry, "and that they told you where they had hidden it. Damn—no wonder he's obsessed with finding you."

"Good," Lore said. "He's more than welcome to find me. We'll be waiting for him."

"We need a different strategy," Castor said, shaking his head. "One that doesn't put you directly in the path of his blade."

"Yes," Miles said quickly, pointing to him. "That option, please."

"What are you thinking?" Van asked.

"We need to find Artemis," Castor said. "And convince her to ally with us."

Athena scoffed at the idea.

Even though Lore knew the other reason why he wanted to find the goddess, she was still startled at the thought of searching for a being who so badly wanted to kill him.

"I can try searching again," Van offered. "I haven't spotted her since she left Thetis House . . . Are you sure you actually want to find her, Cas? I can't imagine she's going to be a happy recruit."

"I am well aware of the fact that she wants to rip my heart out and eat it," Castor said. "She's the best tracker in the hunt. Better than any computer program—no offense."

Van waved his hand.

"If anyone can find Wrath and figure out whatever his bigger plans are without being detected, it's her," Castor said. "And, frankly, we could use more power to push back against him when the time comes."

"If she doesn't kill you first," Lore reminded him.

"I agree. That is an absurd idea," Athena insisted. "Set aside that distraction and focus your efforts on the matter at hand. We do not need Artemis to kill the imposter, nor do we need her help to find the aegis and the poem inscribed on it."

Lore drew in a sharp breath, better understanding the goddess's reluctance now.

"I didn't bring up the aegis at all," Castor told her, "or the poem. But it's good to have confirmation you'd rather see your sister dead than risk her getting to them first. Are you really that scared there can only be one victor, daughter of Zeus?"

"Artemis will never consent to working alongside the slayer of Apollo," Athena said, ignoring the bait in his words. "And as she wounded me to save herself, I feel no urge to come to her assistance. However, I concur that a new strategy is necessary to disrupt our enemy's plans and his search for Melora." She turned to Van. "Do you possess further knowledge of his holdings and property? Perhaps there are vulnerabilities there."

"Of course I do," Van said. "I have files on all the leaders and elders of the bloodlines. Believe it or not, I was once naïve enough to believe I could neutralize the bloodlines by releasing all of their shady dealings and having their assets seized and their leaders arrested."

"Why didn't you, then?" Lore asked.

"Because the Agon is a hydra," Van said. "It doesn't matter if I cut off the heads of the bloodlines. There are always more hunters to replace them, and even if I had exposed the Agon to the wider world, some of them would have still found a way to continue the hunt."

It struck her then, in a way it hadn't before, that all of them truly wanted the Agon to end—just for different reasons, and by different means.

"I get what you're saying," Castor said. "But is there anything that could be released to the press to draw unwanted attention onto Wrath? He might have some city and police officials in his pocket, but he can't own all of them—"

"Do you know where their weapons stocks are?" Athena interrupted. There was a frightening look of concentration on her face. "Where their vaults are hidden?"

"A few of them," Van said. "I have no doubt they have more than I know about here in the city and abroad."

"A few would suffice," Athena said.

"Where are you going with this?" Lore asked.

"There is more than one way to kill a king," Athena said. "You can bleed the life from him, or you can sap his men's confidence in him."

Van caught on to her meaning. "Hitting his weapon stocks might shake his hold on the hunters who flocked to him thinking he was the more powerful leader and protector."

"As he has dedicated so many hunters to searching for Melora and his rival gods, these vaults and weapons stores may not be as well-guarded as in the past," Athena said.

"The remaining Achillides still loyal to Castor *are* in desperate need of weapons," Van said. "And I have to imagine it's the same for Iro and her hunters. The locations all observe the same shift-change hours. We could strike as early as tomorrow morning."

"We can find other weapons," Castor said stubbornly. "A raid isn't going to do anything but make him double his efforts to find Lore and speed up his plans. We need help. We need someone with Artemis's skills—"

"We are not going to waste time looking for Artemis right now," Lore cut in sharply.

Castor tried to seek out her gaze, his brows drawn in surprise. A lance of guilt shot through her, but Lore pushed it away. Athena was right. Artemis was nothing more than a distraction at this point.

"Guys," Van said. "It's not an either-or. We can do both at once. I'll run a continuous search for Artemis in Argos—"

"You just said a minute ago you haven't been able to find her," Castor said. "We need to go out and look ourselves."

"You keep forgetting that you're a target, too," Lore said, "and that there are still hunters looking for a shot at godhood."

Castor's jaw set.

"We'll look for her after the weapons raids, all right?" Lore said, softening her stance. "The Kadmides will be distracted and trying to regroup. It'll be safer for you to be out in the open."

"I don't care about being safe," he told her.

Her nostrils flared as she drew in another long breath. "Well, sorry.

I do." She turned to Van. "Tell the Achillides which weapons stores to raid and give me one or two locations and a time I can text to Iro."

He looked to Castor. The new god nodded.

"I'll run the search," he promised Castor. "And I'll put out more feelers through my sources, too—"

Van's phone vibrated on the table. He scooped it up, the screen flashing against his dark skin as he scanned the new message there. "The Kadmides contact says he has something on Wrath's next moves we may be interested in."

Lore's heart leapt. "But?"

"I don't think it's a good idea anymore," Van said. "Not after what happened with Belen and now this—something about it doesn't feel right. He's insisting he'll only meet with Miles."

"Because he hates you," Miles reminded him. "I can do it."

"You can, but it doesn't mean you should," Van said.

"How many times do I have to prove you wrong?" Miles demanded. "I can—"

"*No,*" Van snapped, rounding on him. "You're not one of us, and you don't get a say, all right?"

Miles rose, confusion twisting into anger at the ice in Van's expression. "And you don't get to tell me what to do. Do I really have to keep reminding you that you wouldn't have gotten this far without me?"

"Wrath just had two innocent children killed," Castor reminded him. "If this is some kind of trap, I can only imagine what he'll do to you."

Miles moved closer to Lore's side until he was on the opposite side of the room from the others. "Good thing he won't catch me, then."

"We're doing this *for* those little girls," Lore insisted.

Castor leveled her with a piercing look. "Which ones?"

Lore's body went cold. She drew in a deep breath, holding it until her chest began to ache.

"I'll go with Miles," Castor said. "I'd feel better knowing he has someone there to protect him."

"Because I can't?" Lore shot back. "If anyone is going, it's me."

"No," Miles said. "I mean, thank you both, but no one is coming with me. The guy is super tetchy and won't go through with the meeting if he suspects I brought someone with me. And he might have something we really need, or at least a lead on Wrath's current location."

Van kept his eyes on Castor, gauging his response. "He wants to meet tomorrow morning. It would be around the time we'd need to launch the weapons hits, when there's a shift change on the hunters guarding them."

"If clever Miles believes he will be successful," Athena said, "there is no reason for you to stand in his path and deny him."

Lore felt Castor's eyes on her again. Her heart began to riot in her chest, even before she heard Miles's faint "Lore?"

Maybe . . . maybe it was too much of a risk to do the meet right now, given Wrath's anger. If he did somehow get his hands on Miles, Lore would never forgive herself.

The more she thought about it, the more Lore wondered if Castor didn't have the right idea about laying low and focusing on searching for Artemis now, instead of carrying out the weapons hit. If they could convince the goddess to ally with them—and that was a big, deadly *if*—they might not need to rely on the asset's information or risk the meets. Artemis could track anyone or anything, gathering information as needed.

As if sensing the storm in her mind, Athena drew closer. Calm certainty radiated from the goddess, and, somehow, just being near it was clarifying. It gave courage to the need inside Lore—it gave strength to what Lore knew to be right and necessary.

For the girls, she thought. What Wrath had done deserved a retaliation.

"Miles will do the meet," Lore said at last. "We'll carry out the weapons hit in the morning, at the shift change. And if the asset doesn't have information on Wrath's location, we'll start looking for Artemis in the afternoon. All right?"

But even as she said it, Lore knew Athena was right. Artemis would never agree to work with them, and she would never give Castor the information he wanted on Apollo's death—if she even had it at all. Maybe by then, though, Wrath would have emerged from whatever hole he was hiding in, and they wouldn't need to risk Castor's life trying to persuade a goddess whose will was as unyielding as steel.

Van nodded, his face betraying none of his emotions. "I'll text you the information for Iro, then."

Lore barely heard the others as they climbed the stairs, no doubt to crash for the rest of the night. Only Castor lingered, one hand on the banister as he watched Lore pull out her phone. She typed out a message to Iro with trembling hands.

I need your help.

The rage building inside her rose like the smoke from the body of the bronze bull, until she could taste ash in her mouth and her mind blazed with the bloodred words that had been left for her on the wall.

By the time she looked up again, Castor was already gone.

THIRTY THREE

THE LATE-AFTERNOON AIR WAS HEAVY WITH MOISTURE, BUT IT WAS nothing compared to the oppressive atmosphere that had taken hold of the town house.

After they'd had word from the Achillides that the raids had gone off without any problems or casualties on their part, Lore had gone back to sleep for a few more hours. She hadn't heard back from Iro yet beyond the girl's single-word response to Lore's text with instructions for the weapons hit: **Confirmed.**

Lore wasn't worried, though, especially after Van met one of the Achillides hunters and brought home an array of the Kadmides' weapons. Athena had taken obvious pleasure in laying them out and examining each one, including a proper dory. But any excitement Lore had felt at the success disappeared into the emotional black hole of Van's and Castor's silence.

When Lore couldn't take any more of Van's judgmental looks as he sat watching Miles's progress on Argos, let alone the sight of the closed door Castor was hiding behind, she had gone back into her bedroom. There, she finally noticed what Miles had left for her on the dresser.

The feather charm on the necklace winked at her as it caught the sunlight. She hesitated a moment, her finger brushing against its edge.

Never free, she thought.

Lore swept the necklace off the dresser into the small trash can beside it. But she felt its presence, even if she could no longer see it. Needing to escape it—to escape the house—Lore opened a window and crawled out onto the fire escape to make her way up to the roof. There, she watched the heavy gray clouds roll in from a distance.

Lore looked back over her shoulder at the sound of someone on the fire escape, but relaxed when she saw who it was. "You shouldn't be up here."

Athena looked around the town house's bleak roof. There was nothing much to see beyond Lore, two old lawn chairs, and the air-conditioning unit. Truthfully, no one should have been up there, but Miles and Lore sometimes made the climb when the weather was nice and they had wine to drink. They'd talked about doing something with it—a little garden, maybe—but that had been before Gil died.

Before Hermes left, Lore corrected herself, rubbing her arms. She turned back toward the silver thunderclouds gathering to the east.

The goddess avoided the other chair, choosing instead to sit on the rough surface of the roof. She drew her dory across her lap and began to sharpen both points with the whetstone she'd taken from the kitchen.

"It was Hermes."

She wasn't sure why it was easier to tell the goddess. Maybe it was knowing that Athena, blunt as the flat edge of a blade, wouldn't try to console her or make her talk through it.

"What of him?" Athena asked, setting the whetstone aside.

"The man I worked for—the person who owned this house and left it to me." Lore swallowed. "It was Hermes the whole time. When he disappeared, he came here. The Reveler told me in the museum."

"Ah," Athena said. Then added, carefully, "And you believe the imposter?"

Lore nodded. "Apparently Hermes also thought I had the aegis. It must have been a massive disappointment to him when he realized I didn't and he'd put in—" Her voice caught in a way she hated. "And he'd put in all of that effort cozying up to me for nothing."

Athena's lips compressed into a tight line.

"I don't get it, though," Lore said. "The Reveler said that Hermes felt indebted to me, and that he had wanted to keep Wrath from getting the aegis . . ."

"Hermes clearly discovered the existence of the poem," Athena said, "and hoped to use it to escape the Agon."

"That," Lore agreed, "or he had no idea and just wanted the shield to use in the next Agon, and thought I might give it to him willingly if he showed me enough kindness. But why did he feel *indebted* to me? Why go to *such* elaborate lengths to maneuver his way into my life when he never asked me about my past, or pushed me on it? He even gave me an amulet that hid me from the sight of gods. He left me this house."

"I had wondered as much," Athena said slowly. "As I told you, I had followed your tale through the years and searched for you. I saw you only once, three years ago, walking through the nearby streets, and followed you home. Yet I never saw you again, and at the start of this hunt, all I could do was hope you might still be there."

The thought of passing within feet of the unseen goddess filled Lore with a strange, delayed dread.

"Do you remember if I was wearing a necklace?" Lore asked. "One with a gold feather charm?"

The goddess considered her question carefully. "You were not."

337

It must have been just after Lore had returned with Gil—with Hermes. It had been another two weeks before she'd woken to find the necklace on her nightstand. He'd seemed to believe her birthday was the date on her fake passport. Her real one had already passed.

"You ask why Hermes would enact such a charade?" Athena said. "It is because he is cunning and because he delights in it. Yet he is no fool. If he believed you possessed the aegis, he had a reason. So I must ask you again, Melora—do you possess my father's shield, and is it in danger of falling into the imposter Ares's hands?"

Numbness pricked at Lore's fingertips, her palms. Her mind looped her thoughts into circles, one dark fear chasing the next. She jammed her nails into the skin of her arms, using the pain to break through it.

"I don't have it," Lore said. "Maybe he found out that Aristos Kadmou bragged about its location to my father."

"Indeed." The goddess let out a low hum.

She remembered then what Belen had said. *You are a distraction.* It *is a distraction.*

Lore hugged her arms to her chest, leaning forward over her knees. "Do you think it could be about more than the poem—that it could be that the idea of a *girl* stealing it cuts at Wrath's pride?"

"He may have many reasons for desiring it. He wishes to know the secret of winning the Agon. He wishes to mend his wounded pride at being bested by a young girl. He wishes to have the glory of the aegis as a symbol on his arm," Athena said, "and to use it as a tool. It can summon thunder and call down lightning, but it does not have to be used at its full power for it to drive fear into the hearts of those who behold it."

The goddess seemed to consider something else, adding, "If you will not give the shield to him willingly, he will need you to wield it on his behalf, and he will do whatever he must to compel you."

"You say that like you care," Lore said. "Why pretend you actually have some interest in me beyond the terms of our agreement?"

"Like any craftsman," Athena said, tilting her head toward her, "if I see potential in raw material, I have the urge to shape it into something great."

"That's rich, coming from you," Lore said.

"I do not understand your accusation," Athena said plainly.

"You've never guided women," Lore elaborated. "Not the way you did for your heroes. But you were always more than happy to punish them."

"Women and girls belonged to my sister and were beyond my responsibility," Athena said, the words edged with warning. "I owe you no explanation."

Athena's face dared her to continue, and Lore had never backed down from a misguided fight.

"Do you know why female hunters aren't supposed to claim a god's power—how the elders of the bloodlines have always justified it?" Lore asked, letting years of quiet anger fill her chest like steam. "They point to the origin poem, but they also look to you. To the fact that you only ever chose to mentor male heroes on journeys. You only helped *them* attain battle-born kleos—the only kleos that matters to the elders. To them, you have always been an extension of Zeus's will."

"I was born from my father's mind. I *am* an extension of his will."

The goddess's jaw set, turning her face into a mask of fury.

"My presence here, now, is all that is needed to understand what becomes of those who upset the natural order of things. Who betray the father."

"Weren't you angry?" Lore asked, hearing her voice break. "How can you not be furious that even *you* weren't completely free to decide who or what you wanted to be?"

The goddess remained silent, but there was something to her expression now—a narrowing focus.

"You let men use your name and image to reinforce their rules— you represented what they alone could strive to be," Lore said. "But what about the rest of us? Those of us called women, and everyone who isn't so easily sorted?"

"I did not realize my gift of artful craft belonged solely to men," Athena said. "Or that I did not acknowledge those women who displayed excellence in their home and the care of their family."

Lore drew in an unsteady breath. "You know, what almost makes it worse is that you actually see yourself as the myth men created for you. Just now you claimed you were born from your father's mind— but you had a mother, didn't you? Metis. Wisdom herself. That was her gift, not Zeus's, and he devoured you both to save himself, and claimed it. Denying her is denying who you are. It's denying what men are capable of."

"I know precisely what they are capable of, child of Perseus," Athena said coldly.

Lore flinched at the name of her ancestor.

"You cast your opinions with unearned certainty," Athena said. "However, I am not the one you do battle with now. Your anger lies not with me, but with yourself. Why?"

Lore ran her hand back through her hair, gripping it.

"You are so very angry. I felt it from the moment I first laid eyes upon you, and it has only grown more powerful as you have tried to stifle it," Athena said. "You ask me why I did not see fit to use my power the way you might have, and yet, you hold yourself back from your own potential. I would not have thought you to be such a coward."

I am not special, or chosen. Lore pressed her fists to her eyes. The memory of the realization was just as agonizing as what had happened. "I'm not holding myself back, I just . . . I just can't make another mistake."

Athena made a noise of derision. "The false Apollo has weaseled his way into your mind and made you doubt yourself. You know what must be done. He does not even know how he came to possess his power."

Lore looked up sharply at that.

"Did you think I would not unravel the truth?" Athena asked. "When he has been so very forward with questioning those he meets about my brother's death? Why else would he seem to despise and resent his power? Why else would he want to seek out my sister, knowing she only wishes him dead?"

"He . . ." Lore began, uncertain. She didn't want to talk about this. It felt like a betrayal of Castor. "He doesn't want me to go too far."

"And you are not capable of determining that limit yourself?" Athena asked. "You rely on his judgment over your own?"

"He's trying to protect me," Lore said. It was what Castor had always done, as much as she'd tried, in her own way, to protect him.

"From whom? From what?" Athena asked. "Yourself? All that you might become if you embrace who you are and not who he wishes you to be?"

Lore trusted Castor with her life—she knew he would never intentionally hurt her. But the way he had looked at her when he'd caught up to her in Central Park, the shock and disgust on his face . . .

Maybe he really didn't understand. The seven years they'd lost had never felt longer.

"I hate the Agon," Lore began.

"No," Athena interrupted. "I think not. You hate what it cost you, but this world bore you. You belong to it. That is your birthright. You were always meant for glory, but it was taken from you, and now you will never feel satisfied—never *whole*—until you possess what you deserve."

In her mind, Lore heard her younger self say the words again. *My name will be legend.*

"It's not about deserving," Lore said, forcing herself to get the words out. "I don't want to become the kind of monster they are."

"You are no monster. You are a warrior," Athena said. "And were you not meant for some greater role, you would have perished with your family."

"Don't say that," Lore whispered. *Please don't say that.*

Longing tore at her. The thought that everything that had happened hadn't been her fault, that it hadn't been for nothing—her whole soul ached for it to be true.

"There are far worse things to become than a monster," Athena said.

"Is that what you told yourself when you punished Arachne for her hubris?" Lore asked. "When you turned on Medusa?"

The goddess seemed confounded by the question. "What is it you accuse me of with Medusa?"

"Poseidon raped her in your temple, and instead of stopping him, instead of punishing *him*, you—" Lore choked on the word. "You made being the victim the worse crime. You made her a monster, and then you sent someone to kill her."

"Is that what you believe?" Athena asked.

"Your father, your brothers . . . they took so many women against their will. How could you not understand Medusa's experience, when Hephaestus had tried to force himself on you?" Lore took a deep breath, steadying herself. "They took whatever they wanted. Why would the men of the Agon treat their women and girls any differently? They make us believe our lives are our own, even as they slip the collars around our necks. Even G— Even Hermes. At any point, they can pull the leash."

"Is that why you abandoned your path as a warrior?" Athena asked. "You did not wish to be controlled? I would have thought the deaths of your family were at the root of the decision, but you continued your training, did you not? Yet something drove you from the hunt . . . from this world."

For years, Lore had steadfastly refused to recall what had happened that night. She'd hoped that if she buried it deep enough in her heart, it wouldn't make her feel half as sick or terrified of being made to answer for it.

But Lore found herself speaking now, the words unfurling with such force, she wasn't sure she would be able to stop them if she tried.

"When Iro's father ascended to become the new Aphrodite, he had no son," Lore began, "and no immediate male relatives. A second cousin became the interim archon of the Odysseides. He never came to the estate for the first two years I lived with them. During that time, I focused on my training with Iro. I told myself that even if I had nothing else, there was the Agon. I could still bring honor to my family."

Athena watched her, waiting.

"And then the new archon of the Odysseides came. He stayed. He seemed to be everywhere at once, his eyes always trailing after

343

us. Watching us from the window as we drilled and sparred, across the table at meals, as we swam in the lake . . ." Lore said, her hands curling at the memory. "He would find any excuse to touch me—to correct my stance when I didn't need it, to stroke my arm or leg as he passed. My instructor told me to never speak of it to anyone, or else the archon would find out how ungrateful I was for his favor and attention. I would be thrown out into the street without so much as a knife to defend myself. No money, no future."

Lore's hands tightened into fists.

"One night, after dinner, he told me to go to his office and wait for him there," she continued. "The others at the table must have known what would happen, but they did nothing. The servants looked away. Iro was so excited. She thought he was going to offer me a place as a léaina."

She needed to draw a deeper breath, to collect the right words. Bile rose in her throat.

"His office was dark except for the fire in the hearth. He locked the door. He told me that I wouldn't be continuing my training. That I would serve only him. His needs."

Athena hissed.

"I knew he was right. I had no one else. I had no family. It was the moment I realized my future was entirely in his hands—it just—"

Lore drew in another breath. "He put his hands on me . . . He forced his mouth on mine and pinned me to the desk. He was bigger. Heavier. And I thought, *I am not special, or chosen*. That was the shield I'd used against the truth for years—the certainty that I was meant for something more. But that moment, with him over me, that's when I understood what that world was. There would always be a man deciding my fate, whether it was my father, an archon, or a husband."

344

The goddess's eyes glowed, the sparks flaring into riotous spirals. It made Lore think of the fire in the office again, how much brighter it had seemed as her terror set in.

"I never had a choice," Lore said.

At least, not one whose consequences she understood before giving her answer.

"He took away the last of the illusions."

The archon's breath had hitched with excitement as he'd watched her realize as much.

"Gods were supposed to be my enemy. The other bloodlines. Not the archon of my mother's house—the one that had taken me in. Sheltered me."

The knob to the desk drawer had dug into her hip. Her body moved to protect itself, when her mind couldn't. Her fingers closed around the cold metal. She pulled, slipped her hand inside. He pressed himself to her, and it was like nothing she had known in a fight.

"I found the letter opener. I cut myself pulling it out from the drawer. He gripped my chin and forced my head back, so I would have to look at him."

He pulled the collar of her shirt until it tore. The fabric gave easily, but not as easy as the skin across his throat.

"I realized I had always had choices, even if I hadn't seen them," Lore said. "And I made one. I chose not to belong to him. I chose to kill him, so he couldn't hurt me or anyone else."

The memory of his blood spilling, staining his white skin and her dress, the weight of him slumping against her as he struggled to kill her in retaliation, even in the throes of his own death, came back in a cold rush. She touched the long scar on her face, the last cut he'd made as she'd slipped out from under him. Sweat broke out across her body,

345

and she was shaking, scarcely able to draw a breath.

But what Lore remembered most from that night was her rage. The way it burned through her fear and shock and devastation and gave her what she needed to survive.

Lore had done what she'd been trained to do, knifing his body until it was still and there was no air moving in his lungs. It had been rage that carried her on bare feet across the fields and unpaved roads. It had been rage that kept her alive and moving. Her rage had fed her when she went hungry.

And then Lore had done exactly what Athena accused her of. She had suppressed it, making it smaller, making it feel irrelevant and undeserved. And then Hermes had found her, when she was almost empty.

"That's . . ." Lore began. "That's what's so— It kills me to know that I was wrong about Gil. I knew better. I did. I let my guard down, even after what happened with the archon, because I thought I was the one making choices. That he wouldn't be able to hurt me or control me like the men in the Agon had tried to do."

"But you do not regret your actions against the archon that night?" Athena asked.

Lore shook her head. She had never, beyond knowing she had left Iro behind.

"That is because they were justified. You did what was necessary," Athena said. "Just as we act out of necessity now. You fear the judgment of others in our pursuit of the imposter Ares, but you will not regret your choices once he is dead—only the opportunities you will lose if you allow others' fears to keep you prisoner to your doubt."

"It's . . ." Lore closed her eyes. "It's not that simple. I don't—"

I don't want to remember how good it felt to have a purpose, she

346

finished silently. *I don't want to forget why I had to leave the Agon when it feels so right to me.*

Children shouted to one another as they sped down the street on their bicycles. Their light laughter seemed to sparkle in the silence. Lore wondered if she had ever been that carefree.

"I gave her fury power," Athena said quietly.

Lore turned to her, confused.

"I transformed Medusa," Athena continued, "so that she would have protection against all those who would try to harm her."

"That's bullshit. You didn't give her a choice, did you?" Lore bit back. "And now history remembers her as a villain who deserved to die."

"No. That is what men have portrayed her as, through art, through tales," Athena said. "They imagined her hideous because they feared to meet the true gaze of a woman, to witness the powerful storm that lives inside, waiting. She was not defeated by my uncle's assault. She was merely reborn as a being who could gaze back at the world, unafraid. Is that not what your own line did for centuries, staring out from behind her mask?"

Lore almost recoiled as her words sank in.

The Perseides had worn the gorgon mask—the mask of Medusa, her ringlets of snakes, her mouth set in a line of grim determination—for centuries. Both of her parents' masks had been taken when their apartment was cleaned and their bodies buried.

Lore hadn't been old enough to have her own made, though one of her clearest memories was of taking her mother's out of its silk wrappings and bringing it close to her face. In the end, the feel of the bronze snakes against her small fingers, and what she saw reflected in the mirror, had made her feel powerful.

Now she only felt her stomach clench. How many men, her own beloved father included, had worn that mask and the anger of Medusa's gaze, twisting it into something that served them? The bloodlines wore masks of their ancestors' greatest accomplishments and kills, not to honor them, those terrible monsters of their age, but as trophies.

"Your ancestors carried the shield that bore her head," Athena said. "They wielded her power until they lost her. If the shield should be carried by anyone, it should be you—you, the one who knows the darkness of men yet refuses to be afraid."

Lore could picture herself with the shield so clearly, the way her face would mirror Medusa's grim expression cast in silver. There was no fear or shame in the thought, and none of the agonizing regret that had kept her from so much as speaking its name for years.

The aegis should be carried by her. It was her birthright, yes, but it was more than that—it represented everything that she stood to gain, and everything she had ever truly wanted to be. Not the lie that Hermes had convinced her she needed, but the powerful hunger that lived in her still.

If she could use it against Wrath, if Medusa's face and her own were the last the new god saw as his life bled from him, it would mean it was all worth it.

It would mean her family hadn't died for nothing.

Go get it, her mind whispered.

"But . . . you gave Perseus the shield," Lore said. "The one he used to kill her. You guided him, and were a friend to him."

Athena rolled the dory across her lap. "I have played my part in wicked games, and lived at the mercy of more powerful gods. I have been quick to temper and relished striking at those who wounded my pride or dishonored me."

The first droplets of rain began to fall, pattering softly against the roof.

"You could have stopped it," Lore whispered. "You could have stopped Poseidon."

Athena's face became hideous with cold anger. "Know this, Melora: Even the gods are bound by fate. Even the gods serve a master. I have done many things, among them lashing out at a weaker being when I did not have the strength to punish one more powerful than even myself."

Athena paused, smoothing her fingers along the staff of her dory.

"There is a story greater than all of us, a fabric that spreads far and wide, guided by hands more powerful than my own," Athena said. "You may call that complicity, and perhaps it is. But I deemed it survival."

"How could you be sure that your path was written for you?" Lore asked. "What if you always had the chance to live on your own terms, and you didn't see it?"

Athena made a sound of derision. "All I have ever desired is to do that which I was born to do."

"Which is?" Lore prompted.

"To guide the hearts of warriors, the minds of philosophers, and the hands of artisans," Athena said. "And to never again fail to defend a city under my protection."

The goddess rose to her feet, taking in the sight of distant buildings.

"On one last matter you are wrong," Athena said as she turned to go back inside. "I did not choose to mentor a woman through great adventure, but I gave them counsel. It was not done out of malice, or the belief that they were inferior creatures. Rather, I felt that elevating

349

one in such a way would dishonor my true friend, who had no earthly equal in life, or in death."

Pallas. She was speaking of the companion she'd been raised alongside, the one she had accidentally killed while sparring.

Athena returned to the fire escape at the back of the town house, climbing down to the window below.

"The only thing I've ever been afraid of is being powerless. Of not being able to protect the people I love. But I don't know what will happen to me if I give in to it," Lore said. "Everything I feel. Everything I want to do."

The goddess did not turn around. "You will be transformed."

The rain picked up, drumming harder against her skin, but Lore couldn't bring herself to move. She felt drained, but not in a way that left her feeling weak. For the first time in days, maybe even years, her mind was clear. Lore held on to the sharp hurt inside her and didn't pull away. She held firm, waiting for her claws to come back to her.

Thunder pealed over her like a shield striking a shield. Hours had passed since she'd first climbed the fire escape, and Miles would be home soon, but she still couldn't move. She couldn't do anything but let the rain wash down over her.

Her phone buzzed in her pocket, startling her from her reverie. Lore stood, pulling the phone out. The message was from Miles; she released a small sigh of relief and began to log in to reply to it, only for her phone to buzz again and again, the same message repeating.

help

help

help

THIRTY FOUR

"WHY ISN'T IT WORKING?"

Lore's hand shook as she held out her phone to Van. He took it from her, struggling to master his anger.

"He made us share locations," she continued. "That was our deal—"

"You're sharing locations with him," Van said sharply. "He probably forgot to share his in return, or someone disabled it. In either case, we need to leave. If they can track your location, this house is now compromised."

Castor stood behind her, his back pressed up against the stairs. He said nothing, which said everything. Neither he nor Van would meet her gaze.

"We're not leaving," Lore said. "He might not have been taken. Maybe he's just hurt, or in hiding or . . ."

"Or dead," Van finished coldly. "Which is exactly what I told you would happen if you didn't convince him to leave."

"Do not cast her as the enemy for believing in his abilities," Athena cut in. "You have maligned him repeatedly and tried to force him from a choice he made voluntarily. Melora is not responsible for whatever has happened to him."

Lore wanted to believe her. She wanted to believe her more than anything. "I thought you were supposed to be watching him."

"I was, but I needed to take a call," Van said. "Don't you dare turn this back on me. If you think that I don't feel—"

He cut himself off.

"Run another search for Miles in Argos," Castor said quietly, already turning to go. "I'll keep watch from the roof. I should be able to see anyone coming and buy us some time to escape if Wrath and the hunters try to attack."

Athena moved to stand beside the bay window, cracking the roman shades open to peer out into the street.

Van went to the kitchen to retrieve his second laptop. While one ran Argos, actively searching for Miles, he used the other to bring up saved videos.

"This is archived footage from a street camera a few hours ago," Van told her. He played it through and, together, they watched as Miles disappeared around a corner.

"There's no camera at the meet spot," Van said, frustrated. "It was offline."

Lore leaned closer to the screen. "There's no way to know if he actually met the source?"

Van shook his head. "I have to imagine he would have texted or called right away if there was a problem."

Miles appeared in the same feed a few minutes later. There was none of the triumph he'd had after his first successful meet—now he only looked afraid. The program jumped to the next camera, picking up his trail as he turned onto Lexington. Another captured him crossing the street against traffic, still looking around.

Then the video cut off.

"That's it?" Lore choked out.

Van's face was as grim as she'd ever seen it. "That's where Argos lost sight of him. Either he's hiding himself well, or he was taken."

"Shit," Lore breathed. Her pulse was hammering, her breathing growing shallow. The darkness edged into her vision as her thoughts began to spiral toward the worst possible outcomes.

The other computer beeped. Van grabbed it, straightening as his fingers flew over the keyboard. *Not Miles,* she begged silently. *Please, not him, too . . .*

New security camera footage loaded. In it, a small figure knelt in some kind of lake. His hands were tied behind his back and only his profile was visible, but Lore recognized Miles's clothes.

"When was this?" she asked.

"It's right now," Van said, glancing at the time. 6:21 p.m.

"Can you zoom in at all?" Lore pleaded.

"I can't," Van said. "Do you recognize where that is?"

She leaned closer, scanning the live feed. Terror made it hard to focus on any one detail. "It looks like . . . the lake and the waterfall behind him—I think that's Morningside Park? It's not far from here."

"He has been left there as bait," Athena warned. "The imposter Ares must have discovered what he means to you. We will need reinforcements if we are to help him."

Lore's mind raced. "How fast can the Achillides get here?"

"They're back in Brooklyn," Van said. "Even by car it's at least a half hour. Is it possible the Odysseides never left Manhattan?"

She pulled out her phone. "We're about to find out. Go get Cas."

As Athena watched, Lore typed a message to Iro.

I need your help. Come to pond in Morningside Park ASAP.

But there was no reply.

Morningside Park served as the narrow boundary between Morningside Heights, poised high on its hundred-foot cliffs, and

Harlem below. Lore and Miles had walked the length of it from 123rd to 110th Street any number of times; she sometimes met him there after he finished classes, or for the promise of lunch on his dime.

It had always unsettled her to see this piece of Manhattan's original landscape standing defiant in the face of the modern buildings around it. Its rough terrain had refused to be tamed by developers. Dark cliffs interrupted several streets, and the only way to directly continue from one part of a road to another was to pass through the park on foot and use its many staircases to ascend or descend the sheer drop.

As they walked to one of the park's entrances, Lore spotted a security camera nearby and pointed it out to the others.

"I looped the feeds in all of the park's cameras," Van told her. "We're covered. For now."

High in the distance, the pale cathedral of St. John the Divine was just visible through the gloom. Lore thought it was as scenic a place as any for a deadly confrontation.

Even considering the impending storm, the park was eerily quiet. She finally understood why when they came across the first body just inside the gate. A woman, with an arrow in her back.

"What news from the Odysseides?" Athena asked.

"Nothing," Lore said. "But I don't want to wait any longer. If they come, they come."

Castor nodded, steeling himself as he rose from his crouch. "Let's go."

Then dogs began to howl.

Lore slowed as the realization set in.

"Oh no," she said softly.

"What?" Van asked. "What's happening?"

"Wrath isn't the one who set the trap," Lore choked out.

"It is my sister," Athena said, holding her dory firm. "Artemis."

354

THIRTY FIVE

"INCOMING," VAN WARNED.

Dozens of dogs, their fur matted and mud-splattered, bounded down the path, barking and yelping. Some were strays, others had seemingly escaped their owners and still had leashes attached to their collars. Saliva foamed at their mouths.

"Bay hounds," Athena said in disgust. They had armed themselves with the superior Kadmides weapons, and while Lore had chosen a dagger, the goddess had taken a small knife and dory, the latter of which she now used to keep the dogs back.

Bay hounds were used by hunters to chase, then circle up, their prey. They'd bark and howl to keep them cornered until the catch dogs, or the hunter, arrived.

Out of the corner of her eye, Lore caught a certain darkness gathering in the trees just behind Athena's head. Birds and squirrels packed the branches, perched side by side in unnatural stillness, their eyes glowing gold with Artemis's power.

They couldn't even run. The chase would get the hounds' blood up, and they would tear them apart.

"Ideas?" Castor asked the group. "Anyone?"

All at once, the dogs fell silent. Lore's scalp prickled and tightened at the feeling of the unseen gazes around her.

Cats began to gather on the grass, the fur on their backs sticking up like knives.

Lore should have known Artemis's instinct would be to hide amongst the wild things, even within the boundaries of a concrete-and-steel city. They'd be lucky if they even heard the whisper of the arrow before it pierced their hearts.

The dogs circled them. The ones at the back edged forward, closer, while those in front of them turned and started down the trail. Not to guide them, she realized, but to keep them from escaping.

"Are we just standing here like assholes and waiting for her to come kill us?" Lore said, removing the knife from the sheath strapped to her leg. "Come on."

Her breath was loud in her ears as they followed the trail south. They were surrounded by full-bodied trees and a thick border of shrubs. As the path narrowed, it became claustrophobic. There were more bodies—men and women who had gone out for runs, others clearly coming and going from work or school. Lore's whole being twisted at the sight of them, feeding her anger.

Artemis would answer for their deaths. Athena had been right all along. Her sister was beyond reason. Castor could try, he could hope, but Artemis would never ally with them, and now Lore would never accept the goddess's help even if it was offered.

"This is your last chance to turn back, imposter," Athena warned. "I will waste no breath protecting you from her."

Lore looked to Castor. "Maybe you should . . ."

He wouldn't hear it. "I'm here for Miles, and I won't leave without him."

"How did she even know he was involved in this?" Lore whispered.

"Isn't it obvious?" Athena asked. "She has been watching and tracking our movements. She needed a way to draw us out."

"Is there really no way to get through to her?" Van whispered. "She's your sister."

Looking at Athena now, though, Lore wondered if she had made a mistake in bringing her here. Athena wouldn't do anything to endanger Lore's life, as it would mean endangering her own, but . . . she hadn't bound her fate to Castor's. What was to stop Athena from serving Castor up on a platter to her sister to reignite their partnership?

Me, Lore thought, watching the powerful muscles of Castor's back work with each step he took.

"She is not a beast to be soothed," Athena warned. "When Apollo fell, her mind frayed and she became half a soul."

Castor said nothing as he gazed into the dimly lit park.

By the time they reached the pond and its waterfall, the faint drizzle had picked up into a punishing rain. It slashed down onto the spread of green-tinged water, sending the surface into a frenzied dance. At the very center of it, positioned on his knees and slumped forward until his face was nearly in the rising water, was Miles.

Lore darted forward, but Castor held her back, forcing her to take cover with the others behind a nearby park bench.

She scanned the area around them, searching for any sign of movement. The dogs fell back to line the water's edge. They sat, obedient, waiting for their next command. Lore followed their gazes across the pond.

"There!" Lore said, pointing. "There she is!"

The archer was balanced on one of the smaller outcroppings between the waterfall and a weeping willow dripping with rain.

Lore shielded her eyes against the onslaught of the storm. The goddess's face was striped with dirt, and a crown of leaves and thorns rested on her pale hair. Her once sky-blue tunic was nearly black with blood and grime. She raised her bow, turning the nocked arrow toward Miles.

"*No!*" Van leaped over the bench and ran for the pond, splashing into the dank water as Artemis let her arrow fly.

THIRTY SIX

"CAS—" LORE BEGAN, BUT THE NEW GOD WAS ALREADY ON HIS FEET. Power blazed from his hands, incinerating the arrow and exploding jagged stones around the waterfall.

Artemis leaped away just as Van threw himself over Miles to shield him, disappearing into the trees. Castor and Athena ran around opposite sides of the pond in pursuit of her. The dogs bounded after them, snapping and snarling.

That's going to get someone's attention, Lore thought. She jumped over the park bench and splashed down into the pond. "Is he—?"

Van held out a hand, blocking her path. His voice was low with fury. *"Don't touch him."*

Lore froze, her stomach knotting. "We need to . . . We need to get him out of here."

Van's voice was low with fury, and his whole body shook with the force of his words. "You always—you always do this. It's always about what you want and everyone just has to— Just . . . don't touch him."

She didn't know what to do, other than hold herself back as Van dragged Miles out of the pond. He knelt, securing Miles over his shoulder, then ran back into the safety of the nearby streets.

"Godkiller!" Artemis cried out from the darkness. "I've waited for this!"

Lore shook herself. She could deal with the fallout of what had happened with Miles later—right now, he was safe with Van, and there was another, more pressing problem at hand.

She ran up the nearest set of stairs, stopping as she reached the narrow walking path. She couldn't see anyone else through the veil of rain and the thick brush, but she could hear bodiless voices as they echoed off the cliffs. She stopped as she reached the next level's walking trail, scanning the trees.

"Leave, sister!" Artemis shouted. "You know this kill is mine! If you betray me again, it will be your life I take next!"

Betray her? Lore thought incredulously.

"You wish to speak of betrayal?" Athena thundered back. "After leaving me to become the new god's prey?"

"And now you betray me with every breath my brother's killer draws," Artemis said. "You should have brought him to me. You promised he was mine!"

Lore tried running toward the sound of their echoing voices, but they seemed to come from everywhere at once.

"*Listen* to me," Athena called to her. "Control your feelings before they destroy you."

"Listen, listen, *listen!*" Artemis snarled back. "I will never again listen to you. You weave lies and spin promises that you never intend to keep. You have done this to us—*you*! We followed you, and you led us to ruin!"

"Yes, sister, but now we have found a possible end to the hunt," Athena said. "New instructions. Help us find them and we will return home. The hunt will end."

"We will *never* be allowed to return home!" Artemis growled. "When will you see this? We will *never* bask in our father's light again.

360

We will *never* know his favor. All that is left is to kill the hunters and false gods for what they have done to us. To punish them for their lack of faith. If I must die, then so must they—beginning with *him!*"

Lore raced up another long flight of stairs for a better vantage point. The cliffs there were reinforced with stone blocks, making her feel like she was scaling the walls of an ancient castle as she reached the lookout at the very top. She leaned over the cement railing, searching the park. Fear rose in her like mist.

There, Lore thought. Athena and Castor were both in pursuit of Artemis as she led them off the lower trail. They disappeared beneath the cover of the foliage.

Lore bolted back down the slippery steps. She was soaked through, but no longer felt the rain's cold touch. The crash of falling tree limbs was her lodestar as she made her way to them.

The gods had circled back around to the waterfall, to the copse of trees at its crest, not far from one of the trail paths. The rock outcrops on either side of it seemed more like conjoined, flat-topped boulders when viewed from above. They jutted out over the pond like smaller cliffs and fed the waterfall with more rain.

Athena was a short distance from the other gods, ripping apart the tangled net of thorns, twine, and branches her sister had woven and thrown over her.

Castor and Artemis rounded on each other, slamming through the trees as they wrestled for control. Artemis struggled to get her carbon bow up. She reached back, only to find she was out of arrows.

Tossing the bow aside, she pulled out a small hunting knife she had strapped to her arm. Castor was forced to weave back and forth to avoid her erratic slashing. He hissed as it sliced across his forearm, and

361

she redoubled her effort, darting forward to drive the blade through his throat.

"No!" Lore dove for the dory Athena had dropped, and sent it hurtling toward Artemis.

The goddess knocked it away easily with a humorless laugh, but Lore wasn't trying to kill her. She only needed to give Castor a second's chance.

He took it. When Artemis leaned back to avoid the spear, he punched her wrist, forcing her to drop the knife, and wrestled her to the ground.

Finally free of the net, Athena lurched toward the other gods at the sound of Artemis's ravening scream. The ferociousness of it made the nearby birds call back in a screeching cacophony. Artemis kicked Castor off her, sending him sprawling back onto the grass and mud.

She grabbed her knife again and held it out in front of her, warding off both Castor and her sister.

"Listen to me—" Castor said, gripping his side. "Please—we need your help—"

Artemis moved with the grace of a stag and the uncontrolled fury of a raging boar. Where Lore could occasionally see a touch of humanity in Athena's calculations, there was nothing but animal in Artemis. She was incomprehensible in what one of the ancient writers had described as her *cruel mysteries*. She was as unpredictable and merciless as nature itself.

"Stop this, Artemis!" Athena said. "The hunt is as much our enemy as the hunters. Together, we can end it—"

"Oh, you fool!" Artemis sneered. "You cannot even see the truth before you. The Agon cannot be won. It cannot be escaped. It is our own Tartarus."

"I do not believe that," Athena said, taking another step toward her sister. She held out an arm to keep Lore from following.

Lore bit back a sound of frustration, but understood—Artemis would only grow more agitated if she felt the situation had become three against one.

"Calm yourself, sister," Athena continued. "Listen to what I am saying to you now. You are lost in your fury, let me lead you out once more. I understand—"

"You don't!" Artemis shouted. "Or else you would have brought him to me! We were meant to kill them—all the imposters! All of them!"

Water streamed around Lore's ankles, flowing down to, and over, the waterfall. But as Artemis shifted, Lore noticed that some of the runoff from the rain was disappearing into a nearby patch of leaves and mud. As she watched, a layer of dirt washed away, revealing the edge of a hole and the careful layer of thin branches that had been placed over it.

Lore gasped as a weight slammed into her from the side. A large Labrador was on her, then another—snarling and snapping at her.

"Stop—it—" she bit out, struggling against their frenzy. Hot spittle flew everywhere.

One sank its teeth into her forearm, and Lore let out a pained cry, throwing the animal off her, into the other dog. More and more were gathering around them. She rolled to her feet, gripping a large branch to ward off the dogs and keep them away from the others.

"Yes, you are right," Athena said, keeping her eyes on her sister. She approached slowly, showing her empty hands as Artemis clutched her knife. "Sister, have you forgotten? Can you not see it, even now? The first light breaking from high above the clouds, the way it swept over the gardens and halls of our home, the purest of golds . . . the air sweet with incense and smoke . . . the hearth, ever-burning . . . the world below us, so green and vast with promise . . . our unconquerable father, the others . . ."

Lore was shocked at the emotion underlying the words, the well of deep-seated pain they revealed.

Artemis moaned, clawing at her face as she shook her head. The severity of her expression was shattering. Athena had pierced her armor.

But all at once, Artemis straightened, her eyes narrowing in pure hatred as she took in the sight of her sister.

"*You*," she said. "You stole that from me."

Artemis had momentarily turned her back on Castor, allowing him to approach from behind her. She spun, but he was faster, locking his arms around hers and pinning her.

One of the dogs tried to break free to attack Castor, but Lore pushed it back with the branch and craned her head, just for a moment, to see what was going on.

"No—*no!*" Artemis's body twisted, and there was a sickening, wet pop as she dislocated her shoulder to free herself. Her mind was somewhere the pain couldn't reach. Using her other hand, she plunged her knife into Castor's upper thigh.

He fell back with a shout, grimacing as he removed it.

"I feel my brother's power, but it is far-reaching, it is so far," Artemis snarled, her eyes wide. Her heel had dropped at the edge of the trap as she'd backed toward the waterfall, and she narrowly regained her balance. "You feel different than the others—what are you?"

Lore looked back at the goddess's question. *What?*

Castor came toward her slowly. Artemis was shaking her head, unable to tear her gaze away from him as she retreated toward the edge of the nearest outcrop over the pond. The waterfall rushed down beside her, drowning out some of her words.

"Did you see how he died?" Castor asked desperately. "Were you there? Do you know what happened?"

Thunder boomed over them. Artemis launched another barrage of attacks, slamming her fist into his stomach, his kidneys, wherever she could reach. Blood gushed from his leg, mixing with the rainwater.

Artemis shoved him back with a single kick. He used one arm to block her and the other to stab her own blade through her shoulder.

She shrieked in pain, clawing at Castor's face. Artemis ripped the blade out of her shoulder and tackled him again. Castor knocked it out of her hand, sending the knife spinning through the air and into the pool below.

The ledge of the outcrop was at a slight angle and slanted down toward the pond. Artemis had gained the high ground, leaving Castor to fight for his footing as the wind and running water conspired to drag him over its edge.

"Don't move," Castor warned. "Please—he wouldn't want you to—"

"If you speak his name I will tear the tongue from your head!" Artemis raged. She stalked toward him.

"Don't come any closer!" Castor warned her.

"Stop!" Lore called. "Please!"

"Stay back, Lore!" he shouted over the rain. "The current is too strong—"

Artemis's body heaved with breath after labored breath, her dislocated arm hanging useless at her side.

"It does not matter what you are," Artemis told him. "It does not matter who you were, or what you might have been. For now you are dead."

"Artemis!" Athena called. "Do not destroy yourself over this mortal!"

Lore knew the look on the huntress's face, the burning resolve behind it. Artemis had always been a creature of solitude, even as she had run with a small coterie of favored hunters and nymphs through the wilds of the world. Lore felt the ache of it then, and it echoed through her. The goddess was singular in her nature, shrouded in shadows and silence, but without her twin, she was truly alone. There was nothing left for her to lose now.

"There's a monster in the river." Her voice frayed as it built into a frenzy. "A killer of gods and mortals. It'll devour all—even you, sister."

"A monster?" Athena began. "Tell me—"

"Your death is fated, imposter," Artemis told Castor. "My path is righteous."

Castor threw another bright burst of power at her, then another, trying to move her toward the trail and away from the outcropping. Wind whipped at them from all sides, forcing Castor to kneel and use a hand to brace himself to keep from going over the edge.

Artemis kicked her bow up off the ground, holding it out in front of her like she would a club, then made her way back toward him. Castor threw one last blast, and, without thinking, Artemis stepped left to avoid it.

"Stop!" Lore shouted.

Artemis's foot caught the edge of the trap she'd set. It collapsed, falling in on itself to the jagged wood points arrayed below. Athena reached for her, but Artemis spun away from both her sister and the trap.

366

"He's mine!" Artemis snarled. "His life is mine! His life is *mine*!"

That small movement brought her foot into the heavy stream of running rainwater that fed into the waterfall. Howls filled the air once more. Artemis bared her teeth in defiance as she righted herself and tried to jump the open air between the head of the waterfall and where Castor knelt at the edge of the outcrop.

A flowering bush hid the true edge of the cliff. Every muscle in Lore's body clenched as Artemis's foot hit it and slid out from under her. Castor reached out, trying to catch her before she plunged down into the pond, but Artemis pulled back, repulsed.

And fell.

THIRTY SEVEN

UNTIL THE DAY HER LIFE LEFT HER AND SHE WOKE IN THE DARK WORLD below, Lore would remember the crack of bone and the strangled cry suddenly silenced.

Castor dropped down onto his knees, gripping his hair and releasing a ragged cry of frustration.

Lore fought her way forward, bracing her hands on the trees and rocks, crawling until she reached the edge of the waterfall.

The strap of Artemis's quiver had caught on a long branch hanging over the waterfall, and it had turned into a noose, breaking her neck in an instant.

And the goddess's face . . .

The shocked scream was still lodged in Lore's throat, trying to claw its way out. She thought she might choke on it if she tried to breathe.

Athena came to stand beside her, staring down at Artemis's crown of leaves and thorns. The only sign of emotion on her face was the tightening of her jaw. It was a warrior's countenance, too hardened by centuries of death to be at the mercy of grief.

"I'm . . ." Lore began, uncertain of what to say. She wasn't sorry. But . . . "What do we do? Do you want me to cut her down so you can . . . so you can bury her until the Agon ends?"

"How do you bury a god?" Athena said. "She was power, not flesh.

This was little more than a crude vessel. Now she is . . . free."

And, Lore realized, Athena was the last of the original nine.

The dogs on the trails began to whine and howl in mourning. In the face of everything that had happened this week, Lore hadn't felt nearly as close to blowing apart as she did in that moment, hearing them drown out the creak of the quiver as Artemis's body turned and turned and turned like the endless wheel of life and death and rebirth.

Lore moved toward the small sloped cliff beside the waterfall, toward Castor. He had remained in place to heal his leg. He still looked agonized as he rose, though it clearly had nothing to do with the pain.

"You all right?" She held out a hand to help guide him over the last few perilous steps of the outcrop.

"Been better," he admitted as he reached out toward her.

Suddenly, Lore heard a whirring. At first, she thought it was the wind picking up again, rasping through the branches and stones. Then came the searing pain in her left shoulder.

Lore looked down in disbelief at the new split in her shirt, at the blood welling at her shoulder. Behind her, an arrow shivered where it had struck the trunk of a tree.

"Lore—"

Castor's expression was pained and frightened. She watched, her hand still outstretched, as blood blossomed on his drenched shirt, pouring from a single gaping wound on the left side of his chest. Through his heart.

Lore screamed, surging forward to catch his arm, but she was too slow. His lips formed a last, silent word.

Lore.

The life left his eyes, extinguishing the sparks of power. Castor slid back over the edge of the outcrop, into the water below.

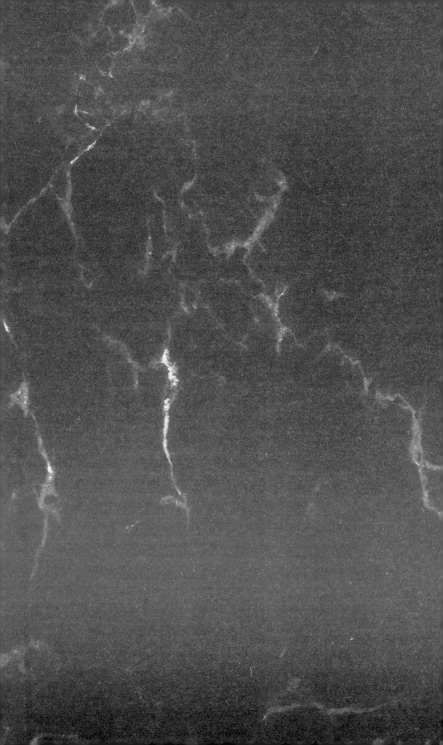

PART FOUR

—

DARK RIVERS

SEVEN YEARS EARLIER

Lore had sparred with Castor enough to know when something was wrong.

The others were distracted with excitement over the start of the Agon in two days' time, electrified by the preparations being made as the rest of the Achillides gathered in the city. Lore was distracted by something else: the countdown that Aristos Kadmou had initiated two days before, when she and her father had gone to see him.

Send me your answer by the end of the Agon.

That was nine days from now. Her father had told her not to worry, that he would never say yes. But Lore couldn't stop thinking about it.

Castor wasn't preoccupied like she and the others were. His movements seemed to drag through the air, as if his body had become too heavy for him. They had always been perfectly matched in speed—or, at least, he kept up with her, the way she tried to match his strength.

His face worried her, too. She had seen a shadow drift over it, the way a cloud passed over the sun and dimmed the world below.

Tap-tap-tap.

Lore pushed harder with her training staff on the last strike. Castor retreated a step, his back foot slipping through the pool of sweat gathering beneath him.

"Again!" the instructor ordered. "Faster!"

Lore raised her staff once more. Castor was bent slightly at the waist, shaking his head. His eyes blinked rapidly, struggling to focus on her face.

She tilted her head, silently asking, *Ready?*

He brought his own staff up. She read the answer in the set of his mouth.

Lore began the drill again—*tap* high, *tap* center, *tap* low, over and over. Castor blocked her strikes, but as he slowed, she was forced to as well.

The quick clattering of the staffs around her served as the drumbeat to a song of battered shields and ringing blades. The room was hot with the afternoon sun pouring through the windows high on the walls. The other training classes were blurs around them. The stench of bodies, oil, and rubber mats was heavy in her lungs.

On the last *tap*, Lore tested her theory, hitting harder than she needed to. Castor lost his balance, slipping down onto his knees with a faint gasp.

Lore glanced back at their instructor. The man had his back to them as he circled their section of the training hall, giving corrections and faint praise. "Good, Abreas—harder, Theron—"

As Castor righted himself, Lore feigned a wrestling hold, leaning forward until their foreheads touched and she had a hand on the back of his neck. It was the only way she'd figured out how to talk to him between breaks.

"Are you all right?" she whispered. "If you're sick you should have called out."

"I'm fine," Castor promised. "My rank is bad enough without getting more points docked. And you wouldn't have anyone to train with now that Van went home."

Evander, one of Castor's distant cousins, had come to stay at Thetis House for a few months in the lead-up to the Agon, but had been taken home by his parents after a disastrous series of training sessions. Lore had resented him for invading her time with Castor, but even more for the lessons the instructors had made her sit out so Castor and Evander could partner.

It had made her so angry—Evander couldn't block a blow without flinching and covering his head. She deserved to train more than he did, even if she wasn't born of the Achillides.

"Water!" the instructor said. "Quickly. We'll finish with knife work."

Lore took Castor's staff from him before he could protest.

Go, her eyes ordered him. She nodded toward the long bench at the back of the room where their water bottles were lined up. Castor waited for her anyway.

"Give it up, Cassie," came a snide voice. "You can't even keep up with a girl anymore."

"Jealous, Orestes?" Castor shot back, still breathing hard. "As the instructors say, we're only as good as our partners. Poor Sabas has no chance, does he?"

"Better anyone than a sick, weak worm," Orestes said. "Hurry up and die already, will you? If your mother hadn't been such a coward she would have left you on a hill somewhere."

Lore slammed her water bottle down on the bench and rounded on him. Castor kept a faint hold on her wrist, stopping her.

"You would know all about that," Castor said, "living so bravely with half a brain. Don't worry, no one notices that you still haven't mastered the first-year sword skills. We're all pulling for you, though."

Their class traded whispers around them, glancing back at

the instructor to see if the man would intervene. He was busy consulting with another instructor. Others grinned, anticipating the fight to come.

"At least I'm not going to become a snake bride," Orestes snapped.

Lore drew in a sharp breath. Castor glanced at her, dark brows furrowed. Orestes looked like the crow who'd caught the worm.

"She didn't tell you?" he said as they made their way back toward the thin training mats. "This is her last day here. Patér is furious that her ass of a father agreed to marry her off to the archon of the Kadmides. The elders met last night and agreed to kick her out. My father told me so. The only reason they didn't send her home this morning is because her father begged and begged for one last day."

Hurt and confusion wrestled on Castor's face as he watched her, waiting for confirmation. Lore's only heated with a flush of blood.

"It's not true," she told him. "It's not!"

She hadn't told him about the meeting with the Kadmides because . . . because she still didn't really understand what had happened. But her father would refuse Aristos Kadmou's offer. He would never give her to him.

"No one refuses the Kadmides archon," Orestes told her smugly. "Maybe he'll smother you while he ruts over you like—"

Castor slammed his fist into the side of Orestes's head, knocking him sideways. The others were brimming with glee as Orestes tackled Castor.

If he had been at his full strength, Castor never would have fallen the way he did then.

"Enough!" the instructor said. "Take your positions. We'll start again—"

But Castor didn't move. Couldn't move.

"Cas?" Lore said.

He didn't respond. His eyes rolled back and his whole body began to convulse.

Lore dropped to her knees beside him, trying to hold him still.

"What did you do?" she screamed at Orestes. But even the boy seemed shocked. Their instructor dropped a hand beneath Castor's head to keep it from banging against the wood floor.

"Call for the healer on duty!" he barked at one of the trainees.

"What did you do?" she demanded again. Orestes backed away as she lunged at him, beating her fists into Orestes's stomach. It was the last thing she remembered before her mind blacked out. The next she knew, her instructor had his arms locked around her center and had lifted her off Orestes. The boy's face was a bloody, pulpy mess. Her hands were covered in it.

"I'll kill you," she swore. Orestes coughed, spitting up snot and blood. His own hetaîros knelt beside him, wide-eyed as he stared at Lore.

"You'll have to wait another seven years to try, little gorgon," her instructor growled. "If the serpent ever lets you out of his den."

Lore tried to break out of his grip, but he had a master's hold on her. Her hand strained toward Castor, but she couldn't see him, only his sandaled feet sticking out among those gathered around him.

Hours later, after Healer Kallias had come bringing unwelcome news, Lore was finally allowed into the rooms Castor and his father shared at Thetis House to see him.

Lore stood to the left of his bed, watching the rise and fall of his chest, counting them as she would her steps in a drill. Chiron slept at Castor's feet. He licked at her hand as she gave him a good scratch behind his ears.

"Do you think I was wrong?" she whispered to him. She saw the *no* in Chiron's dark eyes, and agreed.

Her heart hammered in her chest, echoing the blows she had given Orestes. She touched the rough bandages Castor's father had wrapped around her knuckles after Healer Kallias had refused to. Orestes, apparently, was her nephew.

She heard her parents arrive through the crack in the bedroom door. As the building's caretaker, Castor's father could slip them in through a side entrance and the service elevator, lessening their chances of being seen by the Achillides. Lore was ashamed by how badly she wanted to go to her mother—to be held until the healer's words disappeared.

There is nothing more to be done. No Unblooded treatment can cure him.

Fragments of their hushed conversation drifted through the room, interrupted by the soft whirring and beeping of the strange medical devices around Castor's bed. Lore drifted toward the door, ears straining to hear them, but reading half of the words on their lips, the way she and Castor had taught themselves to in order to spy on the bloodline's elders. A sound like radio static grew in her ears.

"What am I supposed to do?" Castor's father whispered. "Is he suffering because I can't let him go? Is this only hubris, thinking I can change an impossible outcome?"

"No, of course not," Lore's mother replied, her voice low and soothing as she clasped his hands between her own. "There is always hope."

"Hope has abandoned us," Cleon said. "The elders informed me that they will no longer pay for treatment, and he is too weak to travel abroad to those who might help us."

Lore's hands curled into fists at her sides, and her whole body, from her skin down to her soul, began to vibrate with fury. This wasn't right. This wasn't how it was supposed to be—

"There's nothing to be done but surrender to the weaving of the Fates and allow him the dignity of death," Cleon said.

"*No!*" She burst out from behind the door. Chiron barked behind her, startled by the noise and movement. Her body felt like it might explode as she lashed out at Castor's pathetic excuse for a father. He wanted Castor to die—he was going to let Castor go. A hunter always fought, like the men in the legend; they were never supposed to give up.

"Stop this, Melora," her father ordered, grabbing her by the arm and pulling her back. "Stop this at once!"

"You coward!" Lore snarled at Cleon, struggling against her father's hand. "Hades take you, you soft-bellied dog! You're the one who deserves to die, not him!"

"Melora!" her mother said, aghast.

But Castor's father only wept. "I wish he would, I wish he would . . ."

"Apologize at once," her father said, shifting her toward Cleon Achilleos.

Lore turned her head away, her jaw clenched. *No.* The gods hated cowards, and so did she.

Her father drew her back into the bedroom with a sharp "Stay here until you calm down."

The door shut behind him. Lore banged both hands against it, hot tears streaking down her cheeks. Inside her was a riot of pain and confusion, and she couldn't stand it.

The instructors said, over and over, that there was no greater dishonor than cowardice. Castor's father might give up, but she wouldn't. She would bring Castor to every doctor in the city if she had to carry him on her back. She would fight until her body gave out, and then she would crawl if she had to.

"He's just sad, Lore."

Castor's voice was barely a whisper by the time it reached her.

Lore looked up, dashing the tears in her eyes against her arm. She went to him, crawling onto the narrow bed. Castor shifted over on the mattress as much as he could to make room for her. She lay back, her hands still shaking as she let them rest on her stomach. Chiron let out a grumpy noise as he moved to make room for her feet.

"I don't care," Lore whispered, turning to look at him. His skin was still pale, almost as translucent as the tubes in his nose feeding him oxygen. But then he smiled, and it made her feel a little better.

"You'll be fine," she told him. "There's always another way."

"I don't think so," he said. "Not this time."

She pressed her hands hard against her stomach to force them to be still. "I have an idea for how we can watch the Awakening without anyone knowing."

"Healer Kallias said I can't leave this bed," Castor said. "That . . . I need to rest."

"And then," Lore continued, sitting up. The words babbled out of her, but she didn't care. "After that, we can go buy ice cream in that place near our apartment that's always open. Our neighbor gave me a few dollars for watering her plants while she was out of town—"

"Lore," he said, and then used that word she hated almost more than any other. "Stop . . . It's okay. Really."

She drew in a deep breath. Something wild clawed at the inside of her chest. "It's not okay! You'll be fine. Healer Kallias is stupid. She doesn't know anything."

"It's all right," he said softly. "I'll see my mother again. I won't be alone. I'm not afraid."

"I won't let you go," she told him, her voice low with promise. She wouldn't. He was her friend and hetaîros, her companion and partner in all things. She would defend him if he fell, cut at anything or anyone who threatened him; her blade was his, and his hers.

"Hey," he said softly. "Did you hear the one about the dancing dogs?"

Lore's brow furrowed as her spiraling thoughts suddenly stopped. "What?"

His smile was weak, but still there. "No one wanted to partner with them because they all had two left feet."

Lore shook her head. Even Chiron seemed to groan. "Castor Achilleos, that is the worst joke you have ever told."

He gave a small shrug, but even his little grin fell as silence descended over them, and his breathing became more labored.

"You won't die," Lore whispered. "You won't. And if you do, I'll follow you to the Underworld and drag you back. I'm not scared, either. I'm not scared of anything."

Her hand closed around his thin wrist, as if she could keep him alive by the force of her will alone. His pulse fluttered beneath her fingertips.

He watched her, his lips pale as they pressed into a thin, bloodless line. He was fighting his exhaustion, blinking against the pull of it. She didn't like that, either, so Lore forced herself to nod.

"No," he said. "No, Lore—swear you won't."

When she didn't, he gripped her by the back of the neck, bringing

381

their foreheads together. His hand shook from the effort it took, but Lore pretended not to notice.

"Swear it," he whispered. His eyelashes were dark against his cheek as he closed his eyes. The tension in Castor's body released with sleep, but her mind, her very soul, blazed.

"I know my fate," she whispered to him.

And I will change yours.

THIRTY EIGHT

For one terrible moment, Lore could not move, could not think, could not do anything other than stare at the place where Castor had been standing. The rain washed the puddle of his blood away, feeding it to the growing stain in the water below.

Dead.

Just beyond the pond stood a dozen hunters. Some wore masks—but not Iro. Not the tall male hunter who stood beside her. The one who still had his crossbow trained in her direction.

Across the distance, through the rain, Lore's gaze met that of her friend. Iro stared up at her, her eyes defiant, her face cold.

"Get down!" Athena was yelling to her. *"Melora!"*

Another arrow flew, this time from a different hunter. It sliced along Lore's upper arm. The searing pain tore through her shock. Iro barked something at the hunters, a few of whom scattered, falling back into the city streets. The others turned their bows away from Lore, toward where Athena sheltered behind a tree.

More arrows flew. Athena sank even lower, careful to keep her head covered as the tree trunk splintered above her.

Lore's whole body throbbed with her heartbeat. She couldn't seem to bring her mind back into her body.

Dead.

"We must leave this place," Athena called to her. She slid something across the wet distance between them. Lore stared down at the silver of Artemis's hunting knife, watching the rain slide off it.

Dead.

A small flame grew at the center of her chest. She held on to that, she let it burn, because it was *something* in that numb nothingness. Lore held it until she recognized it for what it was.

Fury.

She seized the knife and stood, keeping low among the brush. Every part of her was straining to rush forward and cut the killer's throat. To punish Iro. It would be justified. Demanded, even, by the rules of their hunt.

Iro and the hunter who had fired the killing shot stepped over the ledge of the pond and trudged forward through the relentless rain. He dropped his bow and unsheathed a sword slowly, his gaze fixed on Castor's dark shape face-down in the water. Iro had a dory in her other hand, and used it to check her balance as they made their way across the pond's unseen basin.

Weapons they had taken from the Kadmides, at Lore's insistence.

And they had repaid her by doing *this*. By taking Castor from her.

Her head pounded with the blistering force of her thoughts. Lore reached the lower level of the park, riding the river of mud, rain, and loose rocks down to the edge of the pond.

"Iro Odysseos!" she shouted, her voice hoarse.

Iro spun as Lore jumped into the water, raising her dory. She waved back the other hunters hovering by the pond. "Stay back, Lore!"

"How could you?" Lore snarled. "After everything we did for you—"

Her foot slid against something long and thin in the soft bottom of the pond. An electric trill moved up her spine when she realized what it was.

Athena's dory.

She pulled it up with her foot, lifting it from the water with relish. The length of the spear would give her the biggest advantage over the hunter.

"We need a god in our bloodline," Iro shouted back to her. "You've turned your back on this world, but we haven't! If we're to ever repay Wrath for what he did to our line, we need our own protector!"

Lore turned the dory in her hands, still striding toward her. The hunter beside Iro shifted, uncertain of what to do.

"You couldn't even do the dirty work yourself," Lore snarled. "You let a man kill him for you."

"I had hoped it would be Artemis, or Athena," Iro said, fighting for a measure of calm in her voice. She didn't back away, even as Lore threw the knife in her left hand, flinging it into the other Odysseide hunter's throat.

He went down with a startled gasp, choking on his own blood. Iro whirled back to Lore, shocked.

"You'll—you'll ascend," Iro managed to get out. "Why hasn't the power taken hold . . . ?"

The words washed over Lore as if they had been spoken in a language she couldn't understand. There was nothing else in her world aside from the weapon in her hand and Iro.

Lore whipped the dory's sauroter up, catching Iro under the chin and slicing the right side of her face. She might have split the girl's eye like a grape if Iro hadn't leaned back, slamming the staff of her own dory against Lore's to drive it away.

You took him from me, Lore thought, letting her pain feed the explosion of hatred building in her mind. *You're not going to touch him.*

"He might not be—" Iro pressed a hand to the blood streaming down her face, spitting a wad of it from her mouth. "You are not my enemy, Lore!"

"You've *made* me your enemy!" Lore spun the dory high overhead, allowing Iro to block her strike so she could kick the other girl in the chest. The water saved Iro's balance, but slowed her advance on Lore.

She leaned right as Iro thrust forward—Lore tried to stab the sauroter down onto Iro's foot, but it was almost impossible to see anything beneath the frantic shivering of the water. Rain poured over them. Iro stooped, pulled the knife from the dead hunter's neck, and threw it. Lore repelled it with the metal body of the dory with enough force to cause a spark.

The rhythm of the fight set in, and Lore disappeared into the strength of her body, into the past, until she found the little girl who would have clawed the heart out of her opponent to claim victory.

Then she unleashed her in all of her ferocity. Every agonizing loss, every humiliation, every memory of that suffocating hopelessness raged in her like a tempest.

Iro finally landed a hit, splitting the skin of Lore's upper arm as she parried her attempt to shove the head of the spear through Iro's chest.

She deserves to die, Lore thought viciously. *They all do.*

Let her become the monster who haunted their legends. Her kleos would be glorious infamy.

Lore feinted a low hit to Iro's stomach to skim her hand beneath the water in order to pull up the knife again. The whites of Iro's eyes flashed as Lore stabbed it through the girl's thigh and flipped the dory to bring the sauroter to Iro's throat.

Athena's form appeared at the edge of the pond, not far from where the bodies of the other Odysseides were now scattered.

Iro was struggling to back away with her wounded leg, looking for a quick escape. Blood ran down her face. Lore had the distant thought that Iro's wound could be a twin to the scar the Odysseides' archon had given her the night of his death.

Lore stalked toward her again. The wound wouldn't have a chance to scar.

Iro held out a dory to ward her off, struggling to stand to her full height.

The weapon began to turn a molten red. Heat seemed to radiate from its tip, turning the rain around them to steam. Iro stared down at it as the heat spread, the steel becoming soft in her grip. She flung the weapon away into the water before it could singe her hand.

Lore turned.

Castor rose slowly from the water, his face expressionless, his eyes burning gold.

THIRTY NINE

THE AIR SHIMMERED AROUND CASTOR, ALIVE WITH POWER.

As the dory slipped from Lore's fingers, she lost all sensation in her body.

Not real. This was . . . It was impossible.

She had watched him die. Her gaze dropped to his chest, to the place the arrow had pierced his heart. Beneath the bloodstained tear in his shirt was new, unmarred skin where the wound should have been. Which meant . . .

The light and power around Castor intensified. He took in the sight of the dead hunter, then Iro.

"Leave," he told her.

"What—is—this," Iro gasped. "Who are you? You were . . ."

"*Leave,*" Castor thundered.

This time, Iro had the sense to run. She struggled through the rain and water, clutching her wounded leg. Castor paid no attention to her, but looked again at the body of the hunter.

"Did you do this?" he asked softly.

Lore's jaw clenched painfully at the distress in his voice. "Yes. And I would do it again."

His eyes closed and slowly opened again, as if waking from a dream. "It doesn't matter what happens to me—you can't do this to yourself."

The brief joy she'd felt turned to ashes in her mouth. How dare he—how dare he pass judgment on her like this, like they were children again and she didn't know right from wrong?

"I can do whatever I want," Lore said coldly.

"But you're not," he said. "I don't believe this is really what you want—to kill people, to be a hunter."

"I make my own choices," she said. "You're the only one who won't play by the same rules as everyone else. It's not complicity. It's survival."

He stared at her in disbelief. "Do you hear what you're saying? Do you think this is what your parents would want—for you to lose yourself avenging them?"

"Don't you dare use them as a weapon against me!" Lore snarled.

Whatever Castor would have said next vanished as Athena stormed toward them.

"What are you, imposter?" Athena demanded. "You are not mortal, which means you are no god. *What are you?*"

"I'm . . ." Castor looked down at his hands, tendrils of power still wrapped around them like golden rings, then touched the place the arrow had passed through him.

Artemis had asked the same question. *What are you?*

"How do you live?" Athena demanded. "What are you keeping from us?"

"Nothing," he said, looking to Lore. "I can't explain this—I don't remember what happened that day—"

"What do you know about the Agon that we do not?" Athena continued. "I do not believe that you remember nothing. If you are immortal these seven days, you have learned something—*done* something—and you have withheld it from us, your allies."

"I don't—" Castor's voice was low, rough. "*I don't remember.* There

389

was pain, and then darkness—and then I woke up."

"You *lie*," Athena told him. "You are here, but not part of the hunt. Not truly. Tell me what you are. My sister was correct—your power feels different, somehow. It always has—it flows through you, but is not born of you."

Lore turned to her in shock. "What does that mean?"

The goddess only stared at Castor until, finally, Lore looked back toward him, too. Her pulse spiked and she suddenly felt like she was drowning in the air as one clear voice emerged.

None of this is real.

"Your lost memory is a convenient lie to cover the truth of how a god might escape the hunt," Athena said. "Is that why you did not present yourself in physical form these last seven years? Were you even in this realm at all?"

None of this is real.

Not Gil, not her life here, not even Castor and the shelter his familiar presence had given her heart.

Castor didn't acknowledge the goddess, but tried to catch Lore's gaze again. "You don't believe me."

Lore couldn't be caught in another god's deception. She couldn't surrender to becoming a game piece moved against her will. But this was Castor.

Wasn't it?

"We are just trying to figure out what's going on," Lore said.

He watched Lore, his devastation clear.

"*We*," he repeated.

Lore replayed her own words in her mind. Athena's presence was steadying behind her. It bolstered her, giving her one last bit of strength to keep from unraveling.

"*We,*" she confirmed.

She and Athena would do whatever was necessary, whatever was justified, until the last breath left Wrath's mortal body.

Castor had never wanted to help them see this plan through. If he truly didn't know how he ascended and that he couldn't die . . . If he truly had no ulterior motives for working with them . . . Lore needed him to prove himself to her now. It would be her last offer: join us, or leave.

With one last look at her, he turned and walked away.

He crossed through the water, his head down and shoulders hunched. Panic seized Lore at the sight of him growing smaller and smaller and the rain engulfing him.

Lore took a step forward, but Athena lowered an arm, blocking her. The sound of emergency sirens blared toward them, growing in intensity and pitch as they neared.

"He is not needed," the goddess said. "We were chosen for this, you and I."

Lore's body felt wooden as they climbed the stairs toward the quiet of Morningside Heights. As they reached the lookout point, however, Athena suddenly pivoted back toward the park, her face strained with concentration. She studied the red and blue lights of the emergency vehicles as they appeared below, racing down the street.

"We need to go," Lore said.

Athena held out a hand to silence her.

A tremor moved through the ground like a serpent through sand. The vibration raced up Lore's legs and along her spine, setting every nerve ablaze. Thunder let out a low murmur of displeasure.

Only, it wasn't thunder.

It stormed through the streets with a monster's roar, overpowering

391

everything in its path as it charged forward with a violence that stole the breath from her lungs.

Dark water. So much of it—more than Lore had ever seen, rushing, rushing, rushing from the nearby river, tearing through the streets. The ambulances and cop cars along the park disappeared beneath the surging wave, rolled like toys, their lights suddenly gone. The officers and emergency workers ran, but they weren't fast enough to avoid being carried away.

And still, the water wasn't satisfied.

It rose higher with each passing second, swallowing signs, street-lights, and buildings—drowning the city whole.

FORTY

HIGH UP FROM THE LOOKOUT POINT, LORE WATCHED HELPLESSLY AS the punishing crush of water broke through brick walls and carried the debris like prizes of war. She heard screaming and started for the stairs. Athena caught her wrist in a steely grip, stopping her.

"We have to help them!" Lore said, trying to extract herself from Athena's impossibly strong hold.

The goddess looked out onto the rising waters, taking in the sight and smell of it churning and churning.

Lore closed her eyes, but the cataclysmic sounds of the water smashing through windows, the honking and crashing of cars, the small, distant voices begging for help, drilled into her mind until Lore thought she would scream, if just to drown it all out.

Athena's face was inscrutable. There was none of the horror Lore felt, or the helplessness. If anything, there was recognition. She had seen bigger, worse floods—floods meant to wipe humans from the face of the Earth. Floods meant to begin life on Earth again after the failures of the doomed men of the Silver and Bronze Ages.

"This can't just be a storm surge," Lore choked out. "There's too much water, and it's not stopping—this has to be unnatural. And the people who live on lower levels of the buildings and town houses . . ."

Lore couldn't bear to finish the thought aloud. *None of them would have had time to get out.*

All along Manhattan and the outer boroughs, evacuation zones for hurricanes and other superstorms would be flooding. Manhattan's natural elevation rose the further inland you were, but the lower-lying waterfronts—the neighborhoods along both rivers—and their southernmost reaches up through Thirty-Fourth Street were prone to flooding.

If it was this bad *here . . .*

All of those people, she thought, desperately.

Fear sliced through her, stinging her down to her soul. If Van hadn't gotten Miles far enough away, to higher ground . . .

Lore pulled out her phone, but there was no service. *Shit.*

"This is not the rivers," Athena said, her face shadowed. "It is a god."

"Tidebringer," Lore whispered.

The goddess nodded. "Evander of the Achillides was mistaken. The false Poseidon lives, and she is allied with our enemy."

Lore let the venom of anger burn in her again at the sight of the dark water pouring through the streets. At the destruction the Agon had brought to her city.

"You are certain there is no chance the false Ares has found the aegis?" Athena asked again. "As one of the Perseides she would be able to decipher the poem—"

"No—I mean, I don't know." Lore's fear grew fangs at the idea that she hadn't been as careful as she thought she had. "It could be worse than that. Even as a god, she could be able to wield the aegis on Wrath's behalf."

And the flood might be only the first phase of Wrath's plan to win the Agon.

Lore forced herself to take a deep breath. "I don't think he has the aegis, at least not yet. We still have time to kill him and end this."

Maybe a part of her was beginning to believe in the Fates again, and that there was a pattern to this. One that had always called for her and the goddess to finish this together.

Lore turned back toward Morningside Heights, her body straining with the need to move. "So we hunt."

"So we hunt," Athena echoed, and followed.

Lore had always taken a certain comfort in the unseen movement of her city.

Even when the streets were empty save for a handful of early-morning cabs, she knew they still had a pulse. That there was water rushing through the pipes below. That trains were pulling their empty cars from station to station. Buried power lines hummed a song that only the cement could hear.

Now the city's stillness brought a feeling of decay.

From six stories up, Lore had a clearer view of the flooded city blocks and those New Yorkers brave enough to try to wade through waist-high water. City crews were trying to pump it out of the streets, but the rivers—both the East and Hudson—continued to swell. The stagnant water was so deep in some places that the NYPD and Coast Guard were using boats and helicopters to rescue those people who had become stranded, or to deliver supplies.

Lore could no longer feel the city's heartbeat.

She and Athena had collected scraps of rumors on their slow crawl downtown, braiding them together to create the bigger picture of what the city had become. *A historic storm. Mistaken weather predictions. Rising sea levels. A freak convergence of events.* Everyone had a different theory.

Emergency workers and city officials were issuing directions over the radio while cell towers were down. Hospitals were being evacuated first as their backup generators failed one by one. Whole sections of Central Park were being turned into relief camps. Red Cross volunteers, along with the National Guard, tried distributing supplies, but as the hours passed, they were overwhelmed by demand.

Convenience and grocery stores were being pillaged by desperate city dwellers, and there was nothing anyone could or would do to stop them. Subway tunnels were inaccessible, and no trains could get in or out of the city. Bridges were closed to traffic. A constant buzz of police and news helicopters flew by overhead, crowding the skies.

New Yorkers were some of the best people in the world, but even Lore recognized they had their limits. The isolation had been instant and devastating.

This is what Wrath wants, Lore thought. To put the city on edge, to strain its resources.

She closed her mind and heart off to the flooded streets, the sight of injuries, the sobbing. She closed her heart off to anything but what needed to be done now.

She and Athena had spent the entirety of the night searching for Wrath's hunters, continuing into the morning. Around ten o'clock, Lore had spotted a Kadmides lioness near the Empire State Building, recognizing her from the assault on Ithaka House. They had tracked her uptown until she'd disappeared into a small boutique hotel on the Upper East Side. Now they watched the entrance from the roof of the building across the street, waiting for her to finally reemerge.

"You love this city," Athena said. "It is your pride."

The goddess all but glowed in the midday sun. The brief respite had given them both the opportunity to dry their shoes and clothes, though it was pointless, given they'd be returning to the floodwaters soon enough.

Lore lifted a shoulder in a shrug. "I might have to share it with eight million other people, but it's always been my least complicated relationship."

"Hm." Athena's presence was oppressive in more ways than one, but as the last few hours had passed, something had shifted. She was brimming with eagerness, or maybe just the simple anxiety of knowing that it was Wednesday morning, and they had less than half a week left to finish this.

"Hold on to what you feel for your home," Athena told her. "It will never abandon you if you serve it well. It is not so fickle as mortals."

Castor's face rose in her mind. Lore stamped it out before it could linger there long.

"That's probably true," Lore said, finally. She leaned over the edge of the roof, quickly searching the sidewalk below. "Where is this girl?"

Athena drank the last of her water, tossing the bottle away. Lore sat back on her heels, and, for the first time, began to doubt their plan. They didn't have time to wait for the lioness to rest or meet with whoever was inside. They needed another lead.

"What was it that your sister said?" she asked. "That there's a monster in the river? A killer of both gods and mortals?"

"I would not spare any great thought to my sister's words," Athena said. "She was unwell, and did not know her own mind."

There was something about that, though—something Lore couldn't place.

"There is still much we do not know," Athena said. "I feel as if the shards of the truth lie scattered before us. Hermes, the imposter's desire for the aegis, even the false Apollo." Her gaze sharpened. "Perhaps he is somehow a true god—or yet another god in disguise—and wished to enter the hunt to ascertain some information?"

"He's Castor," Lore said, more sure of it now than she had been with him standing before her. "Somehow . . . he's Castor. He knew too much from my past to be anyone else."

"Any god would know such things," Athena said. "They would ingratiate themselves into your life, subtly guiding you onto a path of their choosing, all with you none the wiser. As I said, we appear to you as what you need or desire."

"Like Hermes," Lore said softly. The god had become the one person Lore would have trusted in that moment—a compassionate friend far removed from the world of the Agon. He had played to her fear and anguish.

"Perhaps you are correct and it is Castor of the Achillides," Athena said. "Apollo is gone. The false god possesses his power, though the feeling is strange—I do not understand it. It has no logical explanation."

Lore shook her head. Thoughts swirled in her, all those countless doubts and coincidences trying to connect like lightning whipping across the sky.

"There is a lesson to be had in even this. Take my counsel on this matter: it is acceptable, even preferable, to be alone," Athena told her, "when those around you would hold you back or deceive you. The exceptional among mortals will always stand alone, for no one in the world was made for their task. Take confidence in that, and let it be a poison to your fear."

A small smile curved on the goddess's face.

"What?" Lore asked.

"I had forgotten what it felt like," Athena said. "To take on the mantle of Mentor."

Lore's heart gave an involuntary kick in her chest when she realized what that meant.

"No disguise necessary this time," Lore pointed out, leaning over the edge of the building again. A National Guard patrol was still moving slowly up the street, within eyeshot of the building. She pulled back.

"Indeed," Athena said, a note of amusement in the word. "It is tiresome to wear another's face, but men will so often only listen to other men."

Lore raised her eyebrows, but couldn't argue with that. "Do you still return to your city? The one named for you?"

"I return to them all," Athena said. "And I always will, until the last voice calling out to me is vanquished by time."

"And then what?" Lore asked.

"I will continue to strive to return to my father, and my home," Athena said. "That is all I desire now."

Whatever softness had slipped into the goddess's features disappeared in an instant. Lore felt a touch of ice at the base of her spine at the sight.

"I must tell you something, Melora," Athena said, the sparks storming in her gray eyes. "And give a warning. I am becoming less certain I can fight the imposter Ares alone. Unlike the false Apollo, I can be killed. As strong as I am, our foe will whittle that strength away. I will need your help to overcome him . . . Unless, of course, you wish to claim his power."

Lore drew in a sharp breath. "No. I don't."

She never wanted the feeling of being hunted, being trapped, ever again. Ares's power would drive her mind to the brink.

And make you invincible, her mind whispered.

No. Ares's power was as much a curse as it was a boon, even as it had brought countless hunters kleos as they'd claimed it. Lore had caused enough damage and death in her short lifetime. But there was that girl inside her, hungry still. The last of her name in all the world. Who would remember her?

Lore shook her head, hugging her arms to her chest. She would fight to restore her family's honor and glory as herself. She would avenge them as Melora Perseous.

Go get it. The thought moved through her, warm and powerful. *Go claim your inheritance. Use it against him.*

Even with the aegis, Lore would wither beneath Wrath's power. But if it was in the hands of someone stronger . . . someone who knew how to wield it, and at its full potential . . .

"You really think you can't handle him?" Lore asked slowly. It would be a terrifying thing to behold—Athena reunited with the aegis, roaring into battle.

"Only the Moirai could say with certainty," Athena said. "It pains me to admit such things. Do not ask me this again."

"But if there was something that could level the playing field . . . ?" Lore began, her voice tight.

The goddess's gaze slid back toward her. "It would be most welcome."

The static in Lore's ears returned, quickening her pulse.

But the poem . . . she thought.

Would it really be that awful if Athena emerged as the victor, if it meant that the Agon would finally end?

After centuries of being hunted, Athena only wanted to leave this world and return to her own realm. She had said it herself, both to Artemis and just now.

Giving the shield to Athena wouldn't change the past, but it might start Lore—and Athena herself—on the path to absolution.

There was movement at the edge of her vision. The lioness finally emerged from the hotel, clutching a manila envelope. She started north again on Park Avenue, weaving through the partially submerged cars and debris.

Athena nodded to Lore. They took to the fire escape, climbing down into the cool water. They had to move slowly to avoid alerting the lioness with splashing. The distance between them and the girl grew, but so few people were outside, tracking her wasn't difficult.

When they reached Seventy-Eighth Street, the lioness made a sharp right—and stopped Lore in her tracks.

She *had* forgotten something. Years ago, she and Castor had made a game of finding all of the bloodlines' hideouts within the city. Many were open secrets, but even more existed somewhere between rumor and fact. They had only found this place after hearing one of the instructors talking about it, himself guessing where it might be.

Athena slowed, looking to her. Ahead of them was the East River, and between it and them was a series of impressive prewar ivory apartment buildings.

"One of the Kadmides' properties," Lore explained. "I completely forgot about it. Let's see if there's a place we can get a good view of who's coming and going."

That turned out to be a gated window of Public School 158 across the street. After breaking in through a door on York Avenue, they navigated the school's halls until they found an unobstructed view of the Kadmides' building.

Within minutes, three figures in traditional black hunter robes waded down a paved lane between the west side of the building and the one next to it.

The gate there was open, but the lioness waited for the hunters to meet her on the street. One of the new arrivals opened the manila envelope and pulled out a set of what looked to be keys. He distributed them to the others, including the lioness.

She was the first to leave, heading back the way she'd come. The others stopped to remove their robes before following. Lore waited until they were well away before speaking.

"If it's anything like Thetis House, the entrance isn't the front door . . ."

Almost as soon as the words were out of her mouth, more hunters appeared. All of them coming down toward the street from that same tight lane, dripping wet. The entrance had to be somewhere along that narrow driveway, she realized, and had to be underground if they were soaked through. A basement maybe?

They spotted a brass plaque engraved with its building number and name. RIVER HOUSE III.

"There *is* a monster in the river," Lore said.

Athena turned to her, eyebrows raised in invitation.

Lore took it.

SEVEN YEARS EARLIER

LORE WAS IN THE MIDDLE OF WASHING HER DINNER PLATE WHEN HER mother and father returned from the Agon one day too soon.

Her father dropped his travel bag beside the door, his face tense as he absorbed the sight of the dimly lit apartment. Her mother gripped his arm and gave it a reassuring squeeze.

Lore couldn't understand what she was seeing. Her parents had told her that they would stay away for all seven days, sleeping in a hotel in the city, to ensure no harm followed them home.

Lore had tried her best to keep the apartment tidy and clean in the meantime. She'd put the dishes away, stored Damara and Pia's bright toys in their assigned drawers, and locked her grandmother's blades back in their chest after she'd sharpened them. Her sisters were too young to touch them, but she wasn't. Lore liked to run her fingers over the patterns carved into the hilt, to close her eyes and imagine.

One more cycle, her mother had told her. *You only need to work hard and be patient until then.*

One more cycle, then she could prove herself.

One more cycle, then she could save Castor. He was still alive, and he would keep fighting, she knew that in her soul. If she helped her papa kill a god, they would have enough money to find better doctors and medicine for Castor.

One more cycle.

She had kept herself and her sisters in the apartment all week, finding games and activities to occupy them. Tonight should have been no different: she would put her plate away, throw the frozen pizza box down the garbage chute, brush her teeth, kiss Damara good night in her crib, and then climb into bed with Pia, wrapping the blanket that smelled like their mother's orange-blossom perfume around them both.

"What are you doing here?"

Both turned at the sound of Lore's voice.

"Oh—I didn't think you'd still be awake," her mother said, moving toward her.

Lore jumped down off the stool, backing away from her outstretched arms.

"What are you doing here?" Lore asked again.

Her mother and father exchanged a look that Lore did not understand. Her father hadn't shaved in days, and his face was prickly with a new beard. There was a cut above his left eye, and he seemed to be moving with a slight limp. Lore scanned her mother, only finding a bruise on her cheek and a wrapped wrist. Neither of them had an injury severe enough to force them to leave the hunt early and face the shame of that choice. Not that she could see.

"I was taking good care of them," Lore insisted. "I was being a good girl. I did everything you asked me to."

"I know you did," her mother said softly.

Then why?

Her father knelt in front of her, trying to gather Lore into his arms. She pulled back until she bumped into the counter. "Won't you give your papa a kiss?"

Lore turned her head away, her heart beating hard, her thoughts shooting in a million different directions at once. "You shouldn't be home. It's not over."

"It is for us," her father said gently.

One more cycle.

She whirled toward him, her breath catching. Lore hated the way her voice quivered. "Until next time?"

"Until forever, chrysaphenia mou," her mother said. "Your father and I came to a decision, one we should have made years ago. We will hunt no more."

Lore shook her head, covering her ears to try to block the words. Her mother exchanged another look with her father, who rose onto his feet.

"We have waited as long as we could," her father said. "The situation has become grave, and we need to use the distraction of the Agon to leave the city. Tonight, we'll pack what we need and, tomorrow, begin a new life elsewhere."

It didn't make sense. What could have changed?

"Are you scared of Aristos Kadmou? You told me the Perseides are afraid of nothing," Lore said. "You told me the House of Perseus was the most noble of them all. You said . . . You said . . ."

All the other bloodlines spat at them, laughing each time her father had asked to ally. Their line had lost its inheritance; they fought with flawed weapons other lines had discarded. But Lore had never thought they'd lose their pride. Honor was the most important thing—and the only thing—left to them.

More important than the very breath in your lungs, her instructor had said. *You cannot survive without it, and you would not wish to.*

"I know what I told you, Melora," her father said. "But this can't

405

continue. We can't endure this world. Aristos Kadmou has claimed the power of Ares. Do you understand what that means?" Lore resented his careful pause, the assumption that she could not handle the truth.

She ignored the spike of fear at the thought of a man like Aristos with immortality—with power he didn't deserve. She did understand what it meant.

She understood that, in seven years, she would cut him until his mortal blood rained down, and then she would bring him to her father to kill.

"We're doing this for you and your sisters," he continued. "We *are* leaving the Agon and this city, and we're going as far as the winds will take us."

I will never hunt.

The words brought a cold, terrible feeling into the pit of Lore's stomach. She would never be more than what she was now: a girl standing at the threshold of a secret world, without a key to unlock the way.

"No," Lore said. Her grandmother's knives were waiting for her, a promise yet to be kept. "You are cowards. You are *cowards*, and if you won't fight, then I will!"

Her mother looked away, pressing a hand to her mouth in obvious distress.

"You will not speak to us that way, Melora," her father said. The anger in his words made her feel sicker.

"I hate you," she whispered between clenched teeth.

"Lore," her mother said. "Please."

"I *hate* you," Lore repeated. "And I'll hate you forever!"

"Very well." Her father stared down at her, his face shadowed. "At least you'll be alive to do so."

She pushed past him, storming across the apartment and into the bedroom she shared with her sisters. Her body shook as she stood in the dark, tears streaming down her face. The floorboards creaked on the other side of the door. She heard the soft exchange of her parents' voices.

Not wanting to speak to them, not wanting to *look* at them, she climbed into bed beside Olympia and pulled the blanket over her head.

"Leave her, Helena," her father said. "She's got my temper, and we both know only time can settle it."

"She needs to understand," her mother whispered back.

"I don't want the girls to live in fear," her father said. "I won't have it haunt them."

Her mother persisted. "She needs to know that he's ascended. We should have left before the week began."

"We had to at least try," her father said. "If one of us had been able to ascend, we could have protected them."

"She needs to know the consequences," her mother said. "That we cannot hide ourselves from him. That he won't just come for her, but for all of us . . . and for *it*."

Their footsteps receded, taking their voices with them. Lore clenched her fists, squeezing her eyes shut. Her body shook with anger, and she thought she would explode if she didn't scream.

Olympia turned and curled up next to her like a sleepy puppy, butting her head of dark curls against Lore's chest.

Tears came, hot and stinging. They streamed like a river with no beginning or end, dripping down her cheeks, into the pillow, into the mattress.

Her parents were taking everything from her, all because they were afraid.

Lore wasn't afraid of anything—not the gods, not death, and not Aristos Kadmou and his snakes.

"Don't fight, Lolo," Olympia whispered, clutching at the front of Lore's night shirt. "Don't fight. Go to sleep."

But fighting was all she could do.

Her parents had been humiliated and scorned for years; they'd struggled for so long just to bring food to the table. She'd been ridiculed and mocked every day at Thetis House until they finally found a reason to send her away. But Lore had practiced her skills for hours on end while her parents were at work, because she knew what her parents had forgotten.

They were meant for this life.

They were meant to attain kleos and live forever.

They would not be the last Perseides, and she would not let Castor die.

Her parents only needed to remember. They needed a new reason to believe in the Agon, and in their own power. They needed what was rightfully theirs.

Lore strained her ears, listening for the sound of her parents and hearing nothing but the soft breath of the AC unit in the kitchen. She slipped out from under Olympia's grip and changed out of her pajamas. Her heart jumped into her throat as she tied her tennis shoes and stood, giving her sister a kiss on the forehead. She moved toward Damara, leaning over her crib to give her one, too.

Her father wasn't allowed to brick over any of their rented apartment's windows, but he had reinforced them with extra locks and an alarm system. Lore had figured out months ago that this alarm worked like the one at Thetis House. All she had to do was place a magnet from the refrigerator on the sensor, and it wouldn't go off.

She'd kept one at the bottom of her drawer ever since.

Lore slid through the opening of the window, looking down into the small courtyard that ran alongside their building. They were on the sixth floor, but the pattern of bricks would give her a good enough grip to climb down without using the fire escape. She would be back before her parents woke up.

The thought of their faces then, when they saw what she had done, made her grin, and her heart gave another excited leap.

"Lo?" Olympia rubbed her eyes, but her voice sounded too sleepy for her to be fully awake.

"You're dreaming," Lore whispered. "Go back to sleep, Pia."

Soon enough, she did, hugging the pillow tight. Lore slowly closed the window, but left it open, just a crack, for when she returned.

Then she descended, dropping the last few feet to the ground, and ran into the dark streets.

FORTY ONE

THERE WAS NOTHING IN THE LANE ALONGSIDE RIVER HOUSE.

Not a dumpster, not a car, not even a door leading into the building or a basement. The driveway cut a straight path to Seventy-Ninth Street, blocked only by gates on either end.

"Huh." Lore kept her back to the building's wall, trying to give herself a wide enough view of the lane to see whatever it was that she was missing.

Athena stood a few feet away, her gaze sweeping over the filthy water and ground below.

"Maybe we should go," Lore said. "Someone could come back—"

The goddess stopped and stomped her foot, shifted slightly, and then did it again.

Lore shoved off the wall. "What are you doing?"

"Come," the goddess said, kneeling in the water. A moment later, she dragged open a hatch—one covered with a thin layer of cement to help disguise it.

"Not bad," Lore told her, fighting the water as it poured past her and down through the doorway. She leaned forward, taking in the sight of the tunnel below.

"Quickly," Athena urged.

Lore nodded. As she made her way down the slick metal ladder, she eyed the way the space was rapidly filling with more water. By the time Athena had joined her and shut the hatch, it was up to Lore's knees—but it was moving, flowing away from them, heading down the length of the tunnel.

Lore switched on her phone's flashlight app. The pathway was crudely constructed, but wider than Lore had originally imagined.

The tunnel stretched on and on, winding right, then left, seemingly without reason, until, finally, it split. She stopped at the juncture, shining the phone's light down one tunnel and then the other.

"Which way?" Athena asked quietly.

Lore was about to speak when she heard it—a distinct *thud-thud, thud-thud, thud-thud*. Almost like . . .

A heartbeat.

Her hand tightened on her knife. She turned right, tracing the sound through more turns and splits.

How far does this go? she wondered. *All the way to the East River?*

Their path was cut short by another, this one perpendicular to the one they were on. The *thud-thud* continued, louder and more insistent. They were close.

Lore switched off the phone's flashlight. She flipped the camera lens and, crouching at the very edge of where the paths met, leaned the phone out just enough for it to capture the image of the hunter there.

The man looked familiar to her, but not familiar enough for a name. *Thud-thud.* He bounced a small rubber ball against the ground, then against one of two metal doors in the wall opposite from where he sat on his stool. A lantern-style flashlight glowed at his feet.

Lore let her head fall back against the wall, rolling her eyes at herself. Not a heartbeat. Not a monster.

Athena stood over her, eyes narrowed on the screen. Lore switched it off, storing the phone back in her pocket. Pressing a finger to her lips, she motioned for the goddess to wait, then stepped out.

"Excuse me," Lore said loudly. "Could you tell me how to get to the Statue of Liberty?"

The man startled, jumping to his feet with a sharp inhalation. Lore started to throw her knife toward his heart, but Castor's face flashed in her mind. At the last second, her hand shifted and she struck his shoulder instead.

"You—" the hunter howled.

Lore dove for the stool and smashed it over his head. The hunter fell face-first into the water pooled on the ground, forcing her to roll him onto his back so he wouldn't drown.

Her heart was still pounding as Athena stepped over the hunter, pulling Lore's blade from his shoulder and passing it back to her. Lore had a fleeting memory of what her mother used to tell her and her sisters, the old superstition that a knife passed between people would invite conflict between them.

"Kill him," Athena told her. "He will be a problem."

Lore frowned. The man was unconscious. "Yesterday's body count wasn't high enough for you?"

"I do not keep tally of such things." The goddess turned suddenly on her heel, spotting the hunter's dory leaning against the nearby wall. She made a small noise of pleasure as she lifted it, testing its weight and balance.

Lore returned her focus to the first of the two metal doors in front of them, pressing her ear to its cold surface. Athena guided her back out of the way, then jammed a hand against the heavy padlock. It broke in two, falling heavily at their feet.

The door moaned as she pulled it open.

The chamber was larger than it had seemed on the outside. Metal supports, almost like feet, had been left behind along with a few scattered tools.

Lore retrieved the lantern. "Weird. Why leave a guard down here if there's nothing to guard?"

Athena's head tilted back toward the door, catching the sound before Lore did.

"Hello?" a voice called faintly. "Is someone there?"

Lore's pulse spiked with sudden adrenaline. "Who's there?"

Athena stepped back over the guard and approached another door on the opposite wall, one Lore hadn't noticed, which the hunter had been leaning against. She followed close behind the goddess, raising her knife and lowering into a defensive stance behind her. Athena broke the lock, ripping the heavy door open.

A woman cowered at the back of her cell. She was streaked with grime, her dark skin shining with it as Lore lifted the lantern in disbelief.

Struggling onto her feet, the woman shielded her glowing eyes as she rose to her towering height.

This, too, was a face that Lore recognized. This time, however, she knew the name.

Tidebringer.

FORTY TWO

"WHAT ARE YOU DOING HERE?"

Tidebringer's voice was hoarse, but the melodic undertones were still there, each word rising and falling like the endless pulse of the sea. The embers of power in her dark eyes flickered as her gaze moved from Lore to Athena. Confusion crimped the new god's face. Lore wondered if Tidebringer was afraid that she was hallucinating.

"We're . . ." Lore's voice trailed off as she stared back.

While Lore was the last of Perseus's mortal descendants, the new god had once been Rhea Perseous, the ruin of her bloodline. It took Lore's mind a moment to actually understand that Tidebringer was real, that she was right in front of her—a living, breathing being, not simply the cautionary tale Lore and the other hunters had reduced her to.

"This is Melora Perseous," Athena said. "And I am—"

"I know who you are," Tidebringer snapped. The chains attached to her ankles dragged against the damp floor as she took an unsteady step forward. She looked past the goddess to Lore, as if to say, *I know you, as well.*

Lore moved to examine the new god's restraints. Athena blocked her path.

"Tell me," Athena said. "Why is it that you agreed to serve the false Ares?"

414

"Just as the sea has no master," Tidebringer growled back, "I serve only myself."

"Then why did you bring the flood?" Lore demanded.

The new god regarded the thought with outright disdain. "The Perseides were weak and foolish, unwilling to accept change. That which refuses to grow destroys itself."

"I asked you for answers, not a soliloquy," Lore said.

Tidebringer leaned back against the wall, snorting. "If you want the story, you'll have to bring me the keys from the guard."

Lore ignored the warning look Athena sent her way and went to do just that. As she stepped back into the small, dark hell of the prison, the smell of human waste emanating from a nearby bucket almost overpowered her.

The new god's body shook, and she never once, not even as Lore approached, took her gaze off Athena. Lore started to kneel in front of her to unlock the restraints, but quickly thought twice.

Even chained, Tidebringer was still dangerous—she could snap Lore's neck before she'd registered the pressure of the woman's fingertips on her skin.

She passed the keys to the new god. "I'll give you the pleasure."

Tidebringer nodded. "I will gladly take it."

"The rest of your tale?" Athena prompted, impatient.

Tidebringer slid back down the wall, motioning for Lore to bring the lantern closer, so she could better see. The new god's brown skin had shrunk tight to her muscles, and there were distinct hollows beneath her high cheekbones. Judging by her appearance, Lore couldn't begin to guess the last time Tidebringer had any sort of food or water.

"The Kadmides swarmed me at the Awakening. I was brought

415

here and given a simple choice—die, or serve with my power when Wrath required it. I thought it best to live, discover what his plans were, and take my revenge in the next cycle."

"And you were foolish enough to believe that he will allow you to live?" Athena said.

"He does not see himself as needing to be the last god," Tidebringer said. "Merely the one who will bring about the end of the Agon. He believes he'll usher in a new age once his divinity is permanent and he has access to his full power."

Lore rubbed her arms, trying to dispel some of the cold crawling along them. Standing between the burning gazes of the two gods felt like being trapped in the path of two stars about to collide.

"Does he mean to overthrow my father?" Athena asked.

"He thinks your father has completely retreated to the realm of the divine and left this world to be claimed by the victor of the Agon," Tidebringer said.

"Preposterous," Athena said sharply. "My father does not control the whole of the world. There are many lands and many gods."

"Well, how many still reign now?" Tidebringer asked. "Wrath seems to be laboring under the impression that he will crush all of his rivals and their worshipers through war."

Athena recoiled at that, pulling back like a snake poised to strike. Rather than let her, Lore pushed on.

"That's only if he gets the aegis," Lore said. "And he won't. Do you know anything about the inscription on it? How to read it?"

Tidebringer stared at her, and the slow, dawning horror in her face, plain as anything, set off a shrill noise in Lore's ears.

"Oh gods," Tidebringer said. "You think he still needs to find the poem. That he doesn't know how to read it."

The feeling left Lore's hands. Her body.

"They had the shield for years—you really believed they didn't comb over every inch of it? The inscription is on the inside of the interior's leather lining. All they had to do was remove it." Tidebringer shook her head, releasing a noise of frustration. "You're already too late. He didn't spend this week searching for the shield—he's been putting his plan into motion. He's within days—hours—of winning the hunt."

"I just—" Lore replayed it all in her mind, everything Iro had told her, her conversation with Belen, the message on the wall. Vomit rose in her throat, leaving a bitter tang in her mouth. She swallowed it, and her fear. "No—it's not too late. He still needs the aegis, otherwise he wouldn't be searching for me."

"I pray that you're right," Tidebringer said. "He does need you. I can't wield the aegis or give it to him, even if I were of the mind to. It can only be done by the last of the mortal bloodline."

"And you don't know what he needs it for?" Lore asked. "He didn't give any kind of indication?"

The new god shook her head. "By the time he found me, he was already well into his plans. He's a hundred steps ahead by now."

"We can still stop him," Lore insisted. "We can kill him."

"It won't be enough," Tidebringer said, prying off one of her cuffs. "His followers will just continue whatever work they were doing down here."

"Work?" Athena questioned. "Of what kind?"

"I can't be certain—it was chemical, based on what I could smell and hear. Explosives of some kind, I think," Tidebringer said, prying off her other cuff. Her eyes shifted quickly to Athena, then back to Lore. "Whatever it is, it killed a few of them while they were working.

A few hours ago, before the flood, they took their work out through the tunnel."

Athena's nostrils flared. "That information is useless—"

There was a panicked intake of breath outside the cell, followed by quick steps splashing through the water coating the ground.

The guard.

Shit, Lore thought.

She started toward the door, but Athena was already there.

"No," the goddess said. "*I* will take care of the problem you have failed to."

She took off, not needing to run. It would be a slow, confident pursuit.

A hand clamped over Lore's wrist and wrenched her back. Pain shot up her arm and her wrist bent as it hit the ground.

Tidebringer lunged forward to block the door. Lore scrambled up onto her feet, lungs squeezing tight as she reached for her knife.

"You stupid girl!" Tidebringer hissed to her. "What are you doing with her?"

"I— We have a deal," Lore told her haltingly.

"What could she offer you that could ever be greater than what she's taken?" Tidebringer shook her head. "Go now, before she comes back!"

"What are you talking about?" Lore demanded. That cold dread, the one that seemed to have awakened in her the first time she laid eyes on the dying goddess outside her home, slithered through her blood, whispering, *You know.*

"After I learned what happened I searched for you across the world, but you had vanished—I could never find you," Tidebringer said.

"I was with the Odysseides at their protected estate, and then

418

Hermes gave me an amulet," Lore said. "It hid my presence from gods—"

Tidebringer swore viciously. "He should never have tried to protect you alone, the fool!"

"Is that why you were looking for me?" Lore asked, trying to understand. Tidebringer had been a god for so long that Lore was shocked she even cared to remember her mortality, let alone the last remnant of her doomed family.

"No, child, to *warn* you—I would have come to you days ago if I hadn't been taken at the Awakening," Tidebringer said. "I only agreed to Wrath's terms because I thought it would keep me alive long enough to escape and find you. To tell you that Hermes saw you that night, and that he told her. He told her, knowing how badly she wanted it back—how she thought she needed it—"

"What?" Lore asked rolling up onto her feet. "What did he tell her?"

You know.

Tidebringer's eyes widened as she released a thick, wet gasp. Blood poured from her mouth as the jagged metal tip of a dory punched through her chest. She struggled, her body lashing back and forth in the doorframe like a fish caught on a hook. As her gaze locked on Lore, the sparks of power there faded.

"Everything," Athena said, pulling her weapon free. Tidebringer's lifeless body collapsed to the ground. "He told me everything."

SEVEN YEARS EARLIER

It was easier than she had ever imagined.

Lore had hated the Kadmides for a lot of things over her ten years of existence, but just then, standing in the cramped back courtyard behind the Phoenician, she hated them most for acting like they didn't have to try. That no one would dare to take what they themselves had stolen.

There was a narrow, fenced-off gap between the restaurant and the building beside it. They'd made the mistake of leaving its gate unlocked to bring their bags of trash up to the street level for collection in the morning. Lore had slipped inside and crouched behind the rows of trash cans, watching as hunters came and went like bees to their hive.

Between their trips, the restaurant's back door always shut firmly behind them. They all entered the same code on its keypad.

3-9-6-9-3-1-5-8-2.

She repeated the series in her head again and again. She wouldn't forget it.

The moon was nearing its pinnacle in the sky when she felt a prickling at the back of her neck.

Lore turned, searching the courtyard and nearby windows for another shadow. The only camera that she could see was the one posted above the door, and that was easy enough to avoid. She and Castor—well, really just her, but Castor kept watch—had practiced staying outside the field of security cameras to slip inside Philip Achilleos's chambers at Thetis House. She hadn't been caught then, and she wouldn't be now.

She would be like the heroes in the stories. She wouldn't fail.

"Just do it," Lore told herself, pulling the hood of her sweater up over her ears and tucking her wild hair inside. When no new people came or went for another ten minutes, Lore approached the door, keeping her back tight against the wall to avoid the camera's eye. She input the code and, with a deep breath, let herself flash across the camera's sight to slip inside.

The kitchen was still steamy from the dishwashing and smelled of damp onions. A young man kept his back to her at the sinks, softly singing along to the radio. Lore moved slowly around the darkened edges of the room, her steps light and her breathing lighter.

A rumble of voices sounded nearby. Lore slipped beneath one of the stainless-steel worktables and retreated into its deep shadows. She pressed a fist to her mouth and waited.

Several hunters entered the quiet kitchen with a roar of laughter. They'd taken off their masks, but all were still armed within an inch of their lives. One waved to the boy at the sink as they made their way toward the large freezer.

"How'd it go?" the boy asked eagerly, trailing after them, eyes wide.

"Disappointingly quiet for the last night of an Agon," said one of the hunters. "Though I don't know that our newly divine lord would have appreciated a rival deity in the family."

Lore's top lip curled at the thought of that disgusting old man as a god.

Another hunter shushed him, but the sound ended on a drunken laugh.

"What?" said the first. "He got what he's always wanted, but he still doesn't have ears everywhere. At least not yet. I can't wait to see what his commands are."

Lore leaned forward again, squinting to see what code they entered on the security pad to the right of the freezer. 1-4-6-9-0. She smirked as they disappeared into it and reemerged a few minutes later with no weapons or robes.

That answered her biggest question. As he'd taunted her father, Aristos Kadmou had revealed that they kept the aegis somewhere beneath the restaurant. And here she'd thought it would be a challenge to find where to access their vault.

"Let's go, Chares. I'll take you home to your mother," the first hunter said to the boy as the others shuffled off toward the side entrance. As they passed by Lore's table she shrank back and held her breath.

"But the dishes—" he began, his voice cracking.

"There'll be time to finish in the morning before the ritual," the man said gesturing to them. "The restaurant will be closed for our celebrations."

The boy nodded, untying his apron and eagerly hanging it on a wall hook. Lore's hands curled against the cold tile floor as she counted their footsteps toward the door. She waited for the telltale click as it shut and locked, and then counted to a hundred before sliding out from beneath the table.

Lore felt light and giddy as she opened the door to the freezer and stepped into its icy arms.

Thinking twice, she caught the door before it shut behind her and used a heavy cut of frozen meat to prop it open, letting in more heat and light.

The surfaces of the freezer were covered in a thin sheen of frost, including the floor. The area around the rubber mat at the center had recently been disturbed; Lore lifted the mat with her foot before kicking it off all the way.

Her lip curled at the sight of the trapdoor, unsecured by a lock— her family wouldn't make the same mistake.

Lore lifted the hatch open and climbed down the steps beneath it. Lights flickered on around her as they sensed her movement, revealing shelf after shelf of weapons, money, and tech. Her eyes went wide at the sight of it all, even before she saw the treasures at the center of the room. One, draped over a mannequin, was what had to be the hide of the Nemean lion. The House of Herakles had traded it willingly to the Kadmides centuries ago in exchange for desperately needed weapons. And just beyond that, in a glass case, was the aegis.

Thoughts fled her mind, replaced by an involuntary shiver that crawled over her scalp.

Even cast in silver and gold, Medusa's visage was still so lifelike that Lore's feet rooted to the ground. She flinched as the gorgon's lips seemed to part to draw breath—but it was only her own reflection shifting in the glass.

Medusa's face, and the wild knot of snakes in her hair, protruded slightly from the shield, as if the gods had melted her severed head down into the stiffened leather and metal. A delicate filigreed pattern of lightning and vines framed her visage. The gold tassels that hung from it were still in place after thousands of years, as bright and gleaming as the day they had been made.

I see you, the gorgon seemed to say. *I see you, Melora.*

Lore drew in a deep breath, trying to shake the nerves firing through her.

"Stop it," she ordered herself. There had to be cameras hidden around the room. Someone would be coming to stop her. "Get going."

There was no latch to open the glass case, and it was too big for Lore to lift on her own. She had one option left to free the aegis, and that was a very, very bad one.

Lore circled the case. Judging by the thickness of the glass, it was reinforced, likely bulletproof. She glanced to the trapdoor.

There would be an alarm. She would have only seconds . . .

Lore backed away, retrieving the heaviest-looking sword she could find from the nearby rack, and climbed the stairs to the freezer. She laid the blade across the opening of the trapdoor. Just in case.

Then, without risking another minute to second-guess herself, Lore returned to the aegis. With a grin, she used all the strength in her body to shove the case and its pedestal over.

A siren screamed as the room flashed red around her. There was a loud *bang* that made Lore nearly jump out of her skin. She whirled around. The trapdoor had swung shut as the alarm was triggered, but the sword had stayed in place and kept it cracked open.

As she'd expected, the glass case around the aegis hadn't shattered when it hit the ground. She picked up a nearby dory and wedged its head down where the glass had been sealed to the flat surface of the marble pedestal. Her arms strained as she cut away at the sealant until, finally, the case and pedestal separated enough for her to draw the shield out.

It was almost as big as her, but despite its size, the shield felt lighter than the arm she hooked through its leather straps. Her heart punching up into her throat, Lore turned and fled up the stairs. The trapdoor pushed back at her, still struggling to shut, but she braced the shield against it and shoved up.

A blast of pressure and light exploded from the shield, whipping the door open. It crashed against the freezer's floor so hard it broke from its motorized hinges and slid under a nearby shelf. Lore stared at it a moment, then at the aegis. The dull thudding of the freezer door opening and shutting against the flank of meat drew her back into the moment and set her running again.

Lore barreled through the opening into the dark kitchen. The door to the outside had locked as the alarm was triggered, but Lore, quickly developing a theory, smashed the aegis against it. The metal door fell flat against the uneven asphalt of the courtyard.

Lore ran until the world blurred around her. The shield bumped against her side and beneath her chin, but she felt like she was wearing winged sandals as she fled up the east side of Manhattan, weaving in and out of its grid of empty streets.

Every part of her, from her bones down to her soul, felt suffused with glee and pride. The aegis was back where it belonged and the Kadmides would never forget this night or her name. Her family wouldn't be leaving the Agon, or the city, and Lore wouldn't be leaving Castor.

By the time she reached Central Park, however, that same fizzing giddiness in her blood began to still, and then cool. She started to turn toward the west side, toward home, but her feet refused to move.

Realization set in the way Medusa's gaze had once turned men to stone.

The Kadmides wouldn't forget her name, because they would know exactly who had taken their prized treasure. She hadn't been careful about checking for cameras in the vault. Any number of them could have captured her face.

Lore sagged against a nearby bench, her thoughts spinning dark, terrifying patterns in her mind.

If the Kadmides had caught her on camera, they would know where to look for the shield. Who to blame and who to punish. And now, with their archon a god, no one and nothing would stand in their way.

Lore let out a choked sob, her heart punching against her ribs until she thought she might throw up. There were so many Kadmides, and so few Perseides.

For the first time, courage abandoned her. Her trembling body took over, jumping the stone wall to retreat into the familiar safety of the park. She needed to find a place to hide.

She needed to do more than that.

I have to take it back, she thought, choking on the realization. *They won't punish us if I take it back.*

But the aegis didn't belong to the Kadmides—it wasn't *theirs*, and now that they had a new god, now that Aristos Kadmou had shed his mortal skin, he might be able to use it. Her father told her that wasn't true, but her father had been wrong before.

Lore crouched behind a bench near the Mall, her body feverish with fear. She smeared the sweat from her face with dirty hands.

And all the while, Medusa watched her. *I see you. I know what you've done.*

No. She could still fix this.

Lore stayed there, her body curled and her face pressed to her knees, until, finally, she decided what to do.

FORTY THREE

Lore's chest burned with a scream that wouldn't come. She was gasping for it, ripping it from the deepest part of her soul, but only a low cry escaped her lips.

Her body no longer seemed to be completely her own. Lore stumbled into the wall, disoriented.

"You . . ." She tried to get the words out. "You . . . you knew . . ."

"Do you see it now?" Athena asked, speaking in the ancient tongue. Any warmth, any sign of humanity had gone out like a doused flame. "The steady hand guiding the loom?"

Lore's body shook with enough force that it was a struggle to keep her grip on the hilt of her blade. Her vision swarmed with black. If Hermes had told Athena that Lore took the aegis . . . if Athena had known where to find her family and had come looking for it that day . . .

The poison of truth moved through her, turning her insides to ash.

As if knowing her thoughts, a faint smile touched the goddess's lips.

She killed them.

Not Wrath. Not the Kadmides. It had always been Athena.

As Lore's shock faded, a feral panic set in.

"I thought—" she began.

She had left her alone with Miles and Van . . . She had trusted her to honor her oath to not harm Castor . . . She had . . . She had . . .

Believed her.

"You thought what, that I possessed a heart?" Athena said. "The heart is only a muscle."

"You killed them." Her voice was barely a whisper. *"Why?"*

"I almost didn't believe Hermes when he told me what he'd seen. The aegis, the object I had spent centuries searching for, found by a child. Carried by a *child*," Athena said. "I knew where the last of the Perseides resided. The hovel they called a home. I was delighted to discover a window had been left open for me, almost as if in invitation."

Lore clawed at her hair, her breathing growing erratic, her heart on the verge of shredding itself against her ribs. Desperation flooded her veins. *No—please no—*

"But as I stood inside the room I thought, surely, the thief could not have been either one of these tiny, insignificant creatures. They were smaller than the shield," Athena said, taking a single step forward into the cell. "I stood over their beds and thought about how easy it would be to simply smother them."

She moved another step closer to Lore. "But I waited, until your mother and father came to look in on them, until my powers were fully restored to me at the cycle's end." Athena stopped before Lore, looming over her. "And then I claimed one piece from each girl for every question they refused to answer. About their missing child. About where you might be hiding."

The memory of her sisters, carved up beyond recognition, burst the pressure trapped in her chest. Rage and grief ripped through her; the world swung off its axis, and Lore attacked.

She slashed her blade down toward Athena's chest. The god used her dory to parry it with little effort, her face expressionless, then swung it down, battering Lore's right shoulder.

"No restraint, no discipline, no strategy," Athena said. "Only *anger*. I saw it in you immediately. Like molten bronze waiting to be shaped by skilled hands. I merely had to plant the suggestion of the new poem. I knew you would find out where it was inscribed, and you would return for it. It became a matter of patience."

Lore was knocked back by the force of the blow, but used the distance to toss the knife to her left hand, changing her grip. She feinted right, and when the goddess moved to block it, Lore sliced up. Athena leaned back, but the tip had caught her chin. The gash painted the side of her neck with blood.

Athena let out a single caustic laugh. She rubbed a thumb against the cut, studying it for a moment. "The problem with mortals that small, of course, is that there is only so much lifeblood in them. They die too quickly."

Lore screamed. The sound was ragged, torn from the broken part of her. She gave herself over to the pain, cutting and clawing and slicing until the cell disappeared around her and she began to dissolve into instinct.

The hit from the dory came from behind, smashing against her skull. The knife flew from her hand as Lore fell to the ground. She rolled to face forward, but Athena clubbed her once more, then plunged the dory's sauroter into her thigh. With a single stroke, she had pierced muscle, cracked bone, and pinned Lore in place.

The agony was so complete, Lore could barely draw enough breath to sob. Athena turned the spear, digging the tip deeper. Survival and instinct roared in her. Lore slapped a hand against the dank ground, feeling for the knife, and she seized it in triumph.

But before she could lift it, Athena gripped that same hand, wrenching it away. Then, with all the effort it would have taken to crumple the head of a flower, she tightened her fingers around Lore's and crushed every bone in them.

Lore shook violently with gasping cries. Sour vomit rose in her throat at the pain, at the sight of her mangled hand.

"Why?" she begged. "*Why?*"

"They called for you," Athena said. As the goddess pulled the dory free, the sauroter broke off, still buried in Lore's leg. "Both of the girls. Do you think they knew you were the one who killed them?"

The memory of that night assailed her. Lore did not have to close her eyes to see it—the blood smeared on the walls and floors, her sisters thrown down on their beds, the dark gaps where their eyes should have been.

"They were just little girls," Lore sobbed. "Damara was a *baby*. They were innocent!"

"None of you are innocent," Athena growled. "Least of all you, Melora. Your father died first, begging, then your mother, who at least knew it would be wasted breath. I waited hours for you to return, and when you did, it was no longer in your possession. I watched as you stood in the doorway of your home, as you saw the gift I had left for you. But you did not cry. You did not make a single sound. You were stronger then than you are now."

"Why didn't you torture me to find out what happened to it?" Lore gasped out, one hand clutching at her face, her hair. "Why didn't you just kill me?"

"I needed you to show me where you had hidden it," Athena said. "And to give it to me willingly. Of course, once I learned of the poem, I had yet another reason to keep you alive. I could not let it disappear

430

with your death until I read it myself."

Lore clawed at her throat. She almost *had* given the aegis to Athena, only an hour before. It had felt like her own idea. An inevitability.

"All those years with the House of Odysseus, I watched your pathetic existence, waiting for you to one day retrieve it or to reveal where you had hidden it," Athena said. "I might have intervened and come to you in another form, to ingratiate myself to you, had Hermes not found you first."

Lore shook her head, trying to shut out the words.

"I followed him to this city, curious as to why he was wearing a false face," Athena said. "I had my answer soon enough. I felt the power of the averting charms he cast on his home. I could not enter it, nor even approach. There was but one reason he would go to such lengths to deny me. Only one mortal he would go to such lengths to protect. The fact I could not see you—that I could only catch the sound of your footsteps, the smell of you—confirmed it."

The goddess studied the tip of her dory. "Hermes made such an effort, and all out of a misplaced sense of guilt. You see, he had traded his sighting of you and the aegis to keep his lover alive. He knew I had found the false Dionysus's hiding place," Athena said. "And when this hunt began, and I watched Hermes die from a distance, I saw my opportunity. His power would not hold beyond his death. I could finally go to you, unhindered."

Keeping her blade up became impossible as Lore's body turned to lead. Blood poured from her leg. It throbbed with every heartbeat. She pressed her back against the wall, its dampness soaking through her shirt.

"But Artemis attacked you . . ." Lore began weakly.

"As if my sister could strike such a blow without my consent,"

Athena said. "We had planned to kill all the imposters this cycle, but she agreed to aid me in the deception once I told her of your connection to the boy who had murdered our brother. But he is so curious, is he not? I knew the moment I felt his power we could not kill him. Not until I found out what he was. It angered her, but it allowed me to get close enough to some of the other imposters to ensure they died by a true god's hand."

Artemis hadn't been raving as her sister had claimed—Athena *had* betrayed Artemis by not giving Castor to her.

"You told Artemis to track me that first day thinking I would go to find him, didn't you?" Lore said, finally putting it together. "And then you just—you watched her die?"

"We were not all meant to return to Olympus," Athena said coolly. "Only the strongest among us will be recognized by the Horae and allowed to pass through the gates once more. Artemis faltered."

Athena's hand lashed out, catching Lore's chin in a painful grip. "Shall we end your suffering and go retrieve it at last?"

Lore looked up at her, pouring every ounce of her trembling fury into her gaze. Her mind was a torrent of terror and disbelief. "It won't be willingly given if you torture me for it. You wouldn't be able to use it."

"Not yet, no. However, I *will* have the inscription. I will know how to end the Agon," Athena said. Lore felt her jaw begin to crack under her grip. "And when I am restored to my full power, I will be able to wield it once more."

"But Wrath will . . . He'll come for it," Lore rasped out. "He won't let you have it—"

"When I achieve the final ascension, he will be nothing more than a worm I crush beneath my heel," Athena said. "Along with all those

432

who dared to turn away from their true gods. I warn you, Melora, I will destroy everything and everyone you love, one by one, until you bring me to it."

Lore's heart lurched in her chest.

No.

Not Miles. Not Castor. Not Van. Not Iro.

Not her city.

A calm certainty took control of Lore's mind, quieting the chaotic storm of her thoughts and clarifying the choice. Accepting it, even as she saw all their faces—even as she thought of her family and knew their souls would never find peace.

There was one last choice. At least she would be the one to make it.

I'm sorry, she thought. There would be a single god left for Castor to face, but no one would ever possess the aegis again.

Lore's unmarred hand gripped the broken piece of the spear's shaft still attached to the sauroter and, with a cry, she pulled it from her leg. She thought of her sisters. Her fearless mother. Her father's face glowing in their campfire's light, showing her how to grip the hilt of a dagger.

Shift your thumb to the spine of the hilt, Melora. It'll give you better control.

"No." She raised her voice, making sure the word thundered.

Athena's nostrils flared. "Impertinent child—"

Lore stared up at her through the strands of her dark hair. "The choice is mine."

She turned the blade on herself and slid it into her chest.

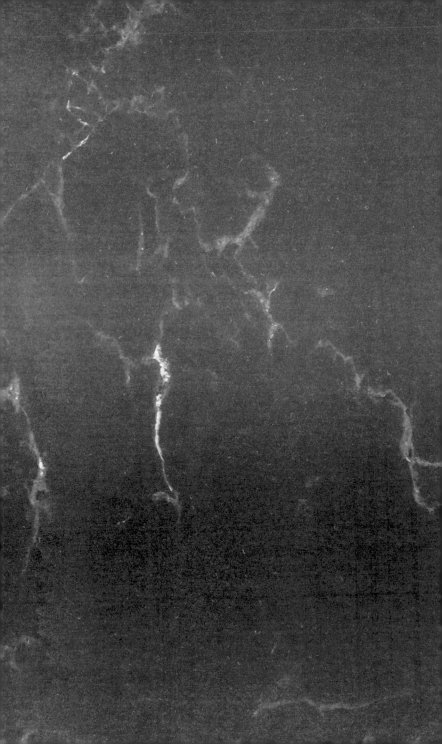

PART FIVE

—

MORTAL

FORTY FOUR

Lore had always thought that there would be more to death than this.

The hunters believed that there was no greater honor than to die on the hunt in the pursuit of glory, rather than be taken by Thanatos, the god of gentle death. She knew better than to buy into the bullshit, but some part of her still wanted to believe that the last fire of pain would burn away her past and transform her into someone who would be judged worthy in the world below.

Instead, death was only numbing. Her mind shut itself down to protect her from the shock of the steel parting her skin and scraping across bone.

Her hand slid from the makeshift weapon, falling limply into her lap.

There was a terrible scream, like the screech of a saw against metal.

Look, Lore thought. *Open your eyes.*

It was the gray-eyed goddess.

"Oh, you fool," Athena snarled. "I will not let you do this—I will not allow you to take it from me!"

"You won't need it . . ." Lore got out, "where . . . you're . . . going . . ."

One hand closed around Lore's neck, tightening as if to break it. Athena's face was rigid with fury, her teeth bared. Undaunted, and unbowed by the weakness of impending death.

"You truly believed it all," Athena said, her voice grating. "You thought I would be so foolish as to bind my life to an impetuous mortal. To *you*? You have done this for nothing!"

Horror sliced through Lore. She stared up at the goddess, struggling to focus as blackness stained her vision. Soon, she could only see the maelstrom of sparks swirling in Athena's eyes.

Not for nothing, Lore thought, the words faint in her mind.

It hadn't just been to kill Athena. Lore had wanted to ensure no one could ever possess the aegis again. She had done that, at least—that one thing, after so many mistakes, she had done right.

Athena pulled back, drawing in on herself. She remained there, her gaze bearing down on Lore. The intricate machine that was her mind whirled until she found control once more.

"I will force the false Apollo to heal you," Athena said. "And you will take me to it."

No—

Lore dragged herself away, digging her nails against the rough ground to claw her way forward. The goddess had leaned her dory against the wall; Lore could reach it if she could will her body to move. *Not before I kill you—*

Athena gripped her by the hair, ripping chunks of it from her scalp. She dragged Lore toward the door and the tunnel beyond it.

But a moment later, the goddess released her. Lore fell to the wet ground. The impact split her chin open. Blood poured down over her throat, hot against her cold skin.

"No . . ." the goddess said, taking a step back and reclaiming her dory. "I think . . . not."

Lore's lips parted, but the words she wanted to say sank into the

438

growing darkness in her mind and disappeared. Ice flooded her veins where her blood had once been.

"There is another way," Athena said slowly, as if unwinding her own reasoning.

Lore let out a strangled roar—of rage, of anguish.

The goddess turned to leave, but paused in the doorway of the cell. She cast one last look over her shoulder, making a noise of false sympathy. "It is a shame you did not even possess the courage to drive the blade through your heart."

"I'll kill . . . you . . ." Lore whispered, but there was no answer.

There would never be an answer.

There was only the dark air, and the silence, and the waiting.

SEVEN YEARS EARLIER

Somehow, despite the hour, the moon was still up in the sky, even as it faded with the arrival of the pale dawn. Lore had kept her gaze on its milky crescent to avoid having to look at the streets of her neighborhood. Now, as she stood in front of her family's apartment building, she forced herself to look at the window she had slipped through a few hours before.

It was closed.

She let out a soft breath, fear biting at her again. Her father and mother were up.

She balled her fists and pressed them against her eyes, forcing herself to breathe and not cry.

The lies were so easy—she went to see Castor, she wanted to watch the last few hours of the Agon, she thought about running away but came back—but the truth made her feel like she had stabbed a knife into her belly. She had to tell them. Their punishment would never be as bad as the Kadmides' would be. Her parents would know what to do.

Lore didn't bother climbing to her bedroom window. She used the building's front door.

Squaring her shoulders and swallowing the sour taste in her mouth, she made her way up the many flights of stairs, to the sixth floor. Already, the previous night was starting to feel more like a dream than a memory.

Their apartment was at the very end of the silent hallway. Lore's heart hammered in her ears. They were going to be so angry. She would have to try to find a way to make them understand, to convince them to stay in the city despite what had happened. She didn't want to leave Castor or New York City. Not like this.

Lore paused outside their apartment's door, pressing her forehead against its smooth surface and closing her eyes. She listened for the sound of her parents inside. Making their coffee, feeding Damara, talking quietly as they listened to the news.

But she heard nothing.

Something wet soaked through the toe of her old tennis shoes. Lore opened her eyes at the sensation.

Dark blood seeped out through the crack below the door and pooled around her feet.

FORTY FIVE

Olympia was waiting for her in the night's shadows.

She sat at the edge of the bed they shared, her hair rumpled by sleep, her eyes too tired to focus. Lore claimed the space beside her, watching as the wind sneaked through the nearby window and ruffled the drawings of Olympia's that Lore had taped to their wall.

Her sister turned toward her. Lore began to cry.

"Don't fight, Lo," she whispered, clutching at the front of Lore's shirt. "Don't fight. Go to sleep."

Lore closed her eyes, but the tears wouldn't stop.

Go to sleep.

It was so easy. Such a simple thing. But just as she was at the edge of it, she was pulled back by the smell of something sharp and metallic.

Don't fight.

She opened her eyes to find the dark hollows of her sister's empty sockets staring back.

Blood flowed around them on the bed, coating Lore's skin, filling her mouth as she screamed. She rolled out of bed and hit the floor, but it was there, too, running between the bars of Damara's crib. A wail pierced the silence, cutting deeper with each of her frantic heartbeats.

The door to the bedroom was open, and a single spark of light was visible in the blackness of the space beyond it.

Lore staggered forward. She couldn't look around her, not when she knew what she'd find—her mother stretched out by the door, slashed from belly to throat, her father in the kitchen, his back broken, his skull crushed. She had been here before. She had seen this before.

The light—if she could just reach the light . . .

Go to sleep.

Her mind fell silent and her body went still as Lore passed through the door of her bedroom. A cool mist brushed against her cheeks.

The light was still there, just beyond the veil of silver fog, but now it was many. Now it was seven, and the lights had forms, faces that watched, expressionless, from the other side of a river. One broke away from the others and floated toward her, growing larger and brighter with each of her slow heartbeats.

The gray world seemed to breathe, as if trying to inhale her. Cold water lapped at her toes.

Melora. The damp air whispered her name, until it became a question with no answer. *Melora?*

A heavy hand fell on her shoulder. She turned slowly.

Her body came alive with a pain that sawed at her. Her limbs contorted into agonized shapes. She gasped for air and clawed at the ground. She was cold—so cold—cracking like ice . . .

The dark world of the river flickered in and out of the underground cell, until Lore could no longer tell one from the other.

"Steady, Melora," the same voice said. "The worst, I'm afraid, is yet to come."

A glowing face hovered before her own. He was young and beautiful, his lips cast in an impish line. His hair curled almost sweetly; above it, wings fluttered on either side of his helmet, keeping time with her pulse.

"You . . ." she whispered. "No . . ."

The figure shifted in the strange light. His form unraveled like ribbons, the layers of him pulling apart to reveal what was hidden beneath.

Someone else.

Lore lifted a shaking hand, swiping it against her eyes to clear the haze from them. An old man hovered before her now, his feet not quite touching the ground. His silver hair seemed to rise, shimmering like waves around his head, above his long face. His white skin was lined with age and veins, his shoulders stooped. His green eyes sparkled as he looked her over.

"Hello, darling," Gil whispered. "Are you all right?"

"You're not . . ." Lore began, unable to catch her breath at the sight of him. He was perfect, in his familiar tweed jacket, that knowing look on his face.

"Real?" he finished. "Stand up and discover for yourself."

Lore's eyelids were too heavy. They drifted shut as she gave a single, small shake of the head.

"*No*," Gil said sharply. "Look at me. I need you to look at me."

Lore tried.

"Do you want to live?" Gil asked. The words echoed through Lore's mind, twining with memories.

Lore took in a slight breath. The others . . . the city . . . She wasn't finished yet . . . but her body . . . she couldn't . . .

"You already know that you are enough," Gil told her. "Stand up, Melora. Come on. Prove me right."

She had thought she was enough to hunt, to save her city, to protect her friends, and avenge her family. And now there was nothing left. Everyone who loved her was gone.

Not everyone.

Not everything had been a lie.

"Do it for yourself," Gil said, his voice a balm to Lore's confused mind. "Not to get back at her. Not out of anger. For yourself."

Humiliation and rage and betrayal had all fused in her, but there was something else. She could . . . There was something left in her . . . *something* . . .

"You have to stand up on your own. I can't carry you the way you once carried me," Gil said. "And I can't take you far, only to the boundary, as he'll permit. Only as I am meant to do. You must stand up on your own and follow me to it."

That—she had enough left in her for that. To stand. To get to the others. To warn them . . .

Lore reached out, bracing her hand against the wall behind her, feeling for something to anchor herself. Her fingers hooked into a depression the uneven drilling had left behind. Her shoulder and arm ached as they absorbed her weight, but she set her jaw. She hissed with the effort it took to get her feet beneath her.

"Good," Gil said, sounding relieved. "That's it, darling."

Her right leg was fine, but her left, the one Athena had impaled, was broken. The smallest bit of weight sent white-hot agony shooting through it. Lore's knee buckled as she took an experimental step, but she braced a shoulder against the wall.

Hot blood escaped the wound in her chest as she bent, forcing her to press a hand there to stanch the flow. She shivered; the pain was so bad now, she felt almost drunk with it.

"Follow me, darling," Gil said. "Keep your eyes on the light."

Lore limped forward, one shuffled step, then the next. Water sloshed at her feet. The world of the river and the world of the tunnel bled into one another until everything was darkness and stone. But there was light ahead of her now. She could see it—that spark.

Her right hip swung forward again and again, her muscles seizing up with the effort it took. Forward. Forward. Their progress was excruciating and slow.

Gil knew the way, as he always did, taking each curve and turn with confidence. Lore let him lead, her eyes fixed on the light emanating from the torch that now appeared in the man's hand.

Its flame was hypnotizing, playing tricks on Lore's eyes. Making them see things that weren't there.

Gil's tweed jacket broke apart like dashed embers, revealing an ivory tunic below. In his left hand, a winged staff with gold snakes twining around it appeared. Their small scaled heads stroked against one another, then turned to watch her.

Help me, Lore thought, because she could not say the words. *Stay with me.*

As if she had called them to her, shadows appeared along the walls of the tunnel. The silhouettes of a man and woman, of two small girls, glided beside her, keeping her tortured pace. Faces she knew. Faces she loved.

Lore reached out a hand toward the woman, her fingers skimming her face.

Stay with me, she thought. *Stay with me . . .*

Gil's form blurred as Lore's vision failed. She leaned heavily against the wall, using the last of her strength to draw herself forward with her uninjured hand, crawling through the cold water. Fighting to keep her head above it.

Maybe it was her punishment for what she'd done. She'd be forced to make this journey in the darkness, to live in the small eternity of it, for all time. Repeating the agony, repeating the realization she would never make it back to the entrance of the tunnels, or find the strength to climb the ladder out.

A small chime sounded sweetly somewhere behind her, then another, until it became a song, like birds in the morning.

Gil stopped, turning back to her. "That's far enough, then."

Lore took in a shaking breath, her back pressed to a rough wall. She tried to grasp at the shadows, to pull them to her, but the sight of them had faded with her vision.

Stay with me.

"For my part in this, I am sorry," Gil said, his voice near. There was a gentle, warm touch on her forehead.

Lore could no longer tell if her eyes were open. Her body drifted beneath her, her mind untethered. When Gil spoke again, the words bloomed inside her mind, his voice melting into a clearer, deeper one. *The eyes of the gods are upon you.*

The dim light of the torch vanished, but the presence of those around her lingered.

Stay with me, Lore pleaded, aching with desperation. *Stay . . . Don't leave me . . .*

The shadows curled around her, and when her thoughts turned to cinders and the world disappeared, she was no longer afraid.

FORTY SIX

A HEARTBEAT FOUND HER IN THE DARKNESS.

Lore followed the sound of it the way Orpheus must have looked to the light above him as he tried to lead Eurydice out of the Underworld. She knew that if she glanced back to search for the face of the cold presence lingering behind her, she would be lost to it.

Instead, she drifted toward the growing warmth—toward the familiar power that wrapped around her senses.

Her eyelids were crusted with grime, but she forced them open.

Castor's eyes were shut, his face tilted up to reveal the sharp line of his jaw. His power pulsated around them, burning away the bleakness of the tunnel. It had turned the standing water into a thick haze that clogged the air.

She was draped across his legs, lifted from the rough floor. One of his arms was wrapped around her shoulders to support her weight, and the other hand rested against her side, where the blade had cut her.

Tears slid down her face, catching in her hair as she looked up at him. Her body felt like it was filled with air and sunlight, too insubstantial to move. Castor barely seemed to be breathing.

She reached up with her free hand, tracing a light fingertip down his cheek. Castor reached up to press the hand against his chest, right beside where his mortal heart was beating.

He met her gaze. He said nothing, but, then, he never needed to. His face was a book that had been written only for her. Its story unfolded while he watched her watch him.

But as the gentle, drugging feeling of his power eased through her, knitting together skin, mending bone, she began to remember.

Shame wove through her confusion and her anger, until she was crying again, this time in earnest. For not seeing the truth about Athena. For the knowledge of how close she'd come to leaving this world and everyone she loved.

For the mistake she had made that could never be fixed, and the precious lives it had cost.

Lore looked to the walls around her, searching for the shadows again. But it seemed they'd stayed only until Castor's light could replace them.

Castor smoothed the hair away from her wet cheeks, easing the curls back around her ears. She wanted to tell him what had happened, to explain it herself, but he already knew. As easily as she could read him, Castor had always had the measure of her.

"You were ice-cold," he said, the words halting. "I didn't know . . . I wasn't sure . . ."

She pressed her forehead to his shoulder. "This is fine. A nice change, even. Our reunions usually involve a lot more punching."

"Not always," he said softly. "Sometimes we chase our enemies."

"Variety," she said, "the spice of mortal combat."

Castor blew out a hard breath, pulling back slightly to examine the wound on her leg and the new, pink skin there. Lore's hand rose, feeling along her ribs.

It is a shame you did not even possess the courage to drive the blade through your heart.

"Hey," he began softly. "Are you still in pain?"

She shook her head, wondering how to tell him everything that had happened.

"I shouldn't have left, but I thought it was the only way to get through to you . . . I should never have left you alone with her." Castor released a shuddering breath. He closed his eyes again, but this time, when he opened them, there was a look of cold intent there.

"I'll kill her." The words were low, without any varnish, without any hesitation. And so unlike him.

"No," Lore said.

"What she did to you—" he began again.

"No," Lore continued, her voice hoarse. "It was me."

Lore saw the exact moment he figured out what she meant. His shock deepened to horror.

"She was the one," Lore whispered. "All this time, she was the one who killed them."

"Why? Why them and not any of the other bloodlines?"

"Because of me," she said. "And what I did during that last Agon."

Castor gave her a questioning look, waiting for her to elaborate.

"And I thought . . . if I could stop Athena and take her out of the Agon . . . if no one could have the aegis . . ." Lore shook her head. "But the binding oath wasn't real."

Castor brought her hand up, pressing a soft kiss onto her callused palm. He seemed to sink into his thoughts as his power faded around them.

"Even if it had worked, wouldn't you have just taken her power?" he asked finally.

"No," Lore said. "Not according to the stories. I think I would have had to use the blade on her, but I was . . . I was in bad shape."

450

Her hand curled at the memory.

As her nerves jumped and her thoughts sharpened, Lore suddenly remembered the first question she should have asked.

"How did you find me?"

"Your phone," he said.

Lore stared at him, not understanding.

"Miles did a friend . . . tracking thing?" Castor repeated, suddenly looking uncertain. "He had to accept your request. We all found one another near the brownstone after the flooding and spent most of today looking for you. Cell service was restored about a half hour ago. Van and Miles went to regroup with the Achillides and find a safe place for us to shelter."

And you came here, she thought, overwhelmed with gratitude. *You came to find me.*

"Miles is okay?" she whispered. "You're all okay?"

"Everyone's okay," he promised.

She lifted herself up just enough to slide the device out of her back pocket. The screen had cracked, but the message and missed-call alerts were still visible. There was a string of panicked texts from Miles.

Are you there? Just tell us you're ok.

She fumbled with the phone, her hands trembling as she responded to that message with:

am ok. text when safe.

The responses were immediate, making the phone vibrate and sing a familiar high note.

Ding.

k. Will send new address to meet.

Ding.

Be there in 2 hours. Need to hire a boat back.

Ding.

What happened?

The chimes. The sounds that she'd heard had been real, not hallucinations. But then . . .

Had everything else been real, too?

She looked around them, only to realize she was a few feet away from the ladder leading back up to the street. Deeper in the tunnel, in the cell, there wouldn't have been reception.

Castor followed her gaze down the length of the path behind them.

"Tidebringer's body is down there," Lore said haltingly.

She knew that the mortal remains would disappear at the end of the cycle, but the goddess deserved more than to be left to rot.

He nodded, helping her to her feet. "I'll take care of it."

Castor made his way down the winding tunnel, disappearing at the first turn. Lore leaned against the wall, imagining she could see the golden glow of his power as it released Tidebringer's body to ash. Sooner than she would have expected, his footsteps were coming toward her again, splashing in what was left of the standing water.

He shook his head. "I've never seen anything like this . . ."

"I hope to never see anything like it ever again," Lore said. "I'll tell you everything—just not here."

"No arguments from me," Castor said, starting toward the ladder. "I'll go up first, in case anyone's waiting. Step back—there's still some water."

She tucked her dagger between her teeth. The trapdoor groaned open. Dim light and water poured in. Lore turned away, letting it fill the tunnel around her feet.

"All clear," Castor called down. "Ready?"

452

Lore nodded, gripping the first rung until her hands stopped shaking. There was a hollow ache in her healed leg, but even that faded as she reached up for the next rung and, bit by bit, drew herself up toward Castor and the fiery sunset that crowned him.

FORTY SEVEN

THE NEW ADDRESS CAME IN JUST AS THEY FOUGHT THROUGH THE floodwaters and barriers around Central Park to cross to the west side. It was a vacant office space situated above a boarded-up clothing store, not far from Lincoln Center.

Castor melted the lock on the door, prying it open, then sealed it shut behind them. Lore looked around. Judging by the city seal etched on its glass, it was likely being renovated to become some sort of government office. The smell of new paint and the plastic tarp covering the stairwell seemed to confirm it, even before they found the spread of empty cubicles upstairs. Toward the floor-to-ceiling windows, all papered over, was a small sitting area, complete with a table, couch, and chairs.

Unoccupied and unguarded by security, it was a good choice— and all thanks to Miles and the access he had at his internship. She hoped he and Van would be back sooner rather than later. She needed to see with her own eyes they were both all right.

Castor removed the plastic covering the couch, guiding Lore over to it. She sat heavily, exhausted. As night fell, and the city's power remained off, her eyes began to adjust to the growing darkness. The new god squeezed his hand into a fist, gathering a faint glow around it.

"Very impressive, big guy," she told him.

"I'm getting better at controlling it," he told her. "I can now take it from zero to thirty instead of zero to a hundred."

Her smile slipped as she watched him explore the kitchen area, then disappear into a back room. When he emerged, Castor carried a five-gallon water bottle, clearly destined for a water cooler, on his shoulder and a package of brown paper towels under the other arm.

He knelt in front of her, wetting some of the towels. Lifting Lore's hand from her lap, his sole focus turned to wiping away the dirt and grime and blood. She hadn't realized how cold she was until the warmth of his skin spread over her again. She tried to help him by lifting her arm as he rolled up her shirt at the shoulder, but her body wouldn't obey her.

For the first time in days, Lore felt safe enough to stop pretending she could keep pushing through the pain and fatigue.

This is why, she thought. Athena had worked a slow, methodical manipulation. Each suggestion was designed to separate her from the others, who might have been able to recognize what was happening, and deepen Lore's belief in her and her alone.

Castor gave her a small, reassuring smile as he retrieved a new paper towel and began on her other arm, gently dabbing at the dark stains on the hand Athena had broken and he'd healed. Lore watched him, her heart full to bursting.

The goddess wasn't mortal, and she didn't have a human's understanding of the world. Emotions were nuisances to a purely rational mind, but even Athena had recognized the threat the others posed simply by being near. A person alone could be controlled, but a person loved by others would always be under their protection.

Lore had been angry for so long—at the world, at the Agon, but most of all at herself. It wasn't that anger was inherently good or bad. It could lend power and drive and focus, but the longer it lived inside you unchecked, the more poisonous it became.

Even now, every fiber of her being was straining to head back down the staircase, to go out into the city with nothing but a blade and the image of the god it was meant for burning like a star in her mind. The impulse shoved at her from all sides, and her whole body shook with the effort of forcing herself to stay still.

Castor brought a fresh towel along her neck, and there was a brief flicker of distress in his expression as he ran the cool water along the curve of her jaw. Lore wondered, for a moment, if Athena had broken it, and if the pain elsewhere in her body had been so tremendous she hadn't noticed it.

He gave a playful flick of water against her cheek, startling her out of her thoughts. Lore let out a faint laugh. To her surprise, he moved next to her hair, running damp fingers back through the tangled mess of it with as much care as he could. He braided it over her shoulder, but had nothing to tie it off with.

Finally, he turned his attention to the tear in her shirt, stiff with dried blood. The place she had driven in the blade.

Lore loosely grasped his forearm with both hands, stilling him. "I need to apologize to you."

He shook his head. "Lore, really—"

She pressed on. "I'm sorry for the way I treated you. For not immediately siding with you about searching for Artemis, even though I knew why you wanted to find her, and for not fulfilling my promise to help you find out what happened to you."

"It's all right," he said quietly.

"No," she interrupted. "It's not. If there's only one thing I've been certain of for most of my life, it's that you're always on my side. That I can always trust you."

She drew in a shuddering breath.

"You said something before that I didn't completely understand," Lore said. "Not at the time. That the reason you needed to know how you killed Apollo was because you needed it to mean something. You needed it to be for a reason, and not just chance."

His fingers curled around the soft skin of her inner arm, stroking it.

"I couldn't recognize it in myself," she said. "I told myself I didn't believe in the Fates, but some part of me always hoped they did exist—that they were the reason it happened. Because otherwise, my family died as a result of a choice I made."

"What?" he whispered.

"I blamed the Agon. I blamed Aristos Kadmou and the Kadmides. But it was me. It was—" Lore felt like she was carving the words from her heart. "It was my—it was my fault."

"No," he began, "I know it might feel that way—"

Lore shook her head, her throat tightening. "It was my fault, Cas. My parents came home from the Agon and told me that we were leaving the hunt. That we were leaving the city. I couldn't . . . I couldn't understand. I thought they were weak and cowards, but—"

Castor let out a soft noise, already knowing where her story was headed.

"They knew that once Aristos had ascended he would punish my father for refusing him me," Lore said. "And they knew that if he discovered that he still couldn't use the aegis as a god, he would find a way to force us to use it for him, or give it to him of our own free will. So I thought, it doesn't belong to him. It's *ours*. It should be ours. I was so convinced that if my parents had it again, it would be enough to make them stay."

"You did take it," Castor breathed, half-amazed at the thought.

"You stole it."

She nodded, gripping his arm. Needing to hold on to something steady before the riptide of her regret and grief carried her under. "I did. I was just a stupid kid, and I wanted so badly to be fated for something bigger. For something more."

"That's not stupid," he told her. "It's how they raised us. It's not a thing you just get over."

She nodded, taking in a shuddering breath.

"I took the aegis and I was so . . . excited. So *proud*." The memory filled her with shame now. "But then I started thinking about how badly the Kadmides outnumbered us, what the punishment for theft was, how cruel Aristos Kadmou had been to my father . . . I thought, I'll bring it back. I'll bring it back and they can punish me, not my father, not my mother, not Damara, not Olympia. But I couldn't do it. I couldn't give them back our inheritance. So I hid it in the one place I knew they wouldn't think to look."

Her whole body heaved. She forced herself to continue.

"By then, it was morning. The Agon had been over for hours."

"And then you went home," he said softly.

"And then I went home." Lore shook her head. "I . . . found them."

Her eyes burned. She pressed one hand against them. "I thought that the Kadmides must have seen security footage of me and sought permission from their new god to kill my family outside the Agon. A part of me always knew the timing didn't line up, but I was so sure it was him—all of them. But it was *her*. It's always been her."

"What happened isn't your fault," Castor said, his voice full of intent. "You were only a child. You couldn't have known."

Lore began to cry, letting the tears come fast. "They must have been in so much pain. The girls would have been so scared . . . I can't stop thinking about it. I'm worried that one day it's the only thing I'll remember about them. When I lose their faces, their voices . . ."

Everything her family owned had been destroyed, including photographs, journals, and heirlooms. There was nothing left.

Castor leaned forward, wrapping his arms around her. She leaned into him, listening to rain patter softly down the windows.

"I spent the last few days lying to you about taking the aegis," Lore said. "To all of you. I told myself that as long as it was hidden, Wrath couldn't have what he wanted—if we had found it, I would have done everything to make sure only you saw the poem. That you would be the one to win and escape the Agon. But in the end, I almost went and got it for her. That's how much I wanted Wrath dead."

She looked up at him, the words trembling as they slipped from her. "Do you think they hate me?"

Castor shook his head, pressing his lips to her temple.

"No," he said fiercely. "They love you. They will always love you."

Tears slid down her cheeks. She wanted to believe him. "I should have gotten the shield for you, but I couldn't. I couldn't face it."

The inheritance she had wanted more than anything became the weapon that destroyed her life.

"Neither of us can change what happened," he whispered. "I wish it had all been different. I wished that a thousand times these last seven years. But your parents wanted to leave the Agon because they wanted you to be safe. To be happy. You still have that chance. That's what matters to them now."

Her grip on him tightened, and she tried not to picture her family there in the gray gloom of the Underworld, forever trapped by what she had done to them. She breathed in the scent of him and closed her eyes again, waiting for the clench of pain in her chest and skull to ease.

"If there's one thing I've learned this week, it's this," Castor began after a while. "When we can't change the past, the only thing left is to move forward. I need to do the same. I need to stop questioning a gift that's let me protect the people I care about most."

Lore pulled back. "You deserve to know what happened to you."

"But what's the point of a selfish god?" he said. "Or . . . whatever it is that I am."

"I don't think you could be selfish if you tried," Lore said.

"That's where you're wrong," he said. "The truth is, I wasn't completely honest with you either. I don't remember how Apollo died, but I do remember the moments before it happened. Everything after that is gone, right up to the moment I woke up and realized I had no body and the life I'd known was over."

The pain in his voice made Lore's chest clench.

"I didn't see him at first. He knew how to play with the shadows and light." Castor drew in a breath. "I was bedridden. Barely alive at that point. Thetis House had been emptied as the hunt went on, and my father had left, just for a little while, to run an errand. I woke up and Apollo was there, standing at the end of my bed."

Lore's lips parted in surprise.

"He looked . . ." Castor's voice trailed off. "He was covered in blood. There was a wound in his side."

"What did you do?" Lore asked. "You couldn't have been armed."

He shook his head, turning his palms up to look at them. "I wasn't. I asked him if he needed help."

Lore stared.

"I know. It's ridiculous to even think about. A twelve-year-old, believing he could help a god?" He let out a faint laugh. "I should have been terrified. All those years we'd been taught to hate them, but I saw him and

460

I just thought, *He looks sick*. I saw something in him, in his face, in his eyes, that I'd seen so many times in the mirror. He was aníatos, like me."

Aníatos. Incurable.

"He asked what my name was, and laughed when I told him. It was a horrible sound, like a clarion. But there was this pull to him. It was . . . It felt like all those times you're told not to look into the sun, but something tells you to try, just once," Castor said. "He asked why I had offered him help. I told him that he looked like he needed rest."

Castor finally looked up at her. "That's all I remember. I wish it was a better story. I wish that I could tell you that I was brave and strong, and that I deserved this power, but I can't, and even though I know I might have to let that go, the thought kills me. I would do anything to prove myself to you."

"You have nothing to prove to me," Lore said. "Why would you think that?"

Castor turned to look at her, a faint smile on his face. But his eyes blazed with power, and with that same wild, irrepressible feeling she was drowning in.

"Isn't it obvious?" he asked quietly. "I wanted to be worthy of you."

"Worthy of me?" she began. Her words often came out too quick, too clumsy, too sharp, and she didn't want that. Not this time. *"Cas."*

"Lore." He kept that same soft tone. "I was born knowing how to do three things—how to breathe, how to dream, and how to love you."

Lore began to tremble. Her breath turned shallow, as quick and light as her pulse as it caught fire in her veins.

How did she say this? How did anyone say this? It was like untying her armor, setting aside her blade, and exposing every soft part of herself to the world. Yet the moment he'd said it, Lore had recognized that sense of inevitability that had woven through all their moments together, old and new. How she'd been stumbling toward him, even as she pulled back against the tether between them.

Tears dripped down her face, curling over her cheek. She had always been that girl, her feelings unbearable, her hair wind-matted as she ran through the city. But then, Castor had always been that boy who ran alongside her.

"Did you hear the one about the turtle on Broadway?" he said softly, touching a finger to one of the tears.

Lore gave up on words and kissed him.

Castor drew in a sharp breath as her lips touched his, uncertain at first. Lore pulled back, holding his face in her hands as she studied him and his bright, burning eyes; she wondered if it would be her last kiss, or if any of that mattered when this was now, and they were here, and the growing wind was singing through their city's streets.

Castor wrapped an arm around her waist, carefully drawing her into the heat of his body. He ducked his head and found her mouth again, brushing her lips with his smiling ones, like a challenge.

When had she ever refused a challenge?

Lore kissed him again, meeting him there, pace for pace, touch for touch, until she became lost in it, rising and falling with the push and pull, the advance and retreat. She'd acted on instinct in the park, giving in to the pull of him, but this—this was intention.

Lore had kissed others before. Almost always drunk and in the dark, letting alcohol become the barrier between her and the emotions she hadn't wanted to feel, and the things she wanted to forget. What had happened that night in the Odysseides' home was like a phantom tide that swept in and out of her mind, etching deeper into the sand with each return. Sometimes she could go weeks without thinking about it, sometimes days, sometimes only hours. But then it would come again: disconnection from the body she fought so hard to strengthen, the suffocating feeling of powerlessness.

Maybe it would always be part of her, but she was learning how to move through it and reclaim herself with choice. Right now, with Castor, she didn't feel powerless. She felt triumphant. Like everything in her body had suddenly connected and electrified.

His lips were soft as they brushed against hers, capturing the last of her tears, but grew insistent, harder, at her urging. It wasn't enough. She wanted to touch him everywhere, to melt into the warmth pooling low in her body that was desire, and the tender ache in her heart that was love.

A peal of thunder finally broke them apart. Lore started to drift back, but Castor held on a moment longer, running his hands down her arms, absorbing the feeling of her skin against his.

She pressed her face to the warm curve of his shoulder, breathing in the scent of him. Her hand trailed along his chest to the place where he'd been shot.

"What's going to happen to you when the Agon ends?" she whispered.

Lore felt him smile against her skin. "You gonna miss me, Golden?"

"Maybe I like having you around," she said. "You're easy on the eyes."

She was tempted to stay there forever, listening to the storm, imagining a different life. But as thunder broke over the sky again, Lore made a decision.

"I'm going to the Phoenician," she said. "Will you come with me?"

His eyebrows rose. "The old Kadmides place? Why?"

"Because," Lore said. "I left something there, and it's finally time to go pick it up."

FORTY EIGHT

"Can't say they didn't improve the place . . ."

Lore glanced at Castor, allowing herself a little laugh. "I got a big hit of nostalgia being up here again."

A day after the ill-fated meeting between her father and the Kadmides, Lore had brought Castor into the Murray Hill neighborhood to spy on the Phoenician with her. They'd climbed the fire escape of the building across the street, the exact way they had that evening. Back then, Lore hadn't told Castor the truth of how she'd found the location—she just said that they were on their own kind of hunt.

After the Kadmides sold the property, it looked like it had become a fitness boutique, which also closed. In the months between then and now, rats had invaded, it had been bombed out with pesticide, and now a pita restaurant was being put in. A true New York City circle of life.

Lore looked over to Castor's face, his striking profile outlined by the night-stained clouds. The air had taken on a warm, drowsy quality as humidity settled back over the city. If it hadn't been for the reek of stale water and rot, she might have felt like she was dreaming.

The floodwaters had been slow to recede after Tidebringer's death. To Lore's eye, everything was starting to look as if it had been painted with watercolors; edges were softened and colors stained darker.

Lore pushed up from where she'd been flat on her stomach at the roof's edge and scanned the nearby buildings one last time. It was just shy of midnight and the start of the Agon's fifth day, but there were no New Yorkers out and about—or, it seemed, hunters.

Castor straightened as well, letting out a soft hum of thought. His hair was curling and glossy in the damp air.

He really was beautiful. Lore had wondered, from the moment she'd found out what he'd become, how much of the old Castor was left—as if their years apart hadn't dismantled and remade her, too. She had asked her father once if inheriting a god's power meant absorbing their beliefs, their personalities, and their looks.

Power does not transform you, he'd said. *It only reveals you.*

From what she had seen, immortality turned back the clock on the older hunters who claimed it, returning them to their physical prime and imbuing them with more power, more beauty, and more strength. But it couldn't fix what was broken or missing inside them.

The same was true for Castor, but power had only strengthened the good in his heart. Each time she met his gaze, she saw all those things she'd lost when he left her life. Things she never thought she'd have again.

Things that would be taken from her once more at the end of the Agon.

It was too painful to think about, so she didn't.

"I have to admit," Castor said, "I'm a little sad it's gone."

For a moment, Lore wasn't sure what he was talking about.

"The last time we were here, I imagined us older, sneaking inside the bar under all of the Kadmides' noses and ordering a drink," he said. "Do you remember the serpent mask they hung in the window?"

"The one that supposedly belonged to Damen Kadmou?" Lore asked. The first new Dionysus. "Yeah, why?"

465

Castor had a faint smile on his face as he said, "I imagined us stealing it to check if the stories were true and the inside was still stained with his blood."

"I really *was* a bad influence on you as a child," Lore said.

He winked at her. Lore flushed, turning her head away so he wouldn't see the wash of pink spreading over her face. She lay down again beside him, her fingers brushing where his gripped the cement ledge. Castor shifted his hand, curling his pinkie finger over hers.

"You really thought about that?" she asked quietly. "Us going together?"

Back then, Lore had mostly thought about setting the place on fire and watching the Kadmides flee like rats from their dark booths— probably more than was strictly healthy for a child of ten.

"Stupid, I know," he said, "considering how little time I had. But you were like this invincible force to me, even then. You were a safe place to hide my hopes."

Her lips parted and her body flooded with sensation and sudden awareness. She didn't know what to do with it, so she looked out onto the street again.

"Come on, big guy," Lore said, pushing up off the roof. "I just hope it's still there."

They climbed down the fire escape. Lore kept herself alert, one hand on her small blade, as she crossed the street.

The gate protecting the narrow path to the courtyard behind the old restaurant was blocked by trash bags and fallen scaffolding. Castor broke the padlock on it with ease.

Filthy water swirled around their ankles as they trudged forward. The stench of trash instantly brought her back to this same place, seven years ago.

466

Lore searched the wet ground, making her way toward the piles of construction supplies in the courtyard. Dread ran a cold knuckle across the back of her neck.

Where is it?

"What's wrong?" Castor asked.

"The storm drain—" she began, only to notice that the water was slanting down, toward the stack of plywood lined up against the restaurant's wall. "Can you help me? We need to move these out of the way."

They made quick work of it together. As they removed the last of the wood, water rushed around her feet, pouring through the rusted iron grate covering the storm drain.

When she tried to lift the cover, it wouldn't budge.

"If you're not too busy standing there looking pretty . . . ?" she said, gesturing to Castor.

He pretended to push up his sleeves. The movement only highlighted how his shirt clung to the ridges of his shoulders and chest. A warm thread curled low in her stomach as she watched him bend over to grip the grate.

He grunted, bracing his feet. The muscles of his arms strained as he pulled at it, until, finally, he used his power to heat the rust seal that had formed. Castor set the cover aside with a look of relief. "How did you lift this as a kid?"

"Panic," Lore said, crouching beside the opening. The force of the water flowing by her nearly pushed her in.

She shifted, sitting at the edge to lower herself into the drain.

"Wait," Castor said, suddenly serious. "You're actually going down?"

It wasn't much of a drop; the darkness made the drain pipe seem much deeper than it actually was. Water roared around her, racing down to meet the bigger drain it connected to. It *was* fuller than the last time she had done this, but she wasn't afraid.

Lore looked up, shooting a visibly worried Castor a reassuring look.

Instead of following the path the water took, Lore went the other way, crossing through the waterfall created by the drain. There was a small alcove-like space where the drain met the wall of the restaurant's basement. She stopped, staring at the dark garbage bag resting there, exactly where she had left it.

There was a sound like whispering, a thousand silky voices talking over one another, urging her forward.

Lore moved, and the world fell silent. Power seemed to burn through the bag, making her fingers spark where she touched it.

"Lore?" Castor called.

She shook herself out of the stupor. "I'm going to pass it up to you."

Lore fought the rushing water to lift it into his hands. Castor let out a small gasp of surprise as his arms locked and he nearly tipped into the drain.

"What did you put in here with it?" he asked, struggling to draw it the rest of the way up.

"Very funny," Lore said, accepting Castor's help as he hauled her out, too.

She sat for a moment, trying to force her breathing to settle.

"I'm serious," Castor said, giving the shield an accusatory look. "It must weigh close to a thousand pounds. How did you lift it?"

Lore shot him a look of disbelief, reaching over to untie the knot in the garbage bag. She pulled it down to reveal the curve of the round shield and the gold key pattern inlaid into the leather.

468

Then, with another breath, she pulled at the bag until Medusa's ferocious face glared back at them from the center of the aegis.

I remember you, it seemed to say.

The first time she looked upon the aegis, Lore had seen a monster made into a god's trophy. Now, as Lore met Medusa's sightless eyes, she only saw herself gazing back.

Castor did not seem to be breathing. "You put Zeus's shield in a trash bag."

"And hid it in a storm drain," Lore confirmed.

"You . . ." he began, only to let the words die off with a strangled "How?"

"I told you," Lore said. "I put it the one place they would never think to look—the same place I had taken it from. Well, on the other side of the wall."

Lore touched the edge of the aegis, feeling that same buzzing sensation move through her fingers, to her hand, to her heart.

It was hers. How she would use it now was up to her, and her alone.

Castor said nothing, but she felt his eyes on her all the same.

She turned it around so the inner curve of the shield faced them. Feeling along the edge of the soft, worn leather that covered the interior, she found a small catch and pulled it away. There, just as Tidebringer had said, was the inscribed poem, written in the ancient tongue.

Castor let out a soft gasp at the sight of it, pulling closer to read it over her shoulder.

"It's almost exactly the same—" she began.

Except for the final lines.

"So it shall be until that day," Lore read, loosely translating them,

"*when one remains who is remade whole and summons me with smoke of altars to be built by conquest final and fearsome.*" She glanced up at his pensive face. "What do you think that means?"

"I have no idea," Castor said. "But I don't like the sound of *conquest final and fearsome.*"

"*Summons me . . .*" Lore read again. "Athena said the aegis could be used to call down lightning. I wonder if Wrath wants to hedge his bets when it comes to summoning Zeus, and use the shield to call on him to witness whatever he has planned?"

"Maybe," Castor said. He drew in a long breath.

"What is it?" Lore asked him.

"I don't know . . . This has given me even more questions than I had before. I'm still stuck on whether or not there can only be one of us left alive," Castor said. "And how can a god be 'remade whole' if they don't have access to their full powers even while in their divine form? And is this act—whatever it is—something only one god can perform to win the Agon? Or do all of the surviving gods have to individually perform it to release themselves and the hunters from the Agon?"

That last thought scorched her with the kind of blistering hope Lore hadn't been sure she was capable of anymore. *Free.* All of them.

Athena had seen the secret longing in her to be *more*. Lore had only ever been kidding herself when she thought she'd be able to shake off this week and return to the life she'd created. The Agon was an addiction, and only its true end would purge it from her—and not just her, but all the others who fought and killed for centuries in the search for that same *more*.

Even if Castor was forced into the realm of gods and separated from her again, he would be alive. The pain of knowing what she would gain and lose made Lore feel as if she'd torn her own lungs from her chest.

In time, she could accept it, though. She could be content knowing he was out there . . .

Well, maybe not *content*.

"In that case, you'd think Zeus would have been a little more specific," Lore groused.

"Not if the Agon was meant to be more than punishment . . ." Castor said, trailing off. "Never mind. I have no idea what I'm talking about. We'll take this back to Van and Miles. I'm sure they'll both have thoughts."

She nodded.

"You know," Lore began, something else occurring to her. "Athena wondered if you were somehow a true god, or another god in disguise—but that would mean you were somehow borrowing Apollo's power, and wouldn't he have to be alive for that to be true?"

"Artemis said something similar," Castor said. "That I had his power, but that I was different . . . I'm limited in the same way they are, though, even in full immortal form. I don't have all of his abilities, only the ones I've used."

She gave him a thoughtful look. "Do you think Apollo figured out the meaning of this and escaped? Maybe he *did* need you to help him in some way, and you can't remember because Zeus wants all of the gods to unravel it for themselves."

Castor looked down at his upturned hands. "But then why do I have his power? Athena wasn't wrong. When I call on it, it's more like . . . dipping a hand into a warm river and pulling from it. Or . . . there's always a candle inside me, but I can feed it with more fire if I reach for it. Am I making any sense?"

"You are," she reassured him. "The little shred of good news is that we don't have to figure all of this out right now. I think we have to focus on stopping whatever Wrath has planned. Cas, he still has to die. We can't let him regain his immortality and come back for Van or Miles or any of the others."

"Athena is still a problem, too," Castor said. "She won't hesitate to punish you and the others."

Lore rubbed her forehead, trying not to imagine her family. What the goddess had done to them.

"I can do it," Castor said.

"Cas—" she began.

"I can kill them," he insisted. "That way, no mortal can claim their powers. And if I really can't die myself—"

"Can we please not test that theory again?" Lore asked.

"There's no other choice," he said. "When they're gone, and the week is over, we'll have seven years to figure out the riddle of the inscription before the start of the next hunt."

And seven years to figure out how to lose you forever, Lore thought, miserably.

Castor took her hand, giving it a squeeze. "Did Athena give you any sort of indication about her plans now?"

She shook her head. "She doesn't even know I'm alive."

Thunder boomed overhead, shaking the buildings around them. Lightning traced a path across the clouds, illuminating Castor's face.

Lore picked up the shield, sliding her arm through its leather straps. Somehow, she knew what to do.

She slammed a fist against the front of the shield, and the roar that burst from it was deeper than thunder—it was primordial.

It raged through the air, bellowing through the quiet streets. She struck it again, and again, until her ears rang and she heard the call echo back to her from distant buildings. The power blazed through her. She felt invincible.

Castor turned and turned, as if the noise was a monster to be chased. He paled as he took in the sight of the aegis again, pulling away from it. Lore drew it closer to her.

Stop, she thought. *I don't want him to ever be afraid.*

Yes, a voice seemed to whisper back. *He is not our enemy.*

He rubbed a hand against his chest as he faced her again. This time, his posture and expression relaxed.

Thank you, Lore thought. *One last thing.*

She took her small blade, slashing across the shield. The dark air flashed white with lightning.

"Now she knows," Lore said.

FORTY NINE

MILES WAS WAITING FOR THEM AT THE TOP OF THE STAIRS AS THEY arrived back at the office space, turning his phone over and over in his hands. He was so deep in his thoughts that it took him a moment to notice them.

In the second it took him to jump to his feet, Lore had already run up the steps between them, nearly knocking Miles over as she threw her arms around him.

Miles let out a shocked, breathless laugh before giving her a hard squeeze.

"Are you all right?" she asked him, near tears at the relief of seeing him.

"Am *I* all right?" he repeated, pulling back to give her a thorough once-over. Lore's gaze landed on a brutal-looking bruise on his forehead.

"I'm so sorry about what happened," she began. "With the meet, and Artemis—"

"I wanted to go," Miles said. He glanced over to Castor, a silent question on his face.

"Right where you said she would be," Castor confirmed.

"Where the app said she would be," Miles said, miserably.

Lore hugged him. The new skin over her ribs pulled with the

movement, but she held on, clinging to Miles the way he clung to her.

"Thank you," she told him.

"Thank technology and the magic of cellular service," Miles said. "All I did was worry."

"You did more than that," Lore said.

"You're right," he said. "I also stress-ate the entire sleeve of crackers that was supposed to be our meal for the day. Van had to go out and try to find more food and water."

"I'm serious," Lore said.

"No, it's true," he said. "My mom also called. A lot. So that was fun. She was about to get in her car and drive up here. I told her not to, but she refused to hang up until I sent her a hostage-style photo to prove that I was fine."

Miles ran a hand back over his dark hair. He was starting to get a bit of a shadow as a beard grew in, and there were dark bruises beneath his eyes. But when he smiled, all of the week's wear and tear seemed to vanish.

"I have some clothes for you," he said, leading them into the vacant office space.

Van and Miles had done some mild redecorating in the last few hours. Scattered bags of supplies were stacked here and there on the plastic tarps covering the floor. Miles went to one of them, digging out a small bundle of clothes.

"Van didn't think it was safe to go back to the town house, and the selection at the shelter wasn't great," Miles said, handing them to her. "I figured you'd want another pair of jeans that actually fit you, but I have to warn you that the wash on them is very two seasons ago."

Lore unfolded the pair in question. "Should I be unnerved that you know my jean size?"

"Should I be annoyed you always leave your clothes in our washing machine so I end up having to dry and fold them for you?"

He'd grabbed her a sports bra, a black T-shirt with some mysterious faded logo on it, and fresh socks.

Lore smiled. "Thank you."

"No problem," he said. "Your brand of 'I don't care' is very easy to shop for."

There was something in the pocket of the shirt. Lore dumped it out into her hand, only to find herself staring down at the gold necklace Hermes had given her. The feather amulet was cool to the touch.

She brushed a light finger against it. *The eyes of the gods are upon you.*

"I thought you might want it," Miles said quietly.

Lore couldn't bring herself to speak. She nodded, opening the clasp to put it on. Whatever power it might have had was gone, leaving behind its slight weight and the meaning she had come to attach to it. The one that had never been more important than now.

Not lost. Free.

Castor went still beside her. Lore followed his gaze to the door.

Iro stood there, breathing hard. She was no longer wearing the black robe of a hunter, but the typical clothes worn beneath them—dark shirt, loose-fitting pants, body armor.

The look she gave Lore was one of pleading, but she didn't speak.

Lore stepped in front of Castor. "What are you doing here?"

"She's helping us," Miles told her.

"No. She's not," Lore said coldly.

The other girl flinched, her eyes darting to Castor. "I—I know I made a mistake. What happened was a mistake. I—all of us—wish to make amends. We wish to fight. To stop Wrath."

Lore looked at her in disbelief.

"It's true," Miles told Lore. "Iro found us while we were on our way to meet the Achillides. They've shared supplies and information."

Lore opened her mouth to speak, but Castor's quiet voice cut in.

"Do you mean that sincerely?" he asked Iro. "What changed?"

"*I* changed," Iro said. "Someone told me that there is a better world waiting to be chosen, and I know that it will vanish the moment Wrath's plan comes to pass. If you can believe nothing else, believe that I will not allow my father's killer to emerge the victor of the Agon."

Castor seemed to consider her and her words carefully before he said, "All right."

Lore spun toward him. "What?"

"I accept your apology," he told Iro. "Thank you for helping the Achillides."

Lore blew a piece of hair out of her face. "This is why I always had to hold all of our grudges as kids. You've never had the heart for them." To Iro she said, "If this is another trick . . ."

"This is no trick," Iro said. "I'll swear an oath to you now—"

Lore held up her hand. "Please. I can't take any more oaths. I'll just take your word for it."

Heavy steps bounded up the stairs behind Iro. They all turned to find a slightly winded Van sagging against the stairwell rail. A plastic grocery bag, laden with water bottles and packaged food, hung from his wrist.

"Are you all right?" Miles asked.

Van held up a hand, waving him off. He turned his face back down toward the stairs behind him, but not quickly enough for Lore to miss the way his lips compressed and his eyes squeezed shut in the kind of relief that was so sharp, it became painful.

477

This, she realized, was her family now. This was what had been right in front of her, waiting to be seen, the whole time she'd been chasing the past.

When Van looked at them again, he noticed who wasn't there. "Where's Athena?"

Miles shook himself, as if he hadn't even realized it. "Wait . . . I just thought she was—actually, I don't know what I thought."

Lore drew in a deep breath.

"I need to tell you all what happened," she said, leaning the covered aegis against a nearby wall. "And then we need to figure out a plan."

"Well," Van said elegantly as he rummaged through one of his bags of supplies. "Damn."

It was a while before anyone else spoke.

"Gil . . . was Hermes . . ." Miles said, looking like he might faint out of his chair. Lore sat beside him on the ground and placed a steadying hand on his leg. "A god . . . washed my unmentionables . . . He came to Family Weekend at Columbia with me . . . We ate pizza together." He whispered the word again in disbelief. *"Pizza."*

"Yeah," Lore said softly. "We did."

"Why did he take me in?" Miles said. "Why offer me a place to live? It must have been to help disguise the fact you were there, I'm just not sure how."

"Maybe he just liked you," Lore said. Maybe Hermes had thought she would need someone like Miles.

"No wonder you were so upset," Castor said, his voice strained. "I knew it had to be something terrible, but I'm not sure I could have imagined that."

"And Athena . . ." Van shook his head. "I should have seen it. I should have believed the stories about her, even as she worked with us."

He opened a small white package, then he crossed the short distance to where Miles sat and carefully brushed the hair from his forehead so he could apply the bright-blue ice pack to the bruise.

Miles stared up at him, eyes wide. Van, as if realizing what he'd done, pulled back, quickly handing it to him.

"Here," he said. "I . . . It looked bad."

"Where did you find an ice pack in a city with no power?" Miles asked faintly.

"Still doubting my abilities, I see," Van said. "I always get what I want."

"Here, let me heal you," Castor said, starting to rise.

Miles waved him off, holding his ice pack to his bruise.

"I really should have figured it out," Van said, finishing his earlier thought. "If not her role, then the fact that Wrath already knew what the poem said."

"He gave no indication that he already possessed knowledge of its contents," Iro told Lore apologetically. "I would not have kept that from you."

"I know. And if it's anyone's fault, it's mine," Lore told them. "I'm the one who brought all of you into this. I'm the one who let her in."

"You're really okay?" Miles asked Lore, reaching over to grip her hand.

"I've been better," she told him. "But Castor found me in time."

Van pressed his cellphone to his forehead, thinking. "And the new lines . . ."

He trailed off in thought again.

"And you did take the aegis," Iro said, her dark eyes soft. "All this time, you never said a word . . . not even when we talked about it while training."

"I didn't let myself think about it," Lore said. "Let alone talk about it."

"Where is it now?" Iro asked.

Lore stood, working out the stiffness in her joints as she went to retrieve it. She didn't bother with the knot this time. She tore the bag off it, kicking away the scraps as she held the aegis out to show them.

The phone clattered from Van's hand.

"I *know*," Castor said to him.

Van and Iro came toward the shield slowly, stunned. Iro pressed a hand to her mouth, crouching in front of it.

"That's—" Van began.

"Yes," Lore said.

"Carried into the Trojan War—"

"Yes."

"Born from Hephaestus's hammer—"

"Yes."

"Bearing the Gorgoneion—"

"Do you need to sit back down?" Lore asked him, seriously. Van stretched his hand out toward it, only to pull it back before his fingers could touch Medusa. As if she might bite. But none of them were afraid—Lore wondered then if she had to be holding the shield to use it to instill terror in others, and if she had to will that effect into being.

"This is so cool," Miles said, dropping onto a knee. He glanced up at Lore. "Can I take a picture with it?"

"What?" Lore said, pulling it back. "No!"

"Was that you, an hour or so ago?" Iro asked. "It sounded like thunder at first, but . . ."

Lore nodded. "I wanted Athena to know that I was alive, and that I had it. I might not know what she's planning, but at least this will help draw her out."

"Do we need to draw her out?" Miles asked, pained.

"We do," Lore confirmed. "If we're going to end the Agon, she can't survive it, otherwise there'll be no place in the world we'll be safe from her."

The new god let out a noise of frustration. "We're missing something, here."

"Of course we're missing something," Van said. "You can't remember how you became a god, but you seemingly can't be killed. Why is that?"

Castor had told the others the truth about his ascension, but the story had only brought more questions.

"It might not be connected at all," Miles pointed out. "Maybe it's just Apollo's power healing him fast enough to prevent any injury from killing him."

"If that's true then I doubt the original could have died," Lore said. "And he was shot through the heart."

Iro looked to Castor. "Sorry."

Castor's shoulder lifted in a shrug.

"What if Wrath is taking the lines literally?" Van said. "Instead of building a temple or calling worshippers back to honor Zeus, he's planning a ceremonial sacrifice of animals or something else in Zeus's name? *Conquest final and fearsome . . . conquest . . .* Do we know where he is now?"

"He's back at the Waldorf Astoria," Iro said, pressing a hand to her face. "I almost forgot to tell you, and that was the whole point of my coming here. We have eyes posted nearby, and they reported that all the Kadmides returned. I can only assume that he did as well."

"He was at the Waldorf Astoria?" Lore asked, looking between them. "Did I miss something?"

"Oh, yeah—you actually did," Miles said. "That's what the source in the Kadmides told me during that last meeting. The hotel has been closed for remodeling for years now and isn't set to reopen for a few more months. The Kadmides paid an eye-watering amount to the owners to stop construction work for the week. They're using the penthouse suites."

The prestigious hotel undergoing renovations in midtown east seemed like a strange pick to her, aside from it being empty, but Lore let it go. "But he left at one point?"

"All the Kadmides evacuated during the flooding," Van explained. "Interesting that they came back . . ."

"He would only go back if he *had* to go back," Miles said. "Don't you think? If Van's right, maybe that's where they've built their altar for the sacrifice."

Van rubbed at his chin. "Why would he need Tidebringer to cause the flood, then? He could have just taken people off the street— Oh."

"Oh what?" Lore pressed. "Oh *no*?"

"They're not going to attack the Waldorf Astoria," Van said. He looked to Miles. "It's empty except for the hunters. But what happened when the floodwaters came in?"

"It broke water mains, disrupted our electricity and all of our transportation systems . . ." Miles stood up. "Oh."

Van nodded. "It forced people into shelters. That was the whole point of it: to ensure that people—a lot of people—would be gathering in a few places around the city."

"You think he's planning a *human* sacrifice?" Iro asked, aghast.

482

"Knowing it is forbidden?"

"*Conquest final and fearsome,*" Van repeated again. "It's a conquest of those who worship rival gods—at least it would be in Wrath's eyes."

"But at any point during a weekday there are thousands of people in office buildings, schools, trains, and in subway stations," Lore said. "Why did he need Tidebringer to cause a flood?"

"To render city services useless, and keep everyone preoccupied with relief efforts," Miles said. "To move around the city unnoticed because of the flood and its fallout. Everyone they haven't paid off will be overwhelmed by ensuring the city's security."

"Where are the biggest shelters?" Iro asked.

"A lot of the usual designated shelters were also affected," Miles said. "They've been using big structures like Madison Square Garden, Central Park, Grand Central Station . . ."

He went very pale, then looked at the time on his phone.

"Miles?" Lore queried.

"I know why they picked the Waldorf Astoria," he said. "And if I'm right, we don't have until the Agon ends on Sunday at midnight. We only have until tomorrow to stop them."

FIFTY

"I MEAN . . ." MILES CONTINUED, TAKING IN THE FACES AROUND HIM. "I might be wrong. I *hope* I'm wrong."

"Let's operate under the assumption you're not," Van said, guiding him back over to a chair.

"They're evacuating the people in Grand Central and the other temporary relief points starting tomorrow night—Friday night— and taking them to a better-equipped shelter in Queens," Miles said, sounding more and more disturbed. "But construction aside, it's definitely not a coincidence he chose that particular hotel."

"What makes you say that?" Lore asked.

"Have you ever heard of Track Sixty-One?" he said, pulling out his phone and quickly searching. "It's a so-called 'secret' subway track beneath the hotel, built for President Roosevelt—the F. D. one, not the teddy-bear one—so he could move between Grand Central Station and the Waldorf Astoria without the public seeing that he couldn't walk. I got to take a tour once with my internship boss—but most people have no idea it still exists."

Miles handed Lore his phone. She scrolled down through the article there as Castor read over her shoulder.

"It looks like FDR would be put in his armored car and they would drive that into an elevator, which led into the Waldorf Astoria's

484

parking garage," Castor said. "Whatever the Kadmides brought over from River House could be hidden there, on the track."

"But I thought the subway tunnels were flooded?" Lore asked.

"Some of them are," Miles said. "I can see if there are any updates through work, but they might have their own motorized system for getting around without using the tracks themselves. What do you think it is, though? A bomb?"

"A sacrificial offering to the gods is usually made with fire," Lore explained to Miles. "So the smoke rises to where they were believed to reside in the sky. If it's not a bomb, it's most likely some other incendiary device. Are we betting on Grand Central Station as their target?"

"They could connect to a number of different subway lines there," Miles said. "But they would definitely need to pass through it."

"You are forgetting a few steps," Iro said. "For it to be a proper sacrifice there would need to be libations. An animal's throat would be cut—there'd be prayers."

"I think he's likely moved beyond *proper*," Lore said.

Iro nodded. "Fair point."

"There's another problem," Castor said. "Even if we're right, how are we going to narrow down the potential window of the attack?"

"Leave that to the Odysseides," Iro said. "We will discover when they mean to attack, and we will cut them off at the knees."

"The remaining Achillides would help with any sort of assault on the Waldorf Astoria," Van said. "We'll still be greatly outnumbered by Wrath's forces, but if we can catch them off guard and preempt their plans, the element of surprise will level the playing field somewhat."

"All right, all right," Castor said. "But there's still Wrath to contend with. And Athena."

"That's the uncomplicated part," Lore said. "I have something they both want, and now they both know it."

Castor sighed. "You want to use the aegis as bait?"

"I don't know . . ." Van shook his head. "He needs it for *something*. Is it really wise to bring it to him? If he finds a way to force you to use it—"

"That will not happen," Iro said firmly.

Lore looked at her, surprised by her old friend's show of faith.

"It won't," Iro insisted.

"It won't," Lore agreed. "Both he and Athena are deluding themselves if they think they can use it once they're in divine form, I really do believe that. And I will never give it to them willingly."

"Haven't we tried this plan a few times already?" Castor asked gently. "What makes you think it'll end any differently?"

"Because of the aegis," Lore said. "It's about more than setting a trap—it's about playing them off one another. Wrath is obsessed with it, and Athena will never let him have it when she's so close to having it herself. Cas, if we can draw them into a one-on-one fight, we'll be able to take care of whoever emerges from it alive."

Van seemed to run the scenario through his head, but he didn't immediately shoot it down. Castor wore his familiar look of worry.

"There are still a lot of *maybe*s and uncertainties," Van said. "But at this point, it's probably the best we're going to come up with. Our goal is to ensure the device never goes off and that Castor is the final god."

"That won't be enough to end the Agon outright," Miles reminded them. "And we still don't know what the new lines mean."

"I know," Lore said. The thought filled her with bitter frustration, but what could they do? They were out of the one thing they

486

needed most—time. "If we can get you through today, tomorrow, and Saturday, then we have seven years to figure it out before another Agon begins."

Iro rose from her chair. "If we are to attack tomorrow, I will need to move quickly to learn the timing of their plans."

"And how are you going to do that, exactly?" Miles asked.

Iro's eyebrows rose. "I only need to find one of Wrath's hunters who knows these details. I will enjoy . . . discussing it with however many it takes to find out."

"Text me when you learn anything," Lore said.

"Yes, I will," Iro said. "I nearly forgot . . ."

She moved toward the stairwell, retrieving the heavy black duffel bag that she had left there as she'd come in. "I thought you might need weapons, given all that's happened."

Iro removed them from their wrappings, laying them out on the floor. Castor unsheathed the sword Van handed to him, inspecting it.

"You remember how to use that thing?" Lore asked.

He sliced it through the air, admiring the flash of the pristine silver blade. "I think I've still got the gist."

It was a xiphos, the shorter straight blade that the ancients had traditionally favored. Only, the bloodline's weapon makers had long ago substituted iron and bronze for superior steel. Decorative silver vines were inlaid in the hilt; that small bit of artistry was a signature of their metalsmiths.

"These are from your own stores?" Lore asked, surprised.

Iro nodded. "It would not do to fight with our enemy's steel. I wouldn't be able to trust it."

Iro passed Lore her own xiphos, the scabbard, like Castor's, attached to a baldric—a long leather strap that cut from her shoulder to hip to allow the blade to hang there. Her sword had no real embellishments, but Lore liked the feel of it in her hand.

When Iro rose to go, Lore followed her to the stairs.

"Are you sure you're going to be all right?" Lore asked her.

Iro nodded, seeming to struggle with her thoughts for a moment.

"I meant with everything," Lore said. "This isn't just stopping Wrath. It's the end of the Agon and the destruction of everything you know. Everything you've wanted."

All the things she, too, would have to face.

"We all cast votes on whether or not to help you, and it was unanimous," Iro said. "The Agon has never been a kind master, but this hunt nearly destroyed us. Everything has changed now. Wrath tore down all of the rules and beliefs that carried us through the centuries, only to reveal the rot that has always been there, just out of sight. If we do not end the Agon, it will end us."

Lore nodded. "Yes. Exactly."

"I didn't tell you this before," Iro said when she reached the door to the street, "when you asked me about her. My mother is alive after all."

"What?" Lore breathed. "You're sure?"

Iro nodded.

"She wrote to me at the start of the Agon. In her letter, she told me that she could not stay within our world, that it would have strangled the life from her," Iro said. "She knew she could not take me with her without the Odysseides coming after us. I suppose I did not understand how I felt about it until this week, maybe not until you told us about your own family wanting that same thing. To me, she hadn't achieved freedom, but shame. How could I believe that about my own mother?"

Lore let out a soft sigh. "That hits close to home."

"All I can do now," Iro said, "is tell you that I am sorry for everything that's happened, and come when you call."

Lore drew in a deep breath. "The other bloodlines won't willingly give up the Agon."

"It's a good thing, then," Iro said with a small smile, "that neither of us has ever been afraid of a fight."

She opened the door, only to turn back. "By the way, that sword has a name. Mákhomai."

I make war.

Lore smiled.

FIFTY ONE

LORE SLEPT AND DREAMED OF DEATH'S GRAY WORLD.

A river drifted lazily by. Memory bled into reverie as she made her way forward over shards of stone that littered its banks. The air turned to ice in her lungs and assaulted her bare arms and legs. A simple shift, the kind the hunters used when burning their dead, scratched at her skin.

She heard a soft voice, a whisper of her name, and looked up. Across the waters of the river were seven golden forms, their outlines blazing against the bleak, craggy landscape.

Lore sat straight up, ripping herself out of the dream. The word echoed through her. *Seven.*

Their faces had been indistinct—more impressions than anything else, but Lore had recognized them all the same. Hermes, Aphrodite, Hephaestus, Poseidon, Artemis, Ares, and Dionysus . . .

If they were truly the gods of the Agon, if it hadn't all been a hallucination . . . there should have been eight. But that would mean— what? That she'd been right, and that Apollo had somehow escaped death?

Lore shook her head, pressing a cool hand to her temple. It took her a moment to remember where she was. She scanned the office space, her eyes landing on where Van sat awake in one of the chairs.

Castor slept on the ground beneath him, his fingers woven through one another and resting on his chest, but Van's gaze was fixed on where Miles slept sprawled out on the couch. As Lore's eyes adjusted to the low light, Van's look of longing developed like an old photograph in the darkness.

Finally noticing her, he stiffened. After a moment, he seemed to decide something and rose, motioning to her to follow him across the room, to the far window.

Lore approached slowly. As she came to stand in front of him, she leaned her shoulder against the glass and crossed her arms. In the end, she was the one to break the silence.

"Listen," she began. "I know . . . I know things between us have always been hard."

"That's one way of describing it," he murmured.

"I've never been that good about talking about feelings—" she began.

"Or listening," he interjected quietly.

She gave him a wry look. "Or listening. But I respect you, and I don't want things to be that way between us anymore. We care about the same people, and regardless of how you feel about me, I care about you, too. I'm sorry if I've ever made you feel that I didn't."

He sighed. "It's not like I've ever been that fair to you, either. Though, for the record, you still have an unhealthy relationship with trouble."

Lore let out a soft laugh, and followed Van's gaze as it turned back toward Miles.

"It's okay to want good things," she whispered. "And to believe that you deserve a good life."

Van shook his head slowly, his left hand adjusting his prosthetic one. "I don't know about that. I've never let myself consider it—maybe in those few moments where I believed the Agon could really end, but then there was always more work to do."

"I only got a glimpse of it before," Lore said. "I see that now. I was happy, but the past, the Agon—there was always something that held me back from fully embracing what I have here, and seeing how truly good it is. Don't make that same mistake."

Van shrugged, but his eyes instinctively drifted back toward Miles, who was murmuring softly in his sleep.

"I had a weird dream just now," Lore whispered. "A memory, maybe."

Zeus had blocked the flow of prophecy, but hunters had always believed that dreams could bring omens and messages. She wasn't at all surprised when Van said, "Tell me."

"You think the missing god might have been Apollo?" he asked when Lore had finished.

"They might not have been gods at all," she reminded him. "Blood loss is a hell of a thing."

"There's something else I've been thinking about," he began.

"While you've been gazing at Miles? Do I want to hear this?" Lore shut her mouth at his look.

"It's the idea of sacrifice," Van said. "I don't know if we're thinking about the new lines the right way."

He worked his jaw back and forth in thought. "*Summons me with smoke of altars to be built by conquest final and fearsome . . .* A sacrifice has to mean something. It entails something necessary . . . Couldn't you argue that it's the act of giving that necessary thing up to the gods that makes it worthwhile?"

Before she could answer, Lore's phone vibrated against the external battery Miles had given her to charge it. The cracked screen glowed as she opened Iro's message.

Confirmed—attack at sunset tomorrow.

She and Van exchanged a look.

"Up to you," he said. "We're going to need a few hours to find some last supplies."

Lore wrote back one word: **Noon.**

The hours passed at a slow, steady march. Lore thought she might be able to doze off, if only to pass the time, but her nerves were jumping too hard beneath her skin. She drilled with Castor, careful as they used their real swords. Even that wasn't enough to steady her.

Finally, at half past ten o'clock, Miles returned from an errand he'd insisted on running.

"For you," he said, handing Van a stack of external batteries.

Miles reached into his tote bag and handed Castor a long black shirt and black jeans, and, to Lore, a dark sweater to pull over her shirt. "These should all fit, hopefully."

Castor disappeared into the storage room to change.

When he returned, Miles passed him body armor, then turned to give Lore hers. "That's from the Odysseides. Iro sent a runner to meet me. Just in case you thought I suddenly had access to army supplies or drug cartels."

Lore immediately tried to give hers back to him.

"Absolutely not," Miles told her. "All I'm going to do is run into Grand Central and shout *Fire!* to get people to evacuate the building. I'll be fine."

She offered it to Van, who shook his head.

"I'll get one from the Odysseides when I meet up with Iro and the others at the hotel," he said.

"All right," she said, opening the Velcro straps and sliding it over her head. Castor reached over, adjusting hers for a better fit.

"So . . ." Miles began, taking two sets of wireless earbuds out of his bag. "These are noise-canceling earphones. There's a switch on the right earbud that actually turns the noise canceling on, otherwise they're going to be regular earphones and mostly useless."

Castor held one up, studying the small device, but Lore was still confused.

"For Wrath's power," Miles reminded her. "I don't really know how it works, but maybe if you can't hear him he can't worm his way into your brain to affect your strength?"

"Right . . ." she said, somehow having forgotten that would still be a problem. "Right."

"Did the Odysseides' runner have the other things I asked Iro to get from my stash?" Van asked.

"She did indeed," Miles said. He handed them both a small wire cutter and a pen-size flashlight.

"This is a lot more powerful than it looks," Van explained, taking Castor's flashlight. "At its highest setting, it'll momentarily blind someone, but it'll be fine to use as a flashlight at its lower setting."

Lore tucked both her flashlight and the wire cutter into the back pockets of her jeans.

"Couldn't find leather straps, but here's some tape, if you think you'll need it to support your wrists and hands," Van said.

When they'd trained in hand-to-hand combat, they'd always worn himantes, strips of leather wrapped to protect their knuckles and wrists. The tape would be more flexible, making it easier to keep her grip on her sword.

"Thank you," Lore said, taking it from him.

"And last but not least," Van said, pulling out two little devices on key rings, one gold, the other silver. They would have looked like garage openers if not for the indentations that marked the speakers. "If you pull the cord out of these and hit the button, it lets out a one-hundred-and-forty-decibel alarm."

"What, no mace?" Lore joked.

"Oh! Actually . . ." Miles slid a small tube out of his jacket. He opened her hand and closed her fingers around it. "I thought you'd enjoy using it."

"You know me so well," Lore said.

"We should be able to track you by sharing locations with Lore's phone," Van said. "Service may cut out, though, depending on where and how deep you are."

Lore nodded. "Thank you for this. All of this."

"It may not be enough," Van said. "But it was the best we could do, under the circumstances."

The group held off on their good-byes until they reached Forty-Second Street and Eleventh Avenue. Miles would be heading east, toward Grand Central, Van would be meeting Iro and the combined remnants of the Houses of Odysseus and Achilles to the west, near the piers, and Lore and Castor would be entering the subway at Thirty-Fourth Street and walking the 7 train's line to approach the station from underground.

Just before they split up, Lore drew Miles away from the others.

"Once you warn everyone, try to get off this island," she said. "If something happens and you're caught in the blast . . ."

"I won't be," Miles told her. "But please promise me you'll be all right."

495

Lore hugged him tight. "I'll be fine. After this, we'll go do all that stupid tourist stuff I never wanted to do, okay? So you need to be fine, too."

Miles managed a small smile. "I hope you're hungry for some Coney Island cotton candy."

Lore's face twisted at the thought. He hugged her one last time, then turned. Castor and Van were across the street, clasping one another's arms in the bloodline's secret greeting and farewell. Van's face turned serious at whatever Castor was saying, and he visibly struggled to keep his expression in check.

When they were finished, Lore and Van each raised a hand to one another in farewell.

"Oh, to hell with it," she heard Miles mutter. "If there's a chance we're all going to die—"

He crossed the street in long, purposeful strides, passing Castor without acknowledging him. The new god looked back as he came toward Lore, apparently just as confused as her.

Van had his back to them and was rooting through his bag, searching for something. Miles stopped behind him and reached up to tap his shoulder.

As he turned, Van's brows rose at the sight of Miles and a small, expectant smile lit his face at something Miles said. There was a beat of utter stillness, then Van took Miles's face between his hands and leaned down for a searing kiss.

Lore's mouth fell open as she watched it all unfold. "Oh."

"*Oh*," Castor echoed slowly. "Well . . . well."

Van wrapped his arms around Miles, giving himself over to the embrace, but Miles reluctantly pulled back and straightened.

"*Now*," Miles said, "we can go."

Castor whispered what sounded like a soft prayer in the ancient tongue as the two of them parted, heading in opposite directions. As Van passed by them one last time, his expression was still dazed.

"I guess that's our cue, too," Lore said.

He nodded.

They had covered the aegis in a bedsheet for the walk over, but now Lore removed it, drawing the shield tight to her body.

She looked up at Castor, lacing their fingers together as they continued in silence, moving through the floodwaters until they reached the 7 train's Thirty-Fourth Street station.

Castor melted the lock that kept the security gate in place, lifting it enough for them to pass beneath. Water rushed down the steps into the station, but Lore was surprised to find that it wasn't completely submerged. The subway must have had some way of slowly draining; there was only about a foot of water on the tracks themselves.

"With it, or upon it, right?" Lore said lightly, adjusting the aegis's straps so she could carry it on her back.

With it, or upon it. It was what countless Spartan mothers had said to their sons and husbands as they handed them their shields before battle. For a society that loathed rhipsaspides—shield droppers who turned coward and threw them down to escape, or those men who lost them in the fight—there were two avenues for returning home: victorious, or carried home dead upon your shield.

Castor gripped her arm, forcing her to look at him. The station was dark, making the sparks of power glow brighter in his eyes as he said, "Don't say that. Please—don't say that."

Not even the Spartans were Spartan, her father had told her. *It's not always the truth that survives, but the stories we wish to believe. The legends lie.*

"Then I won't," Lore said.

How they were remembered would never be as important as what they did now. Her father had been right about that, too.

They splashed down onto the tracks from the station platform and fought their way forward through the water.

Lore switched on her flashlight's lower setting. Her sword bounced against her hip as they walked along the rails.

She couldn't resist looking over at him then, drinking the sight of him in deep to ward off the chill growing along her spine.

"If we're wrong about your immortality and somehow they take you," she whispered, "wait for me at the dark river. I'll bring you home."

"Hades himself would turn me back at the gates knowing you're coming," Castor told her, "and that I'd fight like hell to meet you halfway."

Lore relished the feel of his hand in hers for just a moment more before letting it go. Both she and Castor would need their sword hands free.

She slid the aegis forward, but kept her flashlight aimed at the track. It was a slow crawl, the tunnel making it feel as though they were trapped inside a bleak eternity, that they would be walking forever toward a place they would never reach. It was the kind of punishment the gods used to love.

They followed the curve of the track up from Thirty-Fourth Street to Times Square, settling into a careful silence as they waded through the ankle-high pool of water. The air in the tunnel was still and heavy, and the walls around them were slick with moisture. Lore strained her ears, trying to catch the sound of voices or footsteps, but heard only the scurrying of rodents and the steady dripping of water falling all around them.

"The GPS just cut out," Castor whispered, showing her as much on her phone. "But we're nearly to the Bryant Park station."

They walked for a few minutes more before Castor stopped suddenly, reaching back for Lore's flashlight—not to aim it, but to switch it off. Lore tensed, stepping forward to see what had brought him up short.

Her eyes adjusted again to the dark, and each slow second revealed a new detail of the gruesome scene. The bodies of police officers, along with uniformed National Guardsmen, littered the track in front of them. Their bodies were locked in anguished poses, as if they'd been dropped down from a great height.

Red light flooded the chamber as a flare was lit and tossed down onto the back of a dead woman.

Dozens of hunters peeled away from the dark edges of the tunnel, perched up on the slight, narrow platforms that lined either side of it. They turned their masked faces toward Lore and Castor one by one—serpents, horses, and Minotaurs.

Seeing them lined up that way, like sentinels, Lore felt as if she was standing at the start of a gauntlet. Their grunting chants echoed, swirling in the air like wraiths.

"I do not like these odds for you, new god," one of the hunters said.

"Really." Castor lifted his chin, taking the measure of them in one look. "You seem certain about that."

Each second that passed felt like a cut to her skin. Lore stepped in front of him, raising the aegis toward the bloodred glow of the flare.

These, she thought, *are our enemies.*

Yesss, the voice hissed in agreement.

The hunter nearest to her swore, lifting his mask in shock. Others began to shake, dropping down from the ledges and onto the tracks, cowering.

"Steady—" the first hunter called. "Don't look directly at it!"

Those toward the back shielded their eyes.

Castor slid something into her back pocket. Her phone.

Her heart slammed up into her throat. Lore knew—she knew that she couldn't stop, not even for an instant, not when they were so close and time was so short.

I'll catch up, he mouthed, his powerful body tensed in preparation. His eyes flashed dangerously as he turned back to the other hunters. Those who had seen the aegis were struggling against its terror, but the rest began to beat their swords and spears against the shields they carried. The tunnel seemed to press in around them.

No, Lore thought. *Not yet . . .*

Because if she left him here, against all the hunters . . . she might never see him again.

"Go," he whispered. Then, louder, "Last chance to leave. Any takers for walking out of here alive?"

Lore brought up the aegis, drawing in a deep breath. At the faint smell of fire, of burning hair, she lowered herself into a ready stance. The hunters nearest to her had gone through the same fear and pain conditioning she'd been subjected to, but now sobbed with horror, cringing away from her.

She looked back one last time at Castor. She let his hard expression of determination, of confidence, sear itself into her memory.

Then the screaming began.

The two hunters nearest to her began to burn from the inside out, the heat of Castor's power incinerating bones, sinews, muscles, skin.

Lore leaped forward, her blade slashing through the spears of the hunters, still howling as they died. The aegis absorbed the hammering blows of their swords and small blades as she shoved her way through.

500

A spear tip cut across the back of her neck, but Lore pressed forward, hacking her way through the melee exploding around her.

Lore looked back in time to see one hunter break through the lines of bodies falling to ash, jumping as he brought his sword down. The steel caught the strap of Castor's vest, slicing through it into his shoulder.

Castor staggered back, his concentration momentarily shattered as he flipped his sword around and began his own attack.

More hunters spilled down into the station from the street above, swarming the platform behind her. Lore's mind screamed for her to turn back, but she kept her gaze forward, fixed on the darkness ahead, running until Castor's presence no longer burned at her back and the light of the flare disappeared like a dying star.

FIFTY TWO

Her phone didn't link back up with its cell service until she reached the knot of tunnels beneath Grand Central Station. Lore hadn't considered how confusing it would be underground as three different subway lines intersected with the Metro-North rail.

"*Shit.*" Lore struggled with trembling hands to get her text messages open. The new one that loaded was from Miles, saying he was in position in the building above her. They had fifteen minutes until noon.

Cas in trouble, she typed on the thread with the others. **5th ave 7 Train. Going ahead now.**

The GPS map wasn't detailed enough to tell her which tunnels to take, just that she was moving in the correct direction.

By the time Lore found the last tunnel, her whole body was rigid with frustration. As she stood at the head of it, staring down its silky darkness, Lore hesitated, suddenly uncertain.

Lore had lost herself so many times before she didn't completely understand how she'd found herself here. For a moment, she knew how Theseus must have felt in the Labyrinth, only she didn't have Ariadne's thread to guide her back out again.

She forced herself to take a breath. One hand choked the hilt of Mákhomai, while the other curled into a fist behind the aegis. The shield's vibrations fed the roiling mass of dread in the pit of her stomach.

Her first step forward took as much effort as dragging herself through a dark tide. Lore didn't know a prayer to help her now, or who might hear it. She felt the air stir around her, as if beings moved there, unseen, watching, waiting.

She pressed the curved edge of the aegis to her forehead, closing her eyes. She gripped the necklace, the feather charm, until the metal edges left an impression in her palm.

I can be free.

She was not Theseus in the Labyrinth, or Perseus in the gorgon's lair. She was not Herakles, laboring in his tasks. She was not Bellerophon, who rode across the sky, Meleager on his hunt, or Kadmos fighting the serpent. She was not even Jason, triumphant at the edge of the world with the Golden Fleece in hand.

There was nothing fated. Lore had not been chosen for this; she had chosen to come here herself. Every step she'd made, every mistake, had led her here.

She was here because her father had taught her to hold a blade, because her mother had raised her strong and proud, because her sisters were forever unfinished people.

She was here for the city that had raised her, and she came with the pride of her ancestors and the strength of her heart, and neither would fail her.

Lore recognized them then—the shadows moving along the tunnel walls beside her.

"Stay with me," she whispered, taking that next step. She repeated the words until they became the prayer she'd needed, and armor for her soul. "Please stay with me."

Lore sprinted forward, shooting down the tunnel like an arrow released from the steadiest of hands. "Stay with me . . ."

The air changed, and Lore knew she was close. An undercurrent of power licked at her senses, guiding her off that line and into a smaller tunnel.

Lore's focus intensified as she ran along the tracks, water splashing up around her. Sooner than she'd expected, she reached a section of the subway divided off from the rest—the one that led beneath the Waldorf Astoria.

At the sound of voices, she slowed and switched off her flashlight.

"Listen to me, *please*!"

Belen, she thought. Lore reached up and removed one of the noise-canceling earbuds to better hear.

Indistinct shapes took form at the end of the line, in the cavernous space that was Track 61. Lanterns had been hung around, spotlighting sections of the otherwise pitch-black station.

It was nothing like the other subway stops she and Castor had walked through to get here. As Lore made her way forward, she struggled with her footing over two different sets of tracks hidden beneath the water. There were no raised platforms around them, leaving a generous amount of space to the right of the single flatbed subway car that waited ahead. A large silver tank, as big as the car itself, had been strapped atop it. If it was a bomb, it wasn't like any she had seen.

"Do you doubt me?"

Wrath's voice carried over to her, low and menacing. He moved around the flatbed and came into view. Nearby, a massive elevator loomed—one that no doubt led up into the hotel's parking garage.

He was monstrous in his dark sublimity, his body rigid with muscle. He would have towered over even Castor, just as he towered over Belen now.

The young man backed away from him, holding his hands up. He was dressed in what looked to be a ceremonial robe, crimson embroidered with gold. Both of his hands were bandaged in a thick layer of white gauze.

The sheen on Wrath's skin had to be some sort of gold paint. It covered his entire body beneath the ivory silk of his tunic. He wore polished bronze armor over his chest, as well as gauntlets and greaves. Worse, there was a familiar, spikey tan hide draped over him. Its head had been long ago cast in bronze to be worn like a helmet, as Wrath did now. It belonged to the Nemean lion, and it would make any skin it covered impervious to blades.

Panic gripped her. If he was dressed for battle, hours before sunset . . .

The information had been wrong again. Wrath's plan was happening now.

Lore pulled out her phone, but there was still no service. She debated leaving, trying to get to higher ground to warn the others if they hadn't already discovered it for themselves, but Belen spoke again, this time more desperate.

"You are the most powerful being in this world," Belen said. "You have us, and we are devoted to you. All of us, my lord."

"Is that so?" Wrath asked coldly. He circled his mortal son slowly, forcing Belen back toward the flatbed without ever needing to draw a blade.

"You don't need her," Belen continued, his voice pitching up.

Lore's blood turned to ice in her veins at that single word. *Her.*

"Ask yourself why she would agree to help you—why she has come to you now, when you are so close to all that you have dreamed of," Belen said. "She and her sister planned to kill you and all the other new gods, and now she wants to pay deference? She is cunning—she will take your plan, she will take *it*, and she will kill you—she will destroy you, Father. *Please*—"

"*Father?*" a soft voice repeated.

Athena stood at the edge of one of the lantern's lights, her eyes glowing in the darkness.

Lore's pulse spiked and sweat broke out across her body. Belen's head whipped toward the goddess, his breath visibly catching.

"Father?" Athena repeated again. "My great lord, I would not have expected one as powerful as you to have a son so sniveling and weak of will."

Athena moved to stand beside the new god, a dory in her hand. She, too, was dressed in a short ceremonial robe, this one of the purest white, her skin coated in that same shimmering gold. Her armor was as substantial as Wrath's, as was her helmet. It was studded with what looked to be diamonds and sapphires along its white plume.

The hatred Lore felt looking at them now was breathtaking. All the rage she'd told herself she didn't need, that she didn't want, came boiling to the surface.

She forgot her calm, she forgot her plan, she forgot everything but the shame he had tried to use to extinguish her line and his desire to take her life away from her, even as a little girl. She saw nothing but the face of the man who had wanted to destroy her family, and the merciless goddess who actually had.

Wrath angled himself toward Athena, setting his broad shoulders back. He gripped his helmet, but one hand drifted toward the sword at his side.

"She will betray you—she will destroy you, the way she has all the others," Belen said, this time with real fear. "Listen to me—she's fed you lies! You don't need her!"

"I have spoken no lies," Athena said coolly. "The great Wrath and I are meant for this—we have always been meant for this. The meeting of the old way, and the new. The first Ares was weak, too prone to tempers and madness, and the most hated of my father's children. But now I have found a worthy partner in war—the balance of strength to my strategy—and a new king to kneel to."

Belen shook his head. "That—that can't be true—"

"Do you call me a liar?" Athena asked sharply. "I owe my lord Wrath my allegiance after he graciously told me of the new poem, of my father's wishes. I am pleased to serve him as he makes his final, true ascension."

Bile rose in Lore's throat; even after everything she had done, Athena's words, her soft, cloying tone, felt like another betrayal. On the roof of the town house, Lore had told her everything—her past, her fears—and she had believed the goddess, she had *felt* Athena's own suppressed anger and frustration.

You may call that complicity, and perhaps it is, Athena had said. *But I deemed it survival.*

It had to be an act, but it was one the goddess had willingly lowered herself to.

"The Gray-Eyed One is the wisest of all beings," Wrath said, preening at her words. Believing every one of them, the way only a man who saw no faults in himself could. "She has proven herself worthy to serve me . . . Tell me, how have you? A boy—one who cannot even fight—dares to question my judgment? Dares to believe himself wiser than Athena herself?"

Belen shook his head, backing up until he hit the edge of the flatbed.

"My great lord," Athena said, watching the young man with a look Lore recognized. Silent victory. "As you know, all great ventures must begin with a sacrifice seeking favor from Zeus if they are to succeed."

The new god turned toward his mortal son.

Every part of Lore seemed to heave forward, even as she stayed in place.

Belen had time to whisper, *"Please—"* before his father drew a small hidden blade from a sheath at his forearm and slit his throat.

Blood whipped up against the tank with the force of his strike. Belen fell to the ground, his body twitching as his frantic heart pumped the last bit of life from him.

Wrath watched him die, dark elation spreading over his face. When the young man was finally still, he bent down and placed a hand on his son's throat, coating it with blood.

Athena looked on, her top lip curling.

Rising again, Wrath pressed his palm against the tank, leaving a dark smear on it. He backed away, his gaze fixed on it. Slowly, he brought his fingers to his lips. To his tongue.

He didn't turn around again as he spoke, but his voice carried the words across the distance between them. "Daughter of Perseus."

Stay with me, Lore thought one last time as she gripped the straps of the aegis and stepped into the station.

"How good of you," he said, "to bring your god one last gift."

FIFTY THREE

His voice was like the slide of a reptile's scales against skin, stirring an unconscious, primal sort of fear.

Enemiesss, the voice hissed in her mind.

Lore gripped the straps of the aegis tighter, imagining the gods cowering before her under its power. But the thought didn't fill her with satisfaction.

No, she thought back. *I'll need your help, but not for that.*

Lore had her own fury, her own strength, and she wanted them to fear *her*, to know that she had been the one to defeat them.

Her gaze didn't waver as she met Wrath's eyes. He laughed as she approached, the aegis held high, one hand resting on the hilt of her sword. The sound echoed around them, multiplying until it became a roar. Lore refused to look at Athena, but tracked her at the edge of her vision as the goddess spoke.

"How *cunning* you were, my lord," Athena said, voice low and smooth, "to have sent your hunter to give the descendants of Odysseus false intelligence."

Lore's breath caught, burning in her chest.

"I did what you could not," Wrath said, with a condescending tilt of the head. "I drew the little bitch out of her hiding place and got her to bring my shield to me."

The movement was slight, but telling. Athena straightened at *my shield*. But when she spoke again, the words revealed nothing but deference. "Indeed. Shall I fetch it for you?"

The hair on Lore's body stood on end at how subtle the play was.

"No," Wrath told her with an arrogant smile. He spoke with the tone of a parent indulging a simple child. "You are not strong enough to bear it. I will allow you to carry it once our work is through and I've no need for it."

Lore lifted the aegis to hide that she was replacing the earbud in her ear. Her voice sounded muted as she spoke.

"You've lowered yourself to work with him now?" Lore asked, addressing Athena, not Wrath, in a way she knew would infuriate him. "With one of the inferior new gods you claim to despise?"

He stepped between Lore and the goddess, blocking Athena from her sight. His chest swelled as he drew himself to his full height, leering down at her.

She looked past him.

"The Gray-Eyed One recognizes her master," Wrath said, a streak of anger in his words. "Something you have refused to do—but you've always been excitable, haven't you? The little hellion who needed to be broken. From this day forward, you will serve me in every way I desire—you and that girl from the Odysseides. I'll have one on each knee. The wait will make it all the sweeter."

Fury and disgust blazed in Lore, threatening to burn through her control.

Focus, Lore thought. Her plan could still work—she could still play them off each other.

"So you and Artemis entered this Agon with the plan to kill the new gods," Lore said to Athena as she moved right, away from

Wrath and toward the car and tank. "And you got close to me, in the hope that I would give you the aegis and that it would give you the opportunity to kill the new Apollo—maybe even some of the other new gods, too, including this one."

It was so obvious to Lore now, all of it.

Wrath drew in a breath like a growl. Agitation spread over his face as he angled himself between them again, trying to force Lore's gaze onto him.

"She is loyal to power, and recognizes it in me," Wrath said. "I could have molded even you, a hideous, feral little beast, into something. But you'll die the same way you lived, as no one. Powerless and alone."

Focus, Lore thought again, steeling herself against her rising nausea. Her grip on the aegis tightened to the point of pain. Every muscle in her body was clenched with tension, begging for release.

She reached up and subtly found the switch on her earbud. Whatever other smirking cruelty he was about to deliver disappeared into an unnatural, humming silence.

The quiet concentrated Lore's thoughts, sharpening the hunger in her heart. She wanted them to feel her pain. She wanted to watch these gods bleed and suffer the way her little sisters had, and beg her for mercy.

Athena's cold smile was deliberate, as if she knew each and every last one of Lore's thoughts.

Lore knew what she expected—that her temper would take hold and Lore would lash out. That she would be destroyed by that same impulsive streak Athena had helped to stoke.

Instead, she held herself steady. The aegis would never tremble in her hands, not out of fear, and not out of anger. If she had to use her hate to devour those last lingering doubts, she would welcome it. But

511

Lore wouldn't let it incinerate her purpose in coming here, or throw herself onto it and be obliterated.

After years of practice at Thetis House, Lore easily read the clear command on his lips. He stretched out a hand toward her, his gaze focused and face beaming with triumph, and Lore knew he was using his power. She pretended to struggle with the weight of the shield, to sway.

Bring it to me, he was saying. For all his paint and costume, for how imposing the shadows had made him seem, she still only saw the old man he had once been, sitting on a meaningless throne. *Give me the aegis.*

His body quaked with excitement. Lore forced her own to tense, as if bracing herself against the draining nature of his power. She twisted her features, straining her face to show resistance, even as she took a step toward him. Even as she used the aegis to hide that she was sliding her flashlight out of her pocket.

Athena's eyes narrowed, the word *Wait* on her lips, but Wrath had never been the kind of man to listen to a woman, and immortality hadn't changed that.

He held out his other arm, blocking Athena and all but pushing her back from the shield as Lore approached.

Give it to me, he said again, holding out that hand . . . stretching out a long, powerful arm . . . his face already exalting in his victory. *Give it to me, give it to me, good girl.*

She had meant to momentarily blind him with the highest setting of the flashlight. Yet, as hot as her rage had flashed in the moments before, it had condensed and iced over at those two words, *good girl.*

Lore jammed the flashlight's switch up to its brightest beam and watched both gods turn their faces away.

He was never going to touch her again.

The seconds dragged as Lore dropped the flashlight and ripped Mákhomai out of its scabbard, then sped up again as she made a decision. The hide of the Nemean lion protected Wrath's back and draped down over his bronze chest plate—but neither it nor his gauntlets covered the exposed joint of his elbow.

Lore brought the razor edge of her sword down hard, and, in one clean stroke, severed his entire right forearm from his body.

Wrath staggered back as blood sprayed from his open wound.

"This *good girl*," Lore spat out, "is waiting for you to come and get it."

She pulled the aegis flush against her body, but as she spun away from his thrashing form, sound rushed back into her left ear. The small earbud had somehow popped out.

Shit, she thought, searching the surface of the water. But it was gone.

Wrath expelled a bark of pain from where he'd dropped onto one knee. His lungs worked like bellows as he brought his remaining hand up to stanch the flow of blood. A vein throbbed in his forehead as he leveled a look at her that promised pain beyond agony.

"Bitch . . ." he gasped out, "little *bitch*—"

"He's all yours," Lore told Athena. "Might as well take out the competition while he's down. We both know you'll never let him carry the aegis."

The goddess smiled as she came to stand beside Wrath. "Do not listen to her, my lord. She seeks to divide us. Rise, and prove how strong you truly are."

Wrath did, sweating and cursing as blood pumped out beneath his fingers. At the sight of him, his teeth bared and expression livid, Lore wondered if all she had really done was drain the last bit of humanity from him.

"Your false god healed you, I assume," Athena said, a taunting edge to her voice. "Where is he now, Melora? Did you lose him to the dark?"

He's alive, Lore told herself. *He's alive, and he'll come.*

Another thought occurred to her then, breaking through all others.

Lore had assumed that Athena wanted the shield purely for the poem and what it revealed—but Athena had that information now, and yet she had stayed with Wrath and kept up this act.

She still wants it, Lore thought, brow creasing. *She still wants the aegis.*

Then why not use her unconquerable strength to rip it from Lore's hands, the way both she and Lore knew that she could?

Because, a small voice whispered in her mind. *She's become part of his plan.*

"Tell me why you want the shield," Lore said as she backed up—not out of fear, but to bring herself close enough to the train carriage and tank to steal glances at them. There had to be a way to disable whatever motor was attached to the car.

One corner of the goddess's mouth curled up.

Lore's heartbeat grew louder in her ears.

"My great lord," Athena began, a look of clear derision on her face, though the new god couldn't see, "has discovered the true meaning of the new lines, and my father's instructions—I did not realize it myself, until he reminded me of the story of Deukalion and Pyrrha. You are familiar with it, I presume?"

The dark air seemed to press in on Lore from all sides as Athena's words settled in her mind.

Deukalion and Pyrrha had been the only two survivors of the flood Zeus had sent to end the warring mortals of the Bronze Age, having been warned by Deukalion's father, Prometheus. Deukalion and Pyrrha had been the ones to repopulate the world by throwing the bones of the mother—stones—over their shoulders.

"You understand now," Athena said. "For so long, I thought this hunt a punishment when it was merely a test. All this time, my father desired us to prove our loyalty by ending the worst age of man. To begin a new race that pays devotion to its gods."

Lore was shaking her head, fighting the anger that threatened to suffocate her. "You'd need Poseidon's power over the seas and rivers to pull off something like that."

"Are they not already rising as this race of men slowly poisons this world?" Athena asked. "Will they not continue to, as the god of war inflames their hearts and spurs them on and on until the air is choked by smoke and the ground bleeds?"

"Her fear," Wrath said, suddenly behind Lore. "It feels like wine in the blood."

"It is only a taste of what will come," Athena said, not bothering to look at him. "When the world realizes its fate." She took a step toward Lore, her eyes flicking toward the aegis, just for a moment. "But it is not water that will purify the lands. It is not water that will cleanse this world. It is *fire*."

Lore spun toward the car, the tank, her sword raised.

"I wouldn't, if I were you," Wrath taunted her. "It contains sea fire and will ignite on contact with water."

Sea fire. Lore sucked in a hard breath through her nose. A legendary weapon of the Eastern Roman Empire. Once ignited, anything the chemicals touched would burn, and rather than stop it, water would help carry and feed the flames. It would boil the streets from below, causing massive destruction as it fed on the raw material it encountered. In a flooded city, it would take days, if not weeks, to be fully smothered. And by then . . .

They weren't burning Grand Central. They were burning the whole city.

"Yes," Wrath breathed. "The fires will spread below the streets, through all of its many tunnels, devouring from below."

"Igniting it now will also take out both of you," Lore said, drawing back Mákhomai's tip, ready to try to pierce the tank's metal shell. "Is that supposed to be some kind of deterrent?"

"Only," he sneered, "if you want to save your friends from the inferno set to explode above us."

FIFTY FOUR

LORE'S PULSE SURGED AGAIN, HER NOSTRILS FLARING.

"That's an empty threat," she forced herself to say. "They'll figure out what's going on as soon as they see that your hunters have left."

"Child," he said. "Whoever said all of my hunters have left? I needed but two to trap the rest inside and start the blaze."

Shock whipped her from all sides.

"You're—" Lore began. "You're going to—"

"You're, you're, you're," he repeated, over and over, mocking. He came to stand near Athena again, using his belt as a tourniquet for his arm. "All of them must die eventually in order for the world to be reborn. They should be honored to know they are the first sacrifices to a new, glorious age."

Lore turned toward Athena, but the goddess was unmoved.

"You can't do this," Lore begged. "You wouldn't just be killing hunters—if his plan succeeds, you'd be killing innocent people."

"There are no innocent mortals," Athena said simply.

"I will enjoy tearing your life apart, to watch the true end of Perseus's line," Wrath told her. "Kneel to me, and summon the Cloudbringer with the aegis to bear witness to the blaze."

"You really think it'll summon Zeus to come watch you destroy a city?" Lore asked. "It doesn't work like that, asshole!"

"It works the way I say it does," Wrath said through gritted teeth.

Lore lowered herself into a defensive stance as both gods came toward her, Mákhomai suddenly heavy in her hand. Her arm shook with the effort to keep it raised. A fresh fear swirled in her as the subway car suddenly rattled to life, an unseen engine starting.

"Do you feel it now?" Wrath asked her. Lore fumbled for her one earbud again, but it was too late. The power coating his words turned her limbs to rubber.

Lore staggered as sensation left her body. Her grip on the aegis eased against her will, and, for the first time, she could barely support its weight.

"Do you really believe she'll allow you to live?" Lore asked Wrath, fighting to draw the words out of herself. Her body shook as she planted her feet on the ground beneath the water in one last attempt to keep from falling. "That Zeus and the others will let you have this world?"

"Fool," Athena growled. "You know nothing."

It came to her like a slip of sunlight breaking through the clouds— the real reason Athena had come here. Why she had done everything in her power to retrieve the shield.

Wrath forgot his injury and tried to swing that phantom arm forward to strike her. Lore didn't flinch, not even when Athena's dory fell between them, cutting Wrath's second advance short. Her eyes burned in the darkness.

"You're right, I am a fool," Lore told her. "And you were right before, too, to mock me for believing you. The truth is, I didn't just believe you—I believed *in* you. When you kept those people safe from the explosion and the debris. When you told me about Pallas, about your city, about the role you were born to, and the one you wanted for yourself."

A flinch, almost imperceptible, moved through Athena.

"Your temples fell. Men no longer feared you. Your legend, once sung, became a whisper," Lore continued. "But I still believed in you."

Athena's nostrils flared, her hands strangling the staff of her spear.

"This isn't a test, it's a lesson," Lore said. "Why would Zeus ever want you to kill innocent people—worshippers of other gods—when that was one of the reasons you were punished in the first place? Even after everything he's done to you and the others, I never heard you speak about him in anger or resentment. In your eyes, he has no equal. He would never give the world to the victor of the Agon."

"Silence!" Wrath roared, striking at her.

Van's words from that morning came back to Lore in a rush, and she pushed on, unafraid. "A sacrifice has to mean something. You only understand sacrifice as something done *for* you. But Zeus was speaking to mortals at Olympia, and we've always understood it a different way. We make sacrifices to honor gods, to thank them, to request their blessings . . . or to seek forgiveness."

"I will cut the tongue from your head," Wrath said, "as I should have done when you were nothing but a whelp."

"Have you ever done that?" Lore asked Athena. "Have you truly sought penance for what happened all those centuries ago? Or have you spent over a thousand years trying to justify what happened by blaming it on the Fates—all because you can't stand knowing that you—and only you—are to blame for losing your father's love?"

Athena's expression was disguised by the darkness, but Lore knew she was unmoved, and it stole the last of her faith. There was no way to reach her, not now.

"You're supposed to be the protector of cities," Lore said, "not the cause of their destruction!"

Wrath snarled as he lunged forward again, knocking Lore back as water splashed up around them.

Each blow pushed her farther and farther from the tank and car. Struggling against the drain of his power, Lore dropped to a knee, lifting the shield; she couldn't do anything but let the aegis be battered by the maelstrom of his strikes.

Her arms shook with the effort of absorbing each relentless blow, her teeth gritted.

Help me, Lore thought. *Please!*

Yes, it whispered.

She slammed her fist against the front of the aegis, and it roared.

The sound shook the walls of the tunnel, sending loose pieces of stone raining down over them. As Lore drew in her next breath, she felt its power fill her—fill her and fill her, even as Wrath tried to take that strength.

All at once, it stopped. Somehow, Lore knew what was coming.

There was nothing human left in Wrath's face.

"Was that not enough for you, little bitch? Even your father knew when to submit," Wrath said in amusement. "By the gods—sea, fire, and women are the three evils."

Lore hated that saying more than she hated even him.

She drew toward him. He raised his sword once more, undaunted by the blood that still flowed from his other, severed arm.

He's feeding on my strength, Lore realized. It was the only way he could still be on his feet. The high of the fight only buoyed his bloodlust.

Even if Lore could force him back into regular combat . . .

She stilled.

Regular combat. As if she needed to fight on his terms, as a hunter would.

"I've got another ancient proverb for you," Lore said, sliding her arm out from the interior straps of the aegis. *"Go fuck yourself."*

She flung the shield at him. Wrath reached for it, his booming laugh cut off as the shield hit him, cracking bones as it smashed into his chest. Breath raged out of him and he was knocked onto his back, momentarily trapped beneath the shield's impossible weight.

"You may be a god," she told him, relishing the sight of his struggle. "But I'm the Perseides."

Her adrenaline overpowered her reason. Lore dove forward with her sword, her heart blistering with the need to plunge it through his.

Wrath shoved off the aegis, meeting her blow with his own sword. Athena disappeared at the edge of her vision, sending a new wave of alarm through her.

Lore drove down harder, and saw the moment his eyes widened when she didn't take a stance he recognized, and instead drove her knees down onto his lower stomach, just where his breastplate ended.

"Your biggest mistake was trapping yourself in this city with me," Lore said.

"No more tricks, girl," Wrath snarled, clenching his knees around her hips to flip her onto her back.

Lore tried to angle her sword up to drive it into his chest, but the blade slid off the armor covering his torso.

Wrath shifted with a yell, pinning her with his full body weight. But without the use of his other arm, there was nothing to brace himself with as she kneed him as hard as she could in his groin. Lore had just enough room to get a hand beneath herself and pull the small, finger-length canister out of her back pocket.

"Actually . . ." Lore thumbed the lid off the canister and sprayed a torrent of mace in his eyes. "Just one more trick."

She dragged herself out from beneath him, kicking him onto his back as she stood. Lore clutched Mákhomai, raising it over his exposed throat. Years of anger, fear, and pain purified her mind until a single thought remained.

End him.

He deserved nothing less than what she was desperate to give him. Lore drove her blade down—

Only to stop the tip just before it pierced the exposed skin of his throat.

Lore drew in a shaking breath, trying to still her raging heart.

She could kill him—she knew that now. She could kill him and take his power, and use it to truly match Athena, blow for blow. She could burn her name into the memory of every hunter.

But she would never be free.

It was enough to know he had been beaten by her, a mere girl. That, to him, was a fate worse than death. Revenge created the Agon, but it wouldn't be what ended it. Killing either of them would only continue the hunt for another cycle. For her, and for Castor.

The pressure broke inside her chest, like a sudden storm easing to light rain. She seized the aegis again and rose.

Wrath only growled, thrashing around with unspent rage.

The words reverberated through her again. *A fate worse than death.*

Lore turned to Athena slowly, the words ringing through her.

Suddenly, she knew. She understood.

What could sacrifice be for the gods, except to give up the one thing they truly desired beyond their own lives and power? To sacrifice that which they wanted most—a conquest final and fearsome.

The embers in Athena's eyes glowed at the dark center of her helm.

Lore slid her arm free of the shield's straps and held it out to the goddess.

"Take it," Lore said.

The goddess did not move. She did not so much as draw a breath.

Lore moved closer to her, setting the aegis down between them before backing up. "What if I were to tell you that the only way to free yourself from the Agon was to take your fists and destroy this shield? To pound it into nothing but twisted metal and leather?"

The goddess didn't move.

"You were willing to torture and kill two little girls for it. You were willing to murder my parents and countless others to hold it again," Lore said. "I'm giving it to you, of my own free will. At least have the courage to pick it up."

Athena took a single step forward, but caught herself.

"It has nothing to do with the poem, does it? Not really," Lore told her, a strange calmness taking hold. "It doesn't even summon your father, the way you've let Wrath believe."

Wrath snarled behind her. "Is this true?"

"My lord," Athena began.

"You can't let go of it," Lore continued, cutting her off. "Because it was a symbol of your father's love. His *pride* in you. That's what you want back, not the shield. That feeling you lost when you stood against him."

"It *is* true," Wrath said. His gaze was murderous as it fell on Athena.

The goddess didn't seem to hear him. Her whole being was focused on where the aegis lay beneath the shallow water. The goddess's expression turned tortured as the weight of her choice set in.

Athena could escape the Agon—and perhaps end it for *all* of them—but only by destroying the one thing that mattered most to her.

"Do it," Lore told her. "It has to be you. You have to finish this!"

A blade appeared in Wrath's hand, then winged out of it, spinning through the darkness.

No.

Lore felt the certainty of her decision before she recognized making it. In the sliver of time between one heartbeat and the next, she stepped into the dagger's path.

The shock of it cutting into her chest savaged her, even before the pain took hold and blood poured from the wound. She collapsed onto her knees, into the water, but in the moment before she fell, a face flashed in her mind.

Castor.

Wrath roared as he pulled her from the water, slamming her down again. Water flew up around her, lashing at her from all sides until she was choking on it.

Dying—

Her body locked, twisting as she gasped for her next tortured breath. The sight of Athena split like a prism, spinning until, finally, Lore vomited and tasted blood.

Wrath ripped her from the water once more, bending her back over his knee. Her lower back cracked. Lore screamed.

She couldn't fight. She couldn't move. Agony tore into her.

"What have you done?" Athena's voice sounded as though it was carried on the wind.

"It's the hydra's poison, Gray-Eyed One," Wrath said, pulling the knife free from Lore's chest as he dropped her into the water. He raised the blade over her chest, just above her heart. "Taken from a piece of the cloth given to Herakles. I coat all of my blades in it. Would you like a taste?"

"No," Athena said quickly. "Think this through, my lord. Think of the aegis! It will disappear with her."

"What use do I have for it now?" he said, glowering at her. "When my victory draws near? I cannot summon him and I will not be able to carry it. From this day on, I will only ever hold a sword."

"Our victory."

The words emerged through the fog of torment. Lore wasn't sure if she had heard them, or imagined them into existence. Not until Athena spoke again.

"I am sure you meant to say *our* victory," she spat.

The goddess stepped forward, leaning over the aegis. Her hand hovered for a beat, resisting. Then, as easy as drawing her next breath, Athena lifted it from the water, and returned it to her side.

"Just as I am sure that I did not give you my consent to kill this mortal."

FIFTY FIVE

Lore's mind was a riot of fear and pain. Unable to completely trust her eyes, she focused on the sound of metal clashing against metal. She tried to move her body, to rise from the water that washed over her face again and again in a frenzied tide.

The two gods hurtled toward each other, only to be thrown back by the force of their blows.

"Bitch!" Wrath roared. "How dare you!"

Athena smashed the aegis into his breastplate hard enough to send a shower of sparks raining down. The new god flew as the shield roared, his massive body skidding across the tracks and water. She walked toward him slowly, enjoying the way he crawled toward the flat car, and the tank.

Wrath spun quickly, throwing one blade, then another. Athena was fast enough to deflect the first, but Lore couldn't see what had become of the second before it splashed into the water. The goddess waited until he had climbed onto his feet, until he was an arm's length away from the car—just close enough to believe, for a moment, he would reach it.

Athena, wrapped in ribbons of darkness, leaped high into the air, flipping above Wrath's head, the dory steady in her hand. Her face showed no emotion or hesitation, and she did not need to look back once as she stabbed the spear's sauroter behind her, ramming it through Wrath's breastplate, his chest, and back out through his spine.

The new god's sword clattered to the ground as he fell to his knees, his head hanging. Athena retrieved his blade from the water, then came to stand in front of him. She drew the aegis near his face, until he was forced to meet Medusa's gaze.

Wrath lifted his hand. There was something dark clutched in it.

He squeezed it tighter, into a fist. There was a metallic groan as a valve at the back of the tank opened, and foul, oily chemicals spilled from it.

The subway car let out a loud clang as it suddenly rolled forward. It kicked up waves of water as it sped up down the track, leaving a trail of the sea fire behind it.

Wrath dropped the device and struggled to reach something else inside his armor—a lighter.

His bloodied fingers lit its small flame, and he snarled as he tossed it into the chemicals. A line of white-blue fire flared in front of him, blazing down the heart of the tunnel.

The air near Lore shimmered and turned scalding. Just before the car disappeared into the tunnel that would connect it to countless other tracks, she saw there was some sort of metal heat shield covering the back of the car where the chemicals burned. The shield was the only thing keeping the flames from igniting the tank and causing an explosion. For now.

Fire drifted toward her, but Lore couldn't move. The word, the one she'd feared all her life, rang out in her mind. *Powerless.*

The air filled with smoke, but Lore could still make out Athena's form as she raised Wrath's sword.

"You," he panted out, blood dribbling over his lips. *"You—lose!"*

"You die," the goddess said, and, with her usual cold precision, cut the head from his body.

Lore closed her eyes against the heat growing around her. Agony shot down her spine and legs as she was dragged through the water. When she opened them again, the world was lit by fire and Athena was hovering over her.

The goddess didn't look right to Lore. Her skin was clammy with beads of sweat, and the skin around a cut at her jaw was turning black. Even the glow of the goddess's eyes seemed to dim.

Poison, Lore thought. She hadn't escaped it after all.

Athena coughed and it was a vicious, wet sound. She seemed startled by it, pressing an uncertain hand against her chest. Blood dripped from her eyes, her nose, her mouth.

"Tell me—what to do," the goddess demanded. "Tell me—how to—stop it."

But Lore was beyond speaking. Her soul began to unravel from her body, the world fading.

The goddess gave Lore one last look, the skin between her eyebrows creasing, and rose. Lore was so sure that the goddess was leaving, that she was saving herself, that she released a sound like a wounded animal. Her breath rattled as she struggled for it.

But Athena returned a moment later, struggling to hold on to one of Wrath's daggers.

For the first time, a story was playing out across the goddess's face. Emotion rippled through the placid exterior. Anger. Regret. Acceptance.

The goddess slid the hilt into Lore's hand, carefully closing her fingers over it, and her own hand over Lore's.

Lore's eyes widened as she stared up at her; her body seized with fear. With dread.

She wouldn't . . . Athena would *never* do this, and even in her deepest hatred of her, even desperate for a way to protect her loved ones, Lore never would have wanted her to. She never wanted *this*.

"It must be this way," Athena rasped out. Her body trembled violently now, trying to fight off the poison's effects. "I am . . . lost . . . You will be born again. You will have more time. Fight again . . . to the last. It is . . . the only . . . logical choice. The city . . . must be defended."

The goddess positioned the point of the blade over her heart. She gave Lore the final choice.

Never free.

Lore shuddered, squeezing her eyes shut. She wanted to claw at the small, throbbing hope in her, the one she'd carried like a torch against impossible darkness. She wanted the life she'd fought so hard to create, and was as desperate for it as her next breath. She wanted to cry in a way she hadn't since she was a child. She wanted her parents.

She wanted everything, but never this. Never *this*.

Lore had been born into this cage, and now she would die in it—if not her body, then her soul.

But the city had to be defended, and it was hers to protect.

She met Athena's gaze and nodded.

The look the goddess gave Lore was sharp, ever-commanding. "Through the heart."

Together, they plunged the dagger forward, the blow striking hard and true. The goddess shook, her eyes open, flashing silver as she saw something, felt something, beyond knowing.

It was a warrior's kill.

A god's final reckoning.

FIFTY SIX

BREATH EXPLODED INTO LORE'S LUNGS, HER CHEST EXPANDING painfully as she drew in more and more air, trying to ease the boiling beneath her skin. Her heart became thunder, threatening to tear through her rib cage and skin.

Then her body roared with fire.

A storm of light spun down around Lore, swallowing her into its depths. Her body rose from the water. Veins of lightning traced over her limbs.

Athena's mortal remains burned away to ash. The being that emerged from it, drifting up like light breaking over a sleeping land, was nearly indescribable and cast in pure, radiant power.

The goddess looked down at Lore one last time, reaching a hand toward the aegis. Between one heartbeat and the next, both vanished, leaving behind sparks that trembled in the darkness as they fell.

And then the world Lore had once known disappeared with them.

She screamed as the pain set in. Power rippled through her, consuming blood and muscle and bone. It was a hollowing. An eradication of every bit of matter that had once lived inside her.

The seconds dragged by, slowly regaining their speed. Lore felt her consciousness begin to go—to drift. The lightning, that unbridled power, was threading through her, threatening to tear her mortal body apart.

Lore didn't know what she would be left with, only that she might not have the ability to touch the sea fire tank, let alone stop it.

"I need—" She had to shout over the maelstrom of whipping wind and rumbling forces around her. "I need to stay—I need a little longer—*I need to stay!*"

Power blasted down her spine as her body was dropped back into the burning water. Lore staggered upright. Inside her, something was thrashing, pulsing against the barrier of her skin.

Lore looked down at her hands. Strands of that same lightning danced over her knuckles and palms. She hadn't realized how dull her senses had been until they awoke in her again. The air suddenly felt like a living creature, cool in places, damp in others, always moving, always brushing against her.

Her legs were primed as she took off at a run, exploding with unfamiliar strength and speed.

The subway car flew down the tracks, the fire trailing behind it. The flames began to climb up the stone walls, devouring supports and the tracks themselves.

Lore caught up to it just before it broke through the tunnel that would send it beneath Grand Central station. With a cry, she cut in front of it, bracing her hands against the flat edge of the car. Digging her feet into the tracks, she pushed back against the force of the engine.

The car sputtered and creaked as it struggled to press on. Lore set her jaw, releasing a ragged cry as she lifted her foot long enough to slam it down against the front-right wheel, and then the left, beating them both out of shape. She tipped the whole car forward, folding and crushing the metal down as if it were paper, until it could no longer move.

She snapped the restraints on the tank, pulling its massive body toward her. Lore hissed as the sea fire licked at her legs and bare arms, but she held on until she could crush the open valve and stop the flow of the sea-fire chemicals.

Lore rolled the tank as far into the station as her strength would allow, into water that wasn't yet burning.

The flames couldn't be doused by water. Her father had told her about sea fire, he had told her . . .

It could only be smothered by dirt. Starved of oxygen.

Lore turned and looked back into the empty tracks below Grand Central one last time. The distant platforms she could use to climb out of the burning hell and find the others.

She drew in a breath, bracing her hand against one wall of the tunnel.

Not free. The thought pierced her. *Never free.*

But the others would be.

Lore tore at the stone wall, punching her fists into it until the entrance to the tunnel rained down fractured stone and the sight of the station disappeared behind the wall of rubble.

The fire's path was cut off for now, but it wouldn't stop burning as long as there was water. If enough heat built up, it would collapse the streets above. She had to find a way to smother it. To starve it of oxygen.

Lore ran back the way she came. Heat tore at her from all sides, but she didn't stop, not until she reached Track 61. The whole station was on fire; there was no end to it. There was no way to drain the water.

Yes, she realized, *there is.*

She wasn't powerless.

With a deep breath of burning air, Lore waded out into the center of the station, gasping as the sea fire crawled along her clothes and skin. She dropped to her knees and pressed her fists against the ground hidden beneath the burning water.

She could send the water, the fires, deeper into the belly of the earth. Where there would be no air, and nothing but darkness to feed on.

Please, she thought, drawing a fist back. The electric feeling was still building in her core, only this time, Lore didn't resist it.

She unleashed it.

Power gathered around her hand, glowing molten gold. She slammed it against the earth with a guttural scream. The ground roared back as it splintered. Spidery fractures glowed gold beneath the flames and water.

Lore closed her eyes, focusing on the feeling of the heat and energy pouring through her. She felt herself sinking deeper and deeper as her power incinerated the stone beneath her. There was no way to escape it. She would be carried down into the darkness below and extinguished with the flames. Alone. She was alone . . .

"Stay with me." Lore let out a choked cry, sobbing for breath and relief at the crush of it all. *Don't leave me . . .*

They didn't.

She felt her family around her—the soothing touch of them, brushing her cheeks, wrapping around her center. And beyond them, the presence of unseen eyes.

Power raged in her body, as pure as the fiery heart of the world. As old as Chaos and the worlds born from it.

"Lore!" Castor's voice carried across the station. *"Lore!"*

She looked up, searching for him through the smoke and finding him in the elevator.

"Get out of here!" she choked out.

The smell of burnt hair and skin rose around her and she realized it was her. Sweat poured from her face as Lore beat the ground, overturning the hard rock, pulverizing it. The burning water rushed down through the growing cracks. It was working. This was working.

At the edge of her vision, she saw Castor rush forward, shielding his face from the fires.

"Don't do it!" he called. "We need to get out! There's nothing else you can do!"

There was always something she could do.

Sparks of her power flew around her, catching in her hair and turning her skin into a glowing cosmos. Her arms quivered with the effort of trying to keep that last grip on herself. Her hands blazed gold as she slammed them down one last time and finally broke the world open beneath her.

The sea fire poured into the deep crevice, draining out of the station. She punched the tunnel again, pulverizing more stone in order to bury the fire. The tunnel shook with the force of each hit, as if it might cave.

Only one thought made sense to her. She needed to bury the fire . . . But she hurt . . . Every part of her burned . . .

The glow at her hands intensified, spreading up her arms, washing over her, until Lore couldn't tell if the light radiating around her was coming from her or the fires.

"Stop!" Castor's terrified voice reached her. *"Lore, stop!"*

He fought through the heat, bold and shining as her vision started to fade to darkness.

"It's enough!" he said. "If the street caves in, it'll take the hotel with it!"

"The fires—" she rasped.

"They're out!" he told her, gripping her arms, trying to force her to look at him. The walls and ground stopped shaking, and the remaining water hissed as it poured into the crevice she had created.

But Lore was beyond hearing; the same deep pull of power she had felt before returned, threatening to tear her body apart as she ascended. Her veins glowed gold beneath her skin as the last of her mortal blood burned away. She felt as insubstantial as smoke.

Castor pressed her to him, hard.

"No—stay," he begged. "Stay here!"

Her power left brands on his skin. It stirred a thought in her, pulling her out from the fathomless light she was dissolving into. *Hurting him.*

Castor kissed her—kissed her until that blazing power lost its grip on her mind and body. The feel of him became a tether to the world, and she held it with everything she had in her.

The blazing power extinguished around them. Nothing felt real but him.

"Stay," Castor said again, as he pulled his lips away from hers. "Don't go without me . . ."

There was nothing left in her mind. There was nothing left of her in this body. And when the darkness finally came for Lore, it didn't feel like an ending, but a beginning.

FIFTY SEVEN

To her surprise, Lore woke to the world she thought she'd left behind.

The city sang its old song for her, weak but growing in volume and tempo. Dozens of car engines hummed through the streets, the start of what might come in the days ahead. Construction equipment clanged and boomed with the effort of hauling debris. People walked the nearby streets, laughing—and that was the sound that Lore held on to, the one that embedded itself in her heart as she opened her eyes.

Miles's anxious face stared back at her. His hand tightened around hers as he bit his lip and tried not to cry. It looked like he'd somehow had a shower, or had at least a good scrub and shave.

"Your eyes," he whispered.

Lore tried to think of what to say to him. Now that she was awake, that disconcerting feeling was back. Power moved inside her, restless in its confinement. Her body, which had served her so well for so many years, the one she had strengthened and loved and scarred, felt too insubstantial for her now. Instead, she looked around.

They were in her bedroom in the town house.

She was surprised at how close to tears she was at the thought. Lore cleared her throat. "I didn't mean for this to happen."

He gave her a watery smile. "That's why it's probably okay that it did."

Miles had opened the curtains in her room, inviting the golden afternoon sunlight in. Lore felt its warmth pass through her as vividly as she felt the slide of the blanket against her skin.

Lore sat up suddenly. "What day is it?"

"Saturday," he said. "You've been asleep since Castor healed you."

Saturday. The thought filled her with a surge of panic. There were only hours left until the end of the Agon.

"Where is everyone?" she asked, her pulse quickening as she looked around the empty space. "Are they okay?" Lore had a sudden, vivid memory of what had happened in the subway station. "Is Castor—?"

"He's okay. Everyone is fine. I mean—fine in that vaguely traumatized way that comes with not fully processing everything that's happened, but fine." Miles rubbed the back of his neck. "They went up to the roof a few minutes ago to get some air."

A comfortable silence settled between them. Lore breathed in, and out, and in, and out, relishing the feel of it. How easy it came. She realized she was still holding Miles's hand, but didn't let go.

"What's going to happen to you when today ends?" he whispered. "Are you going to disappear? Will you be hunted like the others in seven years?"

She shook her head. "I don't know. But . . . I hope it's over. All of it."

Lore suddenly felt desperate for the sight of her city. She stood slowly from the bed, releasing Miles's hand to make her way over to the window. As she moved, the power moved with her, flowing through her muscles and winding around every joint and sinew.

Miles came to stand beside her. "What if the Agon takes you with it and you can't come back? Athena said that the gods live in a world beyond ours—is that where you'd go?"

537

"*This* is my home," Lore said. "Even if I lose this form, I'll find a way to come back. I'm determined, and you know what that means."

"You get a very intense look on your face and punch someone in the kidney?" Miles said.

"Maybe a little of that, too." Lore let out a true laugh, but saw that he needed more reassurance. "I might need to be gone awhile, but I would never leave you forever. Not if I can help it."

"Okay, but counterpoint," Miles said. "I don't want you to go at all."

Lore turned her gaze back out onto the street below, watching as the first colors of sunset held her sweet neighborhood in a moment of perfect light. A couple walked with their dog and stroller, the men laughing together as the baby tossed a small star-shaped toy into the street.

He glanced at her again, leaning his temple against the warm glass. "You do seem a little different, but also not. I can't explain it."

"Me neither," Lore said. "I just feel . . . light."

She draped an arm around Miles's shoulder. He did the same.

"You know, this city is a lot of bullshit," Lore said after a while. "But it's some beautiful bullshit."

Lore and Miles joined the others on the roof. The sunset had begun in earnest, putting on a spectacular show of rosy gold and violet.

Castor stood to take the plastic bags of snack food Miles carried up. As he saw her, she caught a flash of concern in his eyes that he did his best to disguise.

Iro and Van were sitting on the blanket that they'd stretched over the rough surface. Lore's heart was full at the sight of them, her joy so bright that she was almost startled by it. The two of them shared a glance, an unspoken nudge to each other to say something.

She suddenly felt shy then—as if what had happened, and what she'd become, was a ghost they all could see, but no one wanted to acknowledge.

Lore *really* hated feeling shy.

"Man, we really need to put a pool or garden up here," Lore said, pretending to look around. "What the hell is the point of having rooftop access if you can't lord it over your neighbors?"

"I'm guessing the point is to not violate city building codes," Miles said lightly. "So we don't have to pay an exorbitant fine."

"Don't you have an in with the city government?" Lore asked. "I mean, picture it—some nice lights, a few little plants here and there—"

"You have killed every single plant I've brought home for you," Miles said. "And then I went home to Florida for spring break and you killed *my* plants because you didn't water them."

"I was busy," Lore protested. "They seemed fine."

"How did we get on this subject?" Castor asked, digging out a small package of pretzels and tossing it to Van.

"How did you know I had a hankering for the mini twists?" Van asked, plucking one from the bag.

"Because we've been eating like subway rats for the last two days and you had the cheese puffs for breakfast this morning," Castor said.

"Subway rats at least get the occasional slice of dropped pizza," Lore said.

"Can we please stop talking about rats?" Van asked, pained.

Lore and the others circled up around the bags, stretching out across the warm roof as the sun finally dipped beneath the horizon.

As Miles went on about the updates he'd gotten laying out Columbia's delayed start of the school year, Iro caught Lore's eye.

Okay? Lore mouthed.

Iro nodded. There wasn't a bruise or scratch on her that Lore could see, and that didn't seem possible, given the fight she'd likely had in the hotel. Castor must have healed all of them after caring for Lore.

She leaned back and turned her gaze upward, toward the heavens. Without the city's usual glow, it was easy to make out the stars.

Castor, Miles, and Van went to the edge of the roof, and the new god pointed out all the same constellations Lore had quietly noted to herself.

Her father had taught them to her and Castor, telling them the myths behind each. Like the heroes of old and so many others, she had believed that the only greater honor than kleos was for the gods to place you among the stars.

Sometimes Lore caught herself searching for her family in those lights. When the heaviness of that grief visited her, when she missed them with the kind of pain that made sleep impossible, she had made up her own constellations for each of them.

Lore pressed a hand to her chest, rubbing it. In time, she knew she would see them again, but not now. She'd outrun death so many times she'd stopped counting, but it wasn't lost on her that the one being who had destroyed her life had also given her a second one.

Iro came and lay beside her, taking in the dark sky. Lore turned to look at her.

"Is everything all right with your line?" Lore asked. "What happened in the hotel?"

"The Odysseides are wounded, but mending," Iro said. "We lost

540

only one hunter in the fight. Once the Kadmides discovered the tank of sea fire, and that they had been locked in with us, the fighting stopped and they were willing to show us how to smother the flames. It was all so strange, in a way."

"The Odysseides were lucky to have you there to lead them," Lore said.

Iro shook her head. "If only it were that simple. I want them to listen to me, but there's still a small part of me that feels like . . . I am not meant to lead."

"You are," Lore told her.

Iro breathed in deeply. "I don't know how to convince the elders that we have to find a new role to play in this world, but I'm hoping my mother can help. She's meeting us at the estate in the Loire Valley. We'll fight for the soul of the Odysseides together."

"Good," Lore said. "That's good, Iro. I'm not sure if there's anything I can do to help you, but I'll try."

Iro scoffed. "What can't you do?"

"Beat you in sparring?" Lore offered.

"Do not ever forget that," Iro said. "No matter how many eternities you see."

"If I'm lucky enough to have that long," Lore said quietly.

"Do you . . ." Iro seemed uncertain of how to ask her question. "Do you want this for yourself?"

"I don't know what I want, or what I really feel. Mostly sad, I think," Lore said. "Maybe that's not even the right word. It's like I'm missing everything, and all of you, and I'm still here. I can't shake this feeling that having Athena's power will only create more problems. That, no matter how hard I try, I'll lose touch with my humanity and find myself in the same destructive patterns the old gods fell into."

Lore didn't want ages to feel like moments, or for time to lose its meaning for her. She didn't want to decide how and when to use her power and know she would inevitably make mistakes.

She didn't want to be alive after all her friends were gone.

"We don't know what will happen until the hour comes," Iro said as the others made their way back over to them. "But until then, we'll stay here together as long as the night will have us."

Lore nodded, but both of them knew exactly how long that would be. The day would turn at midnight.

They ate and drank as night fell. Finally, Lore told them what had happened in the tunnel, and what Athena had done. She answered what questions she could, even as she had more of her own.

As the hours passed, the night felt dreamlike to her. The flow of conversation and laughter, the faces lit by candlelight. Lore watched, too afraid to look away in case she missed a second of the life she loved.

FIFTY EIGHT

L̲ORE FELT THE MOMENT THE MOON NEARED THE SUMMIT OF ITS ARC through the sky.

Extracting herself from the comfortable warmth of Castor's arms, she sat up. The others slept around her, sprawled out beneath the stars. Van and Miles with their hands intertwined, Iro with the soft look of dreaming.

She reached for her phone, checking the time. 11:50 p.m.

Lore had promised Miles and the others that she and Castor would wake them up before midnight. Yet as her hand hovered over his shoulder, she couldn't bring herself to go through with it. She had already faced so many good-byes in her life, all painful, and none of them on her own terms.

Instead, she picked up Miles's phone where he had left it beside him, made a face, took a photo, and set it as his background. Then, in a draft email, she left him instructions on how to access the untouched bank account Gil—Hermes—had left to her and where to find the keys to the safety-deposit box that held the brownstone's deed.

"What are you smiling about?"

Castor had been dozing for the last hour, but he must have felt the shift in the world, too. He stood and stretched now, rolling his shoulders back and swinging his arms, as if to remember the feeling of it.

Lore put her finger to her lips, quieting him as she set the phone down beside Miles's sleeping form. She reached up to take the hand Castor offered to her. They walked, their fingers interlaced, to the other side of the roof.

He looked out over the dark city, still without its dazzling lights. "I remembered."

She looked at him, waiting for him to continue.

"I dreamed it, just now," Castor said. "Apollo let me kill him, but he didn't die. He ascended."

Exactly as Athena had.

"Was that it all along?" Lore asked. "They had to willingly give their lives to a human?"

"I think it's more than that. Do you remember what the Reveler said?" Castor asked. "That even Apollo knew that it would never end, and all of this—the Agon, the killing, it was all just pointless? I saw that in him. The realization was destroying him. He told me that he could feel the disease in me, and he got angry. He tore around the room, destroying whatever he touched. I thought it was because he was enraged that I had dared to meet his gaze, or that he'd been found, but that wasn't it."

Castor drew in another steadying breath. "He went still. All that fury, and then . . . silence. *Thought.* He pulled the blade from the sheath at his side and came toward me."

"Were you frightened?" Lore whispered.

Castor shook his head. "No. There was something different about his expression—there was this *focus.* He asked me if I wanted to live. I told him I wasn't afraid to die. Not anymore. And he said, *If a mere boy is unafraid, I will match his courage.* He put the dagger in my hand and closed his around mine. I couldn't pull back. I couldn't break his

544

hold. He said, *I am not without power, or purpose,* and he pulled the blade in my hand into his heart."

Lore couldn't speak for a moment. "Why didn't he just heal you? He had the ability, didn't he?"

"I don't know," Castor said. "The Agon was nearly over. He'd have his full power back within moments. But I think he wanted to be released from it—he wanted to escape the endless pain and violence and loss as much as we did."

"And he left it the only way he knew how," Lore said. "By letting you kill him."

He nodded, rubbing his face. "I don't know that it was a true sacrifice, because it served him in a way. I think they had to remember their true purpose, and they could only do that by giving up the power they had desperately tried to hold on to."

A soft sigh escaped her.

Where were the other gods now? Lore wondered. Free, or still trapped in the dark world below?

Her hands closed around one of Castor's, needing his touch. "Will it feel the way it did in the station? Will it hurt to leave?"

"I don't know," Castor said, smoothing the hair back from her face. "I'm not sure what'll happen."

The seconds were passing too fast. Lore squeezed Castor's hand. Her heart pounded in her chest, and she wondered what it would be like to no longer feel it.

Lore rolled up onto her toes, capturing his face between her hands and pulling him down for a kiss before it was too late.

"Are you afraid?" he asked.

She shook her head. "Just . . . worried about leaving the others."

But it was more than that. *I don't want to go at all.*

"If you could choose," Lore began. "With everything you know . . . would you keep your power?"

He considered the question, stroking along her jaw. "No. I never wanted forever. When I was sick, I just wanted a moment more. An hour more. A day more. I wanted to wrestle with my dad, continue my training to be a healer, and to run through the city with you . . ."

Lore closed her eyes, concentrating on the feeling of him, the sound of his voice.

"I needed the power this week, no matter what I thought of it," Castor said. "But I still feel the way I did then, when I was a boy. Grateful for good days, when I feel strong in my body. Grateful for any time I have with you."

Lore wrapped her arms around his center. He rested his cheek against her hair.

I don't want to go, she thought. *I don't want to lose this, even for a moment.*

She didn't want eternity. She just wanted to hold Castor. To know that her friends were safe and nearby. To hear her city's heartbeat, growing steadier by the day.

"Please," Lore whispered—to the Cloudbringer himself, to whoever might have been listening. "Let us have a choice. Let it end."

The air shifted around them, as if in answer. She felt a charge, spreading in a wild dance across her senses. A presence gathered behind them, a wall of immense, rumbling pressure. She didn't turn around to face it.

"Please," Lore whispered again, repeating the desperate prayer. "Let us go."

Release us.

Wind rose, ruffling her hair. It sang an ancient song, carrying all

546

that it had seen across lands, seas, and centuries. She drew in a sharp breath as it passed through her—a sudden warmth that spread across her soul. Lore gripped Castor tighter, but there was no pain. There was only light beyond her closed eyelids.

The pressure relented as the power shimmering inside her pulled free from her body like an unraveling thread. She drew in a sharp breath at the sensation, and again as it disappeared. The air settled and the sounds of the city rose once more.

Lore opened her eyes. "Cas . . . ?"

He opened his own. For a moment she could only stare at him in quiet wonder. His eyes were dark again without the sparks of power in his irises. They were the eyes she had seen every day as a child. They were the eyes she loved.

His mortal body was warm next to hers. She felt his heart begin to drum madly in his chest. Pure elation spread through her.

Thank you, she thought. *Thank you.*

Castor let out a soft, joyful laugh, his hands touching her arms, her hair, her face, as if needing to be sure it wasn't a dream.

As the eighth day began, Lore smiled and kissed him.

CAST OF CHARACTERS

GODS

DECEASED AT THE START OF THE AGON

Aphrodite—goddess of beauty, procreation, pleasure, and love

Ares—god of war, valor, brutality, and bloodlust

Dionysus—god of festivity, religious ecstasy, frenzy, theater, wine, and vegetation

Hephaestus (*powers removed from the Agon*)—god of fire, smiths, and stone- and metalwork

Poseidon—god of the sea, floods, drought, horses, and earthquakes

ALIVE AT THE START OF THE AGON

Artemis—goddess of the wilderness, the hunt, wild animals, childbirth, and young girls

Athena—goddess of wisdom, crafts, and war strategy; defender of cities

Hermes—god of flocks and herds, thieves, merchants, travelers, and language; guide of the dead and messenger of the Olympians

STATUS UNKNOWN AT THE START OF THE AGON

Apollo—god of prophecy, song, poetry, archery, healing, and light, as well as plagues and diseases

NEW GODS AT THE START OF THE AGON

Heartkeeper, possessing the power of Aphrodite

The Reveler, possessing the power of Dionysus

Tidebringer, possessing the power of Poseidon

Wrath, possessing the power of Ares

HOUSE OF PERSEUS, FOUNDER OF MYCENAE AND SLAYER OF MEDUSA

Rhea Perseous—mortal woman who became Tidebringer, the new Poseidon; distant relation to Lore

Demos Perseous—Lore's father and the archon of the Perseides; murdered at the end of the last Agon

Helena Perseous—Lore's mother; born into the House of Odysseus; murdered at the end of the last Agon

Melora Perseous—also known as Lore; the last mortal member of the Perseides

Olympia Perseous—Lore's sister; murdered at the end of the last Agon

Damara Perseous—Lore's sister; murdered at the end of the last Agon

HOUSE OF ACHILLES, HERO OF THE TROJAN WAR

Philip Achilleos—the archon of the Achillides; distant relation to Castor and Evander

Acantha Achilleos—former lioness; wife of Philip

Healer Kallias—Castor's former healing instructor

Cleon Achilleos—Castor's father; deceased

Phaedra Achilleos—Castor's mother; killed during an earlier Agon

Castor Achilleos—Lore's closest childhood friend and former training partner

Evander Achilleos—Castor's distant cousin; messenger of the Achillides

Orestes Achilleos—member of Lore and Castor's training class

HOUSE OF KADMOS, FOUNDER OF THEBES AND SLAYER OF THE SERPENT

Aristos Kadmou—former archon of the Kadmides who became Wrath, the new Ares

Belen Kadmou—son of Aristos; born out of wedlock

HOUSE OF ODYSSEUS, THE CUNNING KING OF ITHAKA

Iolas Odysseos—Iro's father and former archon of the Odysseides who became Heartkeeper, the new Aphrodite; after ascending, his position as archon was inherited by a distant male relation

Dorcas Odysseos—Iro's mother who mysteriously vanished; a close friend of Lore's mother during her life

Iro Odysseos—Lore's friend and former training partner

HOUSE OF HERAKLES, HERO OF THE TWELVE LABORS

Iason Herakliou—murdered the rest of his bloodline when he became the Reveler, the new Dionysus

OTHER HOUSES

The House of Bellerophon, slayer of the Chimera and rider of Pegasus (*extinct bloodline*)

The House of Jason, leader of the Argonauts who recovered the Golden Fleece (*extinct bloodline*)

The House of Meleager, prince of Calydon and slayer of the Calydonian boar (*extinct bloodline*)

The House of Theseus, king of Athens and slayer of the Minotaur

ACKNOWLEDGMENTS

MY INTRODUCTION TO GREEK MYTHOLOGY CAME THROUGH A BATTERED copy of *D'Aulaires' Book of Greek Myths*, which my siblings and I inherited from our mom, who was eager to start introducing our Greek heritage to us. I've been blessed with a big Greek family that is everything the hunters in this book are not: incredibly loving, supportive, funny, and always ready with a vast collection of family legends. I would like to start by thanking all of them.

In addition to my family's input on the Greek in this book, I owe a huge amount of gratitude to Brendon Zatirka and Kiki Hatzopoulou for helping me double-check usage and spelling, and for being all-around heroes of the highest order when it came to answering my many questions. They, along with Katalina Edwards and Joel Christensen, were kind enough to also weigh in on transliterations from the original Greek and discuss the different ways of approaching the names of the bloodlines. (If you speak any version of the language, you may notice that I've leaned toward using the Romanized names for the sake of reader clarity, but I've tried to preserve some of the language's "purity," so to speak, whenever possible.)

This book also benefited greatly from the writings of Mary Beard and Christine Downing, both of whom helped me refine my own view of Athena and many of the myths discussed in this story, as well as the translation work done by Richmond Lattimore, Emily Wilson, Samuel Butler, Robert Fagles, and Hugh G. Evelyn-White. My fellow Greek mythology fans will see I've made some calls on which versions of the myths I wanted to use (for instance, having the aegis be a shield rather than a breastplate of sorts)—believe me when I say they were all tough calls and were ultimately made to help tell this story.

Lore and I were lucky enough to have a number of brilliant editorial minds weighing in on this story. Thank you to Laura Schreiber, Hannah Allaman, Marissa Grossman, and Rachel Stark for helping me figure out how best to tell this story. I'd also like to give a special thank-you to Kieran Viola for all of her help.

I feel so much gratitude to Ashil Lee for their wonderful and detailed feedback, which helped me come at this story from a more sensitive and nuanced angle, and added greatly to my own understanding.

To Emily Meehan, Seale Ballenger, Melissa Lee, Augusta Harris, Dina Sherman, LaToya Maitland, Holly Nagel, Elke Villa, Andrew Sansone, Sean Weigold, Jennifer Chan, Guy Cunningham, Meredith Jones, Dan Kaufman, Sara Liebling, Marybeth Tregarthen, Terry Downes, Shane Jacobson, Alexandra Sheckler, Kim Greenberg, and the entire sales team: Thank you for all of your hard work and your devotion to giving books the best lives they can possibly have. Marci Senders: This cover is beautiful beyond words. I'd also like to thank Billelis for the incredibly eye-catching (pun intended) cover art and Keith Robinson for the gorgeous interior art.

I'm sending a big thank-you to Merrilee Heifetz for being in my corner, Rebecca Eskildsen, and the foreign rights team at Writers House for helping this book find readers across the world.

I can't begin to describe how grateful I am to my incredible friend Anna Jarzab for believing in this story and for helping me brainstorm it. Thank you to Susan Dennard for always being game to weigh in when I need another trusted opinion, and for your limitless compassion. Finally, thank you to Erin Bowman, Leigh Bardugo, Victoria Aveyard, and Amie Kaufman for being a chorus of supportive voices!